"*Seven Ways We Lie* isn't an in-depth study on why we lie; it's a study on how our secrets make us human. Riley Redgate's deft prose twines and twists between graceful and gritty, weaving seven unique characters into a story with threads so universal yet variegated, it could belong to any one of us. Don't expect a fairy tale. This is reality at its most raw, most poignant, and most relatable. Art imitating life . . . fiction perfected."

–A. G. Howard, author of the *New York Times* bestselling Splintered series

HELLO my name is LUST

HELLO my name is ENVY

HELLO my name is GREED

HELLO my name is SLOTH

HELLO my name is GLUTTONY

HELLO my name is WRATH

HELLO my name is PRIDE

seven ways we lie

RILEY REDGATE

Amulet Books

Cataloging-in-Publication Data has been applied for and may be obtained from the Library of Congress.

Paperback ISBN: 978-1-4197-2348-3

Originally published in hardcover by Amulet Books in 2016
Text copyright © 2016 Riley Redgate
Book design by Maria T. Middleton

Printed and bound in U.S.A.
10 9 8 7 6 5 4 3 2 1

Amulet Books are available at special discounts when purchased in quantity for premiums and promotions as well as fundraising or educational use. Special editions can also be created to specification. For details, contact specialsales@abramsbooks.com or the address below.

ABRAMS The Art of Books
115 West 18th Street, New York, NY 10011
abramsbooks.com

FOR NOELLE,
the stories we've written,
the ones we've lived,
and the superheroes
in them all

HELLO
my name is

OLIVIA SCOTT

"ALL RIGHT," I SAY, "EITHER THE FURNACE IS ON OVER-drive, or we've descended into the actual, literal fiery pits of hell."

"I feel like 'both' is the answer here," Juniper says. "Assemblies, eternal damnation . . . same basic concept."

"Correcto." I wipe sweat off my face, feeling as if I'm melting. "God, this is horrible."

Other kids stream past to our right, flooding the overheated auditorium's aisles, filling the seats ahead of us. Juniper ties back her hair, looking clean and sweat-free, like those airbrushed girls in deodorant ads who are always prancing through blank white voids. I'm used to it. Juniper is the kind of beautiful that we regular human folk can't quite connect to. With guarded gray eyes, blond hair swept back, and the barest touch of blush, she's a cautiously assembled girl. Always has been.

A noise from across the aisle catches my attention, a noise that could be either a violent throat-clearing or a cat being strangled. Looking over, I catch a glare from Andrea Silverstein that could level a building.

"Oh, good Lord, not this again," I mumble, sinking down in my seat.

"Ignore her."

"Trying, Juni."

Seriously, though, can someone explain why they call it a "personal life" when it's the one part of my life everyone knows? Today alone, I got three death stares in the hall, two whispers accompanied by averted eyes, and one *So* that's *Olivia Scott!* face of recognition. Why do I even have a branded face of recognition?

Okay, granted: Andrea maybe has license to get defensive, since it was her brother I hooked up with. But the rest of the world can shove it up their collective ass.

Andrea's eyes burn into the side of my skull for a straight minute. Finally, Juniper leans forward and gives her a cool, uninterested look. Andrea stops glaring at once.

I've been friends with Juniper since third grade, and I'm still waiting for her to pull out the magic wand she obviously owns. Something in her composure makes people stare; when she talks, she holds attention like a magnet. Juni chews on her words before saying them, as if she's parsing the sentences in her head, ensuring they'll come out perfect.

"Shit. Do you see Claire?" I say, looking around the auditorium. "I said I'd find her." With the fluorescent lights bathing us all in sickly green, Claire's red hair doesn't pop out of the crowd as usual.

"Maybe she's skipping," Juniper suggests with a wry smile.

I snort hard enough to kill off a few brain cells. Claire skipping anything school-related would be the first sign of the apocalypse.

With one last scan of the auditorium, I give up my search, and preoccupation sneaks into my head. God knows what percentage of the student body skips assemblies, but I see a hell of a lot of empty seats—and I can't help thinking that my sister's supposed to be in one of them.

We keep getting calls at home about my sister skipping class. It's the most bored-sounding voice mail of all time: "This is a recorded message from the Republic County School System. We are calling to inform you that Katrina Scott missed one or more classes today. Please send an excuse note within three days."

The messages baffle me. What is Kat doing when she skips? She doesn't have a car or as far as I know friends she could skip with. Not that I know much about Kat these days—she seems determined to delete me from her life by whatever means necessary. If it keeps going this way, I should watch out for snipers.

The lights dim, and the auditorium doors clank shut at the back. Teachers close in, standing guard on either side of the exit, as if they're trying to discourage a revolutionary uprising. The stage lights glow as Principal Turner approaches the podium.

It's a nice gesture, the podium and the microphone and all, but Ana Turner doesn't need any of it. Our principal is a pearl-laden Air Force veteran in her mid-thirties, with the glare of a guard dog and the bark to match. Every time she opens her mouth, everyone under age twenty within a mile has a minor panic attack.

She clears her throat once. Silence drops like a bomb.

"Good afternoon," she says, wearing a weirdly upset expression. I say "weirdly upset" because Turner has always done a stellar job of convincing the school that she does not, in fact, feel feelings.

She folds her hands on the podium. "Faculty and students, I've called this assembly to address a serious issue that has been brought to the administration."

"This ought to be good," I whisper to Juniper, rubbing my hands together. "You think they caught the guy who's been pooping in the third-floor old wing?"

Juniper grins, until Turner says, "We've received word that a teacher at Paloma High is having romantic relations with a member of the student body."

I blink a few times before it registers.

I look over at Juniper. Her mouth has fallen open. Noise swells back to life around us, and Principal Turner clears her throat again, but this time, the chatter doesn't subside. Appearing to resign herself to the chaos, she talks over it. "The message we received was anonymous, submitted via our website. While it didn't include names, we take such accusations seriously. If you have any information whatsoever about the matter, please come forward to myself or a guidance counselor. In the meantime, we've mailed a letter to your parents. It should arrive within two to three days." The talk buzzes higher. Her voice booms out to compensate: "These measures are for the purpose of complete transparency. We can and will resolve this matter soon."

I fold my arms, glancing around. The expressions in the sea of faces vary: shock, nervousness, and excitement. Normally I might wonder why anyone would get excited about a teacher-student sex scandal, but hey, even rumors of regular sex get our delightful peer group stirred up.

Turner brushes sweat off her forehead—apparently, even she isn't impervious to the heat—and glances back down at her notes. "Unsubstantiated allegations like these are worrisome, but they serve as an important reminder that the student body's safety is our first priority. We've called this assembly to reiterate our code of conduct and ensure a safe learning environment. I've asked Mr. García to prepare a brief presentation on how to handle unwanted sexual advances."

Turner nods toward the wings. Our English teacher, Mr. García, wheels out an overhead projector and slides a transparency sheet onto it, a nice little throwback to the mid-1990s. García's whole vintage obsession turns from quirky to exasperating whenever technology's involved. Seriously, who gets nostalgic for overhead projectors?

As Turner exits the stage, García launches into a lecture. The longer he talks, the less sense any of it makes. I've seen shit like this on the news, but it always seems to be a crazy gym teacher and a pregnant fifteen-year-old. The idea of our gym teachers impregnating anyone makes me want to throw up—they're both, like, sixty-five. It makes even less sense to look at it from the kid's perspective. What person my age would get themselves into this? Wouldn't they realize how life-ruining it would be if their name got out?

There are a few teachers young enough for a hookup not to be *that* gross. I always catch guys drooling over the econ teacher, Dr. Meyers, who's short and curvy and in her mid-twenties. The calculus teacher, Mr. Andrews, is handsome in a super pale, vampire sort of way. And Mr. García's definitely hot. Not my type, though. With the way he gets all swoony when he talks about Mercutio, I'm ninety percent sure he's gay.

God, though, I can't imagine any of them hitting on a student. Sometimes girls make eyes at Andrews or García, but if the teachers notice, they don't let on. As for Dr. Meyers, she sent some kid to the office last year for saying she looked "real sexy today, Doc." Points for her.

Half an hour later, the Powers That Be release us from the brick oven of the auditorium into the November afternoon. The chill air tastes crisp. As the sun's harsh glare assaults my eyes, part of me feels as if the assembly weren't real. A heat hallucination, maybe. Juniper and I head down the hill toward the junior lot. She seems just as dazed.

A voice jolts us out of our stupor. "Hey, guys!"

We stop at the edge of the parking lot, a few paces from Juniper's Mercedes. Claire jogs up to us, her frizzy red hair pulled back into a thick ponytail for tennis practice. She elbows me. "Missed you at the assembly, lady."

"I looked for you—promise," I say. "Couldn't see you. There were, like, you know, a thousand people in there."

"True." She clears her throat. "Where are you guys going?"

Shit. That expectant tone means I've forgotten something. "Um," I say, shooting Juniper a frantic look. "To, uh . . ."

"Nowhere," Juniper says. "Dropping off our stuff before the meeting."

Right—student government. Juniper and I both promised Claire we'd run for junior class president, so she had at least two people guaranteed to be on the ballot.

I have a million problems with this, none of which I've voiced, since Claire's so rabid about the whole thing. But Juniper and me running against each other is a hilarious farce of an idea. Juni could ask the whole school to jump off a bridge, and they'd be like, "Brilliant! Why didn't we think of it sooner?"

Juni unlocks her car, and we sling our bags into the backseat. The three of us head across the green. Ahead, at the end of the long stretch of grass, Paloma High School's main building looms above us like an architectural Frankenstein. They renovated the east wing two years ago. It's three stories of glimmering plate glass and steel beams now. The west wing—brick, weathered, sixty years old—hangs off the new section like an unfortunate growth.

We cross the entire green before anyone speaks. "So, that assembly," I say, opening the door to the east wing.

"Yeah," Claire says. "Girl, dat shit be cray."

I wince. "Yeesh, please don't—you are whiter than Moby-Dick."

Juniper laughs, and Claire flushes, flicking a curl out of her eyes. We head down a long hallway filled with afternoon sun. Light glances off the lockers, making them more of an eyesore than usual: red on top, green on the bottom. Our school colors. Also Christmas colors. Every year around the Christmas season, someone tags a red Rudolph graffiti nose onto the Lions logo out front.

"Seriously," Claire says, pushing open the door to the stairwell, "when they figure out who's sleeping with a teacher . . ."

"I know." I jog up the steps after her. "We won't hear the end of it for, like, twelve years."

Claire aims a smirk at me over her shoulder. "It's not you, is it?"

That stings—I bet half the school thinks it's me—but I manage a laugh. "Go to hell."

"Fine, fine," she says, raising her hands. "It's actually me. Me . . . and Principal Turner."

Juniper mock-retches behind us. "Why, Claire?" I moan. "Why do you give us these mental scars?"

We come out on the third floor, dodging the after-school-club traffic. We pass the computer-science room, filled with Programming Club kids on their laptops, and the English room, where Poetry Society meets in a solemn-looking, somewhat cultish circle. We head into the Politics and Government room.

"Good crowd," I say. The room's empty.

"Three's a crowd," Claire says, checking her watch. "It's just juniors today. And the girl who's running for secretary emailed me—she can't come. But there's also a boy running for president, so . . ."

My heart sinks. If there's only one other candidate, the odds of me wriggling out of this contest without hurting Claire's feelings are way lower; and what with her hyperactive sense of responsibility, she won't let it go for a while.

"Who's the boy?" Juniper asks, perching in the empty teacher's chair. Mr. Gunnar must be helping with the assembly cleanup. I bet they need a dozen people to mop up the sweat.

Claire unzips her backpack and thumbs through a folder. She draws out a sign-up sheet with one lonely name sitting at the top. "His handwriting's terrible, but I think it says Matt something? Jackson, maybe?"

"I know him." Juniper raises one thin eyebrow. "We did a group project together in bio, by which I mean I did the entire thing. The guy isn't exactly a paragon of self-discipline."

"Oh, wait," I say, recalling the kid who slouches in late to English every day, reeking of weed. "Tall? Never talks? Kind of a pointy face?"

"That's the one," Juniper says.

"Well," I say. "This'll be, uh. Great."

Claire scrutinizes my expression. "Something wrong, Liv?"

"What? No, everything's fine." I shrug. "It's just . . . not that I don't want to be Paloma, Kansas's new political wunderkind, but I sort of want to drop out."

Claire makes a dismissive *tsk* sound between her teeth, setting her backpack down. "Oh, come on. Don't pull that."

"Dude, I'm being honest. I don't know about this Matt kid, but everyone knows there's no contest if it's me and Juniper."

We both look at Juniper. She stays diplomatically silent, spinning in Mr. Gunnar's chair.

"Well, I guess you do have a lot on your plate," Claire says knowingly.

"What do you mean?"

"Oh, I don't know. Maybe your latest conquest?" Claire wiggles her eyebrows. "Dan Silverstein, huh? Ees vairy eenteresting choice."

I know she's not serious, but it's been a long day of stares. "Hmm, that's funny," I say. "I don't remember telling you about—"

"I mean, no judgment. But, like, did you even know he existed before last Saturday?"

"Claire, give me a break." I try to ignore the tug of hurt. "Can you stop doing this every time I hook up with someone? I know everyone else thinks I'm, like, Slutty McGee, Queen Slut from Slut Island, but you're supposed to be on my side."

"Whoa. First of all, it was a joke, and second, there's not a *side*." She frowns. "Although I'll admit, I don't get why you sleep with so many guys."

"It's not like my reasoning needs to be public knowledge," I say, unsuccessfully attempting to keep my voice level.

"Excuse me? So now it's not my business?" Her blue eyes stretch wide. Surrounded by gold eyeliner, they look like gilded windows framing a sunlit sea. "Do I need a reason to care about you and your . . ." She gestures in the vicinity of my ovaries.

"My what? My sex life? What, want to hop on down to CVS and pick up some Plan B with me? Because I've never seen you or anyone else lining up to chat about that side of things."

"I wasn't going to say your sex life, Olivia." Claire plants her hands on her hips. "Okay, look. You want me to be honest? You've been doing this more and more, and I'm starting to get worried about your emotional well-being."

A million mean responses swell at the back of my tongue— Claire isn't exactly the crying-shoulder type—but before I can snap back, Juniper cuts in.

"Guys," she says, standing in one sharp motion. Her voice is quiet with irritation. "Are you listening to yourselves? I'm not going to tell you to apologize, but this is all objectively dumb." She folds her arms. "Could you please think for ten seconds?"

I stiffen. Juni's voice of reason tends to be more patient than that.

Claire and I trade a glance, chastened. It's not fair of us, drag-ging Juni along for every squabble when she's already got so much to deal with. Alongside Juni's unhealthy stack of AP classes, she's a concert violinist with an obscene amount of Paganini to learn for her December recital. Twice a year, Juni's parents drive Claire and me out to Kansas City so we can watch her recitals—she plays in one of the performance halls at U of M. This season's program seems to be stressing her out hard-core.

I look down at my sneakers and count to ten, focusing on the frayed edges of my shoelaces. When I look back up, Claire's accusatory stare has wilted. "Sorry," she says. "Didn't mean to escalate."

I sigh, my anger still simmering. Every time this happens, it gets a little harder to grin and bear it. Claire was never entirely aboard the *Let Olivia make her own sexual decisions!* train, but she's gotten a million times worse since May, when Lucas—her boyfriend of over a year—dumped her in a random and arbitrary fashion. Which was weird, since Lucas ostensibly is a nice person, but . . . well. There are secret assholes in the world. Big shocker.

She's been single for six months now, and her offhand comments about my hookups have about exhausted my patience, which, God knows, is a nonrenewable resource. Opening my mouth takes herculean effort. "I'm sorry, too," I manage. "I've had a not-excellent day."

"Same." After a long second, Claire tugs her bag from the desk. "Okay, I can't wait around for this kid. I'm going to be late for practice. I'll email you guys the info later." She sneaks a cautious glance at me. "If you . . ."

I sigh, and a grudging compromise falls out with it: "I'll run if you want me to."

"Thanks." Avoiding my eyes, she strides out of the classroom in her usual military fashion. We didn't fix things—not even close.

Juniper leans against Mr. Gunnar's desk, looking weary. "You two. What is happening these days?"

"I don't know. Look, I'm sorry—it's not your job to babysit us."

She shrugs. "No, it's okay. Is something up, though?"

"Not really. It's just . . . I'm used to her worrying. That's how she . . ."

"Of course. Works."

"Yeah, how she works, yeah. But these days it feels like—I

11

don't know. She's tightening in, or clamping down, and I'm like, please, will you back the fuck *off*? I swear to God, sometimes she thinks she's my mom."

The last word fades too slowly from the air.

"That's a lot," Juniper says, tilting her head. Her blond hair, loose again, sways in two thin curtains, framing her eyes. Those chips of wintry gray are as perceptive as always.

"Well, I mean it." I cross my arms, feeling mutinous. "I don't need Claire to replace anyone. And it sure as hell feels like she's trying."

"Have you told her that?"

"Nah. She'd do the whole 'who, *moi?*' thing, and I don't know. I wouldn't be able to take it seriously."

"I can talk to her, if you'd like."

I consider it for a second, but how childish would that be, sending Juniper as my ambassador? "It's fine. We'll figure it out."

Juniper swings her legs, looking pensive. "Do you mind if I ask something?"

"Go for it."

"I'm not questioning your judgment, but I'm curious: you could sleep with just one guy, so why go for more than one?"

I shrug. "Because my body belongs to me, and I get to make my own decisions?"

Juniper raises an eyebrow. "I mean beyond Feminist Theory 101, Olivia."

I give her a sheepish grin. "Well, I'm not looking for anything serious. Somehow I doubt I'm gonna find the love of my life in high school, so . . . might as well have fun, right? Low stress, low commitment." It falls off my tongue a little too fast. I give my head a quick shake. "Ready to go?"

Juni doesn't push. She slides off the desk and follows me. She's a reassuring silence at my shoulder as we hurry downstairs, past the lockers, and out the door.

Her question turns over and over in my head. I do like sex, and I do like making my own decisions, and I do like Feminist Theory 101. But something else about sleeping with people keeps me at it. Winding up beside someone, resting my head on his shoulder, relaxes me. That part outperforms the sex most of the time—no offense to the dudes involved.

But thinking about it too hard feels like second-guessing myself, and I already get so much shit for "whoring around," as so many people have kindly put it—I don't want to give my critics the tiniest hint of validation.

As we head across the green, I fold my arms tight against the chill. I try to forget Claire's hurt expression and try to shake off thoughts of my mom. I shouldn't have mentioned her to Juniper. Now she's at the front of my mind, and she won't go.

I always miss Mom more at this time of year. With Halloween, Thanksgiving, and Christmas all in a row, thoughts of her are packed tight on the road to winter. Keeping everything locked away takes more energy than usual. Sometimes I take the memories out, dust them off, and look at them hard, and they glow a little around the edges. I still have the image of Mom's delicate hands scooping pumpkin seeds into a bowl. "Oooh, pumpkin innards," she'd say in a ghostly moan. "Katrina, Olivia, young mortals, assist me with the pumpkin intestines."

These days, the house stays bare. Dad doesn't say anything about it, but I get the feeling the empty space is easier for him. And Kat doesn't say anything about it, but then again, Kat never says anything.

Juniper unlocks her car. I slip into the passenger seat, sliding it back to stretch my legs.

Juni presses a button. The engine purrs to life. "Kat doesn't need a ride, does she?"

"Nah, Drama Club today," I say. "I think she's getting a ride after or something." My twin sister must have occupied the "talented" half of the womb. Though I've developed quite the talent for sitting in audiences and applauding.

"Oh, hey. Our competition." As she pulls the car forward, Juni nods to one side of the junior lot, where a tall boy sprawls on top of a black Camry. "Over there."

I straighten up and almost whack my head on the ceiling. Peering out my window, I spy Matt Jackson, who lies back, texting. I've never looked hard at the guy before. He looks foxlike, with the forward set of his facial features and the fringe of fire-red dye at the tips of his rusty hair.

Juniper's car dips over a speed bump. From his car roof, Matt Jackson turns toward us, and I look away. Not fast enough.

"Ah, shitshitshit," I say. "He's totally looking at me. He totally saw me creeping."

"Don't worry," Juniper says. "He'll never guess we're planning his political assassination." She lets out a maniacal laugh.

I grin. "Yeah, you've always struck me as a John Wilkes Booth sort of girl."

"June Wilkes Booth, even."

I groan, sinking low in my seat. Juniper, looking pleased with herself, turns the radio on. The sound system emits a deep, start-up hum, and one of Paganini's Caprices sings out of the speakers. Juni's left hand, her nails cut short, plays along on the steering wheel.

By the time we pull out of the parking lot and down the street, the day's problems have faded in the distance, left back at Paloma High School with its waxed hallways, defaced bathroom stalls, and all the students who think it's their job to judge me.

HELLO
my name is
KAT SCOTT

BACKSTAGE, THE CURTAINS SMELL LIKE DUST. IT'S easy to forget myself here, drowned in the dark.

Whispers scurry along the wing from the girls who play my daughters. Whispers that beg for my attention.

Focus, Kat.

I tuck my hair behind my ears, digesting the lines that pass onstage, beat by beat. It's Emily's monologue out there—her plea for relevance.

Focus . . .

The backstage whispers scrape at me again, harder this time. Anger prickles hot in my palms. The others should be listening for their cues. They should be taking this seriously.

"—and I'm tired of waiting," Emily says. My cue.

I stride onstage and lose myself completely.

Here in the blinding lights, I shed layers of myself like a knight casting off her armor plate by plate. I move with purpose, with want, with drive. Kat Scott is nobody. Nowhere. If she even exists, I'm not concerned with her.

"*You're* tired of waiting?" I demand.

The girl across from me takes half a step back. She's not Emily, not anymore. Now that I'm standing across from her, she's Natalya Bazhenova: a mathematics professor who made a promise to my character years ago. She promised to sweep me away from my Russian town to an elite school and nurture my mathematical talent. Between acts 1 and 2, I reached thirty-seven years old waiting for her to rescue me from this life, but she never did. She forgot me. And now she dares to come back.

"You're tired of waiting," I say. "You, Natalya, who left me in this town?" I step closer, snarling my way through the questionable translation, hunting Natalya down with my eyes. "Look at me. Look at what I am now."

"I am looking at you," she says.

"Look harder."

"I see a loving mother, a caring sister. I see—"

"You see nothing," I whisper. "I am nothing anymore except wasted potential. Nothing!"

My voice echoes back from the far reaches of the auditorium, and silence ricochets afterward like a boomerang. Dead, beautiful silence.

I speak more slowly now, tasting the bitterness in every word. "You were supposed to be my teacher. You said I was brilliant—a prodigy, you said. You were supposed to take me away, teach me everything, but instead you ran the first chance you had. And now you come back and say you're tired of waiting?" My voice hardens to a condemnation: "You hypocrite."

"I'm sorry, Faina," she says.

Before it happens, I know our director is going to stop us. "Hold," calls Mr. García from the front row. I drop character, slouching down to take a seat in the kitchen chair. Everything that was held tight in my body goes loose, every muscle, every bit of focus.

It's a relief to get out of that headspace. God, the Russians were miserable. This play, *The Hidden Things*, was written by a man called Grigory Veselovsky around the turn of the century, and by the end, exactly zero of the characters are happy. Our pal Grigory must've been a sadist.

Mr. García hops up onto the edge of the stage. Our drama teacher, Mrs. Stilwater, has to plan some regional conference, so García's directing the fall play. He's technically an English person, not a theater person, but he knows what he's doing.

I've heard he's not getting paid for this, though, which is insane. Not that I'm complaining. There wouldn't have been a fall play otherwise, and most days this feels like the only reason to get out of bed.

García jogs over to my scene partner. "Emily, push it more, I think. You can heighten the physicality of being afraid. And cheat a little to the right; we're losing that section of the audience."

And now the volume problem . . .

"Also, I hate to say it, but we're still losing your lines."

"I'm so sorry," Emily says, obviously on the verge of tears.

I purse my lips. Damn right, she's sorry. He's given her this note a hundred times already. The show goes up in under three weeks, right before Thanksgiving break, and I'm starting to think she might never get it.

"It's okay," García says. "Hey. Emily? Don't be upset. We'll do some projection exercises later, all right?" He gives her a thumbs-up. "It's a matter of trusting your voice—a confidence thing. You have this."

God, García is patient. I would've yelled at half the people in this cast by now, but in five weeks of rehearsing, he hasn't so much as raised his voice.

Emily nods once, her mousy hair falling into her eyes.

"Oh, and that's another thing," he says, scribbling a note on his omnipresent clipboard. "You've got to tie your hair back or something. It keeps hiding your right eye."

I sigh, slouching down in my chair. He's told her that note before, too. I don't get why people can't follow simple directions. Sometimes it feels as if García and I are the only ones giving this show everything.

It's not that I think I'm more talented than the rest of the cast—the other kids are all good, in their own way. But . . . I don't know. They don't seem to need the stage, the space to fill, the echo of the voice, and the punch of the words.

"Kat?"

I look up. "What?"

García approaches me. "You're doing great, but there's something missing in the way you're tackling this scene, I think." He puts his clipboard on the table. "What's your character's objective in this scene? What does she want from Emily's character?"

I figured all this out when I did the script work back in September. I answer without hesitating. "She wants Natalya to apologize."

García runs a hand through his hair, making it stick straight up. He looks like a hungover college student, with his stubble and thick-rimmed glasses and messy hair. He's a new teacher this year, but he's chill and doesn't give too much homework, so he's doing pretty well by most people's standards. "Yeah," he says, "I can see the apology motive. But what else do you think it could be?"

I frown. "I'm pretty sure that's it. Natalya ruined my character's life, so it—"

A fit of giggling bursts out backstage. The frustration that's been burning low in my chest ignites. I twist around in my chair. "Could you shut up?" I snap. The giggles die.

García's eyes glimmer with amusement. "You can let me do that, you know. Believe it or not, I, too, am capable of saying, 'Quiet backstage.'"

"Sorry," I mutter.

"Don't be. Just don't make it a habit." García checks his watch. "Ah, nuts. Okay." He hurries back to the lip of the stage, hops off, and retakes his seat in the front row. "All right, one more thing before it's five o'clock. Let's jump ahead to the last scene."

Emily, who still isn't off-book for this scene, runs to grab her script. We don't have all the props yet, so I mime a chalkboard at center stage.

"Okay," García says as Emily scurries back into place. "Last little bit of scene 6. Let's take it from 'What do you think?' Whenever you're ready, Emily."

A short silence. Then Natalya Bazhenova says to me, "What do you think?"

I look at the blank space in the air, where my fingers hover over an imaginary chalkboard. I scrutinize an imaginary equation. "It's beautiful," I say. "It's beautiful work."

"So you see why I had to go? Why I had to resume my research?"

"No, I don't. But it is still beautiful work." Letting the imaginary chalk drop, I turn around. The lights won't be set for two weeks, so all the brights are on too high. I squint into them.

Natalya approaches me. "Do you want me to show you the rest?" she asks, making me thirsty with imaginary want. "I could try to find a way," she says. "I could go back and ask the other professors if you could join us at the university. I could—"

"Mama?" says a voice. I turn stage left. My character's daughter enters. "I did it," she says. "I made dinner. And—and we are all waiting for you at home."

I study the sight: the lines of my daughter's face painted a harsh white by the stage light. "Thank you, sweetheart," I say mechanically. I turn back to Natalya. "No," I say. "I can't go with you."

"But—"

"I won't go," I say, defeat filling the words. After a long second, I follow my daughter off left. Natalya stares after us.

"And lights down," García calls. "Great. Everyone, onstage."

We sit on the edge of the stage, the rest of the cast talking and joking. The guy who plays my husband flirts with Emily, who doesn't seem to realize it. I sit off to the side, as far as possible from the girls I yelled at. I shouldn't have snapped—I know it's García's job, telling them to be quiet—but it maddens me, people not having the basic decency to shut up during rehearsals.

García runs over his notes from the scenes we worked today. "Kat," he says finally, "what do you think the play's ending means?"

The rest of the cast looks at me. I feel the eleven pairs of eyes like spotlights. I shrug, avoiding their gazes. "I lose," I say. "My character loses. She's been at home waiting fifteen years for her teacher to come back, and by the time it happens, she has this kid to raise, so, like . . . you know. She can't chase her passion. She loses."

"That's what I thought you'd say," García says, dashing off a note on the clipboard. "I want you to rethink that. And I want you to rethink the apology thing from earlier. Okay?"

I nod, almost relieved to have notes for once. Usually García spends so long fixing people's blocking, he doesn't get to characterization.

His questions baffle me, though. How could I want anything but an apology from Emily's character, after a decade and a half? And of course I lose at the end. My character's dream goes out the window, and she's saddled with a life she never wanted.

García tucks his clipboard into his satchel. "Kat, thanks for being off-book already. The rest of you, remember to off-book those last few scenes by Thursday. Nice work, everyone."

I hop off the stage, hurrying out the side door ahead of the others. I jog down the grass of the hill, squinting into the sunset. I'm still not used to the sun setting so early thanks to daylight savings, which doesn't seem to save much daylight at all. Though maybe that's because we're locked in school buildings until sunset.

Crossing the parking lot toward the street, I pass Juniper Kipling's empty Mercedes, a shimmering foreigner in the crowd of scuffed Jeeps and mud-splattered pickup trucks. Weird—I thought Juniper was driving my sister home today.

As I reach the sidewalk, I stick my hands deep in my pockets, steeling myself for the journey. It's not a long way home—two miles, maybe—but it's getting cold these days. Soon I'll have to start asking people for rides after rehearsal. I dread the awkward car conversations already.

No matter what, when I talk to people, I come off as an asshole. They should leave me alone, for their sake as much as mine.

Whenever someone breaks my privacy, my head fills with panic, panic, panic. I lose my thoughts in white noise and fuzz. A short, sizzling fuse. And what comes out of my mouth is always angry bullshit.

Life is better when it's scripted.

HELLO
my name is

MATT JACKSON

AN HOUR LATER, I'M STILL THINKING ABOUT HER EYES
and her attention, lying back and letting that glance loop in endless repeat.

She looked at me. The thought of it keeps turning, replaying,
spinning like a mobile or a galaxy, and it feels even more impossible now that I'm this high.

When you're high, getting stares usually feels fine, because
unless you're having a bad high and feeling paranoid as hell, the
staring person seems like just another citizen of the world, and
that's chill. But even if I weren't high, I'd be freaking out over
Olivia Scott giving me the eye. I sit three rows behind her in
English, and I spend about 108 percent of that class staring at the
back of her head, wondering how she gets her hair that rich and
straight and glossy. Everything I've heard her say is hilarious, and
when she smiles, it's so high-voltage, I start a little, every damn
time. Olivia Scott is magnificent.

Sometimes I can't help resenting her raucous laugh and her
sexy, poised, confident body and her blaze-blue eyes, because she
only notices assholes like Dan Silverstein, and I have no idea why.
But then I remember that if by some miracle she noticed me

instead, I'd feel super-awkward, because we don't have any friends in common. I don't even know if we'd get along. From what I've seen, she's one of those semi-geeks who likes school enough to do well but not enough to try. Who even knows how that works? It's like . . . I don't know, but if you're going to not give a shit, at least devote yourself to not giving a shit, right?

But what the hell do I know? I've never spoken to her. She could be totally different from what I've seen and heard.

Still. She looked at me, and I can't stop thinking about it.

I pick up the joint from my car roof and play around with the smoke, sniffing it, licking it up, rolling it across my tongue and through my teeth. It's not sanitary, letting the thing sit on my roof like that, but I've done worse, and I know Burke's done worse. He picked a joint up off the sidewalk one time and took a drag for shits and giggles, and he didn't get sick, even though I insisted for a week that he was going to get oral herpes or some shit. Then again, Burke has the immune system of a god.

My watch hits five o'clock. The drama geeks pour down the hill from the auditorium, trickle into their scattered cars, and drive off.

I take a hit and stare up at the clouds, those plumes of cotton and Marshmallow Fluff, their underbellies pinkened by the dying sun. It's crazy that they're so huge, and crazier that something so colossal is so temporary, that they'll never be the same as they are now, and as soon as they turn heavy and cry themselves down in sheets of rain, they'll be gone, as if they were never looming a mile above the crown of my head. This day is lost already. This hour is as good as going, going, gone.

I shut my eyes and flush out the thoughts, and new ones float in like breezes, like the sound of chimes. Minutes swirl around me, and seconds fall across my skin with the tingle, the prickle, the itch of dying sunlight, and Jesus, have I ever been this relaxed in my life?

Then a familiar voice splinters my nirvana with an "*Hola*, Mateo," and I keep my eyes closed and slur out a "*No hablo* Spanish," and the voice says, "Yeah, sure, Mr. Half-Mexican," and I say, "Please, man, I'm, like, six hundred percent American," which Mamá would kill me for saying, because it's probably an Insult to My Cultural Heritage or something.

I peer off the side of my car at Burke. In the red light of sunset, and with my head tilted sideways, he looks like something out of a horror movie, his nose and ear and eyebrow piercings glinting, a sleeve of black-and-purple tattoos twisted up his left arm like an injury. He's wearing his bleached hair in gelled spikes today.

"Yo, man," I say, and as he climbs up the back of my car onto my roof, he grunts, "You been out here smoking, huh?" and I'm like, "Yeah, nothing else to do. You?"

"I was reading. Waiting for one of my sculptures to cool." He waves a book at me. When Burke's not welding metal sculptures out of abandoned hubcaps and steel rods, he spends all his time reading, which people never guess, because he looks like every gang-member stereotype ever conceived. In reality, he's probably the most well-read, intelligent person at this school—not counting Valentine Simmons, because I refuse to count that pretentious dickhead—and no one knows it, because Burke's way sneaky about the whole *smart* thing.

Sometimes I'd swear Burke is from a different planet. He's normal if you talk to him, but besides me, nobody ever talks to him, because they can't get past the way he looks. It's not just the ink and the piercings and the hair, which he dyes a different color every other week. It's his clothes, which are weird at best and embarrassing at worst. Last Friday, he strolled into school wearing neon-yellow skinny jeans and platform shoes. Today, he has on a green peacoat, jean leggings, and a kilt. It looks like a Goodwill threw up on him.

He wears makeup, too. Not standard emo-kid guyliner, either. Like, bright blue lipstick, the other week, and orange eye shadow, the day before yesterday. Today he's clean-faced, but back in freshman year, he didn't go a day without it. His whole persona, this whole thing he does with the way he looks—it happened so suddenly, right out of middle school, I wondered if it was performance art, maybe. Some big stunt I wasn't part of. Now, though, I'm so used to it, I hardly notice when he goes crazy with winged eyeliner and purple eyebrows.

At first I thought he'd get beat up, but it turns out that people are terrified to talk shit about Burke because he's six foot five and built like a Mack truck, and sometimes when he's dressed down he looks as if he'd knife you without thinking about it. But Jesus, if he were my size, he'd get laughed out of Kansas.

I take his book and squint at the title. It's called *The Gay Science*, written by some foreign dude whose name looks like a sneeze. How can he read this stuff for fun?

"What?" he says, looking hard at me, and I'm like, "Nothing, man, you do you." I drop the book into his backpack and pass him the blunt. He takes a hit.

"So Dan got with Olivia Scott," I say, and Burke's like, "Yeah, I heard him talking about it. Apparently she was great," and I stare up at the sky, and he's like, "What?" and I'm like, "I didn't say anything," and he's like, "Your silence is more silent than usual silence," and I'm like, "Shut up," and he's like, "So I'm right."

I shrug. "Fine. Olivia's awesome, and Dan sucks, and why does he get to have sex with her, is all I'm saying."

"Hey, why you gotta shit on Dan? Just 'cause you're jealous doesn't mean—"

I chuckle. "Dude, I couldn't be jealous of Dan if I tried." And that part, at least, is true, because it's hard to describe the soul-sucking blandness that is Daniel Silverstein. He has no personality anymore; he just wants to stick his dick in things. Sometimes you look at people, and you can see every second that's going to make up their lives, and it depresses you, because they're clearly fated to do nothing that'll last even a decade after their death, and it's like, why are you sitting all cushy in this suburb when a million disadvantaged kids out there could do so much more with your place in this world? That's Dan these days. It blows seeing him turn into that, too, since he used to be different.

Back in middle school, Dan and Burke and I used to hang out all the time. Middle-school Dan loved dubstep and Mario Kart and late-night walks, where the three of us would talk about everything from what aliens might look like to the meaning of life. But the second we hit freshman year, high-school Dan took over. He stopped talking to us and found new friends, and now every time we pass each other in the hall, he doesn't even nod. Burke and I try not to take it personally, but getting friend-dumped is kind of personal by definition.

Burke taps my shoulder and passes the blunt back to me. I take a long hit—too long—and sit up, my eyes watering, and

Burke says, "So why're you mad at Dan, huh?" and I sigh, because I feel he should get it by now. "Because," I say, "I've had a thing for Olivia Scott for, like, thirty years," and Burke says, "But you haven't ever spoken to her," and I'm like, "*Yeah*, but . . ."

I trail off, floundering to find actual justification for being upset. After a minute, I give up. "Forget it," I mumble. We watch sports teams walking by, red-faced and sweaty from practice. Guys' tennis. Girls' cross-country. Lacrosse. Football . . .

Eventually, Burke says, "If you want to meet up with Olivia, why don't you go to the thing at Dan's this weekend, huh? Maybe she'll be there."

I make a grumbling sound. I'd rather chug cyanide than show up to Dan's sister's birthday party. It's sad, the thought that everyone I know is so repressed, they have to get, *like, oh my God, totally wasted* to have an excuse to act the way they want to act. "Thanks, man, but I'm good," I say. "Like she'd talk to me, anyway."

"Bro, don't be so fucking defeatist," Burke says, and that's a Burke phrase if ever I've heard one, *so fucking defeatist*, but before I can tell him he's ridiculous, an overloud voice butts in:

"Hey. Are you Matt? Matt Jackson?"

I turn. A couple of varsity tennis girls have stopped near my car. The only one I know by name—the one who's talking to me— is Claire Lombardi, who has enough freckles for a family of four, as well as an arsenal of identical tank tops that display *Nike* across her huge chest. The girl is Paloma-famous, since she does every miserable extracurricular this place has to offer: debate team, French Club, Academic Bowl, Young Environmentalists, student government . . . the list goes on.

She moves to the front of my hood, brushing her frizzy red

hair out of her face. Since I can't remember having actually spoken with her before, and since I stay under the radar, it's kind of weird that she knows my name, but I reply, "Uh, yeah. Hey," and she says, "We missed you this afternoon. I can send you the information later by email, though."

"What?" I say, glancing at Burke. "Missed what?"

"Student gov. There are only three candidates, so your chances are pretty good."

"I—chances for—?"

"Make sure you start campaigning next week. It'd be great for the program to have some competition in the presidential race, at least. For, like, visibility's sake."

"Um," I say, trying not to let my confusion show, and she's like, "You're running against Juniper Kipling and Olivia Scott, if you were wondering," and I'm like, "But I—" and then one of her tennis friends nudges her. Claire glances to the right. Her gaze fixes on something near the far end of the lot, and she says too fast, "Heading out—see you," and leaves me sitting there wondering what the hell just happened.

I check over my shoulder to see who scared her off. It's the guys' swim team. For a moment I wonder what Claire's issue is, but then, from the middle of the pack, Lucas McCallum gives me his usual cheerful wave, and I remember his and Claire's heinous breakup last spring, which nobody could shut up about for frickin' ever.

Lucas bounces by, pushing his curly hair back, a smile the size of California plastered across his face as usual. "Hi, Burke! Hey, Matt! How's it going, guys?"

I nod in response, wondering if his cheeks ever get tired. If you turned a six-week-old puppy into a human being, you'd get Lucas. Dude's so cheerful all the time, I keep getting this creeping suspicion that he thinks we're friends because he sells me weed. But that wouldn't make sense—he deals to half the school, providing the teeming masses with an ass-load of pot and cheap beer. Maybe Lucas is just chronically overjoyed to be alive.

He jogs off with the rest of the swim team, leaving Burke and me alone.

"Dude, I don't know what Claire's talking about," I say, looking at Burke. "I didn't sign up for anything."

A second passes, and the corner of Burke's mouth twitches.

"You shithead," I say, realizing. "You did this. You put me on some list for this." And Burke cracks up, and he's like, "Who, me? 'Course not. But I can't wait to see your campaign promises."

I punch him. "I'm gonna kill you."

"Come on, it'll be fun."

I blow my hair out of my eyes, giving him the dirtiest look I can muster, but I can never stay mad long—I don't have the dedication for grudges. Good thing for Burke, too, 'cause he's always doing this, dragging me to after-school clubs or putting my email address on information dis-lists. It's the most random stuff. Last week he signed me up for some national newsletter about clock making. God knows what he's getting out of it.

I lean back on the roof. Dusk hunches over the sky, and the twisted end of our joint blisters on the asphalt beside the car, the bittersweet smell of it floating and fading.

"So, who do you think it is?" Burke says, and I'm like, "Who do you think what is?" and he's like, "Didn't you go to the assembly?" and I laugh so hard, it turns into a coughing fit. "Is that a serious question?" I sputter, and he's like, "Some teacher's sleeping with a student. They don't know who yet."

I give him a confused look and ask, "Am I supposed to care about this?" and he's like, "I mean, it's sort of crazy, huh?" and I'm like, "Not that crazy. It happens everywhere," and he sighs and says, "What's it gotta take for you to be interested in anything, huh, dude?" and I'm sort of affronted. "Hey, get off my case, would you?" I say. "We can't all be, like, conscientious citizens and read *The* fucking *Gay Science* for fun."

Burke shrugs, adjusting his kilt. "It's got nothing to do with reading, man," he says. "I'm talking about, literally, anything. I miss when we used to do shit that wasn't smoking, you know?" and I want to retort, but for the second time in ten minutes, I can't find justification.

The silence stresses me out. What does he want, an apology?

At a loss for what else to do, I pull out my phone. A missed call pops up. It's Mom. "I gotta get home," I say, and Burke's like, "Yeah, it's getting cold," which I guess is sort of true, but I'd stick out even freezing temperatures to remain in the lazy, forgiving environment of late-afternoon Paloma High, because staying here means I don't have to go home. Also, it's nice being around Burke, because he's always thinking something or reading something or making something, and maybe it's pathetic to live vicariously through my best friend, but my hobbies of sleeping, eating, and avoiding responsibilities seem lackluster by comparison. Not that I'd ever tell him that.

My phone rings. I pick up. "Hello?"

"*¿Dónde estás?*" comes the sharp question.

I sigh and look up at the sky. "I'll be right there, Mamá. Calm down, would you?"

She hangs up on me. Nice.

"God, she's the worst," I say, and Burke says calmly, "I'm sure there's been worse," and I give him a glare, because when he gets all reasonable like this, he makes me feel guilty about being unhappy, and that's unhelpful at the best of times. "Later, man," he says, rolling off my car. He buttons his peacoat, loops his scarf twice around his beefy neck, and takes off for his Jeep.

I climb off my car. By the time I slide in, Burke's already gone. Sitting in the driver's seat, I consider rolling another joint to calm myself down, but then I'm distracted by a glimpse of Juniper Kipling hurrying to her Mercedes, the only car left in the junior lot besides mine.

She slips in, takes a second, and starts bawling her eyes out, which baffles me, because what problems could *her* perfect life ever have? And couldn't she go home to do the whole crying thing?

As I shift into drive, I feel like a douchebag for thinking that, because, to be fair, this place is basically empty, and it's not her fault if she's going through something personal. But hey, maybe I'm just bitter because people like Juniper have these roads set up, these highways to success. She's going to go to Yale or Harvard or whatever, partially because she's a music prodigy and smart as all hell, and partially because her parents are filthy rich. And me? Even if I go to college, my parents sure aren't paying for it. Once I move out, college or not, God knows if they'll even stay together. Last night, they argued so late, I had to go in there and ask them to cut it out for Russell's sake. Who's going to stick up for my kid brother when I'm not around anymore?

I stare out my sunroof at the dusk. I hate getting angry or sad or upset. About my parents. About anything. It always seems angsty and undeserved. *What are you, every teenager ever?* says a voice in the back of my head. *Be a little original, asshole.*

I take my time driving home.

HELLO
my name is

JUNIPER KIPLING

Finally,
I am the last car here.
I am an island.

I returned here,
tugged back by some irresistible gravity,
but I hit the ground too hard.
My knees have buckled,
leaving me prostrate.

Stop crying. You're in public.
Grip the wheel tight and
drive. Don't think. Just go.

I'm home, I say,
more a defense than an announcement—
because this place is not home anymore.
The only voice to whisper back is the cuckoo clock,
click, tock, *cuckoo*, crazy.
Crazy, because I hear notes in the silence,

gentle baritone notes,

and no matter how fast I play,

how far my fingers stretch,

how purely the vibrato resonates,

I cannot overwhelm the remembered sound.

The bow trembles in my right hand,

and under my left, my pizzicato slips.

Start again. Again. Over again.

Those two, trying so hard, they cannot know.

Those two, they will never guess.

Every day I have sat like stone at a slab of polished pine,

back-straight/legs-crossed/elbows-in/eyes-down,

dodging questions and hiding from warm voices.

It's been months since I could speak truthfully to those two—

months since I could speak at all without fear tightening my
tongue,

and still they call our house a home.

I am displaced. A watery weight, shifting,

my cup dribbling over.

How have I measured these seven days alone?—in breaths,
blinks, heartbeats?

With numbers, with questions?

No:

with tweezers, I think,

plucking time out from sensitive skin.

Second after stinging second.

I devour my meal in silence.

Last Saturday, I devoured noise and light and the motion of agitated bodies.

I drank with purpose, drank violently,

drank myself to the floorboards.

Last Saturday, I forgot how to feel alone. How to feel.

I forgot clumsy fingers and maple necks,

heartstrings and gut strings,

warm sheets and crisp papers.

I forgot the beginning and the end. *Da Capo al Fine.*

(Hold on until the weekend, Juniper—

you can forget it all again.)

HELLO
my name is

OLIVIA SCOTT

FROM WHERE I'M SITTING IN THE LIVING ROOM, I CAN hear the rattle of keys. Finally. That's got to be Kat.

I flip my textbook shut and walk into the kitchen, hitting the light switch. A chipped lamp sitting on the counter flickers to life, illuminating our wooden table. Our bare fridge is framed by a square gray rug. This house sort of looks as if it took interior-design tips from the little-known "prisons" section of *Better Homes and Gardens*. I ache for drooping pumpkins and trios of pinecones, the decorations our Novembers used to wear when Mom was around. Not even three years ago, but it feels like a different lifetime.

"Hey, where were you?" I ask as Kat shuts the door. "I called you, like, three times."

"I know." She kicks off her shoes beside the fridge.

"Dude, you've been out of rehearsal for nearly an hour."

"I know," she repeats. "Thanks for the update, helicopter sister."

The unwanted nickname hits me right in the pet peeve. I try to muster patience. "Dad's working until eleven, so he said not to be loud when he comes home. He needs a good night's sleep, so . . . I don't know. Use headphones, if you're gonna game."

Kat trudges toward the staircase. I talk faster, calling after her. "And I made dinner. And also, there were two new messages about you skipping class, so can we talk abo—"

She starts up the stairs.

"Jesus Christ, Kat," I say. "Could you—"

She turns. "What?"

When I get a good look at her face, my angry thoughts stop swirling. My sister looks exhausted. Her neck-length blond hair is bedraggled and tangled. It's brittle from too many home-brewed bleach treatments, but her roots have started to grow out dark. The circles under her eyes glare like wine stains on white cloth. Her lips are thin and bitten.

"Are you okay?" is all I say. It comes out timid.

She half smiles. It looks an awful lot like a sneer. "Yeah, sure," she says. "And how was *your* day, honey?"

Hurt bursts in me like a bitter grape. She strides upstairs.

What is her problem? Doesn't she see how hard I'm trying?

Nothing works with her anymore. For hours, Kat locks herself in her room with her best friends: BioShock, Mass Effect, and Half-Life 2. I hear shooting through the walls. Amazing, how loud her laptop gets.

It's not my job to drag her out kicking and screaming, but some days, I wish I had the guts to. Our house has started to feel like solitary confinement.

My phone buzzes with a text. I yank it out—it's Dan Silverstein. **Hey you, how are things?**

I sigh. This Dan thing has been so well publicized, I don't want to reply. But it's not fair to take it out on him because other people are giving me shit.

Things are solidly average, I reply. How about you?

As I wait for his response, I take the pasta off the stove and spoon myself a bowl, then put the rest back to stay warm for Kat. I always hope she'll join me for dinner, but she never does; this might be for the best. Last time we ate together was maybe a month ago. We spoke six sentences to each other. Two of them were "Hey" and "Hey."

I can't help remembering dinners from eighth grade. Better-cooked, for one thing, because my mother—unlike me—was an expert at putting food items into heating implements without causing fires. More than that, though, dinners tasted better with the family around the table. Mom's absence is always glaring, and tonight, Dad's chair is empty, too. He's been working later and later these days. This is the third day in a row he's out until eleven.

I wolf down my pasta so fast, it burns. I flinch, rolling bits of skin off the roof of my mouth with my tongue.

My phone buzzes. I'm doing pretty good, Dan says. I had a nice time Saturday

Me too, I reply. Not too much of a lie. The guy's no Han to my Leia, but he was cute and nice and seemed pretty harmless. A surprisingly rare combination.

So what's up? he asks.

Just having dinner. Pasta yay!

Oh sorry didn't mean to interrupt

No, I mean, I just finished, it's okay, I reply, standing to wash my plate. What's up with you?

Not much, is all he says. I wait for a follow-up, but nothing comes. I can't help but laugh. Why did he text me if he's going to say that "not much" is up? How do male brains work?

Then a picture of his dick pops up on my phone screen.

I let out a splutter and drop my phone. "What? Why?" I say loudly at the phone, sort of hoping Siri will shed light on the situation. There must be a mistake. Did I say something that made him think I wanted a picture of that?

I snatch my phone up and scroll back through my texts. I definitely didn't say anything inviting, unless he has a weird attraction to pasta that I don't want to know about.

It's not even the appropriate time for a dick pic! It's 6:10 PM! Although there really isn't an appropriate time for dick pics you didn't ask for.

I text back, **Dude.**

His reply: **Dude what**

I tap in what I think is a well-measured response. Though it's a little tough to get past the panicked mental loop of *Penis! Penis! Penis!*

What do you expect me to do with that?? I say.

Idk? Enjoy? he replies.

"Enjoy," I say to the phone. *"Enjoy?"* I can't help picturing an ad for Italian food. *Enjoy!*

A laugh spills out, a high, nervous giggle that hardly sounds like my voice. I set down the phone and hunch over the kitchen table. God, if Kat is hearing this, she must think I've had a psychotic break.

An ellipsis bubble pops up as he types again. The next gem of a text: **So I don't get anything back? ;)**

I sigh. Should have seen that coming. "Nope," I say to my phone.

A sound comes from behind me. I whip around. Kat stands in the threshold.

"Hey," I say, shoving my phone into my pocket.

She nods and heads for the stove. With one careless motion, she dumps the rest of the spaghetti onto a plate. Quiet hangs between us as she slumps into a chair, spinning a fork between her fingers.

I ease myself into the chair opposite her. She gives me a look, her blue eyes narrowed. Those blue eyes—Mom's blue eyes—are the only quality we share. Otherwise, we're anti-identical twins. Kat barely stands five foot two, and she's so pale, I used to make jokes about her trailing ectoplasm, back in eighth grade when we did things like make jokes with each other.

"Rehearsal go okay?" I ask.

She shrugs and keeps eating. A long minute passes.

I clear my throat, eyeing Kat warily. "So. About going to things."

"Yeah, relax. I took care of the class skips. Got Dad to sign notes saying I was sick."

"I—but you weren't."

"But he signed them." She shrugs. "Problem solved."

I lean an elbow on the table. I need to talk to Dad, apparently. I understand wanting to give us some leeway when his work schedule is this crazy, but he can't let the reins go completely like this.

Dad's the assistant store manager at the McDonald's on Franklin Road. I would've thought having the word *manager* in your title would mean fewer hours, but Dad always does obscene amounts of overtime. Would he really rather deal with drive-through assholes than us? Or are we having money problems he's keeping quiet?

My phone buzzes. I'll wait if I have to ;)

"Who is that?" Kat says.

"Just this one dude."

"The guy you fucked last weekend?"

"Hey," I say sharply. "Watch it."

"We have a winner." She barks out a laugh. "You and the rando from my algebra class. Match made in heaven."

My cheeks burn. Great. I'm even a walking punch line to my sister now.

Maybe I should go upstairs. Why do I try with her anymore? Why do I do this to myself, sit here and take this?

Because she used to be different, says the voice in my head. But looking at Kat, I can hardly remember her before. The Kat in middle school had long, wispy hair down to the middle of her back. She was always quiet but never a recluse. She used to sit with Juniper, Claire, and me at lunch, occasionally trying to convince us to game with her. The only game we ever played was tennis, though, during the summers, the four of us splitting up for two-on-two. Whichever team had Claire on it always won.

Then we left middle school, and Mom left Paloma, disappearing into the depths of the West Coast. It's been two and a half years since Kat went quiet.

But when did she start being mean? There's no neat dividing line. Would she have said something like that this past summer? Last year? How did we get to this point?

"So, what number boy are you on now?" Kat says. "An even dozen?"

"Dude." I set my phone down hard on the table. "What is your problem?"

"I don't have a problem. You're the one with the problem, obviously."

"Okay, stop. Why are you being like this? I'm not doing anything to you."

"You're still sitting there, aren't you?"

It hits like a kick to the shin. I stand up. "Okay," I manage, keeping my voice as unaffected as possible. "Grow up, Kat."

Nothing would give me greater satisfaction than to slam my chair back into place, but I resist. I turn stiffly on my heel and force myself not to stomp up the stairs. The second I'm at the top, out of sight, I lean against the wall, staring at the dark wallpaper. Family photos hang along the hallway, a nostalgic trail.

Mom, what would you say to her? What would you do?

Mom was scatterbrained, nervous, and kind to a fault. She gave herself away in handfuls to everybody she met. I bet she would hug Kat until she melted, refusing to let go until Kat confessed whatever the hell was wrong.

My fingernails dig into my palms. No matter what Mom would do, Kat will hate it on me. "Helicopter sister," she said—the most infuriating thing I've been called in a while, which is saying something. I'm not trying to suffocate her, but what am I supposed to do? Dad's not going to pull her out of this spiral, and somebody has to. It's not as if I enjoy chasing her down, trying to get her to go to classes and shit. It shouldn't be my job.

I trudge down the hall into my room and collapse on my bed, tugging out my phone. **Cmon sexy, please?** says Dan's latest.

After a second, I realize that I'm actually considering it. Why? There's no guarantee it wouldn't get leaked, and my reputation sure as hell doesn't need helping along.

As I reread his texts, a weird yearning builds behind my sternum. It's sort of sad, but beside Andrea's glare, Claire's judgment, and my sister's scorn, this invitation seems welcoming. The persistence is obnoxious, but it at least reminds me that my presence doesn't repulse everyone the way it apparently does my sister.

I don't send pictures, I text back, after a long minute. Please don't send me that sort of thing.

I turn over, exhausted.

HELLO
my name is

VALENTINE SIMMONS

TOWELING MY HAIR, I SCAN MY BEDROOM SHELVES
again, nurturing the hope that I might have missed something.
Of course not, though. I have every book counted: thirty-seven on
the shelves by the door, eighteen on the shelf above my mirror,
and another sixty-six in the bookcase under my loft bed. As of
this afternoon, I've read every book twice, except *Physics of the
Impossible*, which I never planned on rereading. Not my cup of tea;
it's clearly targeted at people who like science fiction.

I don't know why people find sci-fi so fascinating. Some of it
has a glaring lack of common sense. The inescapable trope of a
future world where flying cars have replaced all other modes of
transportation? Yes, excellent. Have these authors ever given a
single thought to acrophobia? Just a thought, of course, but for
the millions of people with a paralyzing fear of heights, flying
cars might be a tiny bit *absolutely terrifying*. But no; authors never
seem to care about the acrophobics of the world.

"Valentine?" calls my mother. "Are you still in the shower?"

"If I were, I wouldn't be able to hear you," I reply, hanging up
my towel.

"Dinner, smart aleck."

I pull on a T-shirt and head to the kitchen. My mother places a plate before me, and as she settles at the other end of the table, I brace myself for the usual mindless onslaught of *How was your day? Learn anything new? Make any friends?* One of the many downsides of having a guidance counselor for a mother: her endless enthusiasm for small talk.

But the only thing she says is, "Your dad's still at the lab."

"Yes, I gathered that," I say blankly. "From his absence."

She says nothing else. Suspicious, I sip my water and peer at her over the edge of my glass. Her head is bowed, her honey-brown bangs drooping over her eyes. She stares at her fork, stirring the mashed potatoes rather than doing anything productive with them.

I'm not impressed. She's always telling *me* to eat my food instead of rearranging it.

"Something's wrong," I guess.

She looks up at me and smiles quickly. "No, nothing."

"Okay . . ."

"Just . . . the assembly."

"Ah. That." I take a bite and put down my fork. "What about it?"

"Something like this happening at Paloma." She shakes her head. "I hope they figure it all out soon. The presentation upset me a bit."

"Why?"

She leans an elbow on the table, giving me an unusually wry smile. "You'll understand when you have kids."

"Not happening," I mutter, returning to my food. "Anyway, I thought the whole presentation was straightforward. No use being preoccupied over it."

Hypocritical of me to say, maybe, given that I can't stop thinking about the assembly. But that's because my message triggered this whole ordeal.

Two weeks ago, I stayed after school, waiting for a ride home from my mother. At 6:00, long after the halls emptied, I passed the faculty break room in the new wing. A voice seeped through the closed door. I came just close enough to catch it.

"Nobody's going to find out." That phrase caught me mid-step. A girl's unfamiliar voice was speaking, carrying an undercurrent of anxiety. "Please—try not to worry. I'm not in your class, nobody sees us together, and I haven't told anyone at all. I promise." A pause. The sound of a kiss. "I love you."

I backed away from the door. As what I'd heard sunk in, I scurried away, my pulse quickening. I sent the message that evening through the anonymous submission form on the school's website: *Teacher and student in romantic relationship. Overheard in faculty break room after school. Identities unknown.*

It's strange, but now I almost feel as if I shouldn't have done anything, which is absurd. Wouldn't that make me an accessory to the crime?

What little appetite I had vanishes. I excuse myself, and for once, my mother doesn't say a word about my neglected food. I return to my room, but none of it offers any comfort: not the cracked spines of favorite books, not the cool glow of my laptop, not the frame of blackish night through the skylight. I spin the gyroscope I keep on my desk—once, twice—but its hypnotizing whir hardly calms me.

I grab the spare keys to my mother's car from a hook on the

door. Bundling my coat on, I stride through the kitchen, where my mother still sits. "Where are you going?" she asks.

"Out," I say. I don't wait for a response.

DRIVING AROUND AT NIGHT ALWAYS HELPS CLEAR MY mind. I'm not sure why. It's certainly not the view; there isn't much to see in Paloma, Kansas, population 38,000. I suppose solitude just feels more excusable if you're in motion.

I pass the series of glorified strip malls that comprise our downtown, local businesses and antiques shops. After they peter out, a lonely-looking McDonald's stands on the left, the only evidence that corporate America acknowledges our existence. The rest of this small city is a maze of residential neighborhoods. Some are cookie-cutter suburbs with identical mini mansions; some are yuppie projects liberally adorned with round windows and organic gardens; some are tiny forgotten streets with chain-link fences and our meager police force lurking around.

I end up at Paloma High somehow, parked in the junior lot. Our school is a different building at night, an empty body with no light in its eyes. Staring out my windshield at the three-story mishmash of brick and modernism, I can only think about the tiny sound of those two people kissing. The remembered whisper, *I love you.*

Part of me wonders what it would feel like, a kiss. I've never felt compelled to try putting my mouth on somebody else's mouth. I refuse to believe it feels like a symphony of violins, or a ferociously panning camera, or an eruption of emotion in the center of my chest, or anything else it's supposed to be.

I look at my hands. I lift two fingers, close my eyes, and press my lips against them.

Nothing. It feels like nothing at all.

After a motionless second, I take my hand away. I exit the car and slam the door, embarrassed all of a sudden that I felt compelled to do that. Embarrassed that I even wondered. I clamber onto the hood of the car, lean back against the windshield, and stare upward, my hands deep in my pockets. The galaxy is spray-painted across the sky. Looking at it, I feel swallowed up. Infinitesimally small.

I know Earth is whirling on its axis at one thousand miles per hour. I know it is whipping around the sun at sixty-six thousand miles per hour. I know we're all hurtling around the center of the Milky Way at four hundred and eighty-three thousand miles per hour. But lying here, I feel motionless. I take a breath, hold it for a count of ten, and let it go. It billows out over my head and trails off into the black sky.

You've done your part, a voice says in the back of my mind. *You have no more information to give the school. Worrying about this is pointless.*

But the girl's voice lingers in my ears, low, husky, and sweet.

HELLO
my name is

JUNIPER KIPLING

Since Monday, I've heard three days' worth of theories.

Theories about who would be enough of a creep to screw a student.

Theories about who would be enough of a whore to screw a teacher.

The lunchroom has felt like a den of wolves,

table after table filled with sharp teeth.

Strangers in line behind me yap and bark—

they have new meat to tear into, today:

Claire's candidate list, newly posted.

"The student government lists are so hilarious, I almost died—"

"Matt Jackson is on there, what on earth—"

"—and Olivia Scott, which, like . . . you know?"

"Yeah."

"I've heard Olivia is, like, super nice. But she's suuuch a sluuut, it's insaaane, oh my God."

"Yeah, holy shit, did you hear about her and Dan Silverstein last weekend?"

"Who wants to bet it's her who's dating the teacher? Oh my God,

wait. I'm a genius. What if those guys are, like, a smoke screen of
sluttiness?"

(I round on them because this week has built up
and up,
and I can't hold this towering weight anymore.)
"Don't
you
dare!"

This student body is a body
poisoning itself deliberately and intravenously.
Acid and hatred and bile.
No wonder I feel sick.

It's quiet.
Two glossed O-mouths, four lined eyes staring.
I have never seen these girls before.
I hope I will never see them again.
If they'll condemn Olivia's open legs,
they'll condemn me if they ever find out—
and they can go ahead.
Isn't the number of partners as unimportant as the height,
the weight, the eye color?
The age . . . ?
But no, no, *of course not,*
because we've been trained to obey adults;
because rejecting somebody takes a steely, undeniable power
when you've been brought up to accommodate, to appease, to please;

because age does matter—I know that.

I swear.

"*I'm sorry, Juniper,*" one of the girls says, "*I didn't mean—*"

I dash away. Past our table. Olivia and Claire look at me with
widened eyes,

as though I am made of stardust

and they cannot drink in enough of my

strange, unfamiliar light.

A shocked look in the hallway as I walk as fast as I can,

two, three, four scandalized glances for the girl showing emotion in the light of day.

I splay my fingers across my face,

as if no one can see me past them, I wish, *I wish,*

around-the-corner-through-the-door slammed-locked-shut—
shaking—trembling—

safe.

Light echoes off the bathroom walls,

rings off the inside of the stalls.

Minutes. I spread calm like sunblock onto my skin.

There is a scream cupped somewhere in my ribs.

I shove my fingers under hot water. They turn red.

I look at my eyes in the mirror, but something there is not
mine.

I have not settled back into my skin,

and I cannot coerce myself into believing it:

we are through, we are through, we are through.

HELLO
my name is

CLAIRE LOMBARDI

YOU KNOW THAT FEELING WHERE YOU'RE EMBAR-
rassed on someone else's behalf, and you want to dive under a
blanket, thrash around, and yell, *Why on earth would you do that?*

I never thought I'd experience that sort of secondhand humiliation for Juniper, of all people. She's so put-together all the time,
it's sometimes hard to believe she's real.

Not that she's perfect. Nobody's perfect. I'm not perfect.

Still. It's kind of reassuring when Juniper shows the world
she's not. Yelling at two random girls in the middle of a crowded
lunchroom is far from perfect. I've never done anything that
embarrassing.

Go ahead and judge me for this, but her screwing up like that
makes me feel as if I've won some sort of unstated competition.

"The hell was that?" Olivia says, staring after Juniper.

"No clue. I'm going to see if she wants to talk." I stand, crum-
pling my trash into my brown paper bag.

"She's not going to talk, dude," Olivia says. "Remember last
winter's recital?"

I grimace. It'd be hard to forget Juniper's concert last December.
In the middle of the final movement of a concerto, she fumbled

a transition and stopped playing, to crushing silence from the audience and accompanist. She had to restart the movement, a grueling, seven-minute piece of technical wizardry. When the audience left, she locked herself in the bathroom, and nothing her parents, Olivia, or I said could coax her out.

After half an hour, she emerged, quiet and collected. She's still never mentioned it.

"Well, I can try," I say.

"Godspeed," Olivia says.

I head out, frowning as I hoist my backpack higher on my shoulders. Twenty pounds of textbooks and notebooks and overflowing binders. As I leave the lunchroom, a voice in the back of my head says, *It wouldn't kill Olivia to* try *talking to her, at least.* But Olivia never does that with me and Juni. She doesn't push us like that. In my opinion, she hates getting that close.

When Olivia's mom left Paloma, I did something for her every day. I texted, called, visited—I poured everything I had into her recovery. Back then, the summer before freshman year, I was too young to drive, so I cajoled my sister, Grace, into driving me wherever Olivia needed me to be. But when I went through my breakup in May, Olivia hid behind a bland, scared layer of sympathy, offering me platitudes like "It'll be okay soon," and "Tell me if I can do anything."

Looking back, I don't know if that was fair.

As I turn the corner, I catch a glimpse of Juni way down the hall, disappearing into the girls' bathroom. I hurry after her.

When I reach the door, I push against it with my shoulder. She's locked it. "Juniper?" I say. "It's Claire. Want to talk?"

"It's fine," she says, muffled. "Please. I need some time."

"Okay. Let me know." I back away, stifling a sigh. Olivia was right. Of course.

Sometimes I feel as if Olivia and Juni operate on a different plane than me. They love pretending everything's fine. They understand that about each other. Me, though—I hate keeping everything bottled up. I feel messy, compared with them. They're neatly printed arias, and I'm a sloppy sonatina, splattered across loose staff paper. Juniper is elegant; Olivia is stoic. And God knows what I am.

All this squabbling and silence among the three of us has me on edge. Are we drifting away from one another? We've been a trio, inseparable, since sixth grade—the thought of losing them makes my heart squeeze.

I gnaw on my pinky nail. "Losing them"—that's not quite right, is it? It's not that the three of us are moving apart. I'm trying as hard as ever. It's the two of them who are pulling away from me.

That's how it feels, anyway. Juni and Olivia are a matched set as always, and I'm some spectator growing more distant by the day.

I glance back at the bathroom door. The fact that Olivia was right about this makes me angry. She knows Juniper better than I do, is what that says. I was wrong, it says.

I hate being wrong.

HELLO
my name is

LUCAS M^{c}CALLUM

AS I'M DRIVING BACK TO SCHOOL FROM THE LIQUOR store, I keep thinking about this TV show I used to watch in New York, *The Confessor*. The title character, the host, is a dude called Antoine Abbotson, who's short and smiley and wears a navy blue suit. Each show, he brings in three people who each have a secret. The idea is, the Confessor bids up the price to get them to confess that secret on live TV. But if he hits a certain dollar threshold—a concealed number somewhere under $50,000—the contestant walks away empty-handed. Sometimes, though, the people on that show make bank. One woman got paid $47,000 to explain to her husband that the front room in their house smelled awful because she'd pooped into their upright piano while sleepwalking, couldn't reach down far enough to extract the resulting poop after the fact, and never had the heart to tell anyone.

It's strange, watching that show, seeing how people price their secrets. My family hangs their eccentricities around their necks when they walk out the door every day. There's Uncle Jeremy, who won a trophy for having the longest mustache in New York State. There's my cousin Cabret, who dropped out of college to start her own private-investigation service. And you can't forget

Great-Grandma Louise, who at age ninety-one lives alone in a cabin in the Catskills and still checks her traps every morning for dead animals.

My family values honesty for a couple of reasons: first, the Ten Commandments say, "Thou shalt not bear false witness"; and second, my family is full of givers. Givers palm off their secrets with every handshake; they lay it all bare.

Me? I keep one secret from my parents. It's boring, and everyone at school knows it: I sell drugs. Not hard drugs, just weed and booze, but I'm not about to tell my mom and dad. They think my money is leftover from sweeping aisles down at Brent Hardware, where I work over the summers.

It'd break their hearts if I ever told them, but as selfless as they are, what they give me never feels like enough. I always want more, and Paloma only makes it worse. This place seemed unreal when I got here freshman year: a dollhouse town, unimaginably small, and it's shrunk since then. I've met everyone. I've been everywhere. There's nothing left to collect now, except profits from deals. It gets depressing, sometimes.

As I turn into the junior lot, the cases of beer make a chorus of metallic clinks in the back of my truck. Then a scuffed-up Camry looms out of nowhere, its horn blaring. My foot jerks toward the brake pedal. Too late.

The Camry smacks into my front bumper, and I lurch forward. The sound isn't so much a crash as a thump. "Car thump" doesn't sound as dramatic as "car crash." I feel sort of gypped.

In the sudden stillness, I take inventory of my body, scribbling a mental list across my mind's eye:

- *Icy skin.*
- *Pulse in strange places—earlobes, forearms?*
- *No pain.*

I'm in one piece, at least, and I have something to cross off my "Never Have I Ever" list.

The wounded Camry pulls into a spot, and I park beside it, bolting out to check the damage. My truck door squeals as I swing it shut.

The Camry came out unscathed, except for a tiny dent under one headlight. My pickup, on the other hand, looks as if it got into a fight with a Transformer. The Camry must've hit the last thing keeping my front bumper attached. Now it dangles askew, a lopsided leer.

My jaw tightens, and I bury one hand in my hair. Look at me, worrying over a broken, mud-encrusted pickup. What would my middle-school friends think?

It takes a minute to shake the thought. First of all, if everything goes according to plan, I'll have saved up enough for a new car, a nice one, before graduation. Second of all, I'm out of touch with everyone from the Pinnacle School, so their opinions don't matter.

Still, I can't get rid of the complex that place gave me.

My middle school was a private academy in Brooklyn's richest neighborhood. I was a scholarship kid, the poorest person there by a margin so huge, it was humiliating. Everything about me stood out, from my haircut to my clothes to my commute. An hour's trip separated our apartment in Coney Island from Pinnacle's cushy spot in Brooklyn Heights, and I did homework on the Q, wedged into a corner of the train car beside my mother.

Pinnacle kids never seemed to think about money, but around them, it was all I saw. Every break, my Instagram and Facebook feeds flooded: photos of spring trips to the Maldives, skiing trips to Aspen, and summer homes in Europe. They wore their wealth effortlessly. The preppier crowd had polo players and Golden Fleece logos on their pastel clothes. The "alternative" kids wore baggy woolen tops and artfully shredded leggings, but it was the same old story of unspeakable amounts of money, just translated into a different language.

I don't miss that place. I still feel embarrassed about my family because of it. I still worry how we look to people, even here in Paloma, where we're now comfortably lower-middle class.

"Lucas, you okay?"

I look up from my bumper. The sight of a familiar face floods me with relief—I've dealt to Matt Jackson since I started freshman year.

I nod at Matt. "You good?"

"Yeah. You wanna call the cops?"

"Cops." I glance at my truck bed. "Right."

Matt eyes the tarp that covers the cases. "We don't have to. My car's fine, so if you're okay driving around with your bumper half off, be my guest."

"Thanks, dude. Appreciate it."

Matt's head bobs. The kid is low-key cool, but getting him to say much is tough. He's also hot, in a my-type-of-way, but I've gotten good at ignoring when guys are hot, since everyone at this school is so aggressively heterosexual.

According to an article I read, three or four percent of people are gay, lesbian, or bi. Wherever they dredged up that statistic, it wasn't Paloma High School. Twelve hundred kids, and I haven't met a single other queer person. Definitely no Gay-Straight Alliance Club here.

Sometimes I feel like we should have a club for all minority populations, since this place has all the ethnic diversity of your average mayonnaise jar. The culture shock was real at first, moving here, where everyone's the same shade of white and the same subgenre of Methodist.

Matt opens his back door and leans into his car, his shoulder blades pitching tents in the back of his hoodie. His voice is muffled as he rummages through the mess in his backseat. "Hey, are you selling today?"

"Yeah, hit me up after school."

"Sweet." He shoulders his backpack and shuts the door. "It's a date."

Something goes still in the center of my chest. I stay quiet as Matt pulls a beanie over his head. His eyes are light brown and guarded, and I can't help but wonder.

A date?

An impulse hits me. Maybe it's the adrenaline still zipping over my skin, or maybe it's the smell of cold air conjuring the feeling of someone's hand in mine. Winter of eighth grade was the first time I ever held a guy's hand, and chilly afternoons remind me of it every so often: Caleb's warm, uncertain grip.

"Hey, Matt," I say. "You maybe want to get coffee sometime? Or dinner or something?"

His expression freezes. If it were a computer screen, it would read: *404 error. Unable to process request.* "I . . . what?" he says.

Bad guess. Crap. *Say something, Lucas.*

"Nothing, never mind," I blurt out. The least convincing three words ever spoken.

Matt, of course, because he is not a moron, doesn't buy it for a second. He stares at me as if I'm a poisonous snake that's tried to strike up friendly conversation. "Weren't you straight, like, six months ago?"

A gust of wind scurries through the parking lot. I watch it toy with the heavy leather laces of my Sperry Top-Siders. I shouldn't have said anything.

Nobody cared at Pinnacle, home to yuppie liberals galore. My friend Alicia used to kiss her girlfriend in the stairwell, and they were only thirteen, and nobody cared. Paloma High, though, is different. On the swim team, if you make a one-word complaint about a workout, you get told to "suck it up, fag." After a hard test, people whine, "That was gay as shit." And when my teammates compliment one another, they follow up with "no homo." (They do this every time, as if people might've forgotten from the last time that they're not a homo.) I've never seen anyone getting crucified for actually *being* queer, but that's just one step up from, "Suck it up, fag." So I've stayed quiet.

I should say "no homo," pretend I was kidding, but I can't get the words out. They taste bitter sitting on my tongue.

Matt still looks startled. "I thought you dated that Claire chick forever."

"I did."

"So?" he says.

I shrug. "So . . . what?"

"So how does that work if you're gay?"

"I'm not gay."

He looks baffled. "You just asked me out, dude."

"Yeah, well, I'm not gay. It's—"

The warning bell blares, saving me the explanation. Matt hoists his backpack higher on his shoulder and gives up. "Okay, whatever. After school? Weed? We good?"

"Sure," I say. "And, um, Matt?"

"What?"

"Would you . . . don't say anything, all right?"

He shrugs. "Yeah, no."

He walks off, leaving me uneasy but relieved to see him go. I hate the *What is a pansexual?* conversation. It means explaining the same thing I've explained so many times before to every cousin, aunt, and uncle in our address book. I'll come out a million times before I'm dead, and I'm already bored of it.

To be fair, though, the *What is a pansexual?* conversation is a million times better than the *That doesn't sound real* conversation. Uncle Jeremy still stands by his claim that my sexuality is imaginary. Nice to know I don't exist.

Mostly, though, I'm lucky in the family department, since my parents are the type of Christians who don't stick too close to Leviticus. My dad still wants me to settle down with a girl, but he's stopped saying it out loud, at least.

The seed of the secret being out in the Paloma world worries me. I want to snatch it back, put it deep in my pocket. Never talk about it again.

Making sure the lot's empty, I transfer a half-dozen cases of Miller to Dan Silverstein's SUV, grab my cash from the trunk, and head out. Thumbing through the thin leaves of twenties, loving the smell and feel of them, I cross the green at a jog. It's ridiculous, the profits I make, with a couple of extra dollars per case as commission. People always want the same stuff: beer that's basically sugar water and enough weed to sedate a bull elephant.

The only vaguely difficult part of this was getting hooked up in the first place. For the liquor, I called in a favor from back in New York to get a fake ID sent to me here, since fakes in town are way overpriced and way unconvincing. Now, with my magic piece of plastic, my secret identity is local superhero Anderson Lewitt, a twenty-two-year-old from Vermont who always buys in bulk.

I got lucky with the weed. The guy who used to deal to our school moved away six months into my freshman year, and I networked my way into replacing him. My supplier is a morbidly obese thirty-six-year-old named Phil who prefers to go by "Teezy." He has never explained this to me.

The bell rings. "Crap," I mutter, stowing my wallet deep in my pocket. I take the last bit of the green at a run, shoulder through the door, and skid into the Spanish room. Señor Muniz-Alonso gives me a hawklike glare, and I respond with a sheepish grin, scurrying to my table.

"Luciano . . . *tarde,*" Muniz-Alonso says, like a death sentence. "*Y fuiste tarde ayer también. ¡Ten cuidado! No quiero darte una detención . . .*"

I try to translate the words, but they slip away the second he says them. "Sorry," I say, sitting down.

"*En español, por favor.*"

"Uh," I say. "*Lo siento.*"

Muniz-Alonso goes back to writing irregular conjugations on the board, and I relax.

"Yeah, Luke, *ten cuidado.*" My tablemate, Herman, elbows me. I elbow him back, grinning. Herman swims backstroke, and of course, the second he joined the team, people nicknamed him Merman. He has such long, thick hair that some people call him Mermaid instead, but I don't know. I'm into the idea of mer-dudes drifting through the ocean, straggly hair wafting down to their waists.

Muniz-Alonso starts another conjugation chart. I wait for him to finish, stretching my arms out. Herman eyes my wrist. "Yo," he says, "nice watch."

"Thanks," I say. Before I can restrain myself, the brand slips out. "Movado."

He looks mystified. "Huh?"

I clear my throat. "Knockoff," I lie.

"Oh. Thought you were conjugating on me there."

I grin, rubbing my thumb across the watch face. I don't mention the price tag: most of August's profits. I want to regret spending nearly a thousand dollars on a watch—I could be saving the money for my car fund or, hell, helping my parents with the bills—but I can't regret it, as much as I try. With something this valuable wrapped around my wrist, I get a thrill every time I glance down. I'm already thinking of my next buy, Gucci or Citizen, stacked up by the dozens in my online cart.

Muniz-Alonso steps back, revealing the conjugation charts. Sounds of copying break the air, pencils scratching on notebooks, a few fingertips tapping laptop keys. I take my pencil from behind my ear. I bought myself a new laptop last Christmas, but when it comes to notes, the feel of writing satisfies me more.

"Yo, Mer," I say quietly, starting to copy. "Anything happening tomorrow night?"

"Not much. I heard some of the team's doing a surprise birthday party for Layna."

"Probably at Bailey's house, huh? You think they'd mind if I showed?"

"I don't think it's open, man." Herman copies a conjugation chart from the board, brushing his hair out of his face.

"So what else's going on?" I ask.

He lets out a laugh. "You'd know better than me."

"Okay, so nothing," I say, scribbling down *tendré, tendrás, tendrá.* "Know what? I'm gonna get some of the guys together. Nothing worse than a quiet Friday night."

"Dad, come onnn," Herman says, pitching his voice up to a whine. "Give the team bonding a rest."

I chuckle. They can rest when I'm dead. When you move every few years, you live with shallow roots. I've been getting ripped up all my life, and I'm done with it. Time's accelerating. I'm not aiming to end up with nobody and nothing.

Teenage years are the best years of our lives. They keep saying that. I don't know, though. I keep grasping for people, hunting for them. I take people and I write them down, and I think about the ones I want to keep. And sometimes I find people, and I wonder—I don't know. I wonder, are these really the best people we're going to be?

HELLO
my name is

OLIVIA SCOTT

PUNCTUAL AS ALWAYS, MR. JACKSON," SAYS MR. García, opening the door.

Matt Jackson slouches into our English class a full ten minutes late, a new record, looking unapologetic. "Sorry," he mumbles, the cherry tips of his hair dipping into his eyes. "Got in a car accident."

"Everyone okay?" Mr. García asks. Matt shrugs and heads past my desk to the back of the room, ignoring everyone who looks at him.

Mr. García sighs, looking weary. Somehow, I've never seen him give Matt a late slip, although he's been on time all of twice this year. "All right," García says, picking up a piece of chalk. "So, saying good-bye to *The Good Earth* unit. Next up: we're supposed to cover some European books as part of international literature. But for the most part, this list is so standard, I'm sure you've already read some of them. So I've decided to change this unit."

García passes out a stack of sheets, which we hand back, seat to seat. "I've split the eighteen of you into pairs," he says, "and each pair gets a book. Up until Christmas, we'll have presentations on these nine works. Until the first presentation, we'll be reading excerpts in class, so you'll have a homework break for a bit."

Appreciative murmurs rise around the room. García leans against his desk, waiting for the rustling to stop. As he folds his arms, it occurs to me that if it weren't for the jacket and tie, he could pass for a senior. There are actual seniors who look older than he does. I can't help wondering . . .

No, I scold myself. The idea of García creeping on a student is ridiculous. He doesn't seem to care about anything besides English. Most teachers at least mention something about their lives outside class, but not García. With him, it's *the text, the text, the text*.

Still. Glancing around the room, I see seventeen blank faces, and I bet all of them have wondered the same thing over the last few days.

The guy in front of me lets the paper stack flop onto my desk, and I take a sheet, scanning it. García has paired me with Matt Jackson. I stifle a sigh, remembering Juniper's diagnosis of their so-called "joint" biology project. Our book? *Inferno* by Dante Alighieri. At least we didn't get stuck with *Les Misérables*—I could spend three hours a day reading that thing and still not be done by July. Despite my love for reading, it takes me ages to digest each sentence. Mom read to me until I was old enough to want to keep it a secret, for my dignity's sake.

Matt and I have the first presentation date, due to go next Thursday. There goes the next week of my life, sacrificed to the flames of hell.

"All right," García says. "We're going to take ten minutes to meet in pairs and figure out which type of presentation you want to do. The options are at the bottom—you can pick a skit, a game, or a PowerPoint. Though if you're going to do a PowerPoint, you can't just read the Wiki article off some slides and call it a day."

People laugh as we stand and shift around, rearranging ourselves into our pairs. I head to the back and slide into the desk in front of Matt. He's slouched so far down in his seat, his chest brushes the edge of his desk.

"Hey," I say.

Up close, Matt has a weird face. Almost feral, with narrow eyes and a sharp, asymmetrical mouth tilted in a perpetual smirk. He glances at me before going back to the sheet.

I turn my desk to face him. "So, what do you think you want to do?"

He shrugs.

". . . right," I say, clicking my pen. "I'd rather die than do a skit about *Inferno*, so there's that."

"You know it?" he asks.

"What?"

"Like, have you read it?" Matt has a quiet, husky voice. He rushes through words as if he's not allowed to be talking.

"Just excerpts, but I know the plot," I say. "Basically, Virgil gives Dante this guided tour of the nine circles of hell, and Dante wanders around judging people and fainting a ton. Which is kind of like, it seems sorta dangerous to drop unconscious in hell of all places, but I guess my experience there is limited, so."

The corner of Matt's mouth twitches. For a moment I think I might coax a chuckle out of him, but he stays quiet.

I wait for him to offer some sort of opinion. Nothing happens. "Okay," I say. "What if we did, like, a game, where people have to sort themselves into the nine rings?"

Not the tiniest change in expression. Is the dude going to talk at all, or am I going to have to monologue until this project gets done?

I raise my eyebrows and ask, "What do you think, Matt?"

He bobs his narrow shoulders in the laziest shrug I've ever seen. "I mean, suggesting that everyone in our class is going to hell is a good start, I guess."

Taken aback, I laugh. He looks almost embarrassed.

"Cool," I say. "So let's have a presentation poster, and a station for every circle, and we can have sheets outlining which sins are in which place."

He lets out a mumbling noise that sounds somewhat affirmative.

"I'll message you later so we can figure out details," I say. "Are we friends on Facebook?"

He shakes his head.

I take out my phone under the desk, open the Facebook app, and friend him. "Fixed." I squint closer at his profile picture. "Who's the kid in your picture?"

"My little brother," he says, straightening up a bit. "Russell. He's three."

"Cute."

Something like a smile pulls at Matt's mouth again, though it fades fast.

I glance at the clock. We still have a few minutes, and this guy has the type of silence that presses and pushes, begging conversation. "So," I say. "You ready for the election?"

He closes his eyes. "Oh God, I forgot about that."

"Why are you, uh, running, then?"

"A mistake is why."

"Huh," I say. "It'd be hard to get Claire to change the ballot, but I could talk to her for you, if you want to withdraw."

"Why?" he says. "Need something to pad your college apps?"

I blink rapidly. Was that a joke, or does he have a problem with me? "Hey, excuse you."

"I mean, it's true," Matt says. "I'm pretty sure the only reason student gov's starting back up is so people can put 'Sophomore Class Co-Secretary' or whatever on the Common App. I thought I was going to quit, but I don't know. I might as well run, too."

"You sure people are doing it for college apps?" I say. "Maybe some people want to make this school a tiny bit less awful."

"So that's why you're running?" he asks.

"Dude. First off, I don't need the sass, and second, that could a hundred percent be why."

Matt looks up at the ceiling and lets out a chortle. The sudden urge to punch him in the larynx overwhelms me. *Not caring about things doesn't make you cool*, I want to yell. Instead, I force patience into my voice. "So if you're not taking it seriously, and you're not taking yourself off the ballot, what are you going to do if you win?"

"Nothing."

"Oh! Great. Because this isn't important to anyone or anything."

"Uh, apparently it is to one person."

"Yeah, my friend Claire." My fists curl up. "Whatever. You look like you've been hot-boxing for three days, so I bet anyone could get you off the ballot if they wanted."

He frowns. "Wait, is that a threat?"

"It could be."

"Well," he says, folding his arms, "no offense, but you and Juniper Kipling aren't model citizens, either."

"Excuse me?"

"Alcohol." He shrugs. "It doesn't make sense getting self-righteous about weed if you go out drinking every weekend, right?"

I could point out that I don't drink, but frankly, I don't feel obliged to defend myself against that slew of verbal diarrhea. As if this guy knows anything about my life on the weekends. For a second I sit there, my lip curling. "Wow," I say, finally. "I . . . wow."

García calls out, "All right, back to your seats, everyone."

I head back to my desk and fume until the bell rings.

I'm the first one out the door, and I seethe all the way through the halls into the old wing. I smack into Juniper in front of our sixth period, French.

"What's up?" she asks as we head to our row. "You look like someone insulted *Return of the Jedi*."

"No, I just—I talked to Matt Jackson for the first time. García gave us this project, and we're paired up for it."

Juniper pats my shoulder. "My deepest sympathies."

"Sympathies accepted. He is so . . ." I make a clenching motion with both hands. "Oh my God, infuriating, is what."

Juni laughs. "What'd he say?"

"He was normal until we were talking about the election, and then he got all bitchy and just, holy shit." I crack my knuckles. "One of us has to win, Juni. He's not allowed to win. Okay? Deal?"

"Deal, I suppose. Although I thought you wanted to drop out."

"I did until, like, forty-five minutes ago." I flick my hair out of my eyes. "Now I want to win out of sheer spite."

"Naturally." Juniper strokes an imaginary goatee, looking sagely into the distance. "You know what they say. 'Three things last forever: faith, hope, and spite. And the greatest of these is spite.'"

I laugh so hard I have to put my head down on my desk.

HELLO
my name is

CLAIRE LOMBARDI

BETWEEN SIXTH AND SEVENTH PERIOD, I PASS BY ONE of the student-government lists I taped between rows of lockers. A flash of red catches my eye, and I glance up at it. Somebody has taken a pen to Olivia's name. Now it reads: OLIVIA SCOTT SUCKS DICKKKK!!

I roll my eyes and keep walking.

Halfway down the hall, I realize I should have taken that list down, or at least scratched out the graffiti. Why didn't it occur to me to do that? God, I'm the worst friend.

I stop at my locker, loosing a sigh. The way Olivia bounces from guy to guy these days, I can't get away from references to her sex life. It's wearing on me—the graffiti, all the talk in the halls, the muttered conversations I overhear in class.

This stuff doesn't happen in a vacuum—if you sleep around, people think about you differently. Maybe it's shitty, but that's the way things work, and Olivia knows it as well as I do. I've never spoken up. It's not like I condone her sleeping around, and insults have always seemed to roll off her back, so why should I bother interfering?

Still, I have a sneaking feeling that it makes me a terrible person not to stick up for her. A lot of the time, I worry that I am a terrible person and just haven't had it confirmed yet. After all, how are you supposed to know for sure? Who's going to tell you? Who's going to be the one to break the news?

I scoop up my Young Environmentalists brochures and continue down the hall. Why are all my friends going off the rails lately? Juniper has the alcohol tolerance of a five-year-old, but last Saturday she shotgunned three beers in a row for no apparent reason and ended up wasted. Olivia guessed it was because Thomas Fallon kept hitting on her and she was getting annoyed, but I think if Juni wanted some guy to leave her alone, she'd tell him.

She'd tell *us* if something was wrong, right?

Maybe it's good that she's loosening up, making mistakes. That's how you learn, isn't it, through mistakes? Maybe Juni's tired of doing everything right.

Heading back down the hall, I pass Andrea Silverstein. A couple of guys beside me wait until she's gone and then start snickering about the streak of green dye at the front of her hair.

As always, I feel like I should tell them to stop. But—as always—the idea of speaking up paralyzes me, like, if I say a word, their laughter might turn on me. One time, back in sixth grade, I got caught texting in class, and Ms. Rollins read it aloud. **Zomg Eddie is so cute,** I'd texted to Olivia. **I want us to exchange numbers and it'll be super romantic and perfect XD**

People lost their minds laughing. I thought I was going to pop from shame, but Juniper stood up for me. I remember that day like quartz, hard and clear: November, five years ago now. "Grow up," Juniper had said to the other kids. "Would you want her to laugh at you?"

I'd never spoken to Juniper in my life, but she found me after class and asked me to sit with her and Olivia at lunch. I was hideously grateful, feeling so lucky to be with the two of them. They weren't just smart—they were pretty, too, with their straight, perfect hair, their clear skin. I was the kid with headgear for my braces and medication for my acne. I remember how surprised I was that they laughed at my jokes, that they would even look at me, let alone talk to me. I remember adopting their mannerisms, terrified that they'd let me go as quickly as they'd picked me up. I remember easing in, finding my niche with them, sleepovers and movie nights.

I picture a twelve-year-old Juniper swinging a tennis racket around in figure eights one summer afternoon, her hair whirling out in a blond pinwheel. She lost her grip, and the racket spun over our heads and into the lake with a miserable splash. We laughed until our stomachs ached. It was easy back then.

I hurry into the stairwell and leap up the steps two by two. My mind wanders back to the words scribbled beside Olivia's name, and I can't help but think, *At least people* want *to sleep with Liv.* I bet nobody would give me the attention she gets even if I hung a neon OPEN FOR BUSINESS sign on my back. Or on other regions.

It's not like I'm jealous. I went out with the hottest guy at Paloma High for thirteen months. So what if he dumped me and hardly even gave me a reason?

Okay. I am maybe a tad jealous.

He started to tell me why, the day we broke up. He said, "You can't compare . . ." before cutting himself off, falling back on some empty-sounding apology. I didn't push it—I was busy crying—but now I wish I'd demanded that he finish the sentence. *You can't compare—you can't compare—you can't compare, you can't, you can't—* Lucas's words play on a loop in my mind. *I can't compare to what?*

There's only so much you can discuss a topic before everyone hates you a little when you bring it up. For two months, I haven't said a word, but God, it still hurts to see his face. Tall, burly, impeccably dressed Lucas. I remember the warmth of his bear-hug arms, the mint taste of his kisses—everything, down to the texture of his curly hair. I remember the first time he showed me his most personal possession, the journal filled with lists. To-do lists. Bucket lists. Lists of things he's grateful for, people he loves, and people he wants to get to know. I wonder if I'm still on any of those pages. I used to have my own page: *Reasons Claire Amazes Me.*

Now I'm just another face in the halls to check off the *Vague Acquaintances* list. Lucas could find some rando off the street and be their new best friend within five minutes; he is the people person to end all people persons. He collects people like some people collect coins, indiscriminately and greedily. Now I'm lost deep in his catalog, undeserving of any distinction.

I exit the stairwell on the third floor, my teeth buried in my bottom lip. Some guy calls over my head. His friend, leaning on the lockers, unleashes a braying laugh right in my ear, and I let out a measured breath. Ignoring the boys in this school is impossible. They clumsily hit on my friends every hour of the day, and they're so loud in class, making dumb jokes everyone laughs at anyway. Also, of course, the football team, which has never done close to as well as the girls' tennis team, gets everybody's attention just because. Part of me feels like, hello, of course I'm fixated on a boy. Everything is.

I stride into calculus class. Taking my seat in the front row, I wonder: is it like this for all girls, or am I just pathetic?

I don't understand. I still need to know why it ended and what it is I can't compare to.

"ALL RIGHT," MR. ANDREWS SAYS ONCE THE BELL rings. He sweeps down the aisles, dealing out bright green papers. "Questionnaires. Don't put your names on them." He stops back at the front of the room and folds his arms. His eyes glint behind his horn-rimmed glasses.

"We've been asked to give these to our fifth-period classes. I know they're anonymous, but take them seriously," he says. "They're about the, you know, Monday's assembly." He clears his throat, his cheeks coloring.

I can't help wondering if it's Andrews. He's only a couple of years out of college, and single, and way too intense. I bet lots of people think it's him. Since the assembly, I keep looking at teachers with critical eyes, wondering. *Could they be interested in someone our age? Is this one hiding anything? How about that one?*

Yesterday, the letter Turner promised arrived at my house. My parents were horrified. They even brought up the possibility of withdrawing me from school until they catch whoever it is. As if that were an option. Without me, tennis would collapse. And student government. And Young Environmentalists.

Sighing, I look down the question sheet. Three questions and lots of blank space.

Have you ever been romantically approached or sexually propositioned by any teacher or staff member at Paloma High School? Explain.

Have you ever experienced sexual harassment or unprofessional behav-

ior (hugs, unwanted shoulder touching, etc.) by any teacher or staff member at Paloma High School? Explain.

Do you have any information about the identity of any party who may be involved in an illicit relationship?

I scribble *no* under every question and flip the page over. I bet at least one person at this school will write down some stupid joke as an answer.

When the last bell rings at 3:30, the hall echoes with end-of-day noise. Kids in the halls jostle one another, giving exaggerated hugs and pointedly touching shoulders, laughing about "unprofessional behavior." I barely keep myself from rolling my eyes. It might be a joke to them, but there's some teacher whose career might get ruined over this, and some kid who's probably being manipulated. What if the kid needs years of therapy or something? Yeah, hilarious.

I follow the crowd receding down the sun-drenched hall. The light glares off the walls plastered with neon flyers and posters: advertisements for clubs, maybe fifty percent of them mine. I stop off at my locker to stow my chemistry textbook, and as the lock clicks back into place, a cheery voice says, "Claire, hey!"

Sweat springs to my palms. I don't need to look to know it's him.

I turn to find him standing selfishly close. Doesn't he know I can't breathe in this sort of proximity? His closeness fills my head with sickly sweet yearning.

He looks better than ever these days, his loose, curly hair bouncing over his high forehead, his left ear pierced. The sweater stretching across his square shoulders has some fancy-looking logo, and a white collared shirt peeks up above its neck, framing the inside tips of his prominent collarbones.

Looking up into his eyes, I catch a brief camera flash of memory—the look he used to give me before he kissed me. That look rang with warmth, so filled with contentment that every frantic thought in my head stilled. I could lose every shred of anxious energy in the knowledge that we were each other's.

Does Lucas remember anything like that? Does he miss anything about me?

"Hi," I say, with one thought on loop: *Act normal.* I've gotten better at it—I measure my progress against my mental state last summer. Sometimes I think it's another girl's memories I'm peeking into, some miserable stranger with wild eyes and a surfeit of tears.

I try a smile as the current shuffles us toward the door. "What's up?"

"I got in a car accident earlier!" he says with so much enthusiasm, he might as well have said he adopted a kitten.

"What? Are you okay? What happened?"

"It was great. I value life so much more now."

I laugh, but it sounds weak. I watch his hands as he pushes his hair back from his forehead. I ache to trace the chunky silver ring on his pinky finger. He still wears half the money he makes, trading it in for appearance. He buys leather shoes and designer jeans, rich felt coats and flashy sunglasses, T-shirts that used to feel like tissue between my fingers. At home, his room is littered with treasures, too: the newest MacBook Pro and bulky, noise-canceling headphones. In his small, shabby house, Lucas's acquisitions glare like diamonds.

As we clank through the doors, someone calls, "McCallum!" I flinch back just in time—good to see I still have my bro-dodging reflexes. Lucas's teammates swoop down on him from the green. One wiry kid jumps onto Lucas's back, hollering something about weight lifting. Another buries both his hands in Lucas's hair, ruffling it until it resembles a tumbleweed. I swear, the swim team has the gayest straight boys in the world.

"Whoa, whoa, *unprofessional behavior*," says Herman, the one with the long hair. He wrestles off the guy on Lucas's back. "Careful, or they're gonna call another assembly."

"I'll see you around," I say to Lucas, but his only response is a hasty wave as he disentangles himself from his friends. The wordless dismissal stings like a nettle, and I hold my head higher as I stalk down the green.

When I reach my car, I stow my backpack and pull out my gym bag, trying to shake off the sight of him. It clings stubbornly. When I blink, I see him printed in the dark.

Every couple of weeks, Lucas springs himself on me like this, and for the rest of the day, sometimes longer, he's all I can think about. When he dumped me, he asked, "Can we still be friends?" and like an idiot, I said, "Sure." So now I have to grin and bear it every time he treats me with this impersonal brand of friendliness.

As I head back toward the green for the Young Environmentalists meeting, my eyes fix on Juni's car, which sits in a far corner of the junior lot. Behind the windshield, Olivia props up her feet on the dashboard. Juni's eyebrows are drawn together. Is she explaining why she blew up at lunch earlier?

I can't remember seeing Juniper so stressed so often. Usually, nothing fazes her, gets through her seemingly impervious layer of levelheadedness. But I could swear, she looks an inch from tears.

For a moment, I consider veering their way, to figure out what's wrong once and for all. But then I remember Juni's voice echoing through the bathroom door—"I need some time."

Did she need time? Or did she simply want a pair of ears that wasn't mine?

I force myself not to be curious. If she wanted to, she'd tell me what's wrong.

I duck my head, my cheeks aflame. I hurry away from the car and down the green.

HELLO
my name is

KAT SCOTT

"I . . . LINE," EMILY SAYS.

Mr. García calls out her line from the front row. "You are to be married—"

"Married to Faina," Emily finishes. "She is beautiful, brilliant. What could you . . . oh God, I'm so sorry. Line?"

Watching Emily always stresses me out, this scene more than the others. She has a crush on her scene partner, who plays my husband. Every time they make eye contact, she forgets her lines. The obnoxious thing is that he has a crush on her, too—everybody knows it—but they won't stop dancing around it and date already.

I retreat into the greenroom. A pair of sophomores sit in the corner, one on each massive leather sofa. I hate that those sofas are in here. It enables all the theater kids who are obsessed with couch piles and being way too physical with each other.

I sink into the chair at the end of the nearest sofa, stick in my earbuds, and take out my laptop. A paused game opens up, ready for me to resume. I hit play and sneak through the ruins, a huge assault rifle in my avatar's hand.

"I heard some guys saying it was Dr. Meyers," says Ani, the girl who plays my daughter.

Oh, great. They're talking about that whole thing. As if we haven't heard enough about it since Monday. Thank God the week's nearly over.

I let loose a volley of bullets on some approaching zombies. In my peripheral vision, Elizabeth puts her head on an armrest. Ani sprawls across the other couch.

"They probably just think she's hot," Elizabeth says. "Isn't it usually creepy old men who do this?"

"Not always," Ani says. "I heard this one time in Montana—"

I purse my lips and shoot some more zombies. Black blood explodes out of their heads as they keel to the side. Double-tapping the up key, I jump onto a crumbling stone wall, duck behind it, and find two packs of ammo. Score.

"—Kat?"

I jolt at my name. I hit pause and take out one of my earbuds. "What?"

Elizabeth says, "What do you think?"

I look from one to the other. "About the teacher-student thing?"

They nod.

"No opinion."

"Really?" Ani asks.

"Really. Don't care. I'm trying to focus on the show these days."

Ani and Elizabeth trade a glance. Their lips twitch.

"What?" I say, not letting my voice rise. The greenroom's soundproofing leaves something to be desired.

Ani shrugs. "Just, like, there *are* things that matter outside this play."

A response jumps to the front of my mouth—*Is that why you still can't remember your fucking blocking?*—but I manage to keep it from spilling out. Restraining myself to a frosty glare, I stick my earbud back in and return to my game. The looks they give me glow hot on the side of my face. I get those looks all the time: *God, what a bitch. What is her problem?*

They can think whatever they want. I don't need them. I don't need anybody.

It's sort of hilarious, though, how so many theater kids like to think they're social outcasts, talking with people who are obviously their friends about "never fitting in." They have no idea. If they did, they wouldn't glamorize it. The reality of isolation is unglamorous and unexciting.

Going years without talking to anybody—talking about anything that matters—seems hard in theory, but when you give one-word answers to anyone who approaches you, people piss off pretty fast. The last time I had a legitimate conversation was in eighth grade, before Mom decided we weren't worth her time and energy.

To be fair, it's not as if she didn't have a reason to leave. By the time Liv and I hit seventh grade, our parents got into screaming matches every week, about everything from what we ate for dinner to the clothes Olivia and I wore. It always ended with Dad snapping, "Great," sinking into a capital-*M* Mood, and not talking for hours. Mom would run off in an anxious frenzy and lock herself in their room. She was a ball of energy, our mom, and she used to electrify our dad. But year after unhappy year, she grew more unreliable, like a knot of wires fraying through.

I could forgive her wanting to leave. What's unforgivable is the way she did it.

Mom left our last family vacation early, after an all-night fight. By the time the rest of us got back home, she'd disappeared, leaving zero evidence that she'd ever lived there. Fluttery clothing, sketchbooks, tchotchkes that used to line the shelves—gone, gone, gone. She didn't leave a note. She didn't reply to the texts, calls, and emails we sent for weeks afterward.

What gets me the most is that she didn't have the decency to say good-bye. I knew Mom had her issues, but I never thought she was a coward.

Eventually, Dad tracked down her new number out west. Clear message there: she needed distance. But did she need 1,500 miles of it? If she wanted to start over, couldn't she have started over in Kansas City and seen me and Olivia on weekends? She chose the most selfish avenue and sprinted down it, right out of our lives. As far as I'm concerned, she can stay out.

I don't know what Mom said the one time she talked to Dad, but he never called her again. After that, a part of him packed up and left, too. He's hardly a shadow of himself now, worked to death, silent when we see him. Part of me still hopes my actual dad might come back, the dad who obsessively tracked weird sports like badminton and Ping-Pong and who started getting hyped for Christmas in August. When we put up the tree, he'd stuff tinsel in his beard and puff out his cheeks—*Ho, ho, ho! Merry Tinselmas!* Back in the day, it wasn't hard to tell where Olivia got her horrible sense of humor.

I never catch a glimpse of that man anymore. He's gotten lost in there somewhere, lost inside his own body. And I hate Mom for doing that to him. She had so much power that she ended up breaking him completely.

Nobody will ever do that to me.

. . . .

AFTER REHEARSAL ENDS, I HEAD BACK TO THE GREEN-room to collect my things. By the time I get my stuff and come back out into the theater, everybody else is gone.

"Shit." I needed to ask for a ride. My phone says it's already gone down to thirty-seven degrees. With today's wind, I'll be half frostbitten by the time I get home.

"Kat? Everything okay?" asks Mr. García, wheeling the ghost light toward the stage. Supposedly, ghost lights—left out to illuminate deserted stages—are for safety purposes, but I bet they're mostly for appeasing superstitious theater people.

I squint in the glare of the exposed bulb. "Yeah, everything's fine. Just realized I have to walk home."

The ghost light's sticky wheels squeak forward as García sets it center stage. "But it's freezing," he says. "You don't have a ride?"

"I was going to ask the others. Forgot."

"Well, I could drop you off."

"Really?" I stick my hands in my hoodie pockets. "I, uh, that'd be great."

"Okay, then. This way." He hops off the side of the stage and heads down the aisle to the faculty lot. I hurry after him, slipping through the door. Outside, the wind grasps at my hair, clutching it. García stops by a tiny white two-door that looks about an inch from collapse. It makes a clunking sound as I slide in. Still, getting out of the wind is an instant relief.

"So, where am I headed?" García asks, reversing out of his spot.

"Left here. And then a right up at the light." I glance around the car, which smells like Windex. The seats are bare, every inch clean and empty. A long row of CDs, stacked between the driver and passenger seats, are preserved in spotless plastic cases and alphabetized.

"Good rehearsal today, huh?" García says.

"Decent."

He smiles. "You're tough to impress. I'm guessing you want to do theater in college? Maybe a conservatory or something?"

"Yeah."

García turns right. "Well, they'll be lucky to have you." We accelerate down the widest road in Paloma, which runs through the entire city, top to toe. We pass a strip mall on the left. "I did a drama double-major in school," García says. "English and drama."

"Oh. Did you want to act?"

"No, I was a stage manager, mostly." García grimaces. "I got exactly one part in college, and I had two lines, and I messed both of them up opening night. So that went well."

I bite my tongue. I can't imagine college. It feels so far away—not even a distance in time so much as a physical distance. As if I'm trying to cover thousands of miles on foot.

"Left on Cypress Street," I say. García slips into the turn lane and rounds onto a narrow street filled with potholes.

"Out of curiosity," García says, "do you have a sister? Olivia?"

"Yeah. We're twins."

"Ah, okay. I was wondering. She's in my honors class."

"Of course," I say. "She's the smart one."

"Hey, you're just as smart. A different kind of smart," García says. "Believe me, Kat, it takes a lot of intelligence to show a character like you do onstage." He considers for a second. "I guess you can't put it on a scale, but in my book, it means more than a couple points on the SAT. It's definitely going to mean something to the audience on opening night."

I sneak a glance at him. He looks unconcerned, as if those

words weighed nothing at all, but they settle and fasten themselves somewhere deep inside me. I've never felt smart beside Olivia. She's two math classes ahead of me. Even in the subjects I actually like—history and English—schoolwork never feels effortless, not like it seems for my sister.

These days, my grades are circling the drain. I don't have motivation anymore, just exhaustion. I don't *care* anymore, about anything besides the play, anyway.

I sink in my seat, resolving not to answer anything else. This shit's getting too personal.

Mr. García seems to sense me fortifying my walls. He stays quiet.

He probably thinks I'm jealous of my sister or that I hate her. I'm sure that's what Olivia thinks, but it's not true. I'm not going to braid Olivia's hair and make daisy chains with her, but God knows I don't hate her.

We used to be close in middle school, back before she blossomed out and I shrank in, before high school sent us down different roads. I guess we were close up until the second Mom let the door slam on her way out. That did something to Olivia: she got all bright-eyed and optimistic about Mom coming back, but I knew it would never happen. The first time Olivia talked about calling Mom back up, trying to stay in touch, I walked out of the room. Fucking delusional. Sometimes she still seems to be in denial, as if we're still some happy family with anything in common besides living under the same roof.

These past two years, I've gotten so exhausted with everyone, including my sister. It's so much simpler to fall into computer games and solitude, where, sure, nobody offers consolation, but nobody's going to hurt you, either. And at least the enemies there are clearly labeled.

I watch the houses outside my window shrink, the yards dwindling to small green-gray rectangles. The houses here on the western outskirts of Paloma are tiny and dilapidated.

"Left here," I say as we clunk over the eight hundredth pothole. "I'm on the right. Number 243."

"Great." A minute later, he pulls up our concrete driveway. Our house waits to the right, flat-roofed and beige. The sight of it fills me with resignation.

"I'll see you in class," Mr. García says.

"Yeah," I say, getting out. "Thanks for the lift."

"Sure."

I shut his door and head inside, already aching to collapse into bed.

HELLO
my name is

MATT JACKSON

IT'S 10:00 PM ON A THURSDAY, SO OF COURSE MY PAR-
ents are yelling at each other down the hall in the kitchen, and
I have more homework than I want to admit, so of course I'm
dicking around on the Internet. There's a point where procras-
tination turns into resignation that you will never do what you
need to do, and I hit that point, like, two hours ago, after opening
a Word document in a short-lived fit of optimism. At this point,
anything I write will seem like one hundred percent bullshit
when I read it over tomorrow morning, so is this even worth it?
Signs point to no.

The voices down the hall rise to a cracking point.

"We never should have left St. Louis!" my mom yells. "I would
have stayed with my family, stayed near my parents, but no, you
wanted to—"

"Oh, *I* wanted to? Who was it who—"

Sighing, I get up to block the gap under my door. My clothes,
strewn across the floor like storm debris, tend to come in handy at
this time of night. I kick a couple of hoodies against the crack as
a makeshift silencer, glancing back at my bed. Russell lies asleep
between the sheets, his thumb lodged deep in his mouth. If he

wakes up, I'm going to kill my parents. They're not even trying to keep it down these days.

I sit back down, put my headphones on, and open Spotify, twisting the volume up. Avril Lavigne belts out some inhuman high note over my dad's muffled voice. I will guard my Spotify page into the afterlife, because if anyone saw it, I would probably resurrect from shame. I have this thing for whiny pop-rock, lots of Nickelback and Avril and latter-day Weezer, and it's morbidly embarrassing, but it can't be cured, not by my mom's classic rock or Burke's hipster Bon Iver shit. Besides, nothing's better for drowning out an argument than Avril Lavigne yell-singing about how much of a crazy bitch she is, which, like, I guess if that's how you want to describe yourself, go for it.

A red notification pops up at the top of my Facebook page, announcing a message from Olivia. My stomach does acrobatics, and my brain aches as if someone's slammed a block of wood against my forehead. Jesus, crushes are so humiliating.

Hey, Matt,

Following up for the project thing. We should probably meet over the weekend to practice the actual presentation, sort out who's going to say what. I can get supplies for a poster or something. Go ahead and call me at 476-880-1323—we'll sort it out faster that way.

Also, here's a link to read Inferno *online—www.bartleby .com/20/101.html*

Olivia

Without thinking, I take a joint from my drawer. My fingers move like rubber, thick and clumsy, as I open my window and light up. The first hit mellows in my lungs for a moment before I exhale into the night wind, leaning out to keep the smoke away from Russ. It's not long before I feel it: the world engulfing me in its arms. Guitar chords ring deep in my headphones, every note dissipating out into its own rich, vibrating melody.

When I'm sufficiently stoned, I grab my phone, tap in Olivia's number, and hit call. As it rings, I pause the music, sinking onto my desk chair, and the quiet presses in. Voices rise and fall outside my door, lapping against my awareness in gentle waves. My eyes fix on the trail of smoke twining from the joint out through the window, and Olivia's phone rings and rings, and it occurs to me that maybe 10:00 PM is a little late to call somebody I don't know—should I have waited, talked to her tomorrow in class?

The line connects. "Hey, it's Olivia," she says, her bright, quick voice as awake as if it's early morning. I say, "Hey, Matt here."

"Yeah, I guessed," she says. "So, when are you free to work on this thing?"

I want to say *Slow down*; I want to wait; I want to savor the sound of her voice. I reply so slowly, the words barely feel like words at all, just lazy, meaningless streams of syllables. "I'm free all the time. Whatever works."

"Let's get it out of the way this weekend," she says, and I'm like, "Yeah, how 'bout Saturday?" and she says, "Okay. I'm not going to have a car, though, so."

"We could meet at your place," I say, trying not to sound too into the idea, and she's like, "Not advisable," and I'm like, "Why not?" and she's like, "Kat's going to be home. My sister."

"I won't be loud or anything," I say, and she says, "That's not what I mean." And I say, "Then what do you mean? Don't want to embarrass yourself by letting me in your house?" and the second it comes out, my eyes fall shut, and my mind goes, *Shut up, Matt. Shut up.*

Olivia lets out a disbelieving-sounding laugh. "Know what? Maybe you should meet Kat. I bet you guys would get along great," and I'm like, "What's that mean?" and she's like, "It's clear you both have lots to figure out before you can act like civilized human beings," and a defensive instinct surges up, and I say, "Shit-talking your own sister. Classy." And she snaps, "Well, she's been nothing but awful since our mom left, not that my family is any of your goddamn business."

I go quiet.

"Shit. I didn't mean that," she says. "It's . . . she's weird these days, but it's not . . ."

I rub my forehead. "No, don't worry about—"

"All I meant was, if you don't know her, she gets tough to deal with."

"Right," I manage, suddenly hyperaware that although I've gone to school with Kat Scott for years, I've never talked to her, and I guess it's because she's so quiet. I don't know, there's this romantic idea about quiet people in movies and books, like, *Oh, they're so mysterious*, whereas in my experience it's not like that at all. It's more like, *Okay, you don't want to talk? Fine, I'll let you do your own thing, since you obviously don't want to associate with me.*

"Listen," I say, "I'm sorry, okay? I keep . . . things just won't come out right when . . ." I can't finish the sentence. My thoughts are snarling up like yarn inside my head. Jesus, what is it about this girl that wrecks my ability to goddamn *talk*?

After a second, she rescues me: "Well, I sort of snapped, too, so . . ."

I search for words, but the knowledge about her family is a roadblock, detouring my attention. Their mom walked out. She and her sister have been fighting ever since. I've had this thing for Olivia for years, feeling like I knew all about her because . . . I don't know why. Because I've had a couple of classes with her. Because, like everyone else, I know the guys she hooks up with. Now, though, I picture her blue eyes and try to imagine the miles of thoughts hiding behind them, the years of history concealed back there, and I wonder why it took me this long to think of her as someone with a hundred thousand dimensions, of which I know maybe one. It was too easy to see her as a cutout doll of the perfect girl.

Then a shout bursts into my attention, ringing through my door: "—be *quiet!*" and I wince and smother my phone, but Olivia's already asking, "Everything all right over there?" and I'm like, "It's my parents," because it's easier than a lie.

"That's rough. It's pretty late," she says, and I sigh. I don't want her to pity me, but I do want her to know that I get what it's like, coming home to a house you can't deal with, so I shrug and say, "They've been like this since I was, like, ten. On and off. So I get . . . I hope your sister gets better. I hope you guys work it out. Because this shit drives you insane. You know?"

For a long moment, she doesn't say anything. Then her voice comes back, calm and slow. "Yeah, I know," she says. "I get done with school and everything and come home to this, like, hovering atmosphere of—I don't know what I did, you know? I'm going crazy trying to figure out what I did," and I say, "You probably didn't do anything," and she says, "What?" and I say, "I mean, *my* parents are always angry because they're miserable."

Silence. I feel as if the words should have been hard to say, but they slid out as easily as thin liquid, not an ounce of resistance. I stare at my bedroom wall, and my voice trails on without me, careless, thoughtless. "My mom feels like she's wasting her fancy degree out here in bumfuck Kansas, and my dad gets all, *Why are you so ungrateful?* and nothing I do changes that. So, like, your sister? If I had to guess, she's probably going through something personal, and she needs to figure it out before she's ready to treat you like . . . I don't know. A person."

Looking over at the windowsill, I realize my blunt has smoldered down on its plate. I stub it out, not even angry about having wasted half a joint, because, what the hell, when did this turn into an actual conversation? I'm perched, tense, on the edge of my chair, waiting for her answer.

Olivia says, "Where'd your mom go to school?" And I say, "Yale. She's a biologist."

"How do you deal with the fighting?" she asks.

"I don't know." I rummage around for a better answer but come up empty-handed. "I don't deal with it. I'm just here."

"You don't try to stop them?" she asks, and I'm like, "Nah. Last time I tried was freshman year. Now I only speak up when they get Russell involved," and she's like, "Your little brother," and I look over at him, his mouth cracked open in sleep. "Yeah," I say. "He's better than the rest of my family combined." A breeze washes in through the window as I listen to her silence on the other end. I haven't talked like this in a long time, and something in my heart is waking up, lifting its drooping head.

"What's, uh, what's going on with your sister?" I ask.

"She's missing classes, she never comes out of her room, and every time I, like, dare to seem worried, she snaps. It's like living with a . . . I don't know, a Venus flytrap. A large, deeply angry Venus flytrap." Olivia chuckles, and it breaks, and she's quiet, and I rearrange my fingers on the hot plastic casing of my phone and wish I knew what to say.

"It's frustrating," she goes on, "'cause we're both dealing with the same thing, you know? She's the only one who would get it, but we've never spoken about Mom, not once. I wish she'd talk to me. Jesus, I never thought I'd say this, but I miss middle school."

"Makes sense wanting to rewind things, though."

Her silent understanding rings through the phone. Me, I'd go all the way back to elementary school, before permanent lines settled between my parents' eyebrows.

"But also, fuck middle school," I add, and she laughs.

Silence settles carefully, like ashes. "This is weird," she says after a minute, and I say, "Yeah," and she says, "I hate to, like, ruin your night—"

"You're not—"

"Let's just . . ."

"Yeah," I say. "So, Saturday? My house? I can pick you up."

"Okay, sure. I'll send you my address, and . . . yeah, great." Her voice is uncertain, tense with the weird anxiety I'm feeling, too, and I get this image of her eyes bleary and her long dark hair draped over her shoulder, and it startles me a little, the reminder that she's a real, physical person, someone I'll see in the flesh tomorrow at school. What will it be like, meeting her eyes after saying all this? I'm going to mess it up, won't I? The easy slide of this conversation will disappear, and I'll be back to my usual awkward mumbling.

"I'll read *Inferno*," I blurt out, without knowing why. Somehow, even though I haven't done any required reading since I was twelve, it doesn't feel like a straight-up lie.

She chuckles. "I'm holding you to that. See you tomorrow?" And I say, "Yeah," and she says, "Bye, Matt."

When she hangs up, it feels as if I'm surfacing from a deep dream. I draw a long breath, dazed, and carry Russ upstairs to tuck him in. As I shut myself back in my room, easing myself into bed, I can hardly believe that somewhere across town, Olivia picked up the phone and something happened—I don't know what the hell it was—over the line.

A nervous voice creeps into my head, whispering, *You should pull back before this inevitably goes sour.* After all, twelve hours ago, I barely had the nerve to look her in the eye. But something else bounces around inside my head, louder than the creeping worry: the hesitant sound of her saying my name. I want to keep hearing it. I want to keep handing my voice back in reply. I grip my sheets tight at the thought and stare up at my ceiling, my jaw a little stiff and my heart a little fast.

The sound of her voice pins itself to my eardrum, echoing until I fall asleep.

HELLO
my name is

VALENTINE SIMMONS

ON FRIDAY MORNING, I HURRY THROUGH THE JUNIOR lot, counting cracks in the asphalt as my tightly knotted sneakers hit them. *Twenty-three. Twenty-four. Twenty-five.* I don't look up for anything. Unexpected eye contact is one of my least favorite things. What do you do if you're acquainted with the person? Nod? Smile? Stare blankly? *Know thyself,* said the Greeks, and knowing myself, the blank stare is all I would be able to manage.

The passing conversations bore me in three-second increments: grades and teachers, sports and scores, pop music and celebrity breakups. As if any of that matters. Why is everyone around me so vapid? I'm starting to think they should rename so-called intelligent life.

"Freeeak," a voice drones at me. I glance up, narrowing my eyes at the group walking by. It's half the swim team, uniformly tall and muscular, chuckling like one self-satisfied organism.

"Incredibly original," I call after their retreating backs, in as scathing a voice as possible. I don't know why I'm engaging. I'm better than that. I'm better than *them.* I'm certainly better than vindicating their juvenile behavior with a response.

The one in the center of the pack, a curly-haired kid with a long nose, shoots an apologetic look over his shoulder. I glare at him. If he were sorry, he would say something to his douchebag teammate. It must be nice, being surrounded by an army of friends who'll be complicit in your behavior, no questions asked.

The swimmer guy looks at me a moment longer before turning back to his friends. He doesn't say a word.

That's what I thought.

I glance back down at my feet, but I've lost count of the asphalt cracks. Sighing, I look up. A girl leaning against a nearby car—Izby Qing: short, slender, hair dyed pink—catches my eye. She stands, laughing and hair-twirling, next to a freckled boy, transparently reveling in his attention.

For a second, I wonder what it would be like to have somebody's eyes fixed on me like that—or to look at someone the same way.

Soon enough, though, I fall back into dispassion at the idiocy of it all. It horrifies me that kids our age spend so much effort on this stuff. I thought we were all aware that the vast majority of high school relationships are fleeting and meaningless, but apparently not. People spend a huge percentage of their lives playing into this perpetual cycle of interdependence. They're all wasting their time, and on something with zero long-term benefits. God knows why.

"Hey, wait up!" A boy, sprinting to catch the swimmers, barges into my shoulder and spins me off balance. My periodic table water bottle bounces out of my backpack and away under the front of a car, toppling xenon over helium. I right myself, waiting for an apology, but the boy doesn't glance back.

I hate people. I crouch, swatting under the fender to grab my bottle, but it rolls out of reach. A hand grabs it from under the driver's door. "Got it," says the voice attached to the hand.

I straighten up. "Thanks."

"No problem," the girl says. "Did that guy not even apologize? Jeez."

I start, taking half a step back. That voice . . .

"You must've had this for a while," she says, peering at the bottle. "Copernicium isn't named."

Staring at the ground, I nod. "You, um. Like chemistry?"

"I love it," she says, and the girl's voice in my head says, *I love you.*

It's her.

Sudden pressure clamps down on my skull. I look her in the eyes and know so much about this girl, all of a sudden; I picture her standing in the darkness of the faculty break room, staring up at a nameless face, promising that nobody will ever know—and I suddenly wish I could unknow this. It's too much to hold. I could ruin her life.

She tilts her head. Her eyes are beautiful, clear, and piercing. They dig into me.

I don't know her name. That's something. A tiny protection from this responsibility.

She holds out the bottle, and I snatch it. "I have to go."

I hurry down the green toward the school, not looking back.

HELLO
my name is

CLAIRE LOMBARDI

FRIDAY'S LUNCHTIME ANNOUNCEMENTS BLARE OUT, proving me right: people wrote fake responses on the fifth-period questionnaires. Enough people that Principal Turner spends a good five minutes chastising the school through the loudspeaker.

"Lastly," she says after concluding her rant, "these sheets are still available outside the guidance office if, at any point, anybody does wish to come forward. And as always, the submission form on our website remains open. Thank you, and have a good day."

"No, thank *you*, dear leader," Olivia says, brandishing her juice at the speaker in a Capri Sun salute. Around us, the cafeteria conversations rumble back to life. "Also, happy weekend already," Olivia adds to me and Juni.

"Thank God," I say. "Was it just me, or did this week last forever?"

"Definitely not just you," Juniper says, stirring her yogurt. Olivia and I exchange a worried glance. She looks even more exhausted than she did yesterday.

"Hey, Juni," I say carefully. "You okay?"

"What? Yeah." She looks up with a determined smile. "I was up until, like, three last night. Two essays due today, and . . . well, you know. Paganini calls." She glances at Olivia. "By the way, did your unwanted attention blow over?"

The subject switch doesn't escape me, but I'm curious. "Unwanted attention?"

"Bleh." Olivia blows her hair out of her eyes. "Daniel."

"Why's his attention unwanted?"

Juni and Olivia swap a knowing look that makes me feel instantly excluded. "Sure you want to know?" Olivia says.

"Duh, nerd. Spill."

"He sort of sent me a dick pic, and now things are awkward because, like . . . penises."

I choke on my sandwich. "He what? When was this?"

"Monday."

"How dare you conceal this incredibly important information?" I say in a voice laden with sarcasm. The joke lands—Olivia grins—but part of my heart has clenched up. It's not that Dan Silverstein's junk is in any way interesting, but Olivia told Juni already. So, what, because of our not-fight Monday, I'm not allowed to be in the know anymore? And with Juni's excuses and deflections . . . is this the new normal, them keeping things from me?

"My deepest apologies," Olivia says. She lifts her hands in praise to the heavens. "But at last, we greet the weekend! A joyous miracle! Time to sleep in. And marathon *Parks and Rec*. And rage with my favorite people." She gives me and Juni a winning smile.

"Rage, right," Juni says wryly. "You and your nonalcoholic self."

"Hey, sassy, I can rage without dousing myself in Miller Lite." Olivia slurps her Capri Sun. "So, what's our move?"

"Hate to burst the raging bubble," I say, "but nothing's happening this weekend. Like, zero things. Dan's sister is having a birthday party, but if he's persona non grata now, I'm guessing that's not your first choice."

"Nothing at all?" Olivia visibly deflates, chewing her straw. "Damn. There's this one super-handsome guy on baseball I was talking to last week. Thought maybe I could 'run into him' this weekend."

"How about we hang out, the three of us?" Juniper suggests.

Olivia brightens. "Ooh, yes, excellent."

"My afternoon's open," I say.

"I actually can't do afternoon," Olivia says. She tosses her hair, looking off into the middle distance. "I have a clandestine meeting with a gentleman."

Sharp disapproval runs through me. God, how many guys is she juggling at one time? Hasn't she ever heard of restraint?

I clasp my hands tight. *Stop, Claire.* She can go on dates. She can do what she wants. Who cares if she has eighty boys falling at her feet?

I take a deliberate bite of my apple as Juniper says, "Do tell."

"Well, where do I begin?" Olivia says. "It'll be an incredibly romantic rendezvous, where we will make a poster about Dante's *Inferno*." As she gives her eyelashes an exaggerated flutter, I let out a sigh, feeling like an asshole. It's a class project, not a date. Of course. The day Olivia goes on a real date instead of just hooking up with guys at parties, the sun will probably explode.

"How about evening, then?" Juniper suggests. "We can just chill. Watch a movie."

Here we go. I'm busy tomorrow night, and I already know what's going to happen. My absence makes less of a difference than Olivia's, so they'll meet up Saturday night and have an amazing time without me and send me a bunch of Snapchats that'll make me feel left out, and I won't say anything, because if I do, I'll come off needy.

"I can't at night," I say.

"Why not?"

"Grace's birthday. We're going out to eat."

"How about after?" Olivia says. "We could do, like, nine thirty or ten."

"My tournament's this Sunday, remember? I have to get up early."

"Excuses, excuses, Lombardi," Olivia says. "I'm picking you up, and you can't stop me."

"I'm serious. I gotta get up at six." I gulp some Gatorade. "I mean, you could pick me up if you roll my sleeping body into the back of Juni's car."

They laugh. It fades into expectant silence, and I realize they're waiting for me to give them some sort of weird blessing to hang out without me. I don't want to say the words, but they come out anyway. "Well, whatever. Don't have too much fun without me."

I swear, their eyes brighten. I look down at my lunch, nibbling on my nails. Juni and Olivia drop the topic soon, but my mind sticks on the little things from this week. Juniper's silences. Dan's secret advances. The thought of the pair of them without me. As for Saturday, I already get the sense I'm missing out.

HELLO
my name is

KAT SCOTT

"KAT?" DR. NORMAN SAYS.

My head jerks up, my eyes snapping open.

"Do you know the answer?" Norman asks, the first words in seventh period I've listened to. There's no question on the white-board. Not that I'd be able to answer it—chemistry is my worst subject—but knowing the type of question would make a guess sound less stupid, at least.

I glance at the boy sitting next to me. He shoots back a *Don't look at me* sort of glare.

"Uh," I say.

Dr. Norman sighs. "You know, as much as your attendance is appreciated today, Ms. Scott, I have to say, it would mean more if you were conscious."

Snickers spark up around me. I imagine the sounds glancing off my skin, blow by tiny blow. "Kat," Norman says, "I'm going to ask you to stay after class and clean up the lab equipment for the AP students."

"I have rehearsal," I say.

Dr. Norman gives me a feral smile. Not a good sign. He loves making examples out of students for laughs. It makes me think his ego is fragile beyond belief, because, seriously, what forty-five-year-old with any self-esteem gets his kicks by making fun of teenagers?

"Rehearsal?" he says. "That's funny, because I was talking with Dave García the other day, and he was telling me that he gave the cast Friday off. So, if you could get him to explain, that'd be wonderful." His smile stretches wider, scrunching lines up into his white, rubbery cheeks. "Otherwise, you'll be staying afterward to clean up, thank you."

Everyone goes, "*Ooohhh,*" in unison, the universally accepted sound of *Somebody just got their ass handed to them.* I shoot dirty glances around, the humiliation lingering against my skin like a too-close flame. Norman didn't have to say it that way. I didn't even mean to lie—I forgot García gave us today off.

Ten minutes later, the bell rings. I leave my backpack at my desk and head to the front of the room. Dr. Norman waits behind his desk with justice in his eyes. He probably thinks he's fighting the good fight against juvenile delinquency, saying shit in front of the class like that, but all he's doing is making me resent him.

After showing me what he wants cleaned, Norman bustles out of the room, leaving me alone. I trudge toward the black buckets by the sink, old and scratched, filled with graduated cylinders. I test the tap water and pick up the soap.

The door opens behind me. I glance over my shoulder.

A kid stands in the threshold, blonder than I am and barely taller. He has the physique of a stick insect, and his clothes don't help the illusion: his skinny khakis make his legs look like pipe cleaners, and his black peacoat is so huge, it looks like it's eating him alive.

"Need something?" I say.

"Yes, hello," he says. "There must be a mistake. I'm supposed to clean the equipment."

"Are you in AP?" I ask.

He nods.

"Well," I say, "guess you're off the hook, AP. Norman told me to do these buckets."

"Oh." The boy's eyes fix on my hands, still stuck beneath the warm water. A patronizing look flits across his face, his eyes narrowing to slits.

"What?" I say.

"You're not seriously washing graduated cylinders with tap water, are you?"

I'm almost impressed. That level of derision could flay a person with thinner skin than mine. I turn off the tap. "Yeah, what's the problem?"

"Deionized. You have to use deionized water. You're going to contaminate the—it's over the—oh, just let me—" The kid strides toward the cabinets and throws them open one by one, muttering under his breath. He chucks his backpack to the ground. It slumps against the counter.

After a straight minute of muttering, the boy flings open the last cabinet. "Here." He pulls down a pair of plastic squeeze bottles with thin nozzles attached to their lids. As he sets down the bottles by the sink, I catch his eyes. They're sharp, an indeterminate bluish-greenish-grayish color. Chameleon eyes. He doesn't hold my gaze long, though—his glance darts away to my hairline, my neck, the wall behind me.

I wait for him to leave, but he stands there as if he's waiting for a gold star. After the most uncomfortable silence in recorded history, I clear my throat. "So, you gonna go, or what?"

"I'll help." He grabs a bottle of his special miracle water and starts rinsing out a graduated cylinder.

"Uh." What's the politest way to say, *Like hell you will?* "No," I say, "that's really fine."

"I'm going to be here anyway," he says. "My mom's a guidance counselor, and I have to wait for my ride home. So maybe you should be the one leaving. This was my job first."

"Look, AP, I don't need the attitude." A muscle over my left eye spasms. I rub it. Like a retort, it spasms again.

"Looks like what you need is some sleep," he says.

"No shit, genius."

When the guy says nothing, I glance back at him. "Sorry," I mumble. "That just sort of came out."

He cocks his head like a perplexed puppy. "It's all right. Social interaction is generally not my forte, either."

"Your what?"

"My forte," he repeats.

"You mean for-*tay*?"

"No, *that's* an Italian word used in musical notation. The English word is adapted from the French *fort*, meaning *strong*. One syllable. *Forte*."

My mouth droops open, and I try not to let anything too disparaging fall out. Who the hell is this guy, some sort of malnourished TA? It's almost refreshing, his total weirdness.

Something about him in general soothes my nerves, although I can't pinpoint what.

I take a bottle and draw out a cylinder from the second bucket.

Beside me, the kid's pale hands move in jerks and starts, impatient, hyperefficient. "Rinse them three times each," he says, "then line them up overhead. Got it?"

I nod.

He turns to me. "Got it?"

"I nodded."

"Ah. Right." He goes back to washing. "Didn't see."

"Don't worry about it."

"I'm not."

"What?"

"Worrying," he says. "I'm not worrying about it."

I look at him for a second, wondering how long it's been since he spoke to a human being. I'm not a master of small talk by any means, but this kid is something else.

I go back to my cylinders. We lapse into blessed silence, but it doesn't take long for him to break it. "Valentine Simmons," he introduces himself. "Junior."

"Sure," I say, putting a cylinder into one of the cabinets.

"*Despite* common belief," he adds, "Valentine is a boy's name, since Saint Valentine was a man. So. So it's not weird."

"Okay," I say. "I didn't say it was weird."

Another silent minute trickles by before Valentine asks, "What grade are you in?"

Jesus, this guy won't take a hint. "Same," I say.

He squeezes a thin jet of water from his bottle's nozzle, his expression carefully neutral. Still, I get the sense he's disappointed I won't bite.

It hits me why he seems disarming: this air hovers around

him, and I only recognize it because it's familiar. He's one of those kids who, like me, has zero friends. Nice to know my superpower is detecting social failure.

I make a peace offering. "So, how about that assembly? What a waste of time, huh?"

"Waste of . . . ?"

"One email, and they go batshit crazy? It was probably someone trolling."

"If that's what you choose to believe," he says, an air of superiority cloaking him so thickly, I can almost smell it. He goes back to his cylinder, silent at last.

"I'm Kat Scott," I say. "So, why'd Norman put you on cleaning duty?"

"He didn't. I offered."

"Best buds, huh?"

"Well, we ate lunch together today, if that qualifies."

I eye him. "That's, uh."

"You think it's strange."

"I mean, I'm not going to tell you you're wrong."

"Yes, well." Valentine shrugs. "It was raining, so I couldn't eat outside."

"And you couldn't just go to the cafeteria because . . . ?"

His nose wrinkles. "I don't particularly enjoy the company of my peers."

". . . right. That didn't sound rehearsed at all."

"Well, it's true. I just don't do it. The last time I ate with someone my age was four hundred and ten days ago."

"Um." I look over at him. He doesn't seem to register exactly how bizarre that sentence was. "Why do you remember that?"

"I don't know. I like keeping count of things, and . . ." He frowns. "Yep."

Holy shit, that is sad. After a long minute of searching for an appropriate response, I go back to washing graduated cylinders. I can't imagine a torture more excruciating than eating lunch with Dr. Norman, that condescending prick. I'll take being roasted over a slow flame any day.

Then again, how long has it been since I had lunch with anybody? I sure as hell don't keep track, but my score is probably in the hundreds, too. My corner of the courtyard is my lunchtime sanctuary, and when it gets too cold, I resort to empty classrooms or the back section of the library. No company needed.

I can't remember the last time I sat down to dinner with Dad and Olivia, either. Eating alone seems so *sad* on Valentine. Is that what I look like from the outside? Some pariah, doomed to sit, untouchable, away from the rest of the world? I hope to God people can tell it's my choice.

Valentine finishes his bucket first. But he doesn't leave or find some reason to move away from me. Instead, he stands there, looking like the embodiment of everyone who has ever been awkward.

I tuck the last graduated cylinder into the overhead cabinet and shut the door, checking the clock. "Great." The bus is always long gone by four fifteen, and it's raining today. If I catch pneumonia walking home and die, I hope Olivia sues the shit out of Dr. Norman.

As Valentine takes the empty buckets up front, I head to one of the windows and look down at the junior lot. It's a pleasant surprise—Juniper's car is still sitting there. I shoot my sister a text.

Hey, missed the bus. Can you wait for me? Be down soon.

Valentine stops by the window, shrugging his backpack on. He breathes on the glass and draws an indifferent-looking face in the fog. "Is something out there?"

"Just, my sister's still here. So I have a ride." I point out through the drizzle at the silver Mercedes. "That's her."

Valentine's finger freezes over the fogged-up glass. "*Oh*," he says, packing more meaning into that one syllable than I would've thought possible.

"Oh?" I repeat.

"Nothing. Just, oh." He seems to have lost the ability to blink, staring down at Juniper's car. "The blonde, I assume?"

"Nah, my sister's the brunette. The blonde is Juniper Kipling. She's a friend. Why?"

"No reason," he says too quickly.

I lean against the wall. "What, you have a crush on one of them or something?"

"I don't do those."

"Do what? Crushes?"

"Yes, those," he says. "And no. I don't."

"What are you, one of those love-is-a-social-construct people?"

"I don't know about that. I just don't get crushes." He gives me a flash of his laser eyes again. "What, do you think it's a construct?"

"Spare me," I say. "Don't change the subject. What's your deal with Juni and my sister?"

His lips form a thin line. "No deal. Nothing." He shoves his hands into his jacket, turning away. "I have to go. Bye." He walks out fast, head down, staring deliberately at the ground.

As he shuts the door, I lean against a desk, drained by the interaction. I wish I were one of those androids from Electric Forces VI. I could stick a plug into myself to recharge.

I slouch out of the room, steeling myself for a weird drive home.

THE SIGHT OF OLIVIA AT THE STOVE THAT EVENING gives me a strange, sinking feeling. Most days, I move to my room the second she walks into the kitchen. Today, though, something keeps me at the table as I play Mass Effect. I glance at her every so often. She stands with one hip shifted out, her hair tied back in a messy stream. She hums a tune that sounds familiar, but I can't quite place it.

Dad opens the door at a little past seven, his glasses spattered with beads of water. His usual five-o'clock shadow has grown out to a layer of gray-black stubble, making the gaunt peaks and valleys of his face seem rockier than usual. Dad's all bones, a six-foot-five skeleton man with kind eyes.

"Hi," he says, shutting the door. He shrugs off his raincoat, revealing the plastic name tag on his button-down, emblazoned with the Golden Arches.

I lift a hand, and Olivia says, "Hey, how was work?"

Dad doesn't seem to hear. As he meanders toward the stairs, all he says is, "Horrible weather." His voice barely makes it to my ears, quiet and reedy.

"Yeah, it's gross out," Olivia says. "Dinner's going to be ready in about ten, okay?"

"Thanks." He vanishes up to the second floor, leaving silence except for the simmering hiss of hot water. As I look after him, Valentine Simmons's miserable *Four Hundred and Ten Days of Eating Alone* statistic scratches at the back of my mind.

"You want me to set the table?" I ask, pausing Mass Effect.

Olivia turns, her eyebrows raised. "Yeah, that—that'd be awesome," she says. "You eating with us, Kat?"

I nod. "Smells nice."

A big smile lifts her cheeks. Two words, and she lights up like a lantern—I forgot how transparent Olivia can be. "Great!" she says. "Dad'll be really happy."

If he is, though, I can't tell. When the three of us sit down, he eats slack-faced and quiet, despite Olivia's attempts to draw conversation out of him.

I sneak glances at my sister and my dad throughout dinner. Their presence crushes me in. How do I talk to them? They feel so far away, like distant island countries. God knows what's going on inside Dad's head, and I hardly know anything about Olivia anymore. She, Juniper, and Claire are as inseparable as always, and she goes out every weekend. That's all I know, besides the music she listens to in her room.

"What's new, Kat?" Olivia says, meeting my eyes.

I look down at my lap and scramble for words. "Nothing much. Um . . . Dr. Norman made fun of me in chemistry today."

"Why?"

"'Cause he's a dick."

"Language," Dad mumbles. I've never heard a more half-assed chastisement.

"No, he is, though," Olivia says. "All last year, he used to make fun of my height. And I was, like, yeah, I know I'm tall—thanks for the constant reminders." She takes a swig of orange juice. "What'd he say to you?"

"I was asleep. So he, you know. Made an example."

"Oh," Olivia says. I wait for some preachy *Maybe stay awake next time* remark, but she just shrugs and says, "Yeah, dude's voice could put a dolphin to sleep. Amazing."

"What, is that impressive?"

"Dolphins—fun fact—actually don't sleep," Olivia says through a mouthful of noodles. "They only rest part of their brains at a time, so they're always sorta conscious. Also, they're evil. They, like, kidnap people and drag them off to their dolphin lairs."

I laugh before I can help it. Olivia looks at me with this mixture of astonishment and delight, as if I've handed her a winning lottery ticket. Dad glances between the two of us, looking confused, which is fair—I'm a little confused, too. I forgot Olivia made jokes and offered people sympathy. I forgot she did anything but tell me to deal with my responsibilities.

When we finish dinner, Dad stands. "I'm exhausted, girls. Might call it an early night."

"Sure," Olivia says. "I'll wash up. Don't worry about it."

"Thanks, Olly." He gives her an absent-looking smile before trudging upstairs.

"Shit, he's quiet," I say, looking after him. Dad was never loud, but back when we were in elementary school, he and Mom would bounce jokes off each other at dinner until they both teared up from laughter. Mom coaxed a gregarious side out of him. Around her, he acted out. Trying to impress her, maybe—or keep a hold of her. Maybe he knew the whole time that trying to hold on to her was like trying to hold on to ice—a wasted effort that was only going to leave him cold.

Olivia gathers our plates, looking grim. "Yeah, work wears him down so much, there's not much he can do but crash when he gets home."

I trace a stain on the table. God knows I understand that feeling, not that I have the right to. A thousand kids at our school do the same thing I do every day, and they still have energy and motivation. I've got no excuse. Sick of the feeling of self-pity, I stand. "Night," I say, and I head for the stairs. My sister gives me a smile, but it hardly registers.

HELLO
my name is

OLIVIA SCOTT

ON SATURDAY AFTERNOON, MATT PICKS ME UP, ALONG with my bundle of project supplies. His car smells like he's growing marijuana plants in the trunk. The space in front of the passenger seat is so filled with paper, bottles, and trash, it's like a handy cushion for me to prop up my feet.

"Sorry about the mess," he says, not sounding in any way sorry about the mess.

"All good," I say, glancing into the backseat, which is even worse. It looks as if somebody mistook it for a landfill.

Matt doesn't turn the radio down, so I hum along with various bad pop songs all the way to his house. At one point I think I hear him singing along to Avril Lavigne, but when I glance over at him, his mouth is firmly shut.

My eyes linger on him for a second. As if he's trying to look like as much of a stoner as possible, he's wearing a maroon beanie pulled low over his forehead, tufts of hair sticking out from beneath. He drives one-handed, relaxed and silent, but his expression gives me the sense that something's brewing under the surface.

We didn't talk in English yesterday. Didn't even look at each other, in spite of our phone conversation Thursday night, or maybe because of it. Sitting two feet from him now, I can't help imagining his mother, a discontented scientist frustrated by small-town Paloma, and his father, resentful and underappreciated. But as for Matt himself . . . after Thursday night, I don't know what to think about him. He changed over the phone, showed me a new face.

I look out the window, up at the flat blue sky. The way my sister acted last night at dinner—giving me a glimpse of how she used to be—made me think that maybe she can change, too. I hadn't heard her laugh in so long. Hearing it pulled up a well of memories, even nostalgia, like hearing a song I might have had on repeat during a bittersweet summer.

"Here's me," Matt says, turning down the radio. We pull up outside a small white house with black shutters. He parks at the curb.

I sling my backpack on and follow him up a weed-trimmed path. The porch paint is flaking off, and bugs have gnawed holes in the window screens. I shiver, waiting as he unlocks the door with a stained silver key.

Finally, Matt wedges the door open. We enter his living room, a nest of warmth and color. A squashy-looking couch is upholstered in red, scattered with stitched pillows. Above it, a magnificent painting of the sun stretches across the wall, its orange rays lighting the ridges of a mountain range. A deeply scored mantel holds three different cuckoo clocks and a row of intricate crucifixes, and a television sits on an end table. Quilts and blankets and clutter cover every surface. The Jackson household clearly does not go for the whole minimalism thing.

"We can work in here or the kitchen—whatever," Matt says, giving the door a firm shove with his shoulder. It slides back into its ill-fitting frame with a muffled bang.

I look around. The coffee table, like the rest of the room, is overflowing, filled with magazines and half-melted candles. "Do you have a kitchen table we could use?"

"Sure." He heads down the hall. I follow, peering through the doors to the left and right: a whirring laundry room, a tiny bathroom with a stained mirror, and another small hall ending in a staircase. An indistinct smell hangs around—the new air of an unfamiliar house. Different-smelling detergent, maybe, mixed with a few types of scented air fresheners.

His kitchen, bigger than the living room, fits in a long counter, an island, and a fat wooden table with six chairs. Beside the table, three plates hang on the wall, painted dappled blue. Delicate green and orange floral designs blossom out from their center.

"Those are gorgeous." I wave at the plates, setting the poster materials on the table.

"They're my grandma's." Matt draws out a chair and sits. "They're, like, sixty years old."

"Did she make them?"

"Nah. Mom's side of the family is from Puebla. There's this special ceramic style, regional, called Talavera, and those are from the city."

I sit across from him, unzipping my backpack. "Puebla. Is that in . . ."

"Mexico. South-Central Mexico."

"You still have family there?" I ask.

"Yeah, a few great-aunts, but my grandparents moved to St. Louis in the seventies, so all my closer family is up here. Except my uncle. He's, like, a stock market guy in London."

"Fancy." I unroll the poster, flattening its edges under a pair of textbooks. "Man, I want to go to London. Mexico's on my to-visit list, too. I've never been out of the country, so."

"Yeah?" Matt says. "I've visited Mexico a few times, for, like, two weeks at a go, but I always feel so fake-Mexican, 'cause I'm only half. I haven't lived there or anything, so all my Mexican relatives think of me as white-bread American."

"Do you speak Spanish?"

"*Claro que sí.*"

"Aha," I say. "*Yo también*, sort of."

Matt smiles, pulling off his beanie. His messy hair falls across his forehead. "So, this poster thing. Should—"

"Matt?" says a voice.

I look over my shoulder. The cutest child in the world, probably, stands in the doorway. A mop of dark hair tops his tan little face, and unlike Matt's, his eyes are bright blue. When he sees me, his mouth shuts, and he takes a step back.

"Hey, Russ," Matt says, standing. "You came down the stairs by yourself?"

"I can climb down stairs," Russ says, the picture of three-year-old indignation.

I grin. Matt lifts his hands. "Right, obviously, my bad." He points to me. "This is Olivia. Want to wave hi?"

Russell flaps a hand frantically at me. "Hi. My name is Russell."

"Hey, Russell," I say. "Nice to meet you. I like your house."

He doesn't reply, looking back to Matt with pleading eyes.

"What's the matter, Russ?" Matt says.

"I want car. The car was . . . the car was too high. I tried to climb."

"Oh jeez, don't climb your shelves," Matt says. "I'll get it for you." He glances at me. "Give me a sec?"

"Sure," I say. "I'll start this."

"Thanks."

As he vanishes into the hall, I start writing *INFERNO* across the top of the poster. I know perfectly well how to spell *inferno*, but I catch myself starting to draw the wrong letter twice. Something about these giant, red, unsubtle letters makes the word stop looking like a word.

Matt returns before I finish the *N*. "Sorry," he says, sitting down. "I gave him a bunch of stuff to keep him busy, but three-year-olds are sort of, you know. Attention-thirsty."

"He's adorable."

"Yeah, I know," Matt says. "And he's super smart for his age. I couldn't do actual sentences until I was five or some shit, but Russ already knows words like—what did he say the other day?—'effective' or something. And 'philosophy.' It's crazy th—" He cuts himself off. Something in his eyes happens, like shutters closing, hiding away the fondness. "Anyway."

I fight back a smile, returning to the poster. "You're a good brother."

"What?"

"You are. You're, like, enthusiastic about him. It's cute." I glance at him, but he avoids my eyes. "Um," he says.

We sit in silence for a second. I examine him—his narrow brown eyes, his thick, heavy brows—and our phone conversation swims back to the forefront of my mind. I want to tell him how Kat acted last night—progress!—but he could so easily turn back into the kid from English class, the too-cool-to-care guy. He could say, *Oh, I was high on Thursday*, and dismiss it.

"So," he says carefully. I tense up. I don't know why or what I'm expecting him to say.

"What's up?" I ask.

After a second, he picks up one of the sheets of paper strewn across the poster. "I—nothing," he mumbles. "Nothing. I, uh, I didn't finish reading *Inferno*."

"Oh. Right. Me neither." I cap my marker. "I'm a slow reader."

"Really?"

"You surprised?"

"I don't know," he says. "I guess I am, a little. 'Cause you're smart."

I grin. "Hey, thanks, but I'm also slower than a slug in quicksand. Anyway, I got a bunch of themes and stuff off SparkNotes, so we can put the important bits on here."

"I did start it, though," he says. "I swear, I read like fifteen cantos." He sounds so urgent, you'd think his *Inferno* progress was the only thing standing between us and Tartarus. A hint of intensity shows in his face, too, the corners of his thin mouth tightening.

I tilt my head. "I mean, I believe you."

"Right." He flaps the sheet in his hand. "Right, I . . . yeah."

I look down at the poster for a long second, not thinking about the project at all. "Hey, um," I say.

Matt meets my eyes. I've never seen a brown that clear. Like dark honey, or amber, with something bright crystallized deep in the center. The tightness in my chest winds up.

"I wanted to thank you, I guess," I say. "For talking on Thursday. I . . . yeah."

He sits quiet and still. I hold my breath, praying he won't shrug it off. Talking with him felt like it meant something, late at night like that, quiet and unexpected. I don't know why I mentioned Mom like that, in retaliation, but he didn't throw it back at me. He traded me a little piece of his life, instead, and that deserves a thank-you, in my eyes.

"It's . . ." he says, a crease forming between his straight eyebrows. "I . . . it was a good . . ."

He doesn't finish.

"Yeah," I say. "It was a good."

Matt smiles. His cheeks press his eyes up into half-moons.

"All right." I clear my throat. "We should probably work on this thing."

And for two hours, we do, cutting orange paper into tongues of flame, writing quotes, collecting characters from each circle, listing sins and virtues.

It's quiet except for the occasional rumble from the refrigerator, and sometimes we lean close enough above the poster that the light sound of his breathing distracts me. The sight of his dark forearms folded on the table catches me, too, his knobby wrists and the thin hair leading up to his elbows. It feels weirdly intimate, the two of us tucked into a corner of his kitchen, working in silence that's more comfortable than it has the right to be.

HELLO
my name is

CLAIRE LOMBARDI

I WAKE UP AT 11:30 PM TO MY RINGTONE BLARING. Instantly alert, I grab my phone, squinting at the screen. The blue light makes my eyes ache in the dark.

I pick up. "Juniper? What's going on? What's happening?"

"Claire," she sings. "Claire fair, Claire bear. Claire Clah-Claire, Claire, Claaaire. We're hanging out, and we miss youuu."

I shut my eyes, settling back under my covers. So nothing's wrong—just a drunk dial. I'm not sure whether I'm more relieved or irritated. "Juniper, I need to sleep," I say. And I don't need a reminder of how much fun they're having without me. Is a little consideration too much to ask?

"Oh no," Juniper says. The phone rustles. I hear her talking to Olivia. "I woke her up."

"Well, yeah, you dork," Olivia says in the background. "It's, like, eleven thirty."

"Juni," I say, "how much did you drink?"

"Whaaat? Drink? Don't worry about it," Juniper says. "Don't even worry about. Yeah."

I scowl, nibbling my thumbnail. Before I can say anything,

static rubs against my ear. I catch a snatch of a muffled protest. Then Olivia's voice says, "Yo."

"Olivia. Hi. Can you please explain what's happening?"

"Juni drank a little too much and got sick, so I'm spending the night. We watched *The Road to El Dorado*, and Juni wants to do *Finding Nemo* next."

I picture them curled up in the living room, on the plush rug in front of Juni's TV. My frustration builds. "Why is she drinking?"

"I don't know. She wanted to. Sorry about the late call. I know you have to get up early."

"I mean, it's fine." I straighten up, resigning myself to the fact that I'm awake. "Just . . . I thought you two were supposed to be having a chill night in, and this is two weeks in a row she's done the shitty-drunk thing. You think there's something wrong?"

"She hasn't mentioned anything," Olivia says. "But . . . yeah, you're right, she's been weird. I was gonna ask, but I got distracted by the whole impossible-quantities-of-vomit thing."

"Ew."

"That's better, though, right? Get it all out of her system or whatever."

"Is that how that works?"

"I think so," Olivia says. "Science!" The sound of a commercial blares through the phone. Her voice grows distant. "Juni, want to put *Nemo* on? I'm gonna get some blankets."

"So. Did Dan text you again?" I ask. The second the question comes out, I wonder why I brought it up. Talking about boys with Olivia is never a good idea.

"No, thank God," she says. "But Richard Brown got a hold of my number somehow, so now I have to deal with that. Even though I made it totally clear I wasn't into him."

"Someone's popular," I say.

"Not necessarily a good thing."

I sigh. She always does this weird denial thing, as if guys being interested in her is bad.

"I'm serious," she says. "What, you think I'm bragging?"

"I dunno," I say, chewing harder on my thumbnail. From the perspective of someone totally unnoticed by the male population, it's hard not to hear it as bragging.

"Getting hit on is one thing," she says. "But when guys won't leave me alone, even after I've made it apparent I'm not interested? That just means they've heard I'll jump on anything that shows me attention. Not a compliment."

"Okay," I say, still not getting it. If she stopped sleeping around, guys wouldn't expect anything from her anymore, right? Isn't that the obvious fix?

"Anyway, it's stressful," she says. "Like, one time I said no to this guy, and he was all, 'Fine, I'll find someone better, skank bitch.'"

Anger jolts me out of my confusion. I keep my voice from rising, but only because Grace is asleep in the next room. "I—what? Someone *said* that to you?"

"Eh, don't worry about it. He was wasted, so—"

"Is this someone we know?"

"No, 'course not," Olivia says. "I never know guys who act like that. My point is, you never know if you're dealing with some guy who's going to get scary-angry or just plain mean if you're like, hey, sorry, not interested."

"I . . . okay," I say, starting to see it from her angle. I don't know why I feel so reluctant to agree with her. It's not like I *want* this stuff to be her fault. "I mean . . . yeah."

I hear her fumble with what I assume are blankets. "Aight," she says, "I should go care for our dear, drunken June bug."

"Night, Liv." I plug my phone back in to charge and set it on my bedside table, then roll over, burying the side of my face in a cool pillow.

My eyes won't close. My hands wander to my mouth, and I catch myself about to start biting again. I form fists, protecting my nails.

Skank bitch. Olivia made it sound as if the insult meant nothing to her. How many times has she heard that? How many times has she put up with it and not told me or Juniper?

Or is it only you she's never told, Claire? whispers that voice in my head.

Of everything, that's the thought that sticks: that yet again, I'm being excluded. I squeeze my eyes shut, selfishly hating myself, as if it's the time for that sort of thing.

HELLO
my name is

KAT SCOTT

IT STARTS RAINING AT 3:00 AM ON SUNDAY MORNING. The rain starts and stops outside the window over and over. *Sleep,* I tell myself, but it doesn't come, not like the focus I can drive myself into onstage. Lying here, I can't clear my mind, let alone get out of my head into some other safe haven.

I hate nighttime. In the chunks of night before I drift off, my brain bombards me with every thought I've been kicking back since morning. Tonight, the spinning wheel has stopped on the topic of sadness and how unoriginal it is. People have always been unhappy. It's only in the last hundred years—or fewer, maybe—that people have started thinking that unhappiness is this abnormal thing, that we're all entitled to happiness somehow. Such bullshit. That's not how the world works. I bet in Grigory Veselovsky's time in Russia, all the serfs or peasants or whatever were probably major-depressive by our standards.

So for the last three hours, I've lain here being unoriginal. I don't know.

Crying ceased to do anything for me ages ago. I just stare, these nights. Stare at the window, until a fitful sleep drags my mind under, kicking, thrashing, silent.

. . . .

A KNOCK COMES ON MY DOOR. I GLANCE TO THE wall, at the old-timey novelty clock Dad got me for Christmas back in seventh grade. It has a quote from Shakespeare's *As You Like It*—"One man in his time plays many parts"—and the comedy-tragedy theater masks below.

The clock reads 6:00 PM. A whole day gone, and I hardly noticed. Thank God for the Internet. With a little help from addictive games, I can forget myself at home, turn into a shell of my own mind. It's nicely numbing. This weekend, I've been marathoning Blade-X, which, despite its unfortunate name, is not a cheap brand of grocery-store razor, but a first-person shooter involving large quantities of badly animated blood.

Another knock. "Yeah, what?" I say, as my avatar slams a crate into a metal wall. A shiny shield falls out, and I strap it onto my back.

The door creaks open. Olivia slips in and shuts the door behind her. "Hey."

"Yo," I say, not pausing the game.

"Have you been in bed all day?"

"Yup."

"What do you want for dinner?"

"Not hungry." Maybe I shouldn't have eaten with her and Dad on Friday. I hope she doesn't think that's going to be normal. The energy I had the day before yesterday is long gone.

"What are you playing?" she asks, walking to my desk and sitting down.

"It's called Blade-X."

"Sounds, uh, stimulating."

I don't reply, sheathing my knives so I can climb up a water tower.

"Do you meet many people playing those?" she asks.

"I don't have, like, a social life through gaming, if that's what you're asking."

"Okay," she says. "'Cause this whole isolation thing doesn't seem super-fun."

As I edge around the side of the water tower, bullets spray up at me from below. I roll to one side and start climbing the second ladder, tilting the perspective. There's got to be an entrance here somewhere. . .

"I was glad you surfaced Friday, because you've seemed so mad lately," Olivia says. "I've been trying to give you space, 'cause I thought it was something I did."

I'm hardly listening. I'm dying up here. Climbing the ladders drains my energy, and dark, insect-like enemies have started swarming out the top of the water tower. I can't fight them with my vitals bar empty—I have to get inside, somewhere safe.

Olivia continues. "But someone said maybe you were going through something, so I thought I'd ask if—"

I slam the pause button, disbelieving. "Whoa, wait. 'Someone'? You asked someone about how to, like, fix me?"

"What? That's not what I said." Olivia drums her gold nails on the glass top of my desk. "Look. I know it's not my place to tell you what to do with your time, but—"

"You're right. It's absolutely not."

"But, Kat, you've got to get out of bed. You've got to eat and have an actual sleep schedule. That's not a lot. That's, like, bare-minimum, day-to-day stuff."

I don't bother replying. What is there to say? I have all the personhood of a rock these days. No appetite. No circadian rhythm. No interests, except the play. Who cares?

"And if you can't do this stuff alone," she goes on, "someone has to help you. I wish it weren't me, because you hate me, for whatever reason, but—"

"Oh, shut up. I don't hate you."

"It's not as if you like me," Olivia says, her voice rising. "And I don't know when that happened, but you know what? It would've been great if you'd given me some sort of memo."

I'm quiet. As I look at her, unwelcome reminders swim up to my mind's eye: images of us passing notes in fourth grade and climbing trees in fifth, binge-watching movies late at night in sixth grade and reading idly in the same room in seventh. Years' worth of memories start crawling into the back of my mind whenever she hassles me like this.

I unclench my jaw and say, "I don't like anyone."

She stays conspicuously silent. For a second I wonder if I might've hurt her feelings.

Olivia looks away, out the window. I wonder for a second if she's going to cry. I haven't seen her cry since elementary school. Does she even have tear ducts anymore, in those neatly lined eyes?

I look back at my laptop screen and hit play.

She stands. "If you change your mind about dinner, I'm making soup."

I hardly hear her. There it is—a crack between the water tower's metal plates. I shoulder my way through the entrance into the dark. Finally safe.

HELLO
my name is

VALENTINE SIMMONS

PRINCIPAL TURNER GREETS THE SCHOOL ON MONDAY morning with a lighthearted little announcement: "Students and faculty, we have determined that the next step in our investigation process will be to conduct brief interviews of the student body. All interviews will be strictly confidential and conducted in a safe, closed environment."

I glance around, but nobody else in first period seems appalled by this. Apparently, they don't mind that this teacher-student-romance thing has turned into the Spanish Inquisition.

I sit stiffly at my desk, staring down at a list of differential equations. This weekend I batted around the idea of speaking with Juniper Kipling, but the fact that phone conversations are the bane of my existence provided something of a deterrent. Also, calling her up out of nowhere to accuse her of this seemed a bit uncomfortable, to say the least.

Still, though, I have to talk to her as soon as possible. If she's being coerced into something, I can't keep my mouth shut. In fact, these interrogation sessions provide the perfect opportunity to tell the authorities what I know, if it seems appropriate.

At the beginning of lunch, I wait outside the cafeteria, hoping to intercept Juniper. Clumps of people edge around me, their eyes passing over me so smoothly, I might as well be painted to match the wall.

I spot Juniper halfway down the hall. She's flanked by a pair of girls: a tall brunette with the rectangular shoulders of an Amazon, and a short redhead with thick silver eyeliner. The brunette says something, and the trio bursts into laughter, their smiles matching in a way that suggests they learned how to smile together. As they approach, I clear my throat, balling up my fists. I step into their path.

"Excuse me," I declare.

The three stop, looking at me with identical bemusement.

"Uh, hey," says the brunette. "You're Valentine, right?"

"Yes." I address Juniper, my nerves buzzing. "May I speak with you for a minute?"

"Me? Sure." Juniper glances at the tall girl. "I'll catch up with you guys in there."

The brunette and the redhead vanish into the crowd, and as Juniper and I back away toward the wall, a familiar droning voice says, "Freeeak."

I turn, heat prickling my cheeks, as a pair of guys a head taller than I brush by. "Could you at least find something entertaining to say?" I snap after their matching backpacks. They don't flinch at my voice.

"Dean," Juniper calls. At once, both boys glance over their shoulders. One is lean and wiry, his hair buzz-cut short. I recognize the other: the same long-nosed, curly-haired swimmer from last week, who didn't apologize then, either.

Juniper narrows her eyes at the guy with the buzz cut. "Was that you? Did you say that?"

"Um," Dean says, glancing at his curly-haired friend, whose gaze darts around the hall, not sticking anywhere in particular.

"Apologize to Valentine," Juniper says, approaching them.

"Oh God," I mumble. "Please, you're under no obligation to white-knight me."

"It's a public service," she says, looking back up at the guys. They've stayed still too long—the crowd spits them out, and they hover by the cafeteria doors. As Juniper's eyes harden, I thank God that I'm not in her vicious sight line. "Apologize," she insists.

Dean shrugs. "Whatever, sorry," he says with hardly a look in my direction. He nudges his friend. "Come on, let's get our table."

But as Dean heads into the cafeteria, Juniper turns her accusatory stare on the curly-haired boy, and he lingers behind. "Lucas, seriously?" Juniper says, sounding disappointed. "You're going to stand there and watch that happen?"

Lucas wilts, his shoulders slumping. Abysmal posture notwithstanding, he has nearly a foot on me, his shoulders so wide that I feel as if I'm facing down a bear. His guilty eyes are the dark brown of wet bark. Looking at his glum expression, I somehow feel bad for him, although he's hardly a victim here.

He opens his mouth, presumably to apologize, but I interrupt: "It's fine."

Even as my words come out, I wonder why I'm saying them. It isn't fine. From the rough end of things, silence looks an awful lot like complicity.

Before I can speak further, Juniper's brunette friend bounces back out the door to the cafeteria, wheeling to an ungainly halt.

"Hey, Juni," she says. "Can I steal you back? Claire says we 'need to talk' about Saturday night, which is, like, the most terrifying thing in many moons. I think she thinks I funneled the wine down your throat or something."

The sound of a cleared throat makes all of us turn. Mr. García, striding by, has slowed his pace, his brow furrowed. He doesn't say anything, but gives Juniper and Olivia a look.

"I mean, uh," Olivia says as he passes, "nobody here consumes alcohol, because we are all under the age of twenty-one."

García's frown deepens. He disappears down the hall, and Olivia makes a face after him. "How is *he* a hard-ass about drinking? He finished college, like, two hours ago." She glances at me. "Also, hey, sorry for interrupting. Also, also, I'm Olivia. Nice to meet you."

Juniper gives me an apologetic look. "Valentine, do you mind if I catch you later? I kind of need to talk something out with Claire. This isn't something urgent, is it?"

"I mean, it's—" I cut myself off. If I say it's urgent, I'll interest Lucas and Olivia far more than I'd like. I try to say no, but it doesn't come out; my throat has gone tight, scared into disuse by the three of them looking at me at once. They are all taller than me and all very good-looking. This is the most woefully unbalanced conversation of my life. "Fine," I say, lifting my chin as much as I can without feeling ridiculous. "It could be postponed if you . . . yes."

"I'll catch up with you tomorrow?"

"Right."

She stops in the arch, looking back with something like determination. "Also, Valentine, I'm having a thing at my place on Saturday around nine. Feel free to come by if you want."

My first instinct is hysterical laughter. Miraculously, I tamp it down. "Right," I say, trying not to sound too incredulous. Me going to a party: definitely a viable option. "Thank you."

The two girls disappear back into the cafeteria. Lucas dallies by the door, examining me.

"Good-bye," I say pointedly.

But he doesn't move. "I'm sorry."

"I already said it was fine."

"It's just, Dean's swim captain this year, so the rest of us kind of put up and shut up. And since regionals are only a week away, he's twice as hard-core these days, which—"

"I don't care."

Lucas looks taken aback. "Uh," he says. "Fair, I guess. But I am sorry, okay?"

There's something not quite Kansan around the edge of his accent; he spits his consonants too hard, flattening his vowels. He has an overeager sort of voice, quick and insistent, as if he's terrified he might lose my attention for a second. God, people who try too hard are so embarrassing.

I've hesitated too long. He seems to think it's an invitation to keep talking. "I'm Lucas McCallum," he says. "What's your name?"

"Valentine Simmons."

"Quite the name." He grins, and I feel disgusted, looking at his smile. It's stupidly photogenic, the type of Hollywood-handsome that verges on absurd. This kid is going to go through life and get everything handed to him on a silver platter because he looks like some sort of minor Greek god. I hate him a bit already, and it baffles me that he seems so desperate for validation. Hasn't he, like every other attractive person, been trained to expect the world to fall into his lap with no effort whatsoever?

"So," he says, "what up, Valentine Simmons?"

"Not much. Lunch awaits." I turn on my heel and take all of one step before he says, "Not in the cafeteria?"

Over my shoulder, I give him my most contemptuous look. Some people say there are no stupid questions, but here's a perfect counterexample if I ever heard one. "The cafeteria is filled with people I have absolutely no use for," I say coldly.

He lets out a generous, tumbling laugh, as if I've cracked the funniest joke all day. I round on him, not bothering to mask my glare. "What?"

"It was funny," he says. "Was that not a joke?"

"I mean. No."

"Oh. Okay." He forces a serious expression. "So, what, you eat off-campus?"

"No."

"Then where?"

"Why?" I ask.

"Just a question. Doesn't need any analysis or anything."

"Oh." I frown. "Okay. Well. Analysis is sort of my modus operandi."

He's smiling again, for no reason. The unforgiving hallway lights illuminate the crow's-feet at the corners of his eyes. He glows with inner contentment, and I don't know where he gets it, but it must be nice. He's probably from some other planet, where the sun always shines and everybody is unconditionally nice to one another and puppies frolic around the streets.

"Outside," I say. "By the trailers."

"Isn't that cold?"

"Better being cold than having to deal with what's in there." I nod to the cafeteria. "Shallow conversation and popularity contests—ugh."

A line appears between Lucas's eyebrows. What is that? Surprise? Confusion? Irritation? "Other people aren't as cut-and-dry as you think," he says. "Everyone's got stuff they hide."

"Right." I roll my eyes. "I'm sure *you* have so many dark secrets under the surface."

He doesn't laugh. For a minute I think, *Well, then, he must be a serial killer.* Really, though, what secrets could this kid have? Nobody so grotesquely happy is ever interesting.

I shoehorn my hands into my pockets. "Whatever. Regardless of what people show or hide, they annoy me, and I'm weird, and no one likes me, either. It's mutual."

Lucas cocks his head. "Hey. I'm sorry."

"What? Don't be. Who cares? It doesn't matter." I give my head a sharp shake. Why am I still talking to this kid? Not bothering with a good-bye, I stride down the hall.

But before I get too far, I could swear I hear him say something like, "'Course it matters."

THEY CALL ME IN FOR MY STUDENT INTERVIEW AT THE start of sixth period. The brief exemption from class is a blessing. Our AP Latin teacher has contracted a nasty cold, and those of us in the front row keep getting subjected to her sneezes. I'm determined to dawdle all the way to the guidance center and back. Aimless wandering is a definite improvement on the phlegm war zone.

On the way there, I peruse the student-government campaign posters adorning walls and lockers, some taped to the banisters in the stairwell. Most are for the overzealous freshman presidential candidates, of which there are eight. The juniors only have three, one of whom is Juniper. I wonder how she can focus on extracurriculars, but if posters indicate anything, she's set to win: her advertisements are the only ones that look vaguely official. Olivia's blare out from the cinder blocks, so brightly colored that my eyes cry out in protest. And Matt Jackson's, God help us, have the sentence YOUR VOTE MATTERS! written in Comic Sans.

I push through a set of double doors, crossing from the new wing to the old wing. No more plate glass and constant brightness. Here, high windows cast narrow, dramatic shafts of light onto dark, pitted floors. I knock my plastic hall pass against the padlocks on the lockers, making them swing. Getting assigned a locker on this side of the school is a bad draw—they're so spacious that people get stuffed into them, à la every high school movie made before 2000. For somebody my size, it wouldn't even be uncomfortable. I could set up a nice little table in there and finally have a peaceful spot to read.

I trot down to the first floor and enter the guidance center's tiny cluster of offices. My mother, the head of the office, sits at the front desk beneath a poster of a motivational kitten. HANG IN THERE! it says. The kitten dangles from a tree branch, looking as if its life is in peril.

"Hi, dear," Mom says. "Time for your interview?"

"Yeah." I peer around the corner at the closed doors. "Are you really doing this for twelve hundred students?"

"With the eight of us, it goes faster than you'd think." My mom hands me a slip of paper with my name at the top. "Give this to Ms. Conrad when she calls you in, would you?"

I perch on a padded bench between two other kids, trying not to fidget, counting squares of carpet to relax myself. Maybe I should talk. Juniper will take the fall for her poor decision-making, and the sense of irresolution will clear from my head. My part will be done.

"Valentine Simmons," calls a voice from the depths of the guidance center. I head for the last door on the left, passing the most recent interviewee, a small, nervous-looking girl. I close the door gently and sit across from Ms. Conrad, a tubby woman with dreadlocks thicker than my fingers.

She smiles as I hand her the slip. "Thanks, Valentine. You're Sarah's son, right?"

"Yeah."

"Good genes," she says, smoothing out the slip. She clicks a pink pen. "So, I'm going to ask you a few questions, and if you'll answer them to the best of your ability, that'd be great. First: have you heard any theories who the participants in the rumored illicit teacher-student relationship might be?"

I frown. "You're asking me to tell you rumors? You realize how unreliable the high school rumor mill is, right?"

Ms. Conrad sighs. "Work with me here, kid."

"Well," I say, "I heard something about Dr. Meyers, but I don't at all believe it."

"Hmm." She scribbles Dr. Meyers's last name. "And how about the student?"

Juniper's name trembles at the tip of my tongue. I swallow, look down at my lap, and keep it back. "Nothing."

"Nothing at all?"

I look up at Ms. Conrad. Her brown eyes dig into mine, and I force myself to hold them. "Nothing at all," I repeat, not even blinking.

HELLO
my name is
MATT JACKSON

BURKE AND I PULL UP AT MY HOUSE ON MONDAY afternoon as my mom heads out the door for a dental appointment. She flaps a hand at me and says, "Don't let Russell eat any snacks, or he won't eat dinner. *Y cierra la puerta*—it was cracked open yesterday and so cold when I got home." She gives Burke the usual pained smile she saves for him, because, like everyone at school, she thinks his clothes are ridiculous, and today he's wearing leather pants that show every contour of his leg muscles, as well as something hairy and alpaca-looking draped over his shoulders.

"Have a good appointment, Ms. Flores," Burke says, polite as always, as we walk inside. I jam my shoulder into the door to make sure it stays closed, and Russ, who sits on the couch, sticks out his lip at me, looking up from a board book about airplanes.

"Hey, Russ," I say, "remember Burke?" and Russ looks up at Burke, says, "Yes," and waves furiously. Burke grins, sitting down in the armchair near the couch, and props his combat boots up on the coffee table. "Your brother's the only one who doesn't stare at my clothes," he says to me, and I'm like, "Hey, I don't stare," and he says, "You stare the most, dude," and I sigh, dumping my backpack onto the floor.

"Matt?" Russ says.

I sit by him on the couch. "Yeah?"

"Where is Olivia?" he asks, and I say, "I don't know," and he says, "Will she come again?"

"Yo, wait," Burke says. "Like, *Olivia* Olivia? When was she here?" and I'm like, "Saturday—we have this project thing on *Inferno* for English," and Burke says, "Well?" and I'm like, "Well, what?" and he says, "I don't know—how'd it go?" and I shrug, slouching down in the sofa, feeling self-conscious. "I don't know, man," I say. "I can't stop thinking about her." I feel stupid saying it, but it's a serious problem. I keep remembering her hunched over my kitchen table, her teeth buried in her bottom lip in concentration. I keep seeing the way she twitched her head to get her long hair out of her eyes, and hearing her gut-laughter, which came out at things I said without even thinking they were funny. I keep imagining her fast, clear voice and the wide points of her smile, and I keep wanting to see it all again.

I look down at Russell, who's still staring up at me, wide-eyed, waiting for a verdict. "I don't know, Russ," I say. "I hope she'll be back," and he nods so hard, his whole body bounces before going back to his board book.

Burke lowers his voice. I sit forward to hear him, leaning my elbows on my knees. "So," he says, "did anything happen?" and I'm like, "We talked on the phone last week, and it got kind of serious, so on Saturday it was, like, tense, you know?" I fist one hand in my hair. "Man, I'm so into her, but the project's done Thursday, and . . . I don't know."

"So talk to her," Burke says, as if it's that simple.

I give him a skeptical look. "Right," I say. "Like she doesn't have a hundred other guys chasing after her already."

"Never know until you ask." Burke flicks his nose ring idly. "Come on." He heads into the hall to the kitchen, and I follow, glancing at Russ to make sure he's still engrossed in finding which plane fits which silhouette.

Burke sits at the kitchen table, and I drop into the seat across from him. "How would I talk to her?" I say, and he's like, "You have her number," and I'm like, "Well, yeah, but—"

"So text her," he says, and I'm like, "What? No, that's an awful idea," and he says, "Why?" and his eyes challenge me to come up with something that doesn't sound like me being a wimp. Though I guess I am a wimp when it comes to this. "I'm fucking terrified, dude," I say. "I've had, like, three conversations with her, so how the hell am I this . . . *like this*, you know?"

"Like what? Interested?" Burke unzips his backpack, pulling out a stack of books so thick, it's a miracle he fit them inside. "Look," he says, cracking open his econ textbook, "you've got this English thing, so text her a joke or something about it. Act natural."

"You want me to text Olivia a joke about Dante," I say, thinking about the infinite ways this could go wrong. Burke says, "Well, you gotta read the book first."

I straighten up, indignant. "Hey. I did read it."

Burke's head pops up from his textbook. "You read *Inferno*?" he says, and I'm like, "Don't sound so surprised," and he's like, "But I *am* surprised. Like, fucking floored, dude."

I sigh. "I finished it yesterday. I don't know what I thought—it'd maybe give us something to talk about?"

"Wow," he says. "So, wait, hold on, you *don't* just want to get in her pants," and I'm like, "That's what I'm trying to tell you, Burke. Jesus!"

"Hey, chill." Burke messes up his hair, which is dark purple this week. "So text her and say you finished reading it."

"But I—"

"No, don't argue. Just do it. Man, do I have to force you into everything? I swear, when you get married, I'm gonna be standing at the altar pinching you between every vow."

I frown but take out my phone. My fingers move with agonizing slowness, trying to keep the words tied up in my hands, but I make my way through, tap by tap. **Hey so I finished reading inferno,** I type, thinking about all the movies I've seen where guys write girls letters, long, dramatic, eloquent letters confessing their feelings, and as I stare down at this stupid six-word text, I somehow feel that it's totally equivalent, that this is my own end-all-be-all confession that will betray once and for all the fact that I care.

I send the text.

"Congrats," Burke says.

I toss my phone onto the table, scowling. "You're not allowed to leave until she says something," I mumble, and his pierced eyebrows rise, like he's trying to look innocent, as if that wasn't the biggest lost cause of all lost causes.

A minute passes. Then my phone buzzes, skittering over to me like a hopeful pet. I snatch it up, sliding open her response. **You beat me!! I'm on Canto 27. No spoilers, thanks.**

Burke grabs my phone. I flail across the table, trying to snatch it back, but he holds it out of reach, crowing, "Two exclamation points! Not one, but two! Be still, your beating little heart!" and I say, "*Shutupshutupshutup*," and wrench the phone out of his beefy fingers. "Shit, you are so embarrassing."

As I settle back into my chair, I type, **Spoiler, everybody's already dead**, and hit send.

Burke peers at the screen, squinting as he reads upside down. He doesn't say anything, but when he flips his econ book open again, he's wearing a private little smile, and I say, "The fuck are you smiling at?" and he says, "Just nice to see signs of life," and I'm like, "The fuck is that supposed to mean?" and he says, "Hey, cool it with the f-bombs—your little brother's, like, twenty feet away," and I sigh, 'cause he's right, as always. I lower my head to the table, one finger resting against my phone, waiting to feel it the split second she answers.

IT'S A NEW FEELING, AVOIDING THE CAFETERIA DURING lunch on Tuesday. The rigid social structure of the caf makes it easy to navigate: the tables along the front wall are for football, lax, field hockey, and swimmers. The tables on the side wall belong to what douchebags refer to as the Lesser Sports: tennis, track, soccer, and cross-country. The tables in the middle have their own system, an unofficial order I still haven't deciphered. Although I do know that Matt Jackson and Burke Fischer sit closest to the lunch line. It's impossible to miss Burke, with the clothes he wears. Sometimes I get jealous of the guy—he seems so at home with his weirdness. I can't help thinking that if I had his confidence, maybe I'd be out already.

Today, though, I don't get the chance to see Burke sporting fluorescent pants or a suede cowboy jacket. I jog downstairs, head out the front door, and stride across the green.

Kansas can be beautiful. High's a solid sixty degrees today, the sky cloudless. Whistling, I head down the gym pathway, which twines past the auditorium hill. I skip over the roots of the Climbing Tree—a huge oak the swim team climbs after every meet we win—and turn past the trailers. The tiny white huts are clustered at the bottom of the hill, set apart for specialized classes like AP Latin and Creative Writing. Valentine Simmons sits behind them on the hill, alone, his white-blond hair winking like a comet in the sun.

Nobody's ever talked to me the way he did. *I don't care*—a blunt interruption in the middle of my sentence. I don't know what his deal is, but I'm curious to find out.

"Hey," I call, jogging toward him with a lifted hand. As I approach, he gives me the appalled expression of someone who's been interrupted mid-prayer. With a satisfied sigh, I plop down on the grass beside him, shrug off my backpack, and pull out my lunch. He doesn't stop staring at me until I look back at him.

He's dressed the same way as yesterday: brown corduroys, a knit sweater, a leather belt, and an accusatory expression. He looks normal, until you notice the Velcro sneakers and orange socks. It's as if J. Crew handled everything above his ankles, and then a five-year-old took over.

"What are you doing?" Valentine asks.

"Sitting," I say.

"Hilarious. Why are you here?"

"'Cause you said you ate here, and I thought it sounded nice, so I was like, hey, maybe he wouldn't mind if I joined."

"I mind," he says.

"You do?" I unclip my water bottle from my backpack and take a few huge gulps, not breaking eye contact.

He looks away, letting out a sigh that's way too dramatic to be real. "Fine."

Smiling, I fish my journal out of my backpack, open it out

of Valentine's sight line, and cross off a few items from today's to-do list.

- *English quiz*
- *Hand in math homework*
- *Surprise lunch with Simmons*

I shove my journal back in my bag. Valentine, eyes trained on the trailers, drinks his juice box mutinously. I didn't even know it was possible to drink a juice box mutinously.

I let him have his little moment, and then I dive back in. "Your mom works in the guidance center, right?"

"Yes."

"Is she the one with the huge earrings? Earrings lady is super nice. It's got to be—"

"What were you writing?" he asks, destroying the only line of conversation I prepped.

"Hmm?"

"In that book."

"Oh," I say. "It's got my to-do list."

He tilts his face up, an angular receiver for the sunlight. He looses a soulful sigh.

"Why, what'd you expect?" I ask.

"It looked like an important book."

"It is an important book. Lots of lists in there." I pull out the book, flipping to a page filled through the margins with increasingly tiny words. "This one's fun. It's my favorite words that I'm probably never going to use but that I want to hang on to anyway."

He peeks over at the page.

My Favorite Words I'm Probably Never Going to Use
but That I Want to Hang on to Anyway
- *Hwyl—a sudden, ecstatic inspiration!*
- *Balter—to dance without grace, but with joy!*
- *Swallet—a sinkhole!*
- *Clamjamfry—rabble; rubbish!*
- *Olisbos—a dildo!*

I can tell when he reads *olisbos*, because his face goes red all the way up his forehead, right to the roots of his white-blond hair.

"The Greeks, am I right?" I say.

He clears his throat. "Illuminating."

I grin, shutting my journal. The trees around the trailers are bathed in gentle wind, their fingers twitching at me. "So," I say, "what do you usually do out here, huh?"

"Homework. Or read."

"What are you reading?"

He brandishes a thick book at me before dropping it back to the ground. I catch a picture of an astronaut and something about Mars in the title. "Space," I say.

"Space," he agrees.

"I've got a list of constellations in here somewhere," I say, flipping through my journal. "I messed up drawing Orion's Belt, like, three times."

He doesn't laugh or even smile. He hasn't smiled at all yet—his face is perpetually still and serious. "How do you mess up drawing Orion's Belt?" he says. "It's three dots."

I grin. "I mislabeled them." I find the right page and show him the list. The three-pointed Leo Minor buckles across the bottom right; Delphinus stretches across the top; Orion sprawls across the middle with my crossed-out mistakes above the belt.

"Hmm," Valentine says dismissively, but his eyes linger on the page. After a second, I close my journal again, and without warning, he grabs it. With a pitiful little *nff* sound, he pulls hard, trying to wrest the book out of my hand.

"What are you doing?" I say, bemused. Whatever he wants with my journal, he's never going to get it. I've seen celery with more defined muscles than this guy has.

He gives up, scowling. His hair falls over his forehead, and he pushes it back. "I feel like you're hiding some sort of plan for world domination in there."

I flip through it. "I do have a plan to buy an island someday. Does that count?" One of the kids at Pinnacle inspired that plan. She had a family island; her grandfather bought it and named it after himself, and he has a statue of himself at the highest point on the island. I can't decide whether that makes me want to throw up or whether it's my ultimate life goal.

Valentine gives me a pitying look. "How are you planning on purchasing an island?"

"I'm going to be a banker. And make bank."

"You're a math person?"

"Hey, no need to sound so skeptical."

He shrugs. "That . . . may just be my voice."

I laugh. "I feel you. According to some people, my voice is 'scary upbeat.' So. Sorry if it makes you uncomfortable."

"Meh. I've been uncomfortable since you decided to invade."

It's another shot of honesty, catching me off guard. "What? Why?"

He shrugs, staring out at the track. The sun glares off the numbers *1* through *6* painted on the lanes. After a long silence, he says, "I can't believe people find this interaction game anything but stressful, though maybe that's because I don't like people."

"But . . . is it that you don't like people or that they stress you out? Because those are two very different—"

"Spare me the psychoanalysis, please." I can practically see a shield folding over him.

"Hey, sorry," I say. "I'm curious, is all."

"Curious . . . about me," he says, as if it's inconceivable.

"Sure."

"Why would you be curious about—" He sighs. "Forget it." I can't read his voice, which is almost impressive—I can get a lock on nine out of ten people I meet within five minutes.

It's mostly practice. When you move a lot, you get used to people. Faces start to look the same. Their patterns are eerily similar on the surface, and lots of them are eerily similar down deep, too. You start letting go of people as soon as you find them, crossing them off as soon as you write them down. Picking them up like shiny objects and tossing them away like fool's gold. Eventually, you start detesting yourself for doing that, seeing people that way. Mercenary.

Valentine, though—I get the feeling he's something other than fool's gold. He's a fragment of something different. Topaz, or tiger's eye, or petrified wood.

I tuck my journal back into my bag. "It's fine not to be good with people."

"I mean, it's not like I'm envious. I'm perfectly fine." He flicks his hair back. "Still, people like you are so lucky, and you don't even realize it. It's impossible to fake being good at socializing. I get trapped inside my thoughts. I get ensnared in here." He knocks the side of his head with the heel of his palm. "And people only like people they can understand and people who'll be nice and accommodate them, and I couldn't care less about that."

"Are you sure?"

"What?"

"You sure you don't care? I'm just saying."

He meets my gaze properly. His eyes lay me open with a demanding and invigorating edge. I hope that wasn't going too far.

Eventually, he shakes his head. "Why am I telling you this? *You* don't care."

"Yeah, I do."

"What?"

"I care."

"Why? What, do you care because I'm here? Is that how your mind works, you just go around throwing your *care* at whatever's within range?"

"Why not? Not like I'm going to run out."

Valentine unleashes a mighty sigh. "Okay, Lucas. All right."

In spite of the exasperated tone, the sound of him saying my name feels like a tiny acceptance. His voice hangs in the air a minute, bobbing in the wind. We both turn to our lunches, letting the silence settle.

"So," I say after inhaling my sandwich, "you think you'll go to Juniper's party this weekend?"

"No. I'm sure I'll be able to talk to her before then."

"About what?"

He tightens his thin lips. "Something personal."

"Ah," I say. It makes sense, his being interested in Juniper. She was always a different kind of smart from Claire—the quiet, terrifying sort of smart. Seems like Valentine's type.

Strangely, something near my heart feels deflated, but I keep my voice bright. "I could get you her number, dude. She texted me yesterday, asked if I could hook her up."

"Hook her up?"

"With drinks. Liquor."

"What? You're responsible for all that?"

"Oh yeah. Dealing is kind of my bad hobby. I should've taken up, like, scrapbooking or something."

"Is it profitable?"

"Yeah, that's sort of the point." I unzip the front pocket of my backpack and pull out a rubber-banded roll of tens and twenties. Valentine stares. Then he laughs a surprisingly clear, loud laugh. "What?" I say. "What's funny?"

"Nothing's funny. It's just, no wonder you like everyone, when they're throwing their money at you."

"I'd like them anyway. Most people are harmless."

He lets out a disgusted, mumbling noise. "If by 'harmless' you mean boring, hypocritical, and self-serving, then sure, they're—"

"Dude. That's really mean."

His mouth snaps shut.

"Don't give me that look," I say, laughing. It's like somebody smacked his whole family. "I mean, you don't have to love every-one in the world, but you don't have to be all, *I detest humanity and all it stands for!*"

"That isn't what I said," he squeaks, his ears flushing bright red. "All I 'detest' is when people are boring, hypocritical, and self-serving. Which seems to be a disproportionately high percent of the population. So—so there."

I hold the question inside for a long second, but in the end, it trips off my tongue: "Does that include me?"

He stares at his knees for a long minute before mumbling, "We'll see."

That he doesn't hate me yet is a tiny admission, one that makes me feel weirdly proud. I smile wide, fold my hands behind my head, and lean back on the hill with a contented sigh.

Valentine shoots me a look. His gaze is a laser-sharp ray, aimed down at me. He's as narrow as a reed, and if I had to guess, barely five foot five. But with me lying here, and with the power of his colorless, unreadable eyes, he towers like a Titan.

When he looks away, he's just a kid again. "You know, you're interesting."

"You say that like it's a surprise."

"It *is* a surprise. This doesn't really happen, ever, but I am interested by you." He thinks for a second and then says, "So you can cross that off your to-do list, I suppose."

I grin, grabbing and throwing my journal at him, and he lets out a startled laugh, snatching the book out of the air. In retort, he throws it at my face. I don't dodge fast enough. It smacks me right in the head, stars burst in my vision, and he yelps, "Oh my God! Are you all right?"

As the world comes back into sight, the mixture of horror and alarm on Valentine's face emerges, and it's the funniest thing I've seen in weeks. I lean back on the grass and howl with laughter.

After a second, he starts laughing, too—nervously at first, then with something like relief. The clear sound fills up the air like light. Our laughter echoes off the brick face of the west wing. Off those rosebushes pruned and shivering in the shade. Off that vast bowl of the Kansas sky.

HELLO
my name is

KAT SCOTT

I ALWAYS HEAR PEOPLE COMPLAINING ABOUT MONdays, but Tuesday is the true evil of the week. You still have the whole week ahead, and you're already exhausted. During the dragging haze of fifth-period English on Tuesday, I'm so worn down, all I can do is write my first-act monologue on my desk, lazily drawing the words.

You tell me, "Don't be ungrateful, Faina. Don't be loud, Faina; don't question, Faina; don't ask for a thing, Faina! Don't say a word, Faina!" Am I not allowed to speak, to ask? To grasp for more? Am I not allowed to yearn, to live, as my life trickles down like a bead of honey from a comb—it will fall soon, Father, don't you see?

"Kat?" says Mr. García.

I flatten my hand over the writing. "Uh, what?" I try not to feel twenty-five pairs of eyes fixing on me.

"Prospero. Any idea what he might symbolize?"

Shit. *The Tempest.* Definitely didn't read it. "Does it matter?" I say instinctively.

"Ha. Interesting question," García says, resting his yardstick on his shoulder. "Does symbolism matter?"

He pauses for an overlong moment, as if he's legitimately wondering whether it doesn't matter and his whole job is a lie. Then he says, "Here's the thing. When we look at symbols, we're playing God. Symbolism gives us a bigger picture than just actions and events. That lens organizes stories and gives them resonance; it adds an order we never see in the chaos of the real world. As for *The Tempest*, symbolism matters especially with Prospero, who's often read as . . ." He writes across the chalkboard, his handwriting freakishly close to Times New Roman. "Shakespeare's mirror, guys. A shameless self-insertion, basically."

He puts down the chalk and carefully brushes white dust off his jacket. "So, let's turn to page thirty-six in the text . . ."

I go back to writing on my desk.

When the bell rings, García says, "Kat, could I see you for a second?"

The rest of the students mutter and snicker to one another. I shove through to the front, ignoring them. "Yeah?" I say, stopping before García's desk as people file out.

"What class do you have next?" he asks, sitting down.

"Nothing. Free period."

"Great, that's great. Want to sit down?"

"Not . . . particularly?" I glance at the door. The last person out shuts it with a click.

"Suit yourself," he says. "I wanted to ask if you're doing okay."

"Why would I not be okay?"

He shrugs. "There are lots of reasons you could be not okay, from personal issues to a problem with this class, which could explain why you haven't turned in an assignment for three weeks now."

Ah. So it's about that. He could've just said so.

"So I'm failing, huh?" I say. "What do you want me to do?"

"Well, first of all, start coming to class regularly," he says. I'm surprised he hasn't brought it up before now. García has this militant attendance policy for himself—he says that as long as one student shows up, he owes it to us to be there to teach, no exceptions.

It's actually sort of gross. He was sick for maybe half of September and still didn't miss class. Though, to be fair, he didn't get anyone else sick. Probably because, in true germophobe fashion, he has, like, twelve things of hand sanitizer lined up on his desk.

He opens one of his drawers, thumbs through several binders with color-coded tabs, and unclips a sheet of paper. "I've got a makeup assignment here," he says, handing me the sheet. "An essay on *The Tempest*. It'll turn your last two zeroes into fifties. Won't exactly get you an A, but it'll help."

I stuff the page into my backpack, looking at García skeptically. He has to know I haven't read this play. He can't be that idealistic.

He doesn't say anything, so I assume we're done. I half turn, but he says, "Kat, wait."

I stop. "What?"

"I was serious, you know, asking if you were okay." He folds his hands. "This isn't just about the class. It's barely November; the course is graded year-long. You can get your grade up by May. I know you can."

Not the way you grade things, I want to say. The last essay I got back from the guy looked as if it took a bath in red ink.

"I'm serious," he says. "We've got a lot of grades between now and then. You stay on top of things, do that makeup work, and you'll be fine. That's not what I'm worried about."

"So . . ."

"It's that alongside your missing assignments and—today excepted—your lack of class participation, I haven't seen you smile or laugh or even talk to anyone in weeks. Here or at rehearsal."

The accusation jolts me. "Um, okay, have you been keeping notes or something?" I say, knowing how defensive I sound. "What does it matter to you if I'm smiling? Am I, like, obliged to be happy?"

"No, of course not. But if there's anything I can do to—"

"Can you please stop?" I make an exasperated motion. My backpack slips off my shoulder and smacks the tile. "Why is everyone so obsessed with evaluating me?"

García's heavy eyebrows rise. My head pounds. It's quiet.

It sinks in fast: I just yelled at a teacher. As my voice fades from the air, my instinct is to run, but my feet are iron, soldered to the floor. "I'm sorry," I say hoarsely. "I shouldn't have—"

García raises his hand, and I fall quiet. He wipes the chalk dust off his palms with a healthy glob of hand sanitizer. "May I say something?"

"Free country," I mumble.

"You're, what, sixteen?"

"Seventeen."

"Seventeen. Okay." He nods toward a desk in the front row. "Want to sit?"

I sit, looking down at my hands. They're green-white in the fluorescent light.

He takes off his glasses and rubs the bridge of his nose. "So, Kat—and I'm not saying this is the case for you, but the main thing I remember from being your age was feeling trapped. There was so much I was ready to do. Move out, drive off, live alone."

What he's saying feels familiar, which is strange, since I hardly ever think about getting out of Paloma. It takes too much energy to want things like that, to think about the future as less than impossibly far away.

"They'll let you go soon," he says. "It's less than two years before you're through with Paloma High. And in the meantime . . . well, I'm not telling you to keep your chin up and put on a smile. I'm just saying, you've got a million possible futures waiting ahead. Maybe for now, you should focus on imagining what they might look like."

My lips quiver. Then desperate words elbow their way out. "How am I supposed to focus on years from now? Half the time I barely have enough energy to hold on one more day."

"So hold on one more day," he says. "That's all you need, is to wake up and say, *one more*. And once you make it through, you wake up the next morning, and you say it again. *One more.* You hold on for enough one-more-days, they'll turn into months and years, and before you know it, you'll have met so many wonderful people and discovered a million hidden things. All one day at a time."

Without his glasses, García's eyes are so dark, so compassionate, it hurts to look at him. The conviction in his voice stirs something thick and forgotten in my chest. *How can you promise that?* I want to yell, but I don't allow myself another outburst.

"I just scare people off," I say quietly.

"Really?" García says. "Hate to break it to you, but the cast thinks you're cool."

"They what?"

"Emily was telling me after rehearsal the other day that you inspire her. She's only a freshman, you know—she looks up to you."

I nearly laugh. Kind, quiet Emily thinks *I'm* something to look up to? How does that make sense? "It's a matter of time," I say. "Some people might want to try talking to me or whatever, but they'll realize I'm not worth it eventually."

"Why do you think that?"

I open my mouth to tell him how Olivia and I have grown apart, but I stop. It wasn't that Olivia called it quits—I'm the one who's gotten sick of people. Not her. Ever since Mom left . . .

That's it, I guess. She's the one who didn't think I was worth it. A cold, familiar hand presses down on my chest, just as painful after two and a half years. *You're someone even a mother couldn't love.*

I look up at García. I've been quiet a long time. "I don't know why I think that—I just do."

"Kat," he says, his voice soft, "you do not deserve to be lonely."

I grip the sides of the plastic chair so tightly, it hurts.

García studies me for a second, leans back, and puts his glasses on again. A long minute passes. Eventually, I pry myself from my seat, lift my backpack, and go for the door. In the threshold, I glance over my shoulder.

"I'll see you at rehearsal," he says.

"Yeah." I hardly hear the word drip from my lips.

My feet wander. They take me down the hall. I find myself out in the courtyard, dazed, standing in the beating sun and the icy wind.

Standing there, I feel overwhelmingly alive.

HELLO
my name is

OLIVIA SCOTT

AT THE END OF LUNCH ON THURSDAY, I HUSTLE INTO
Mr. García's room ten minutes early to set up for our presentation.

Matt's already moving desks into clusters for stations. "Hey,"
he says.

"Hey." I close the door. "Where's García?"

"He had to go to some staff meeting." Matt maneuvers the last
desk into place, and he sets up a card that reads, *Treachery: Ninth
Circle.*

"What for?" I say, thumbtacking our poster above the chalkboard.

"Apparently they're going to start interviewing teachers next,
which . . ."

"Doesn't really make sense," I finish. "What does Turner expect
them to do, turn themselves in because they're getting asked a
few questions?"

"Yeah, I don't know."

I set my stuff at the Second Circle station with a sigh. If it's
only been a week and a half since the assembly, and they're
already dragging the teachers in for questioning, they'll probably
be planting bugs in our cars over the Thanksgiving break.

Matt's woeful expression catches my eye. "Hey, you okay?" I ask.

"What?"

"You look, uh, sort of woeful."

"Nah. It's nothing." Matt takes a seat at the Fifth Circle station, running a hand through his hair. It phases through a variety of hilarious bed-head positions before drooping back to its usual state. "I'm just not great with the public-speaking thing."

I tug our script out of my bag. "Hey, don't worry," I say, strolling over to hand him a copy. He glances over the highlighted pages as I climb onto the desk next to him, resting my feet on the chair. "Just talk loud. And you only have to fake interest for, like, fifteen minutes."

"I don't have to fake it," he says. "Cool book, I thought."

"I guess, if you're, like, super into agonizing punishments."

After a split second of silence, I realize how that sounded. "Oh my God," I say. "I didn't mean, like. Um."

Matt makes a valiant try at keeping a straight face. Then he bursts into laughter.

My cheeks flood with heat. "Oh my God," I mumble again, burying my face in my hands.

"Let's do our presentation on that, instead," he says. "Way better topic."

I swat at him, and he dodges, grinning up at me.

García enters the classroom, holding a folder overflowing with papers. "Olivia, mind hopping off the desk?" he says. "People put their faces on that. Not that they're supposed to, but they do, so . . ."

I slide off the desk, my face still burning. "Right. Yes."

"Is—is something wrong?" García asks.

"Nope," I say loudly, and Matt sputters back into laughter.

"I see." García sits behind his desk, spinning in his chair.

"Hey, Mr. García," I say, aggressively changing the subject, "how strict is the fifteen-minute rule? Like, if we have fourteen minutes and fifty-nine seconds' worth of presentation, is that . . ."

"Fourteen fifty-nine is fine," García says. "Fourteen fifty-eight, of course, earns an instant F."

I laugh. He flips his folder open and adds, "By the way, I saw you're both running for junior class president. I hope there hasn't been too much, uh, political strife here."

"Yeah," I say, "get ready for the next Watergate."

"No offense," Matt says to me, "but I think we're both sort of doomed, running against Juniper."

"Nope, totally agreed." I glance at Mr. García for an opinion, but he's busy sorting his papers into neat little stacks.

As the class trickles in, I start feeling as nervous as Matt looks. I could probably talk in front of a whole auditorium, no problem, but there's something about standing at the front of a classroom, people's eyes so close and so focused, that makes me lose my shit.

The script hardly feels like five minutes, let alone fifteen, but by the time Matt and I take everyone to the nine stations, letting them sort themselves into circles of hell, we're already pushing twenty. After a heartening round of applause, everyone moves their desks back into place with the sort of horrifying screeching that does, in fact, suggest a land of infernal torture.

As I sit down, Matt's gaze brushes mine for a split second. I give him a thumbs-up. He smiles, a shy smile that lifts dimples into his cheeks. Weirdly, for the rest of the period, I feel his presence three rows behind me, quiet and reassuring.

When the bell rings, Matt and I file out the door beside each other. He turns the same way I do, and we walk down the hall in step, close enough that he must know I'm there, but far enough that the silence doesn't feel uncomfortable. I want to say something about the presentation, make some sort of small talk, but the silence feels charged. I can't make myself break it.

Finally, as we cross over into the old wing, he gives me a quick look. "Olivia?"

A flash of heat darts across my palms. "Yeah?" I say, stopping by the water fountain.

He halts a pace away, his eyes resting on mine. "You're," he says, "I, um. This was . . ." He looks up at the ceiling and takes a deep breath, making the boxy frame of his canvas jacket rise and fall. "I guess, I'm sort of . . ."

"Olivia!" says a voice. Claire jogs up to me, her ponytail bouncing.

"Hey, lady," I say, not looking away from Matt. His expression is tough to read, the crease between his eyebrows half hidden by his hair. What was he going to say?

"Glad I ran into you," Claire says. "Can we walk and talk? I'm starting to worry about Juniper's party. I think we should set up damage control." She glances up at Matt. "Hi."

He lifts his head the tiniest fraction, in something that could be interpreted as a nod if someone were feeling generous.

"Come on, Liv," Claire says, taking my arm.

"Sure, yeah," I say, giving Matt a tentative smile. "Later?"

"Yeah." He rubs the back of his neck. "See you around."

As Claire and I cross farther into the old wing, she says, "What was that about?"

"What, with Matt? English stuff."

"Didn't look like it."

"All right, KGB, no need for the intelligence probe." I try to say it jokingly, but my hold on my binder tightens. She's got to get off my back.

"Hilarious," she says, sharp and scathing. "So, what, is he one of your thousands of unwanted suitors now?"

All right, that's it. I stop short by the stairwell and move out of the path of the crowd. "Claire, why do we keep going back to this?"

"Back to what?"

"Did you not listen to anything I said Saturday? Like, what do you want me to do at this point?" I lower my voice, scanning passing faces to make sure nobody's listening. "You want me to, like, swear off social interactions with male humans and become a nun? You want me to say some dumb, passive-aggressive shit like, 'Sorry guys are into me sometimes'? What is the problem here?"

An honest-to-God sneer curls her upper lip, an expression I've never seen in six years of knowing her. She looks like a different person. "It's not about you," she says. "God."

With that, she strides off, leaving me bewildered and more than a little pissed.

HELLO
my name is

MATT JACKSON

SCIENTIFIC STUDIES HAVE PROVEN THAT FRIDAY during lunch is the best time to smoke outside the gym, because none of the gym teachers wants to eat lunch by the track, so everything is deserted. Burke and I sit under the bleachers, finishing the last bit of a blunt, thin slats of light illuminating the sequined velvet jacket he's wearing today. As the blunt burns down completely, I stamp it out, searching for another rolling paper in my pocket.

"WELL," BURKE SAYS, WAVING AN EMPTY BAG, "WE'RE out," and I say, "I got some in my car—want me to grab it?" and he says, "How long until lunch ends?" and I check my watch. "Twenty minutes," I say, and Burke nods solemnly. "Do it."

I maneuver my way through the maze of bleacher supports and into the open, stroll across the track, and head up the thin, concrete path toward the main building. As I veer past the trailers at the base of the auditorium hill, their white roofs and walls burn with the noon sun, making me squint through a shield of teary water. It reminds me of snow glare, the snow from the banks on Chestnut Peak, where my family went skiing six Januaries ago, where my dad fell and cracked a vertebra but insisted on staying so that my mom and I could have an actual vacation. Probably the last time I can remember him doing anything generous for anyone.

My vision starts blackening and discoloring in the trailer glare, a line of blisters like bruised fruit edging the painful whiteness, and I hold up a hand to block out the light, about to turn away, when I realize there's a tiny figure on top of one of the trailers: Valentine Simmons, clambering toward the edge of the roof. I slow down at a huge oak tree, wondering for a second if he's going to fall off, although it wouldn't do much damage, since the trailers have such low roofs, it's like taking classes in shoe boxes. For a second, the tree bark in front of my face distracts me: a dotted line of red ants scrolls up along the grain of the trunk, and I feel I could have a whole discussion about what this means in the context of humanity, but I forget it fast, because Valentine breaks my focus by dropping off the roof and turning back to the trailer door with a cocky grin on his face, as if he's expecting a nice surprise, which turns out to be true enough, because in the next second, someone steps through the threshold and gets so close to him, I could swear they were kissing—

Wait. Are they?

I peer around the tree, trying to get a better angle, but I can't tell whether they're spit-swapping or just standing at an inconvenient angle to have some sort of intense conversation.

But when they move away from each other, I can tell that the other person has curly dark hair and a white swimmer's T-shirt and a strong jaw and a perpetual eager smile, which all adds up to Lucas McCallum, and given what Lucas asked me the other day, I guess they could've been making out, but holy shit, *Valentine Simmons*? Valentine Simmons is gay?

Then Lucas half turns, and I whip behind the tree, staring down the school building as if it's conspiring against me, and I try to rein in my thoughts. I guess Lucas's got enough smile for both of them. Maybe opposites do attract.

I keep my head down and hurry back up the path, heading for the parking lot, but as the path meets up with the green, I smack into someone heading from the main building. I back up, lifting my hands, and as I realize who it is, I blurt out, "Olivia," cursing inwardly because she's going to ask me what I wanted to say yesterday, and that's not something I want to deal with when I'm this high.

"Matt," she says, and I'm like, "Hey, hello."

We look at each other for a long second, and my eyes brush over the smattering of freckles on the tops of her cheeks and the stubborn point of her chin, and in the breeze, wisps of her hair drift across her face, and she tucks them behind her ears with fingers whose nails are painted bright gold, and I say, "Um," and she says, "Did . . . yesterday, did—" and I break in with the first thing that comes to mind, trying not to sound too panicked: "Me and Burke are smoking under the bleachers. Do you want to join?" and she says, "I don't smoke. Thanks, though," and I'm like, "Right, yeah, you don't seem like you would," and she's like, "Aren't you worried you'll get caught out there?" and I'm like, "Nah, it's a ghost town—only people I saw are, like, Lucas and his boyfriend or whatever," and the second it comes out of my mouth, I freeze, because he explicitly asked me not to say a word.

And the look on Olivia's face. Her eyes—those bright, oceanic universes—are wide and disbelieving. "What?" she says. "His—his boyfriend?" and I'm like, "No, it—" and she's like, "Holy shit," and

I'm like, "No, he told me not to say—don't tell anyone, Olivia, please?" and she backs up from me. "I have to find Claire," she says, and I start to call her back, but she's already disappearing back toward the main building.

"Shit," I say, "shit, *shit*," and I turn, staring back down the path to the trailers. I have to do something. What is there to do? Why am I so fucking stupid?

Heavy iron shame pushes down on my chest, depressing my rib cage inch by inch, and I want to shrivel up and hide from my panic, but instead I yank out my phone and text Burke. **Dude I messed up I messed up**

He's a fast texter, as always: **Orly?**

Yeah I think I sort of accidentally outed someone, like from the closet.

????? Why would you do that though............

It was an accident!

He takes a while to reply. **Well say it was you, they deserve to know it's your fault! Seriously, Matt, what in the hell I leave you alone for like 5 minutes**

I told you. Accident. Plus I'm so high

Dude that is a hilariously bad excuse, I was high during my last calc test and I nailed that shit so you got no license to pin it on that

Sorry

Bro don't apologize to me! You think it's my place to say it's fine?

I tuck my phone away and head back down toward the trailers.

Valentine's already gone when I reach the bottom of the hill, and Lucas is folding his lunch bag into the overflowing trash can. When he sees me approaching, he brightens. "Hey, Matt," he says, and as he meets my eyes, nervousness tremors through me. "Lucas, hey," I say, and every instinct I have screams at me not to admit this, but I fold my arms and think, *You're a coward, Matt*, and with a deep breath, I say, "Look, dude, I've got to tell you something," and he says, "Sure, what's up?"

"Look, I, uh, I fucked up. I just, I was talking to someone and I—it sort of fell out that you . . . that you're not straight."

For a second he looks confused, and his confusion makes the lump of guilt in my chest ache. Then the perpetual smile leaks off his face, sliding away like water downhill, and without it, he looks like a different person, no curved lines in his cheeks, his brown eyes blank and serious. He says quietly, "But why would you do that?" and suddenly I don't want to ever smoke again or give myself any opportunity to screw up someone else's life with my own carelessness, and any excuse I had evaporates from my mind, and I can't think of anything to say except, "I don't know, dude. I saw you and Valentine, and it was on the top of my mind, and I—"

Lucas frowns. "Saw me and Valentine? What do you mean?"

"Weren't you two—weren't you just—?"

"But it's not like that," he says. "Crap. Did you say anything about Valentine?" and I say, "No," and he says, "Thank goodness. He'd hate that, I think."

He's quiet for a long minute, and I can see the smile trying to hoist itself back onto his face, his lips twitching bravely, but it doesn't make it. "What am I going to do?" he says, and thoughts churn in my head, sluggish with guilt. "If anyone says anything to you," I say, "I'll beat the hell out of them," and he says, "I appreciate the thought, but, um, I'm more than capable of punching anyone who's being a douche canoe."

"Okay," I say. "Um, I—I told Olivia not to tell anyone else," and he says, "Olivia Scott?" and I nod, and his remaining composure fractures, his eyes widening and his lips slackening, and he says, "She's going to tell Claire."

I search for words, but he says, "Later, man," and he strides up the path, gripping the straps of his backpack so tightly that all the color drains from his knuckles. I stand there looking after him with the feeling that—just like that, in one careless moment—I might've ruined somebody's life.

HELLO
my name is

CLAIRE LOMBARDI

BETWEEN SIXTH AND SEVENTH PERIOD—SO CLOSE TO
the freedom of Friday afternoon, I can taste it—Olivia finds me in
the hall. She pulls me into a corner, breaking the news so carefully, you'd think she was telling me somebody died.

For a moment, I'm not sure what to do. My first instinct is to
scream it out, because if Lucas would keep that secret from me
for thirteen months of a relationship and half a year of aftermath,
he doesn't deserve for it to stay quiet.

Panic surges in my throat like bile. "I have to go," I choke,
making a beeline for the bathroom.

"Claire," Olivia calls after me, but I don't turn back.

I NEVER SKIP CLASS. SKIPPING IS FOR SMOKERS AND
underachievers. But halfway through seventh period, I'm still
standing in the bathroom, forehead to the mirror.

I gnaw on my cuticles. My third finger beads up with blood.
Who's the boy? Has he ever looked himself in the mirror with
the sole intent of finding everything that's wrong with him?
Has he agonized for months over how to transform himself into
something worthy of Lucas's attention?

The door opens. I prepare to glare whoever it is into leaving, but Juniper's and Olivia's heads poke in. They approach me. Olivia stands stiff and upright, skeleton rigid. Juniper's eyes glisten with sympathy.

I look back at the mirror. They stand beside me, Juniper with her blow-dried white-gold hair, Olivia with slim, dark jeans on her long legs. And me . . . *Look* at me, splotchy-faced and stumpy and never quite assembled correctly.

"You've got to talk to him," Olivia says.

I grit my teeth. I have nothing to talk about with Lucas. Not our relationship, apparently based on misplaced trust, or the breakup, apparently the equivalent of a mercy killing. I have nothing to discuss with the boy who said I *couldn't compare*—apparently comparing me to people I'd never imagined were competition.

Lucas and I never had sex, but we got close. How does that make sense? He wouldn't have been able to do the things we did, right, if he's gay? He must be bi; he has to be.

Leave it. Who cares? He has a boyfriend now. That's the only thing I can think about. Him and somebody else, some nameless male concept.

"It's not healthy, bottling it up," Olivia says. "You stopped talking about it, so I thought—"

"I know." Of course they thought I was over him. I'm supposed to be on top of my shit. I have better things to worry about than boys. Getting stuck like this is so humiliating.

"What are . . . how are you feeling?" Olivia asks.

My throat closes like a drawstring bag. Eventually, I manage, "Like you care."

Juniper and Olivia trade a glance. "Wh—" Olivia starts.

"No," I say. "I've started being the last person to hear about anything in your lives, so why should I tell you what this is like?"

I back up, heading for the door. "I'm just going to shut up. Forget about it." I swallow. "Have a great time Saturday. I'm not coming."

As I walk out, their expressions match. A dose of helplessness, a healthy serving of resignation . . . and the tiniest bit of exasperation.

HELLO
my name is

OLIVIA SCOTT

I OPEN JUNIPER'S DOOR AND STAND BACK, LETTING in the first swarm of people. "Hey, guys," I say. "Drinks are in the kitchen, that way. Right through the living room."

Word has spread fast about this party, but since Claire's blowup yesterday, Juniper's heart hasn't seemed to be in it anymore. We had a miniature pregame with just the two of us, but it was a downer, since we spent most of it talking about our missing third.

"You think she wants to friend-dump us?" Juniper asked between aggressive gulps of hard cider.

"Kind of seemed like it," I said. "But maybe we do need to go on a friend-break while she sorts things out. I mean, she snapped at me for, like, *talking* to a boy. At this point, I'm kind of maxed out on that shit, you know?"

Juniper nodded. "There's got to be something else going on there. I'm trying to see it from her perspective, but that's sort of hard when she won't, you know, talk to us." She took another swig of cider. "Maybe she'll show up tonight, and we can hash it out?"

"I wouldn't count on it, Juni. Especially since Lucas'll probably show."

Barely half an hour in, that prediction comes true. Lucas enters with a bang, tugging in half the swim team, and navigates the crowd with his usual smile. When he waves my way, guilt gnaws at me. I shouldn't have told Claire. He's obviously not out yet—I don't know a single kid at Paloma High who *is* out. A couple of kids seem pretty obviously gay, but it's sure not on their Facebook or anything. At school, the most out-of-the-box person by far is Burke Fischer, wearer of jeggings and heels, who doesn't seem to give a solitary damn what people think. But Burke's a loner, and I doubt Lucas could survive without his constant swarm of bros.

I get that it's scary, and that Paloma High School isn't hyper-progressive-gay-friendly-land, but I still can't believe he didn't tell Claire. That's a huge thing to keep quiet for that long. Especially for someone you say you're in love with.

Though I guess if you love someone, the thought of losing their approval is probably twice as terrifying.

The party's in full swing when I realize I forgot my overnight bag. Juni offers me the use of everything in her house, of course, but I need contact solution, and her whole family is 20/20. She also offers her clothes, which gets a hearty laugh from my end. Wearing Juni's clothes would be like trying to wear one of those little sweaters that people stuff their Scottish terriers into.

I call Kat. "What?" she grunts. About as cheery a greeting as I expected.

"Yo. Is Dad home yet?" I ask.

"Negative."

"I left my bag on the kitchen table. You think you could maybe drop it off at Juni's when he brings the car home?"

Kat heaves a sigh. "Fine. God knows when that'll be."

Dad must be closing up, because by an hour in, Kat still hasn't shown. People have filled the long halls of Juni's house. There's packs of athletes, crews of yapping sophomores, and nervous clumps of freshmen who look so tiny, I get this urge to swat the drinks out of their hands and hand them *The Land Before Time* DVDs. Edging around a guy who's doing a pretty decent Chewbacca impersonation, I enter the kitchen and find Juniper sitting at the counter playing DJ.

I sidle up, eyeing the beer in her hand. "How many is that? Be honest."

"Hey! Three. I'm going slow."

"Awesome. Not that last week wasn't great, but like . . ."

Juni grins. "Vomiting, bad. I know."

"So. Vital question. Do you still have that sparkling lemonade from my birthday party?"

"There might be a bottle in my parents' fridge," she says. "They've been using it as a mixer, though, so no promises. Also, if you find anyone in there, can you kick them out?"

I make a face. "Will do." In August, during my birthday party, we caught not one but two couples making out on Juniper's parents' bed. Simultaneously. Although I doubt anyone's doing that now—10:15 is a little early for those sorts of messy shenanigans.

As I make my way past the study toward the wide, curling staircase, I hear someone yelling, "Shots!"

I sigh. Juniper better not join in.

I jog up the staircase that wraps around the circular foyer wall, framing a heavy chandelier that weeps golden beads. The rug on the second-floor landing is thick under my feet, hushing my steps as I pad toward Juniper's parents' bedroom. Plaques with Juniper's achievements plaster the walls, first place in violin contest after violin contest.

I shoulder the door open. This room is a lavish, two-tiered confection. Oil paintings hang on paneled walls, and a mirrored bar shines on the second level, up the oak-dark stairs. A banister of the same dark wood cordons off the bar area, and looking past it, I freeze. Matt Jackson is standing by the counter. His presence is a strange, warm shock.

I break the silence. "Matt. What are you doing here?"

"I . . . everything downstairs was sort of loud, so, uh," he says. "I don't know. I didn't see anyone I knew, and I felt weird. What are you doing?"

"I wanted lemonade," I say lamely. "But I meant, what are you doing *here*-here? At Juniper's?" I close the door, heading for the stairs. "I don't see you out usually. Ever."

"I was actually . . ." He rubs the back of his neck. I hop up the steps, cracking open the miniature fridge as he searches for words.

"I was hoping to maybe run into you," he finishes.

"O-oh." I look up. "Well. Success."

Matt laughs. His mouth draws a bit to one side, making his laugh goofy and off-kilter.

I wonder what kissing him would be like. I wonder that about most guys, even if it's a passing curiosity, but the thought of kissing Matt twists my stomach up. Which is weird, since, objectively, he isn't that hot. I've kissed way hotter guys, guys with balanced features and actual musculature, guys who could make me forget I'm five foot ten.

But something in Matt's guardedly blank expression makes me feel awake. Every second in his company feels acute. Maybe it's how he holds himself, careful and calculated. Maybe it's the sharp edges of his features and the sharper, shyer focus of his eyes.

I pull my attention away from him, crouching to grab the lemonade bottle. Among the range of fancy-looking metal implements on the bar, I find something pointy to pry the cork back out.

"Juniper's house is, like, holy shit," Matt says.

"I know, right?" I say. "This room is nicer than my whole house." I take a sip. The lemonade fizzes across my tongue, sugary-sweet.

"The hell do her parents do?"

"Her mom worked on Wall Street for however long, and now she's the owner-slash-mastermind person for the Paloma bank. And . . . well, I don't know what her dad does, but he's always traveling. He's probably an international spy." I lean against the counter. "So, what's going on? Why were you trying to find me?" I give a coy lilt to my voice, hoping that it's the reason guys usually seek out girls at parties.

Matt sits on one of the bar stools. "I just—I made a mistake yesterday. I shouldn't have told you about Lucas." My heart sinks—of course it's about that. He goes on, looking lost: "I only found out by mistake that he's, you know, and I was supposed to shut up about it, and he's worried about . . . you didn't tell Claire, did you?"

A lump rises in my throat. "I'm sorry. I told her it's a secret, but . . . yeah, I couldn't keep it from her."

"Shit." Matt closes his eyes. "She'd better not tell anyone."

"I don't know who she'd tell. Claire kind of considers herself above the gossip thing."

Matt's hands fold, unfold, and fold again. He paces down the stairs toward a weird art print on the wall. "Man, I just—I'm an idiot."

"It was a mistake." *And I went and made it worse, telling Claire,* says a merciless voice in my head. I perch on the banister and slide down to the lower level. The wood squeaks. "You talked to him, though?"

"Yeah. He wasn't mad. He just looked . . . I don't know. Like he dreaded having to deal with it. Which makes sense, but if it were me, I would've beaten me up." Matt sinks into an armchair by the banister, stretching out his legs. A line of bare stomach above his jeans glares out, conspicuous in my peripheral vision. "Well, I guess there's not much I can do about it now."

"I can text Claire and be like, don't tell a soul or I'll poison your dog," I offer. "Not that I would poison her dog. She doesn't have a dog. So poisoning it would be hard."

I spy a hint of a smile before Matt goes back to chewing on his lip. His face has this almost-strangled look, as if he's itching to say something.

"What're you thinking?" he asks.

I reach for my usual honesty. *Can you pull your shirt down? It's sort of distracting. Sorry, that's blunt. But you did ask.*

All that comes out of my mouth is, "Uh, nothing."

"I doubt that."

"How dare you doubt my totally trustworthy self?" I say. He gives me a real smile, and my mind goes blank.

With a horrible jolt, I realize I have a crush on him.

No. This cannot be happening. Crushes ruin lives and destroy souls. Crushes either lead to the inconvenience of unrequited feelings or the batshit-insane idea of having a relationship.

I work my jaw loose. "We should, um," I say. "We should probably get out of Juni's parents' room."

"Right," he says, standing.

For a moment, I don't move. He's so close—three feet? Four?—and the proximity doesn't make him any more readable than usual, but it sure makes everything vivid. The point of his nose. The dark tan of his skin. The flecks of stubble on the tip of his chin. For a second, I wonder what his hair would feel like between my fingers.

He meets my eyes, probably waiting for me to say something or act like a normal person in general. This, unfortunately, is beyond my current abilities. I can only look at him, frozen in our eye contact. It's terrifying, eye contact: the knowledge that somebody is regarding you with their whole and undivided attention, that for a moment, you're the one thing in this world that demands their focus.

I could see if he's interested. It'd be easy enough to say: *So, hey, how do you feel about kissing me?* It'd be less awkward than letting this silence stretch on longer, that's for sure. But my voice is on lockdown, which is bizarre, given that locking down my voice is usually about as doable as locking down a rampaging rhinoceros.

I don't want to say anything that might make him go.

Why am I invested? This is a horrible idea. Whoever invented emotions is hopefully frozen in the ninth circle of hell. They deserve it.

"Right, yep, let's go downstairs," I say in a rush, heading for the door. I hold it open, and as he passes, I catch a whiff of the air that sweeps after him. Tonight, he doesn't smell like the usual *eau de ganja.* Tonight he smells like something aged and a bit sweet. Well-worn leather and honey. He walks with his hands deep in his frayed pockets, and I wonder what the tips of his index fingers feel like, and if the flats of his palms are rough or smooth, and if I were to take his hand, what he would say.

HELLO
my name is

VALENTINE SIMMONS

THIS IS THE FIRST SATURDAY NIGHT IN NEARLY A YEAR that I've had plans. Last time, I watched a partial lunar eclipse with my father and a local astronomy group comprised of a bunch of sixty-year-old hobbyists. I don't expect tonight to be anywhere near as fun.

Juniper said her party starts at nine, and the Internet suggests it therefore would be weird if I got there before ten. I don't see why they don't just start it at ten, but who am I to make edits to social norms?

After dinner, I bury myself in a new book, one I stole from my father's study. By the time 10:00 PM rolls around, I'm so invested in the book, I don't want to leave. I dawdle for fifteen more minutes, but eventually, I mumble myself into it, grab the spare keys, and head for the door.

A voice stops me, calling from the recliner in front of the TV. "Going out, kiddo?"

My father seemed to stop adjusting to my changing age when I was ten or so and now only refers to me as "kid," "kiddo," and "sport." Maybe for Christmas I'll buy him a parenting manual that was published after 1960.

"Clearly," I say.

Dad's gray-brown hair sticks up as he shifts his head against his ergonomic pillow, looking up at me. "Whereabouts?" he asks, a hopeful smile propping up his round cheeks. It's almost sad, watching him trying to connect to me in whatever small way.

"A party. I need to talk to a girl from my grade."

"A girl, huh?" Dad winks. "Well, then, I won't keep you. Go get her."

I turn away, restraining an exasperated sigh. "Right. Sure." That sort of thing is exactly why I speak to my parents as little as possible.

"Curfew's midnight, all right?" My father goes back to the History Channel, and I grumble my assent, heading for the door.

I reach Juniper's neighborhood at 10:30. Called Mossy Grove, the place is composed of a maze of cul-de-sacs. The houses look as if some architect Googled "upper-class suburbia" and modeled his designs after the results. Each house has the same gable over the front door, the same carport set off to the side, the same vaulted black roof with a chimney poised near its edge. I get lost not once but twice, thanks to the genius who decided that both "Mossy Grove Place" and "Mossy Grove Court" needed to exist.

I slow down, triple-checking the address. Juniper lives near the back of the neighborhood with the other houses that veer into "mansion" territory. Her house sits on a dark, sweeping lawn, perched far back and high up like a king surveying his realm. Halfway up the yard, a pebbled path littered with flagstones circumnavigates a two-tiered fountain, and tall conifers sway at the edges of the lawn, making the house's driveway seem even longer than it is. The golden light pouring through the magnificent windows, as well as the distant thud of bass, suggest a huge gathering.

My throat tightens. I can't believe I'm breaking my precious sixty-three hours and twenty minutes of weekend solitude for crowds and noise. I haven't even knocked on the door yet, and I already feel on the brink of panic. Yet here I am, cruising past the stream of cars that eats up the curb on Juniper's street.

Part of me doesn't want to find out which teacher it is or learn the whole story. Knowing would make me even more responsible than I already am. I didn't ask to get involved.

Despite my every instinct urging me toward the contrary, I shove the car into park, steel myself, and start the trek up.

HELLO
my name is

JUNIPER KIPLING

The skinny metal neck of the sink clouds
up, up with my breath
how did i get down here? slumped down here, i'm
blackout drunk and it's only 11:00.
pathetic.
the roof of my mouth tastes like vomit.
i can't *get away from me*
(i need you, my one piece of sanity—
you know i do.)
no. what i need is some goddamn self-control.
stand. wipe. breathe. exit.
the smile on my lips tastes like blood and dry lipstick.
where the hell did the blood come from? stomach? throat? heart?
the solution to drunkenness, obviously, is *drink more!*
god, help, it burns.
all i know is this: it has felt like a dark age, an ice age
since you left me.
when you said good-bye, i heard good luck.
i've found no good in anything since.

. . . .

now—minutes, hours, god knows—it's all the same.

stumbling around . . . where am i? hard to tell from the floorboards *(juniper, don't embarrass yourself, stay on your feet)*

(make bubbling greetings; share a laugh with girls you'd recognize were you the slightest bit sober but)

the door opens.

valentine?—word's out before it's a conscious decision.

two years i've known him and never seen him outside a school building.

you'd think he was grown there,

cultivated in a test tube, carefully, carefully cultured,

and now there he stands, as unnatural as anything.

he says, *may we please talk? i tried to find you all week, but i never caught you after school, and lunch got . . . complicated, so may we speak? in private?*

me: *why*

him: *it's a sensitive topic*

my throat chokes on itself. (i'm still swaying, world's still swaying)

i stagger.

my palm slaps the wall—

my stomach twirls inside my torso—

my brain's got its grip on its favorite subject again.

my fingers slip in slick sweat on the phone in my pocket . . .

would it be weak to text? to ask?

(are you okay without me,

don't miss me

i don't want you to hurt like i do)

or would it be cruel?

get your hand out of your pocket, juniper.

he can handle himself.

valentine: *are you feeling okay?*

me: *what yeah fine, i think . . . gonna get another drink*

finding the ground under my feet, toe by toe

valentine: *water. water is what you need.*

water, the prospect tempts me. i reel back

valentine: *good god, let me help.*

his hand brushing my back, we totter past clumps of bodies

we stop by the kitchen counter

and the bottle starts pouring itself.

valentine, quietly: *stop.*

i stop.

but the clear crystal liquid looks so beautiful.

i am so thirsty for it—

i am ravenous—

my thoughts a hundred thousand devouring mouths.

me: *what did you want to talk about?*

him: *may we go somewhere, um, private?*

me, smiling: *hmm, what type of conversation is this? should i trust your motives?*

(am i flirting with valentine simmons?

the idea is so funny, i'm about to cry,

i'm about to)

him: *. . . trust my motives?*

me: *i do trust you, it was a joke, don't worry don't worry*

him: *you do? why?*

me: *what, why do i trust you? i mean . . . i trust anyone reasonable. and nice.*

his laugh is strange, plucks of a guitar string, light tenor. *you think i'm nice.*

me: *you seemed nice when we talked.*

him: *of course.*

me: *so, what you wanted to ask . . .*

he fidgets, shifts, his lips part. *okay*, he says, *this is . . .* and he half laughs, but it dies fast, he takes up a glass, fills it with sprite, smashes it back, and his eyes lose their light and grow soft and the stubborn line of his mouth loosens, and i make him a brief in-depth study.

him: *I'm trying to figure out how to ask you . . .*

david—

this is me giving in.

this is me telling valentine, *wait, hold up, gotta . . . bathroom, be right back*

this is me sneaking through thresholds to a guest bedroom, dark, hidden.

opening the cabinet, rummaging for another secret drink

(one that will freeze and sweat and gasp against my hand)

three twists to the cap

two acid swallows straight from the bottle and then

speed-dial one

the only one.

two rings and a click and there he is. (so easy. too easy.)

I . . . Juniper? Are you okay? Why are you calling? What's going on?

the murmur of his voice is a warm sun, after a chain of chilly, darkened days.

i remember, before our love got lost in labors,

i could see the future mapped out in road signs,

glaring from the sides of dark highways.

i remember, if i gave him a way to wax poetic,

he spoke the full moon to me.

i lie on the bed, take another sip of bitter cold

and imagine the empty space filled with the posture of his
body.

head's gone back to spinning

lazily, like a mobile,

my brain bobbing two feet above this body.

sleepy. *david . . . david*

There you are. Talk to me. Everything okay?

you at home? i ask.

Yeah. (pause.) *Why'd you call?*

shouldn't say it. *i miss you. i miss you.*

(pause.) *You're drinking.*

sorry, 'm not sorry.

Oh, June.

what?

(pause.) *Don't drive anywhere.*

david, i never got to say. i roll over. *i know you did what you did
for a reason, of course, i know—*

Yeah—

i barrel over him. (are my words coming out as words? i feel
them keeling. reeling. falling.) *i can't see them turn you into—i can't
see people judge you for my decisions—*

he sighs. *They wouldn't, is the thing. They'd judge me for mine.*

and i know, i know, i've read every argument, i've read every article, but at the end of the day, i feel like—david, i'm perfectly capable of thinking for myself—

I know you are, but it's—

at last it spills out: *and i chose you, too. you never pushed me, and i still chose you every day, every time i took a breath. maybe you're a bad choice, but you're still mine. mine.*

June, that's not how it—

i need you. (i need you safe, of all the things to risk it couldn't be you

don't you see?)

the dark is a balm on my forehead

his silence a fire.

and his voice comes back a scratch, a stress: *Please don't say that to me. It hurts to hear.*

david, i'm sorry, i'm so sorry, take me back, please, don't leave me like this. i love you. say you still want me, say you—

Juniper, you don't sound like yourself. You're scaring me. Do you have water? Are other people there?

david . . .

teeth in my lip, a bloody taste again. urgency gets its wiry fingers around my throat,

(i need to know i have you, you're the only thing and the only one)

i'm sitting up and the world is toppling head over heels

come see me. i want to see you. right now.

I can't.

please.

i wait for it—
(my goddamned *head*—)
and then—
not his reply.
knock. knock. knock.

he says, *Is someone there?*
no—
(have to lock the door. lock everything out
so i can have this one
safe place)
i stand too fast, head spinning
throat stretching
clogging
retching
Juniper! Juniper?
(the knocking still . . .)
trying to move, trying for the door—
the bottle's crashing to the carpet
(where have my feet gone?)
i'm up i'm grappling for the doorknob in the dark i'm
a chaos
i'm
(*click* there's the lock)
slamming into the floor
did i get my answer?
wake up, juniper—
(somewhere i hear his voice
he's yelling for me

what a lullaby
lull
a
bye
bye
)

HELLO
my name is

MATT JACKSON

BY 11:45, THE HOUSE LIGHTS ARE OFF, SOMEONE HAS rolled the volume up on Juniper's massive speaker system, and an honest-to-God mosh pit has clustered in the center of the so-called entertainment room, which has hardwood floors so slick, I've witnessed five falls in the last ten minutes. The sight makes me think it's time to call it a night.

Deep in the knot of people, five or six voices yell a protest at once—I make out the words *Party foul!*—and the tangle unfurls, revealing a massive beer spill glazed and foaming across the floor. *Yep, I'm done*, I think. But as I turn for the door, my shoulder knocks into Olivia, and my exit strategy vanishes. On impact, a gym bag slips from her shoulder and hits the floor, and a bottle of contact fluid rolls out.

"Shit, my bad," I say, crouching to grab her stuff, and she grins, saying, "We've got to stop meeting like this." My cheeks turn hot. I hand her the bag and mumble, "You, um. Uh. You staying the night?" and she says, "Yep. Forgot my stuff, so my sister brought it." I look around, expecting Kat Scott to spring out of nowhere, but Olivia adds, "She's not staying. She's in the bathroom, and then she's gonna go." Her eyes fix behind me on the dance floor. "Also, dude, that looks like maybe the worst thing ever," and I say, "It really, really is."

She grimaces. "God, I've got to find Juniper. Her parents are seeing some show in Kansas City for their anniversary, but they're supposed to get home at one-ish. I told her she was going to have a nightmare time getting people to leave at midnight."

"I saw Juniper talking to Valentine Simmons over in the, uh, kitchen area."

"Ah, yes, the kitchen wing and suite," Olivia says, sounding relieved. "When'd you see her?" The music pumps louder, and she takes a step toward me, knocking my train of thought off the rails. In the darkness, one side of her face is painted in shadows, the other side lit up by the flashing white-blue of the TV. Her bright eyes mirror the flickering screen.

I force myself not to stare. "Maybe half an hour ago?"

"Shit," she says. "Okay, well, I should start getting people out."

Then Dan Silverstein walks through the threshold, red cup in hand, and when he looks over and sees us, a grin props up his round cheeks. My heart sinks as he heads our way, calling over the music, "Matt, you know Olivia?" and I'm like, "Yeah, we, uh, we have a class together."

Olivia lifts a hand, and Dan says, "You look great tonight," looking her up and down, and I get this embarrassed, self-conscious feeling like, *Why didn't I tell her she looks great?* because she does, wearing a flow-y black tank top and skinny jeans that don't quite reach down her long legs, and call me old-fashioned, but looking at her bare ankles—that weirdly personal inch of skin—makes heat creep up the back of my neck.

"Thanks," Olivia says. "Dan, you haven't seen Juniper, have you?"

"Nah." He takes a step toward Olivia, and I notice her leaning back an inch. An instinct to punch him in the eye flares up, but I keep myself from reacting. Not my business getting protective.

"You want to go get a drink?" he asks her, closing in toward her ear, and she says, "No, thanks," and he says, "Why not? Come on, Matt, let's get the girl a drink," and she says, "I'm serious. I need to find Juniper and start shutting this thing down. Also, I don't drink, so there's that whole thing."

Dan laughs. "I like that. I like you. You're not like other girls."

Olivia raises one eyebrow. "Something wrong with other girls?" she asks. And Dan says, "No, you're just, you're funny," and Olivia says, "You're in luck. Plenty of girls are funny."

Dan shoots me an exasperated look and says, "I'm trying to compliment you," and Olivia says, "I mean, that—" and Dan doesn't wait for her to finish. "I'm glad I ran into you," he says. "I thought you might've left."

Dan gives me another look, and this one reads, *Be a good wingman and leave, already.* But like hell am I leaving, when apparently Dan never learned how to read basic social cues. "Yeah, no," Olivia says, "I'm cohost, can't leave," and he says, "Hey, want to go somewhere quieter to talk?" and she says, "No, I'm—"

"Come on," he says, putting a hand on her hip, and she takes a full step back, and he's like, "Don't be like that."

I break my silence. "Man, didn't you hear her? She said no. Jesus Christ."

Dan stares at me with disbelief. Anger mixes into his expression like blood uncurling in water, and I wait for him to square up to me, tell me to shut up, and start a drunk fight or something.

Then we hear sirens. The tiniest whine at first, but the three of us freeze as one, trading looks. "Is that—" Dan says, and I'm like, "Yeah," and then Olivia charges forward, yelling, "Turn off the music! Everyone out. Everyone, get out—"

Nobody's listening until she bellows, "POLICE!" and then someone kills the music, the siren slices through the air, and panic crashes down like an avalanche.

They run. I've never seen a charge like this, a clot of people dashing for the nearest exit, cramming themselves through however possible. I press back against the wall, hoping to ride out the storm, but a voice says, "Hey!" and I look to my left. A wild-eyed Valentine Simmons forces his way upstream, battered back by person after person, his desperate words not stopping anyone. "Help—anyone—Juniper's in a room over there. She locked herself in, and I can't get her out."

I yell Olivia's name, and Valentine beckons frantically. The three of us duck between fleeing people down the mile-long hall to the locked door. Lucas McCallum is kneeling in front of it, rattling the knob.

As we skid to a halt, Olivia yanks a bobby pin from her hair and snaps it in half. "Let me," she says to Lucas, and as he moves back, she hunches over the doorknob, bending one side of the pin. "Someone check for the police," she says, and I sprint down the hallway, the tasseled rug slipping askew under my feet. I dodge the bathroom door opening as Kat Scott peeks out. By the time I rush into the foyer and stop at the wide-open door, kids are flooding down Juniper's lawn like ants.

It's not police cars at the curb—it's an ambulance.

And a sleek black car is pulling up the driveway, two horrified adults sitting stiffly behind the windshield. Juniper's parents are home early.

HELLO
my name is

LUCAS McCALLUM

EARLIER TONIGHT, EVERY PERSON WHO SET FOOT IN
this house said, "Holy shit," but I haven't let myself stare. Most
of my friends here assume I'm rich, because I went to Pinnacle
and dress like a Pinnacle kid. If somebody asks, I'm not going to
lie, but I'm not going to give away the game by gawking, either.

Now the house merits a "holy shit" for other reasons. The
crowd demolished it the way someone might demolish a decadent
dessert. Every rug is out of place, their corners folded up. A pair
of stout leather ottomans in the front lounge are on their sides.
A crystal decanter lies in shards on the yellow wood floor of the
dining room, bathed in a pool of whisky that probably cost more
than my truck. The hallways ring in the aftermath of Lil Jon's
sneering rap, silent now.

Five of us stand in the foyer, watching the ambulance wail
away from the house into the night, Juniper's parents following
in their Mercedes. Valentine, to my left, shifts his weight from
foot to foot as if he's standing on burning sand. By the door, Olivia
and Kat Scott argue about something in low voices. Matt Jackson
hovers nearby, shooting Olivia looks every so often.

"Okay," says Olivia, turning to the rest of us. Her sister wears the scowl of the century. "We're going to clean up before we head out. Do any of you think you could stay and help?"

"Sure," I say, feeling numb. The sight of Juniper getting carried out on a stretcher, her face as blue-white as marble, glares in my mind. I can't be alone right now.

Matt nods. Valentine doesn't reply, just stalks down the hall, as expressionless as always.

"Is he okay?" Olivia asks, nodding after him.

"I think so," I say. Down the hall, Valentine enters the guest bedroom where Juniper passed out. I jog his way, and the others follow.

Valentine stands at the foot of the bed, staring at the vomit smeared across the floor, disturbed where Juniper fell into it. It's reddish, the color of the punch. The sight of it makes me want to throw up, too. I look away, twisting my watch around and around my wrist.

"I'll clean this up," Olivia says, waving at the vomit.

"You sure? I can get it," Matt says, although he looks a hundred times more grossed out than she does.

"Nah, don't worry. Juni's vomit and I have gotten real friendly these last couple of weeks." Olivia points back into the hall. "Can you get the kitchen, or move the—"

Someone's phone rings. We all check our pockets, but I glimpse a phone that must be Juniper's peeking out from the bedding. I dart around the vomit and grab the phone, frowning when I see the screen. "She doesn't have the number saved," I say. "Should I pick up?"

"Might be important. Let me," Olivia says. I palm it to her, and she hits accept. "Hello?"

A male voice bursts out on the other end, audible from feet

away. After a few seconds, Olivia's face goes slack. She lets out the tiniest noise.

After a few more moments, the voice on the other end stops.

"It's n—it's not Juniper," Olivia says. Her voice is a hoarse whisper. "This is Olivia Scott. Is this . . . ?"

Silence. I trade a baffled look with Matt. "What's going on?" I ask.

"Dunno," he says.

Olivia's voice rises. "Who is this?"

The rest of us flinch, except Valentine. Still staring at the mess of vomit, he has a look of dread on his face.

"Valentine?" I say. He doesn't move.

The voice on the other end comes back to life. Olivia says quietly, "Is this Mr. García?"

The air in the room gets thick and stifling. "Oh my goodness," I say, realizing exactly what we're witnessing. Kat's and Matt's faces go as blank as Valentine's.

A surge of sound comes from the other end of the phone, but Olivia, turning deathly pale, shakes her head hard. "I can't—I have to go," she says.

I catch one word as she takes the phone from her ear. *"Wait—"*

She drops the phone onto the bed, taking a step back from it as if it's about to spit poison. Disbelief washes over me. I hardly believed the rumor was real, let alone that I'd know the culprit. How can it be Juniper Kipling? Claire never stopped talking about how perfect she was, how she had her ten-year plan figured out to the week, how levelheaded and rational she was . . .

"Well. That's that," Valentine says. He sounds like we've just heard a weather report, not discovered the school scandal of the century.

"Hang on. You knew already?" Matt asks, pointing at Valentine. "You knew! What the fuck?"

Valentine gives him the most withering look of all time. "Of course I knew. Why else would I be here?"

"Jesus, I can't believe it's her," Kat Scott says.

"Is it that surprising?" Valentine asks.

"Dude, hello," Kat says. "Megapopular valedictorian girl, God's gift to humanity or whatever? Banging a teacher is kind of breaking the pattern."

Valentine clears his throat and says, "First of all, she's salutatorian if anything. *I'm* valedictorian."

Jeez, Valentine. I nearly laugh.

"Whatever. That is not the point." Kat tugs a hand through the tangle of her ponytail. "We're turning them in, right?"

I nod, looking around. Olivia nods hard, looking like she'll be sick if she opens her mouth. The others nod, too—except Valentine. Doubt tugs his thin lips downward. "Are you sure we should?" he says.

"I mean, we should turn García in, at least," Kat says. "He's a friggin' statutory rapist."

Everybody avoids one another's eyes at the word *rapist*. It sounds like TV-cop-show talk, something for a crime scene, not for five kids trying to clean up after a party. It forces the image of Juniper and García together into my head, and I blink it away.

After a second, Valentine takes his phone out. "How old is Juniper?"

"Seventeen, pretty sure," Kat says, and Olivia nods.

After a minute of typing, Valentine tucks the phone back into his pocket. "Then it isn't statutory rape. The age of consent in Kansas is sixteen."

Olivia speaks up. "That doesn't make it okay," she says sharply. "Just because there's some arbitrary number they pick for consent doesn't mean he can't be pressuring her."

"Did he say they'd had sex?" Valentine asks. "Did she? Did anybody describe to you the level of their sexual involvement?"

"I mean, no, but—"

Valentine folds his arms. "Then we need to at least talk to her."

"Dude," Matt says, "why are you trying to put this off?"

Valentine shoots back, "And why are you so avid to indict Juniper? Look: telling anybody about this has as much of an impact on her life as on his. We don't know nearly as much as you all seem to think, and if this is happening, I presume it's been happening for a while now. So what difference does a few days make? Not a lot in time, but vast amounts in terms of the information we could learn by, oh, I don't know, *talking* to either of these people."

Valentine's outburst leaves a heavy silence behind. His face turns red, that complete red that reaches up to the roots of his hair.

"Yeah," I say. "You're right. We should wait."

Valentine glances up at me, and I catch a split second of gratitude in his eyes.

"I . . . okay," Olivia says helplessly. "I'm so worried, though."

"Well," Valentine says, "the best course of action is not to ruin her life while she's got a tube up her nose in some hospital bed."

Always the picture of tact, Valentine. I raise my hands, aiming for a gentle intervention. "It's going to be okay, Olivia," I say in my most reassuring voice. "We're going to figure this out sometime when it's not one in the morning, all right? Once she gets out of the hospital and rests up a bit, you can talk to her, and we can go from there. Sound good?"

She half smiles. "Thanks, Lucas."

"Great. So let's clean this place up, yeah?" I look around at the others and rub my hands together, offering them the biggest smile I can muster. "Where should we start?"

But in my head, everything is a hundred percent serious. I picture myself walking onto the set of *The Confessor*, this secret locked away, worth the full $50,000. The five of us have been shackled together, forging an imperfect but unbreakable circle.

HELLO
my name is

JUNIPER KIPLING

This bed isn't mine.

These crisp sheets, looking in the light as if they've been frosted with dust. (Is it dust? Is it sugar? Is it ground-up hounds' teeth? Christ, my head, *my head*)—

This sunlight, spotty and broken. Every fragment—

bang

    bang

on the back of my skull.

My rubbery fingers find an IV plugged into my body:

if they yanked it out, would I jerk

slump

shut down?

I am frail, I am fragile, I am flawed, *yes*—and for once, God, for once the world is treating me as such.

I find the clock,

remember how to read *4:00 PM.*

Remember everything and nothing at all.

But David . . .

I whip up. Bad night. Last night.

Eyes piece the world together: rubber and tiled floor and thin, brittle blinds . . .

Hospital. Alcohol. Caught.

Kiss my past future away. (So much for it.)

I'm crying, like I can afford the saline extract.

My mother keeps vigil by my bed.

The newspaper flops, a dead bird in her lap.

She is so confused. It hurts to see.

"Sweetie . . ."

Stop tiptoeing, I want to scream. Stop tiptoeing and storm at me. I deserve it. *Do it.*

This, her feeble tempest: *I hope this won't happen again.*

"You," I say, *"have got to be kidding me."*

People have said I have her eyes,

but I hope I don't look that cowardly,

readjusting at the first hint of steel

the first flash of fire.

Where is the hard-faced professionalism she slips on for work each morning?

She should be raging. Don't you dare, she should be saying. Don't you talk back to me.

You know better.

(I do know better.)

"Juniper," she says, *"tell me how you're feeling."*

"I can't believe you," I mumble.

"Sweetie—why?"

A hell rustles inside my skull and pours out. *"Are you even angry at me? I did everything wrong—why aren't you mad? Aren't you going to ask how I got here? Why don't you stop me?"*

I don't realize I'm screaming until a door hinge complains and I
slam back to the bed,
the pillow engulfing my peripheral in a puff.
(When did I sit up?)
They make her get out, and she looks lost.

I'm home three hours later. My mother's eyes are a swaying
pendulum that cannot fix on me. Her mouth seems wired shut.
    My father will be back this evening. If he so much as raises
his voice,
    it will signify a radical revolution, shaking me from power.
    My mother tucks me into
    my bed's warm embrace.
    The second she vanishes, I pull out my phone to find
    twelve calls, a neat dozen, lined up from last night.
    Flashes linger past midnight. The dim memory
    of the screen pressed to my cheek, heated as a kiss,
    and the static whisper of his sigh. (I picture his narrow shoul-
der blades
    folding in on themselves like origami.)
    I tap voice mail. It conjures up the sound of him:
    *"Juniper. Are you okay? Please call me back. Call me as soon as
you get this. If I don't hear from you in three minutes, I'm calling an
ambulance. Text, call, anything. Please."*
    (a tight pause.)
    "June, I need you. To be all right."
    (click.)
    I listen to it over, over, and over.
    It takes titanic willpower to set the phone down.

"*I need you,*" he said. I am alight with it.

David.

I ache to go back to your home—

(I still have the key burning inside my pillowcase—)

just one more time,

to your bare living room where I shrugged my jacket onto your sofa, or the kitchen where we drank coffee and murmured lavender words at 3:45 AM, or the bathroom where you brushed your teeth bleary-eyed the morning after I dared to stay the night, or the bedroom where you held me, just held me, where I tried to touch you a thousand times and you said, "*No, June, we can't,*" *we can't,*

or the rooftop where we froze together and my fingers kissed your wrist, our words kissed each other, there hanging in the air so softly, mingled like breath in the black sky.

David.

I nurse your name like a wound.

How excruciating, how much I command you, how much you command me,

the power we have over each other.

God in heaven, I wonder what a healthy relationship feels like.

We need each other too much.

Or maybe love is never healthy, and we should guard our hearts in hospitals

for preemptive healing.

HELLO
my name is

CLAIRE LOMBARDI

AS THE SUN SETS ON SUNDAY, I HEAR MY SISTER heading downstairs to set the table. You can always tell when it's Grace. She limps down the steps patiently. A car accident messed up her foot when she was young, so she wants to be a nurse. She's selfless like that. Good at turning bad into good.

I sit at my desk and stare out at the sunset for a second. It's been a strange, quiet weekend without Olivia and Juniper. The solitude doesn't feel good—it aches—but what does feel good is having told them how I feel. Having laid my insecurities bare for once.

I cap the Sharpie, place it beside my poster, and slide back from my desk to admire my handiwork. I'm not the most artistic person, but I've made enough posters for clubs that I'm used to designing them. A MAN WITHOUT A VOTE IS A MAN WITHOUT PROTECTION, this one says. LYNDON B. JOHNSON.

They'll take the vote on Thursday, and the results will come in on Friday. Mom asked me earlier why I wasn't running. *After all, Claire, if you want something done right . . .*

I couldn't explain it to her. Elections aren't like a sport, where you practice until you improve. Some people are blessed with innate likability, and let's be honest: nobody's winning a high school election without it. Me winning a popularity contest? Laughable.

I was a mess in middle school. More of my face was acne than clear skin. My braces went on in sixth grade and didn't come off until sophomore year. My clothes clung to awkward places on my body, as if they'd been stretched over a poorly sized mannequin.

Things are better now, but I'm still not class president material. Politicians have to be stately. Not short and tactless and a size ten.

"Dinner," comes Grace's voice from the bottom of the stairs.

"Coming!" I yell back, but my phone buzzes. I check it—the number of texts from Olivia has grown since morning. And now four missed calls top the list.

I nearly called her and Juni today, but I chickened out. I kept thinking about that look on their faces, the exasperation. It stings to remember. That's me: a frustration waiting to happen. They probably wished they'd never told me about Lucas.

Still, that's a lot of notifications.

"Fine," I mutter to myself, and I unlock my phone. Olivia's texts pop up in a long line.

12:38 am: Hey Claire. Juniper's in the hospital right now. I'm at her house cleaning up with a few people. Her parents are there with her.

Something seizes in my chest. I sit up straight, thumbing downward. God, I leave them alone for one night, and this happens?

2:24 am: Her parents texted me and said it looks like she's going to be all right.

2:32 am: I'm heading home

11:08 am: Claire? It would be good to hear from you

1:54 pm: So she got discharged. I heard from her mom and J is "drained and irritable" but doing fine, she's going to sleep it off. Might miss school tomorrow but they're not sure. I'm going to visit her tonight after dinner if you want to come with.

My mind spins. My first instinct is to jump in the car and drive to Juni's house. A call is the least I should do.

But a tiny, hidden part of me whispers, *Don't bother.* From this text saga, it's clear she's all right. This is just another story to tell, just another bad night.

I read and reread Olivia's texts. In the end, I set down my phone without replying.

HELLO
my name is
OLIVIA SCOTT

WHEN I POKE MY HEAD AROUND JUNIPER'S DOOR,
she's propped up in a mountain of pillows, reading a tattered copy
of *Harry Potter and the Prisoner of Azkaban*.

"Hey," Juni says, sliding a bookmark between the pages. She
looks normal. I don't know what I expected—for her to look like
a disaster, suddenly, now that I know about her and Mr. García?
But no. People don't change because you learn more about them.
Even the ones you think you know are brimming over with foreign matter in the end.

"You're still in bed. You feeling okay?"

"I'm completely fine, but Mom hasn't let me leave my room."
She flicks her hair out of her eyes. "She's acting like I'm dying of
consumption or something."

"Alas!" I fake-swoon onto the bed. "If consumption taketh thee,
I shall perish from grief!"

"Yeah, don't perish or whatever."

"Your concern is overwhelming." I sit back up, bracing myself.
Nothing for it. "So. What was that about, last night?"

"What was what about?"

"The . . . why did you lock yourself in?"

"No reason. Drunk and stupid, I suppose," she says without a flicker in her expression. I didn't realize how good she was at lying.

I avoid her eyes, my thoughts cluttered with ridiculous theories I cooked up in a sleepless haze last night. (What if this has been going on since freshman year? What if Juni has a second cell phone stashed in her toilet tank, like on *Breaking Bad*? What if Juni is secretly fifty years old?)

I remember the day of the assembly—her wide-eyed expression as she sat beside me. I'd assumed it was shock, but now, in my mind's eye, it looks like fear.

"Is something up?" she asks.

My heart flops in my chest like a dying fish. I grope around for words. How do I phrase a question this potentially life-ruining? "Yeah. Can I talk to you about a thing?" I say, keeping my nerves out of my voice.

"Of course. What's the thing? Are you all right?"

"No, yeah, I'm fine." I swallow hard. "Look. We were cleaning up last night, five of us. It was me, my sister, and Lucas and Valentine Simmons and Matt Jackson. And we were . . . and we found your phone. When it rang."

Staring into her eyes, I can pinpoint the exact second she realizes what I'm saying. Her face goes blank. My heart squeezes up tight, like a sponge, quits, and leaves me bloodless.

"Right," she says. "My phone." The words are so calm, it could be a recorded message. *The number you have reached has been disconnected.*

Juniper looks back at the book in her lap. I float in the silence, up toward her ceiling, this tacit admission loosing us from the gravity of the real world. This changes things, changes us. We're going to carry this together now, until graduation and past.

"Five of you," she whispers. "Oh God, that's—this is bad. Did you say Valentine Simmons? And *Matt*? That's not okay—he's an utter douchebag. What am I going to—"

"It's okay; he's not an actual douche," I say, struggling to sound encouraging. "I found out he's, like . . . I don't know . . . a crustacean? He's got this hard shell, but he's soft on the inside."

Juniper stares up at me from her army of pillows. A disbelieving quiver in her lips gives her away. "A crustacean? I'm panicking here, and that's the best you can do?"

The tension snaps. "Hey, that comparison was fine by my extremely low standards."

Juniper tucks her hair behind her ear. "Okay. So. I . . . how did you find out?"

"Your phone was ringing, so I picked up and said one word, and he, like, exploded. He was all, *Thank God, I was so worried*, and he kept going on and on." I bite my lip. "The others were in the room. I should've left when I recognized his voice. I'm sorry."

"Don't be sorry. There's no reason you should've known how to react." She's ashen-faced. "So. Did someone tell the school?"

"Most of us wanted to, but Valentine got all logic-y and talked us into staying quiet."

The relief that spreads across her face is so instant, so full, I feel a weight lift off my own chest. "Oh, thank God," she says. "I was sure someone would've talked."

"Valentine made us promise to talk to you first."

"I'll make sure to thank him," she says. "You can't get David in trouble."

"David," I repeat, the name feeling alien on my tongue. "*David?* Sorry, Juni, but this is so frickin' weird."

Juniper chuckles. The seriousness in the air tilts, but it thuds back into place as her laugh fades. "How did this happen?" I ask. "You're not even in his class."

"Remember when I worked at Java Jamboree over the summer?"

"'Course. Glorious weeks of free lattes."

"Well, he came in for a straight week in June. Trying to work up the nerve to talk to me, he said." Juni looks as if she's trying to suppress a smile. It makes her eyes shine. "He'd just moved here, and on day five, he ordered some idiotically complicated coffee, then came back up to me. And I said, 'Is something wrong with that?' and he said, 'No, I just wanted to say I'm glad I found the best coffee shop in this town. And the prettiest barista.'"

"That was his line?"

"Yeah," she says dryly. "Barely stammered it out, too. For a theater person, he's pretty awful with lines." She sighs. "Anyway, since he's new this year, I didn't know he was a teacher at the time. I mean, we knew there was some sort of age difference, but I kept putting it off, avoiding the subject whenever he tried to bring it up. The first time he told me where he worked, I couldn't deal. I locked myself in my car. I couldn't . . ." Her voice peters out.

She rubs her forearm. A stray bit of tape is tacked near her elbow, beside the puncture mark where the IV went in. I wait, not wanting to push her.

"So," she says. "Start of school, I switched into AP to get out of his honors class. We didn't see each other at school. Maybe two or three times, so it's just our shit luck someone found out. And when he heard what the assembly was going to be about, he broke things off." Her voice falters. "Right now we're . . . I don't know what we are anymore."

Juniper sinks under her covers. I don't move. I doubt I could if I tried.

"I don't know." She stares ahead at the mirror above her bureau. She looks like a specter, drained and pale. "I feel like I've been doing this forever, not five months. Not just covering it up; I mean needing him. Being in love with him is like this steady . . . like music playing in the background. All the time. Sometimes it's comforting, and sometimes it drives me insane."

She frowns, as if trying to understand her own words. "He's brilliant, you know. There's some people—you don't get how they fit together, they're so full, there's so much there. That's how he is, and I knew it from the first time we talked." She takes her hair out of its messy ponytail, letting it fall in a thin blond line over one shoulder. "It's funny, because I never believed in the whole . . . but sometimes you just know, I suppose." Her gray eyes glow in the lamplight. For the first time, I see the full weight of exhaustion behind them. I feel as if I might cry, looking at her.

Her eyes plead with me. "You can't tell the school, Olivia. Nobody's going to care that we met like two normal people over coffee; nobody's going to care that he ended it. Nobody's going to care that we haven't even—" She clears her throat. "You know. Had sex. All they'll hear is 'teacher-student affair,' and his life is over."

I bite my lip. We've reached the question I don't want to ask and have to ask most. "Sorry, but . . . you guys haven't had *any* sex? Like, no type of sex?"

Juni blushes all the way out to her ears. "I mean, it is legal.

But he didn't feel comfortable with it, so we haven't. Strict cutoff at second base."

Relief floods me. That makes me feel a hell of a lot better about García's motives. If he was using her, screw what I promised Valentine—I would turn García over in a heartbeat. And if Juni hated me for it, well, too bad. I'd take the hit to keep her safe.

"Does anyone else know?" I ask.

"Not even my parents." Juniper's thin lips tighten. "I don't know, maybe they haven't noticed anything's different. They're so busy, and they're getting scatterbrained . . . but still. They ignore me doing anything wrong. No consequences. And that sounds great in theory, but it's its own type of invisibility, and it's peculiarly awful." She sighs. "I need to tell them—I know I need to. They don't see it by themselves, though, and it's so much easier not to say anything. But when they open their eyes, then what?"

I flounder in the deluge of her words. How has she been holding all this in?

At a loss for what else to do, I lean forward, wrapping her in an awkward bed hug. Her arms close around my back, crushing the air out of me. After a minute, I pull back. Tears rest in the corners of her eyes, but she blinks them away.

"The worst part was him ending things," she says. "He was the one person I could talk to about it. The last couple of weeks, I've been on my own, feeling like . . . I don't know. Marooned."

"Well, you've got me now, for what that's worth," I say. "I'm not going to give you horrible lines over coffee, but you can tell me anything you need."

Her smile fades as fast as it came. "I don't know what to do about Claire."

I furrow my brow. "I texted her. Like, a lot. Did she get in touch?"

"No."

"Jeez."

"I know," Juni says. "I thought this might . . ."

"Knock her back to her senses? Me too," I mumble, checking my phone. She still hasn't replied to my texts, let alone called back. "I hate to say it, but I'd keep quiet. God knows what it would do at this point."

"Yeah," Juniper says. "It sucks, because I know she would want to know."

"Hey, look." I give a reassuring pat to a lump of covers that looks as if it could be her knee. "Seven people know, and it has to stay that way. She'd understand."

Juni hugs *Prisoner of Azkaban* to her chest and stays quiet.

I check my watch. "I've gotta run a couple of errands, then get home." She nods, and I hop off the bed, leaning down to give her a less awkward embrace.

Mid-hug, she says, "I'm scared." Hearing her admit it terrifies me.

"I'll do everything I can to keep this quiet," I say. "I promise, Juni."

"Thanks. For being here." Her words are strained in my ear. "It means a lot."

"Of course." I back up toward her door, doffing an imaginary cap at her. "Sleep well, fair maid. Die not of consumption."

She smiles as I shut the door.

HELLO
my name is

VALENTINE SIMMONS

"AND I'M DISAPPOINTED, VALENTINE."

I've been lectured before, but nothing has ever sounded as gentle or as horrible as that phrase. If lectures are declarations of war, "I'm disappointed" is like a guerrilla attack, not least when it's sprung on the way home from the grocery store. My mother strategically waited to start this conversation until I couldn't escape without jumping out of a moving vehicle. Clever.

"It won't happen again," I say as we pull up the driveway. I suppose I should be glad she delayed this conversation this long— no escaping it forever.

"Valentine," Mom pleads as I rush out of the car. She strides after me with her arms full of groceries. "How do you know this girl? Are you friends? You weren't drinking, were you? Because your father and I have never been anything but clear on the issue of drinking. Only in the home, around people you trust, and no driving."

I unlock the front door, not turning around. "This girl is not my friend. I was in the wrong place at the wrong time, so you don't have to be so—"

"*Valentine.*"

My mouth snaps closed as we walk inside.

"Who is this crowd you're hanging around? Do we need to talk about—?"

"Oh, for God's sake," I say. How does she not understand that a single incident is not representative of someone's entire life? "No, I wasn't drinking, so can you please calm down?"

My mother's lips tremble. She sets down the groceries and throws the front door shut with a formidable bang. I quail, surprised the window in the wood doesn't shatter. "I am trying," she says, her voice quaking, "to understand what's happening here. Don't you see that? Don't you see how I'm trying?" She holds out her hands, as if offering me a platter with all her failed attempts heaped atop it. "Do you have any idea how scared your father and I were last night? After having no idea what you do with your spare time, the first peek we get into your life is *that*? Phone dead, not a text all night—and you coming home at one in the morning, pale as a ghost, talking about a girl in the hospital with alcohol poisoning? How do you think that felt?"

I'm lost for words. My mother has never let me see anything like this glimpse of insecurity about her parenting. I always assumed she thought she was doing a marvelous job.

"I don't know what to do," she says with a brave, obvious attempt to bolster her voice. "If you don't want to see Dr. Hawthorne again, that's your choice, but—"

"*No*," I blurt. I am never setting foot in that nut job's office again. I've never felt more naked or humiliated than after my one session with him.

"Then what?" my mother says. "What is your plan here? Can you talk to me?"

I wish. But no: I can barely muster words. "Juniper's back

home. She's fine. Everything's fine." I stride down the hall, leaving her silent behind me. My dad peeks out of his office, his bushy eyebrows sky-high.

I close my bedroom door and lean back against it, feeling suffocated. My gaze trails across my alphabetized shelves, across the disaster area of my desk, over the book lying open beside my laptop—a thick reference text about the limbic system. Everything feels too small, and the walls are too close, crushing me with a sudden sense of claustrophobia.

My bedroom has a door onto the side porch. I could walk outside and onto the road, walk until I lost myself in a tangle of streets. Walk off the edge of the world.

My phone buzzes in my pocket. I check it as a text bubbles up on the screen: Hello there!

It's from Lucas, who ate with me at lunch this week and badgered me into trading numbers on Friday. I give myself a second to think before replying: Hello.

How are you on this lovely evening??

Not wonderful.

Oh sorry to hear that! Is it what happened last night? Or is something wrong??

I stare at the gratuitous punctuation and hear his quick, excited voice ringing in my ears. Yes, I type, and press send. After a while with no response, I realize that may have been a bit opaque. I send a second text: My mother reacted strongly to last night's events.

Oh gosh, his reply reads. Well I hope she doesn't disembowel you . . . ?

No, that's not the problem. I'm more worried that, for years,

I may have been misjudging how my parents think of me. But I can't send a casual text saying that.

I toss my phone onto my desk and hunch over it.

Sometimes I wonder why it's so hard for me to talk to them. It's not for the same reasons that I avoid conversation with everyone at school. I don't have the patience for Paloma High kids, plain and simple—but my parents seem trapped behind a foot-thick glass wall; I feel that attempting contact would be useless. The same is true, to an extent, for my sister, although she hardly ever visits, so speaking opportunities are limited. Diana is a senior at Dartmouth, boisterous and tactless but well liked. I don't think I've ever had a conversation with her that didn't end in her laughing, saying "Aw, you little freak," and ruffling my hair.

Of course I'm a freak. Especially compared with my normal, normal family.

My phone buzzes again. Look out your window, the text reads.

My heart gives a strange start. I twitch the canvas curtains open. A pickup truck sits in the road, a glow emanating from the driver's seat.

You are not sane, I type. How did you know my address?

I passed your house on my way home and saw your car!!! Hope that's not creepy. You want to go do something?? :D

Is anyone with you?

Don't worry, recluse boy! Just me

I look back toward my door. Okay, I text him. On my way.

As I slip out my door, over the porch, and through my yard, I cast a glance back at my house. My mom and dad stand in the dining room, illuminated by the chandelier's warm light. They stand too close, talking with arms folded and eyes downcast, like mourners. My dad's hand trails back over his balding scalp. My mom shakes her head, and her gray curls bounce.

My steps falter. They don't deserve to worry.

But running has served me well so far. So I slip into Lucas's car, and we drive away.

"WHERE ARE WE GOING?" I ASK.

"I don't know," Lucas says. "Back when I lived in New York, sometimes my friends and I would get on random trains. We got off at the stops with the funniest names, and then we'd wander around and find the smallest stores and the weirdest restaurants. Talked to strangers."

"That sounds incredibly reckless and borderline dangerous."

"Nah, it was awesome. There were always six of us, and jeez, it was worth it. I remember those days so much better than anything else." His voice floats off, wistful.

Looking out the window, I imagine the New York City skyscrapers. Paloma must be so boring in comparison. The idea makes me feel strangely self-conscious, as if I'm responsible for this town's thorough lack of luster.

"Sorry, by the way," he says. "For kidnapping you. I have a lot of energy today."

"Understandable."

We share the silence for a moment, the knowledge of Juniper's affair simmering between us.

"You really think we shouldn't say anything?" he says.

"I want to know more. That's all I think: that we don't have enough justification to take any position besides waiting."

He doesn't answer. An idea sneaks into my mind. I debate with myself for a second.

"Stay on this road," I say.

"You have a plan, huh?"

I nod.

We pass the strip mall, where storekeepers roll the grates down over their windows. In the evening, the town shuts down piece by piece. The few remaining lights glower like candles that have burned too low. The only thing still alive is the McDonald's, glowing gloomily across the street.

We pass through Juniper's neighborhood, with its arboreal street names and houses almost anonymous in their luxury. Then we twist through another neighborhood, whose wealth is all show: statues posing on lawns; tacky, sprawling villas pinned up in pastels, pillars, and BMWs. Finally, we cross a grid of streets with tiny bungalows crammed two to a driveway, and we leave Paloma.

"I don't know where we're going," Lucas reminds me as we head into the countryside.

"Just keep driving."

After a few minutes of darkening, thinning road, I throw out a hand. "There," I say, pointing. Lucas jerks the wheel with the heel of his hand, and we careen hard left onto a dirt trail. His truck bounces, its frame producing a symphony of creaks and clanks.

Towering, dark trees whizz along to our right; a fallow field yawns unendingly to our left. An abandoned grain silo, half-buckled, juts out of the dirt like the hulk of a sinking ship. We cross a narrow bridge into the woods as the last sliver of sun collapses beneath the horizon. Lucas brings us poking through a copse of trees, casting wide-eyed glances out his side window. "Jeez," he says, "I've never been out here. I thought I'd seen everything within ten miles."

"Slow down," I say. His foot jams the brakes too enthusiastically, and we jolt forward. I sigh, feeling a strange sort of affection for his awful driving.

The truck noses out from the trees, emerging at the top of a steep hill. We halt. Ahead, the road sweeps down and around the edge of a huge hidden lake.

Even from here, I can tell that the lake water is dirtier than I remember, scummy around the edges. It's spiked with deadwood, and its banks are clogged with the skeletons of leaves. But Lucas looks as if he's seeing God. "Whoa," he breathes. He puts the truck into park, hops out, and jogs down the dirt path. I follow at a walk.

"Wow, *wow*," he says, the words lost in the wind whirling down the hill after him. When the bluster calms, silence settles. In the summer, when I usually visit, this place is alive with the humming of insects, the screeching of crickets. Dark and quiet like this, it's austere.

"You come here a lot?" he calls up to me as I walk down the last part of the hill.

"When I need to think." I approach him, hands in my pockets, and stop at his side.

He nudges me. "Thanks for this. Rough weekend."

"Yes," I say.

For once, Lucas seems content to let the silence linger, rather than filling it with talk. I stare at the murky water, thoughts dancing in my head. It's strange, this new capacity to share those thoughts with someone else. I'm so used to ruminating alone that the possibility of bouncing my feelings off another person feels oddly luxurious.

Words come haltingly from my mouth. It's the first time I've expressed something like this, let on to anyone anything besides self-assurance. "It's my fault," I say, "she wound up in the hospital."

There's a brief silence. Within those three seconds, every tiny social fear rips at me. What if he agrees? What if he scoffs at this feeling of guilt? What if he doesn't care?

But when Lucas speaks, it's soft and earnest. "Why?"

"I—she told me she needed to use the bathroom, when of course she wanted to go off and drink more, but I believed her, like a complete moron."

"Hey, no. That's not your fault. Anyone else would've done the same."

"I'm not *anyone else*," I say, affronted. "I should have known better."

"Wait, were you drinking?"

"No, of course not. I'm just—I'm bad at telling when people are lying. It's always been a problem." My cheeks burn. "When I was younger, I didn't understand sarcasm, either. It took me ages to learn it. So would someone else have realized she wasn't being honest?"

Lucas shrugs. "Dunno. We all believe lies sometimes. That doesn't make her choices your responsibility, dude. She wouldn't blame you, and I sure don't."

His confidence is disproportionately reassuring.

"I get it," he says. "Watching things explode like that is hard. You want to do something about it, and there's nothing to do.

But it's not your job, okay? You don't have to worry for the rest of the world. The world will do its own worrying."

"Sure." I look back at the lake. My eyes are bright, cleared by adrenaline, as if I've run a mile, rather than done something as mundane as talking about my feelings. How do people do this all the time, put their vulnerabilities on the line every day? How are they not perpetually exhausted?

"Do you like it?" I ask, gesturing at the water.

He bounces on his toes like a child. A six-foot-three, square-shouldered child. "Do I like it?" He laughs. "Do I *like* it? Come on. Look at this. It's going on my list of favorite places."

But he's not looking at the lake. He's looking at me, as if there's something in me that's deserving of his happiness.

I look away, back out at the still water, which blackens with the coming night, hiding a million complexities. Lucas starts telling me about the pond behind his aunt and uncle's house in Florida; when he was young, he caught tadpoles in that pond by the handful. I tell him about the southern Darwin's frog, whose tadpoles mature in the mouth of the father until he spits them out as full-grown adults. He tells me that's disgusting. I agree.

We settle into a rhythm of conversation—a rhythm that's starting to feel familiar—but it's the pauses that wake me up. The moments where he stops his eager babbling to look out at the lake, or to wait for my voice to have its turn.

It's remarkable. For once in my life, there is nothing here I find unsatisfactory, nothing worthy of critique. There is nothing I would change about standing here on this muddy bank, talking with a friend as the dusk bends down over our heads.

HELLO
my name is

OLIVIA SCOTT

IT'S DARK BY THE TIME I GET HOME. I SET THE GRO-
cery bags on the table, jog up the steps, and knock on Kat's door.
Not that she asked about Juniper, but she could use the knowledge
that one of my best friends isn't dead.

After Kat's usual grumble of admission, I push my way in.
"Hey," I say. "I saw Juni."

She pauses her game and looks up. In moments like this, I
see the old Kat flicker in her blue eyes, a hint of concern giving her away. But her voice, deadpan to the point of sounding
robotic, shields any notion that she might care. "She's okay, I'm
guessing?"

"Yeah."

"She's really let herself go." Kat taps her game back to life.

"Come on. Juni is having a tough time. She's not *letting herself go.*"

"All right, whatever." Kat glances at the door. "So, want to
leave?"

"You realize that's rude, right?"

"It's my room."

I realize my hands are shaking. I've reached the last of my
patience.

"Why are you so angry?" I ask, meting out the words syllable by careful syllable.

"I'm—"

"And don't say you're not. Don't say you're minding your own business, so I should mind mine. You are my business, and you treating me like this? That's my business, too, and it's not normal. At least, it didn't used to be. So spill."

"I'm treating you like I treat everyone," she snaps.

"There it is. There's you lashing out because you've forgotten how to do anything else." I advance on her bed. "Kat, something's messing up your life. You have got to figure it out."

"God, leave me alone, would you? I'm better off alone."

Before I can reply, she barrels on: "You'd be better off alone, too, but you don't know, is the thing. You don't even know who your friends are. Like, Claire? In CompSci, she sits there listening to these guys making slut jokes about you. Doesn't say a word. And Juniper . . . well, Juniper's a whole other story."

"Stop it," I say sharply. "Stop deflecting. My friends aren't the point: you are. Answer me, would you? Why are you so obsessed with shutting me out?"

No answer.

I look hard at my sister, at her sharp chin and her gaunt cheekbones. She stares resolutely at her computer screen. I've lost her. Every time she goes quiet like this, I feel her leaving me a little more, like a word written on the back of your hand that wears away with every washing. Soon she'll be completely gone.

Panic rises in the back of my throat. All of a sudden I feel the last two years draped over me like chains. I'm so exhausted from carrying them this long.

"It's Mom," I say. "Isn't it?"

Kat slams her laptop shut. She says, low and dangerous, "I do not want to talk about her."

"I know. That's why we've never talked about her: because you don't want to. Which, if we're being honest, isn't fair. Like, did you ever think I might need to talk about it? You think anyone could understand as well as my own sister?"

Kat slides out of bed, her feet hitting the floor hard. "Cut the guilt-trip bullshit," she says. "You want to talk about her, and I don't. Your side isn't more valid than mine."

"Kind of looks like it is," I shoot back, "when you not wanting to talk about Mom has turned into you not talking about anything."

A mutinous gleam enters her eyes. "Oh, okay. You want to talk? About *boys* and *makeup* and *parties*? That'll work out great."

"Wait, is that a joke?" I almost laugh. "When have I tried to talk to you about any of that? And when did you start judging me for wearing makeup and going out?"

"Maybe since you started judging me for staying in and gaming."

"I'm not judging you for staying in, I want you to—to—"

"To what? Be exactly like you?"

"No, I want you to tell me what's going on in your head!"

"Here's what's in my head." She stalks toward me. "You always want to talk about Mom, but last time you said anything about her, you acted like she didn't *break* Dad and like we should forgive her." Kat stops a foot away. "Like hell I'm going to forgive her. Forget her, maybe. Throw her out with the rest of the trash, maybe. Forgiveness? Yeah fucking right."

"You don't miss her?" I say, reeling with the onslaught. "Not at all?"

Kat laughs disbelievingly. "Of course I miss her—that's the point! If I didn't miss her, and if you and Dad didn't miss her, it wouldn't have mattered that she left. But we do, all the time, and she dropped us like we meant nothing. No calls, not even a text on our birthday. And the three of us are fucked up because of it." Her thin eyebrows draw together in fury. "I hope it's hanging over her head every day. I hope she feels guilty for the rest of her life, because God knows I'm going to hate her for the rest of my life. That's all she deserves."

"No." My voice surges up. "Mom's a good person, Kat, but she hated this place. What, should she have stayed in Nowhere, Kansas, with someone she didn't love anymore, going through fights and—"

"Yes! Yes, she *absolutely* should have. Would it have killed her to hang on four more years? We only had high school left. Who looks at their kids and says, yeah, high school, that'll be a goddamn piece of cake—they can do that by themselves."

"Four years is a long time—"

"Oh, stop. 'Four years is a long time,'" Kat mimics, looking disgusted. "Jesus. You think you're taking the moral high ground? You're just taking her side. Why aren't you on your own side here?"

"There's no sides anymore. Don't you get it? The game's over, and everyone lost, and sometimes that just happens, and now we've got to clear the field and sort our shit out, Katrina!"

"*Don't* call me that," Kat snarls, slamming her palm into my shoulder. I stagger back against her desk, and she storms up, jabbing her finger between my collarbones. "Stop trying to be our fucking mother, Olivia. Stop acting like she's a misunderstood saint, and stop trying to be my therapist and rescue me. I don't fucking need it. I don't need *you*."

Her words flood cold over me, numbing the ache where her finger hit my chest.

"Being like Mom," I say hoarsely, "is the last thing I want."

Silence settles in the space between us. Strands of my hair have fallen over my face, fluttering with every shallow breath. As I brush them back, my fingers shake visibly, and something like regret slips across my sister's face. But it's gone so fast, maybe I imagined it.

"So. You don't need me?" I repeat.

She opens her mouth. Nothing comes out. Her expression has a note of resolve, like she's determined to stay furious.

"Okay," I say. I slip out from where she cornered me. I walk out the door, and I don't bother to shut it behind me.

HELLO
my name is

LUCAS M^cCALLUM

WALKING INTO SCHOOL ON MONDAY, MOVING
through the halls, I seem to see the same five people over and over.
The Scott sisters, Matt, Valentine. Then there's Juniper herself.
They all pass in the hallways, smiling or blank-looking, preoccupied with their phones or laughing with their friends. It occurs
to me how rarely people see each other afraid.

Every time one of them meets my eyes, the knowledge about
Juniper yells out in the back of my head so loudly, I'm sure people
can hear it. Guilt fills me up, rising like mercury in a thermome-
ter, but I don't know what I feel guilty for. Staying quiet? I would
probably feel guilty if I told the administration about García, too.

I grew up feeling guilty. Given my parents' altruism, growing up to realize I'm a selfish person was tough. I think back on
elementary school, the times I hoarded crayons inside my desk
or didn't share my food when other kids asked, and I remember
overwhelming guilt. These days, I'm better at managing it, but it
still springs up fast. I'm always apologizing. I'm always wondering
what I did—I can look at one angry face and feel I've ruined everything, that I'm responsible for war and disaster and every tiny evil.

So, of course, I descend into panic when Claire finds me at my locker during the break between first and second period.

In the aftermath of Saturday night, Claire's finding out I'm not straight faded into the background, but now the accompanying anxiety revs back up full force. I knew this confrontation was coming the moment Matt apologized to me. I should have saved up my energy, instead of staying out so late last night, driving, laughing, learning about Valentine.

Thinking about him makes me fidget. I'm too interested in him. I want to talk to him and only him. I want to win his laughs, and I want to pick up every word he says and paste it between the pages of my journal. He's an equation I never want to solve.

"Hey," Claire says. "We need to talk."

I catalog Claire. Her voice is clipped, her gaze blistering. She wears green eyeliner today, with the usual thick mascara and glittering eye shadow—a hypnotically weird combination with her pale blue irises. She's zany in her own rigid, dogmatic way. After we broke up, life was too mellow for a while.

She frog-marches me away. We end up in a stairwell in the old wing, beneath the stairs. Gray light echoes through a dirty window. The bad signs check themselves off in my head:

- *Claire's arms, folded—heralding a yell.*
- *That twitch at the side of her nose—she's trying for control.*
- *My attention scattering—I can't defend myself like this.*

Claire dives in with no prelude. She's efficient that way. "How long have you known?"

"Since, um, eighth grade."

Her eyelids press tightly shut, showing off ridges of glitter that have built up in the creases. She takes a deep breath, then one more. "How'd you find out?"

"I mean, I had my first crush on a guy when I was maybe nine, but I didn't really put the pieces together for a bit. Eighth grade, I heard about pansexuality, and it made more sense than anyth—"

"What did you—*pan*sexual?"

"It means I could be attracted to someone of any gender."

"So you're bi."

"It's not quite the same. I . . . so, basically, there's not just male and female. Some people identify with other genders. And yep, now you look like I'm telling you that aliens have landed."

"What are you talking about, *other* genders?"

"Well, gender's something society made up. I don't mean, like, biological sex—that's a different thing. But gender—so people think women are one way and men are this other way, but if you're a blend between the two, for example, then neither gender's a good description, so—"

"Lucas."

"—pansexuals can be attracted to any gender, a boy or a girl or somebody off the binary, which, I mean, you can read about this stuff if you—"

"*Lucas.*"

"What? What is it?"

"I don't understand anything you're saying," she says. "Would you hold on for a minute? Let's just . . . I'm not gonna bite, okay?"

There's a moment of quiet. Claire ties up her hair. It's brushfire orange, crackling with static electricity in the dry air. In my gut,

I have this feeling that none of this is real. Talking to her about this is unimaginably weird.

She fixes me with a skeptical look. "Okay. So. How do you know you're *not* bi? Have you met anyone who thinks they're not—you know, not a—a girl or a boy?"

I shrug. "How do you know you haven't?"

"I . . ."

"It's not like they'd be super public about it. Even gayness still has people being all, 'Whoa, now, don't get so political; this is an awful lot to deal with.'"

"Hmm," she says. Not much of a concession, even by Claire standards.

It's not as if she would care less if I were bi. She just wants to be right.

I abruptly remember how little I miss arguing with her. Memories of our fights snap out of my mind, bite-size pieces of discomfort scribbling themselves down.

- *"I hate when you get like this—"*
- *"Shut up and listen—"*
- *Her gimlet eyes.*
- *My endless apologies.*

Here I go, doing it again. "Look, I'm sorry, okay?"

"I mean, yes, I think you should be. You could have brought it up so many times. Even if you'd copped out and told me through a text, or, for God's sake, on Facebook, it still would've been better th—"

"Claire, look. It was . . . easier, okay? It was easier not to."

"That is such genuinely horrible reasoning."

"Okay." I avoid her eyes. We were together for over a year, and I knew the whole time, but somehow I don't regret staying quiet. I wish she'd figured it out somehow. I wish it didn't feel like this duty I have, to inform everybody.

It's not that it was easy to keep it a secret, either. I remember every time I almost spoke up. Images flash by lightning-fast: every time I lay beside her, kissed her, or held her in my arms, I felt an invisible wedge between us. And every time, I backed down from the plate instead of stepping up, for fear, and I felt choked. It isn't *easy*, keeping quiet.

But it's still eas*ier*. Easier than walking around as myself.

"Look, Claire, if I'd told you . . ." I realize I don't want to finish that sentence. Too late.

She crosses her arms. "What?"

"Well, the thing is, I knew if I told you, you'd make it a big deal."

"It is a big deal."

"Not to me. When we dated, you were the only one I was interested in, of any gender."

"So you're pretending it's not an issue?"

"Don't do that," I say sharply. "Stop ignoring what I'm trying to—don't derail this." I don't snap often, but Claire has a unique talent for yanking it out of me. She makes me feel so much. It used to be exhilarating.

"I'm not derailing." To my surprise, her voice softens. "If you purposefully don't talk about something, that doesn't mean it doesn't matter. If anything, that means it matters more."

I open my mouth, then shut it again.

Is she right?

If they dragged me onto *The Confessor*, would they have to

pay me ten thousand dollars to face the swim team and say "I'm pansexual"? Twenty thousand to look Valentine in the eyes and say it? Fifty thousand to stand on our auditorium stage, walk up to the podium in front of the school, and say who I am? Because I haven't done it for free, that's for sure.

I've been telling myself that this is as much for other people as it is for me. After all, I go to church with kids from this school. I'm in a locker room with the swim team every day after school, and I don't want them to feel like they have to worry about anything. I've been thinking, *it's simpler this way, it's better for everyone, it hasn't come up.* But of course it's come up. It comes up every time they call each other fags, joking, jostling, and I stay quiet.

Suddenly, my silence feels like suffocation.

"And I'm sorry," Claire says, "but let me be honest: it feels weird for me. I'm not saying you being pansexual is weird, but *I* feel weird about it. We broke up, and you've been treating me like—like I'm nobody. You don't say anything that matters. You look right through me. So we go from a hundred to zero overnight, and you turn into this stranger, and since then, I've been looking for a reason *why* you called it off, trying to come up with anything, because you never had the decency to explain. And now this, too? I don't know. There's more and more evidence that you're a whole different person than I thought you were."

"Wait." This conversation is veering off the course I'd expected. "You want to know why I broke up with you? That's what this is about?"

"Yes! I want you to tell me what I, quote, can't compare to, unquote."

"I—what?"

"That's what you said in May," she says, anger choking her voice. "'You can't compare.' To God knows what. You don't remember?"

"Of course I remember." I close my eyes. "Jeez, Claire, I wasn't saying you can't measure up to something or someone. I was starting to say, you can't compare *yourself to other people*, but then you were crying, and you tore off, and—"

She draws back, indignation glowing in her eyes. "I do not compare myself to other people!"

"Are you kidding?" I burst out. "That's all you ever do. Don't you see it? Don't you see how obsessed you are with everyone else? You used to talk about Olivia and Juniper like they were your biggest rivals, like they were teams you needed to take down in your next tennis tournament. And I—" I swallow hard. "I started counting it, I started keeping a mental list of it, and it was driving me insane. You treat everyone like measuring sticks for your own self-worth, and if we're being honest, I broke up with you because I hoped you'd work it out, but you obviously haven't. Look at you, talking to me as if *my* sexuality is some sort of personal insult to *you*. I didn't ask for this, okay? It's not like I asked for it!"

The stairwell is a megaphone. The words seem to go on forever. Twirl and leap off the stone.

I rock back on my toes. My fingers are wound in my hair. "I'm sorry. I'm sorry."

She's crying now. Claire calls herself an ugly crier, but I don't think it's ugly. I still remember the things she used to say about herself. The worst mental list I ever kept:

- *"God, I'm stupid."*
- *"Sorry, I'm so hopeless."*
- *"Ha. I look even worse than I thought I did."*
- *"Why can't I be more like her? Why can't I be like—why can't I be like—why can't I be like—"*

She always turned to me to contradict her, but no matter how many times I told her the opposite, she never listened. I never lied, because what I noticed in Claire first was everything wonderful: how sharp she was, how determined, how challenging, and I used to love every aspect of her. But what did that fix? Nothing I felt could change the way she felt about herself.

"I'm sorry," I say again.

"Don't bother with sorry." She closes her eyes. Wipes the smudged eyeliner away. "Okay, we're done here."

"Claire—"

"And I think it's better if we don't talk again. I think that'll be *easier*." She leaves me to stare out the window at the morning sun, frustration building behind my sealed lips.

HELLO
my name is

CLAIRE LOMBARDI

SECOND PERIOD TRICKLES BY, THEN THIRD, BUT MY teachers' words don't sink in. I look down at my hands, which seem detached from me, trembling intermittently.

I bite my nails. I bite and bite and bite. The bitter coat of polish I slather on every morning sinks into my tongue, but the taste can't stop me today.

By fourth period, my fingers are bleeding. It's only when I see the blood that I realize I'm furious.

I still ache, as if somebody has hit me hard enough to bruise bone. My mind keeps rewinding to what he said, and the words throb in my ears, forcing my attention.

Compare yourself to other people. That's all you ever do.

Well, at least I never lied to him, right? At least I didn't conceal some huge part of my identity from him. How dare he preach to me about self-esteem?

I haven't hated anybody since elementary school. Back then, Olivia was the queen bee of South Paloma Elementary, and I hated her. I was so envious, the sight of her used to make me sick. I wanted to slap her every time she smiled. She'd get that self-satisfied look that only eight-year-olds can perfect, and I'd want to scream. But by eighth grade, I loved her so much, I would've told her anything. With some people, it's all or nothing: fierce affection or total detestation, a feeling like a rubber band in your chest stretched too far, about to snap. And for the first time since elementary school, that feeling's back.

By the time the lunch bell rings, the pent-up energy is too much for me to keep in. I shut myself into the bathroom, grit my teeth, and slam the stall door. One, two, three times. The piercing, metallic banging doesn't help. What could? What could fix the fact that I have, for two *years*, loved somebody who apparently thinks I'm a jealous egomaniac?

I storm out of the bathroom, making some freshman dart away with a terrified squeak. I pass classroom doors and advertisements for school photos. Everything is a blur in my peripheral vision until I reach the main entrance. A poster hangs across from the doors, advertising the swim team regionals tomorrow. GOOD LUCK, LIONS! it reads, with a huge picture of the team. My eyes go straight to Lucas's smile, second from the left in the second row. My fists clench.

Ridiculously, I wish I had hit him. I wish I had gone full bitchy-melodrama-ex and slapped the shit out of him. That would have been satisfying, right? Seeing his stupid, innocent, familiar face go wide-eyed with shock? Even the thought of it is satisfying.

I storm onward, gathering looks as I go, but I'm past caring. I storm by the art room, where we hid in the closet after school last March and made weird collages and kissed against the easels. I storm by the locker he had last year, where he kept lists of inside jokes we had. I storm past the guidance center.

And I slow to a halt.

A terrible thought sneaks into the back of my mind. It feels sickly gratifying, a guilty pleasure even in concept.

A thin plastic sleeve hangs on the guidance center door, filled with the questionnaires we had to fill out. *Do you have any information about the identity of any party who may be involved in an illicit relationship?*

Slowly, I approach the door. I take a blank form, hatred pulsing sluggishly in my veins like mud. Nothing makes me feel more disgusting than hate.

Can I do this? Can I actually . . .

My heartbeat speeds up as I take the pencil from behind my ear and scribble out five words. I slip the questionnaire under the guidance center door.

I don't linger. I take off at the fastest walk I can manage.

Whoever's actually screwing a teacher, I hope they're grateful that I threw the administration off their scent.

I wonder if the school will believe me. Lucas will deny it, of course, and there's no actual evidence. His reputation as Mr. Social Wizard, though? Good as gone.

This is the worst thing I've ever done, and I've never felt more vindictive—or more content. Maybe I am a terrible person, and maybe I'm fine with that.

Was I looking for revenge this whole time? Did I want to find it? It was so easy to find, in the end.

THE FIRST TIME I GOT CALLED INTO A PRINCIPAL'S office, I was nine. I told one of my teachers that his breath smelled like fish and that he looked like my dad, if my dad were a century older. It didn't go over well. I remember telling the principal, "My parents always said to be honest."

The second time, I was fourteen. I had been in a fight. The fight wasn't mine—two girls were screaming at each other, throwing punches in the hall. At age fourteen, I'd hit six feet tall, and they were both five foot two, so I figured I could pull them apart. Stupidest mistake of my life. I ended up with a black eye and a fistful of my hair yanked out.

This time is different. No insults, no fights, no explanations. All I have is one defense: *I don't know anything.* Principal Turner's bare desk glimmers. Pictures of her in uniform dangle along the back wall, and certificates and diplomas stand in a neat row atop her shelves. This place oozes excellence. Disciplinary action from her would be terrifying.

"Did he ever try to make you do anything you didn—"

"Principal Turner, I promise, I've hardly talked to Dr. Norman outside class."

"Mr. McCallum, I'm sorry to keep on like this." She folds her hands, looking at me over the rims of her glasses. "But if there's any chance that you're being coerced into silence by—"

"I'm not being coerced. I have no idea how somebody could think it's me. It's got to be some sort of prank." Could it be someone on the team? Last week, the guys were making fun of this whole thing, joking about which teacher would be the worst in bed. But would they take a joke this far?

No. They wouldn't take the chance of making me miss tomorrow's meet. And if I have to miss it because of this, I'll burn the school to the ground. This was the hardest season of my life—our new head coach is a sadist maniac, but he makes everyone so much better that we can't complain about his methods. He's expecting me to place tomorrow in the 500 Free.

"I'm sorry I can't help you," I say. "I'm really sorry."

"Mr. McCallum, there's no reason for you to apologize. If this isn't true, somebody else is in serious trouble for making false accusations. And if it is true, you're still not at fault here. I hope you trust me when I say I have your best interests in mind."

"Yeah." But I'm not sure, with the unforgiving gleam in her eyes. She wants to find the culprit. Of course—she *should* want that. But how can I convince her it's not me?

The obvious sings at me, trying to lure me in. I could turn in Juniper and García.

But I made a promise to Valentine on Sunday morning. I swore myself to secrecy.

Could one of the others have done this? Olivia could want to get Juniper off the hook. Or Juniper—what if she wanted to frame someone else?

God give me patience. I fidget and shift, disoriented, tossed into a room with zero gravity. I am spinning. The world around me won't slow down.

One thought grounds me: the night before last, the oasis of that memory. What I scribbled in my journal:

The stillness of the lake.
Valentine's stiff, quiet voice.
The echoes of the night air . . .

"For now," Turner says, "you should go back to class. Please don't disclose any details of this conversation."

I let out a slow exhalation. "No, of course not."

"You're dismissed."

VALENTINE DOESN'T BELIEVE ME AT FIRST WHEN I tell him, but after a while, it sinks in that I'm not joking. "Well," he says with his usual reassuring scorn, "why would they believe someone on zero evidence? Don't worry; it'll get dropped as soon as they remember they need proof."

"You think so?"

"I'm sure." He doesn't meet my eyes, but I'm so accustomed to that by now, it doesn't faze me.

"I'm just worried none of my friends are going to take my word for it," I say. "I don't want things to be weird, you know? I want them to trust me, and—"

"I trust you," he blurts out. My heartbeat stutters.

My first instinct is to say, *Of course you trust me—you were there Saturday.* Or to joke, *That's a shame, since I'm hugely untrustworthy.*

But the way he's looking at me—with a mixture of hesitancy and apprehension—keeps me quiet.

I wonder how many people he's said that to before. I'm willing to guess I could count them on one hand.

I lean back on the hill, crossing my arms, still holding his gaze. I've noticed he's better with eye contact when I'm not so close, but his eyes stay as piercing no matter how far away I am. Just as filled with life and thought. I'm surprised I didn't spot him halfway across the country, from back in New York.

"Thanks," I say quietly. "I don't know if everyone will believe me, but I'm glad you do."

"Of course." He swallows, making his prominent Adam's apple bob. It's not until he looks away that I can breathe again.

HELLO
my name is

VALENTINE SIMMONS

THE RUMOR BARRELS THROUGH THE SCHOOL, REACH-
ing everybody by the end of the day. I have no idea who started it,
but they have to stamp it out soon, for Lucas's sake.

I haven't been able to stop thinking about Sunday. The chill
wind, the earthy smell of the lakeside, and the way Lucas laughed,
looking in no way like he wanted me to be somebody more normal. I wanted to ask him at lunch, but with recent developments,
the question didn't seem appropriate: does he think we're friends
now?

The bell rings. I slip into my coat and exit the classroom,
cramming myself into the usual clogged artery of the hallway.

Behind me, two swimmers discuss their meet tomorrow. I
hoist my backpack higher on my shoulder, away from their jostling, and one of them says, "Bro, by the way, did you hear about
Lucas?"

I purse my lips, my shoulders tensing up.

"Yeah, shit," the other boy says. "You think it's true?"

"It's weird," says the first. "If he's gay, I mean."

"I mean, I don't know. The teacher thing is weirder than the
gay thing."

"But dude, it's creepy. He's seen us in Speedos all season. You think he just swims for the dicks?" My fists ball up by my sides. The boy's voice is loud, confident, and familiar. I stop in my tracks and turn, to the protest of the people swarming around me.

It's Dean Prince, who was so friendly with Lucas a week ago when he called me a freak. He's talking about Lucas like this on nothing more than speculation.

"Shut up," I say.

Dean blinks a few times. "What?"

"It's not true, so stop spreading it around."

For a second, he stays quiet, apparently stunned by my audacity. Then his voice rises, and he puffs up like an enraged bird protecting its territory. "You wanna go?" he says, taking a few steps toward me. "What, are you also a cocksucking little—"

I panic for an instant. Then I wind up like a pitcher and slam my fist into his nose.

The thing most forms of media fail to portray about punching someone in the face is that it's as painful for the hand involved as for the other person's facial regions. I suppose I should've expected that—equal and opposite reaction, and everything—but hell if I'm in the mood for information recall.

Essentially, though, it works. I reclaim my hand, cradling it to my chest. Dean clutches at his nose and reels off balance. People around us retreat, exclaiming as he crashes to the floor.

"The fuck?" his redheaded friend says, eloquently.

"Next time, watch your mouth," I say. The redheaded guy makes a grab for me, but I stumble back. Knocking people out of my way, I forge through the crowd.

After I emerge into the chilly open air, I realize what I just did.

The concept smacks me, buffets me: I attacked someone. If Dean tells the school, I'll be suspended. I hope to God that his pride stops him from saying anything.

Adrenaline buzzes in my blood. I stick my hands in my pockets and force myself not to sprint to my car. Panic is pouring around me, liquid in a glass box, drowning me inch by inch. What will Lucas, forgiving nature and all, think of me when he finds out what I did?

When I slide into the garage at home, I bolt out of my car, slamming the door. My mind races as I head inside. I should turn García and Juniper in—I should tell them Dean was saying those things before he can tell anyone I hit him—I should do a million things.

"Hey, kiddo," calls Dad from his study, poking his head into the hall. "How are you?"

I hurry by, not meeting his eyes. When he finds out what I did, he's going to disown me.

"Lasagna for dinner," Dad calls after me, his voice cheerful.

"I'm *so* overjoyed," I shoot back, and on seeing his smile wilt, I instantly regret it. Why did I say that? Why can't my mind cooperate with me? Why can't I just be *normal*?

I close my bedroom door. My cell phone falls out of my pocket, taunting me, reminding me that I have nobody to call. I've pushed everyone in the world away with both hands and the strength of a vicious tongue. If I can't tell Lucas, I'm alone again.

It's stupid. Shouldn't I want to tell him? Aren't we on the same side? I thought a friend would stand up for someone that way. But I've only known him for a week—would a friend go that far, after such a short period of time?

I told him I trust him at lunch, and it's true, but I hate that he's made the mistake of trusting me, with his whole, earnest, stupid heart. He's the first person who's bothered to try; he's taken my every eccentricity in stride. And this is how I repay him: by fighting and running.

Can I fix this? I could clear his name to the administration.

No. I can't abandon Juniper's cause, not after forcing the others to promise their silence. And heaven knows I don't want to feel responsible for Mr. García getting fired.

Sitting down at my desk, I realize how disposable I am, how frail the thread between me and Lucas is. You don't realize how alone you are until you let yourself out of your cage, or until someone finds a way inside. And now that Lucas has found his way in, here I am against the bars, terrified he might slip right back out again.

HELLO my name is

KAT SCOTT

EMILY FINISHES HER MONOLOGUE, AND I STRIDE onstage, striking everything superfluous from my mind. Running to catch the bus in the morning? Gone. Last night's screaming match with Olivia? Gone. Lucas McCallum and Dr. Norman? Definitely gone.

Even though I know it's a lie.

Focus.

Even though I should turn Juniper in.

Focus!

"You're tired of waiting?" I snap at Emily, who shies back. "*You're* tired of waiting. You, Natalya, who left me in this town? Look at me. Look at what I am now."

"I am looking at you," she says.

"Look harder."

"I see a loving mother, a caring sister. I see—"

"You see nothing," I say. "I am nothing anymore except wasted potential. Nothing." I take a step forward. "You were supposed to be my teacher. You said I was brilliant—a prodigy, you said. You were supposed to take me away, teach me everything, but instead you ran the first chance you had!" My voice hits the yelling point.

And then García calls, "Hold."

I hesitate, frowning out into the audience. He said we weren't going to stop this run for anything. I glance down—maybe Emily or I didn't hit our lights?—but we're well placed in the bright spots on the stage.

García leans over the lip of the stage, facing me. It's a jolt. I'm the problem? What did I do wrong?

"The objective here," he says. "Your goal. What do you want from her?"

"An apology," I say. "I . . . I tried to think of anything else. But that's all I have."

His eyebrows knit together. His eyes are reddened, as if he's been rubbing them hard. He shakes his head. "Okay. If you're going to play it like that, you've got to find different tactics. You're just—watching this scene right now, it's like watching you scold her. Not the characters, either. It's like watching you, Kat, scold Emily. It's too harsh, too . . ." He snaps his fingers. "You've got to dial back the anger. It reads as one-note, repetitive. Boring."

I stare at him. That's harsher criticism than he's ever given the rest of the cast combined.

Maybe he's saying that because he thinks I can take that sort of critique. I know I should say, *All right, I'll work on it*, and find subtler notes next time through. But what comes out of my mouth is, "So, am I not allowed to be angry?"

"Excuse me?"

"She left." I point at Emily. "She left me, and what, I'm not allowed to be angry about it? I think that's realistic." My voice rises beyond my control. *Focus*, whispers the voice in my head, but I'm no longer outside myself. Kat has forced her way back to center stage, and her voice keeps going. "I think if someone came back after years, having abandoned me like that, yeah, I think I'd be a little mad."

"Kat," García says, a warning. It incenses me. First Olivia, now this. After last Tuesday, I thought García got it—understood me, like nobody had before—but no. Is anybody on my side?

"Why don't I get a reason?" I say, my heartbeat thudding in my palms. Emily looks at me, eyes wide and shining. "If someone can just tell me *why* I should stop being angry," I say, "I'll do it. But the way I see it, I have plenty of things to be angry about. You keep telling me to rethink this apology thing. You know what? I don't buy it. She *deserves* an apology after getting stabbed in the back by someone she thought she could trust."

Whispers from the side of the stage distract me. The rest of the cast has gathered to watch the new show.

García climbs onstage, striding toward me. The closer he gets, the taller I realize he is, and up close, he looks even worse. His hair is a mess. The red in his eyes makes thin veins visible along the edges of his eyelids.

"Stop it," he says. His voice doesn't shake. It's solid ice. "This is a work space, and you leave everything else at the door, you hear? You drop your day there, and you don't bring it onto this stage. If I carried every problem I have into this theater, you know how many times I would've lost it in this rehearsal process?"

"Oh, I know," I say.

"What?" His voice falters.

I don't stop to explain how much I know. "Besides, maybe you should lose it a little more. God knows *they* could use it." I stab my finger at the side of the stage. The other actors stare at me, askance. "Yeah, that's right," I snap. "Jesus, this is the most attention you guys have paid in any rehearsal. You realize how infuriating that is?"

And García loses it. "Kat!" he yells. "Please. You're here to act, not to bully the rest of the cast!"

His words resound off the back walls, and as they fade second by second, he deflates. The hard gleam fades from his eyes, leaving exhaustion behind.

There's my answer. He's not on my side—nobody's on my side.

Am I on my side?

No. No, I'm not. In the ringing silence, I realize that I hate every tiny fragment of what I've turned into. I should have realized it before, realized that I spend every second trying to escape myself. I'm all I've got anymore, and I don't even want me.

I close my eyes, looking inside myself. Staring at what's in there for the first time, I realize how hideous it is, all this hate. For everyone. For myself. A glaring yellow rage, pulsing there between my ribs.

I let out a breath, and it goes cold and gray like cooling metal.

When I open my eyes, my whole body feels limp. Punctured. All the anger has poured out. I have nothing left, nothing to give anymore—not even to this stage.

"Let's go back to work," García says hoarsely.

"No," I say, feeling detached. As if someone raised my anchor. I am drifting, rootless, in a stagnant sea. "I'm sorry," I murmur. "I can't do this."

I walk to the front of the stage, lift my backpack, drape my coat over my shoulder, and slide off the lip of the stage. Standing at the door, I glance back. Mr. García looks as if I've punched him in the stomach.

"Kat," Emily bursts out. "Please don't. Please."

I push the door open and step through. It shuts behind me with a final-sounding clank. The icy wind clutches at my bare arms, but I don't feel it. I am a drive wiped blank, everything erased.

HELLO
my name is

MATT JACKSON

I'M NOT SURE IF I FEEL BETTER OR WORSE NOW THAT everybody knows Lucas is gay, because on one hand, I might've told Olivia, but at least I wasn't the one who made up that bullshit about him and Dr. Norman. But on the other hand, now his life *is* going to be as stressful as I thought it might be, and holy shit, it's setting in fast. The same afternoon the news leaks, as I'm walking through the swarm of people in the junior lot after school, I catch sight of Lucas. Angie Bedford, this hard-core, post-punk, dancer chick who's leaning against her car smoking a cigarette, calls over to him, "Hey, homo, how's Norman?" and the conversations in the sea of people flicker for a second, and a few people laugh, and others pretend not to have heard, and others give Lucas looks like, *What a loser*, and as for Lucas, he's stopped smiling and waving to people. He's motionless, looking lost and hurt.

I can't help it. Something grabs me somewhere in my chest and fastens tight—warm, escalating rage—and before I know what I'm doing, I'm beside Angie's car, and I'm snatching the cigarette out of her hand and flicking it to the asphalt and saying, "What's your problem?"

Her startled look twists fast into anger. All of a sudden, there's pepper spray in her hand—what the hell, did she have that prepared?—and she says, "Keep talking."

"Like you're gonna hurt me with a million people standing around," I scoff, and Angie says, "Self-defense, bro—you're seeming real aggressive," and I say, "I'm not being aggressive; I'm telling you to shut up about my friend," and she says, "*Friend*, huh?" and she gives me this stupid wink, and why does my neck feel hot with embarrassment? I'm not even gay, and it's just a type of person, for Christ's sake. There's nothing to be embarrassed about.

Before I can fulfill my heartfelt wish to give Angie the finger, some guy's voice calls from behind me, "Hey, fag, you his boyfriend?" and his friends laugh, and for a second I'm flabbergasted, like, *wow*, I thought that was the sort of dumb shit people only did in movies.

My opinion about gay rights has always been that it's none of my business. My mom raised me not to hate anyone for who they are. She said it, and they said it in church, so I learned it, and before this exact second, I sort of thought the rest of our school felt the same, because as far as I knew, nobody was getting beat up or bullied. But I guess I was wrong.

I turn toward the person who called me a fag—some zitty guy with glasses I think is on tennis—and say, "Man, someday you're going to have a friend you don't know is gay, and you're going to say some shit like that around him, and he's never going to trust you again."

His smirk wavers for a second. He comes back with, "So . . . you *are* his boyfriend, is what you're saying?" and his friends hoot with encouraging laughter. My lip curls. "So what? Better being someone's boyfriend than being some dumb-ass homo-phobe."

People mumble to one another as I look around for Lucas, but he's already gone. I head for my car, disgusted with everyone and everything.

By the time I get home, my disgust has whittled itself down to tiredness. I hike up to the porch and yank open the door, letting a crack of afternoon light into our musty living room. The air smells like salt and boiling water, and Russell sleeps on the couch, his dark hair curling at the tips like mine used to when I was little, and I ruffle his hair before heading down the hall.

"Mateo, *ven aquí*," comes my mother's voice from the kitchen. Weird. She rarely speaks in Spanish unless she wants to hide something from Russ. Weirder is the fact that she's in the kitchen at all. When I walk in, the lights are clouded with steam, and I dump my backpack on the faded rug, sit at the table, and say, "What's up? Why are you—" and she says, "Wash some plates, will you? I'm cooking dinner," like it's obvious, like we don't eat out of the microwave seven nights a week, and I'm like, "Uh, okay, but why—" and then I break off, because her hands are shaking, and I'm embarrassed I didn't notice from the careful control in her expression that something's wrong.

"*¿Qué pasó?*" I ask, standing, and she looks up at me and says, "Nothing," still in that light, careless voice, and I say, "Mom, seri-ously," and she says, "I asked you in here to help with the cleanup," taking on a warning tone, and I say, "But tell me what—"

She slams the wooden spoon onto the stove and says, "Mateo, do what I told you, and stop asking questions!" and in the rever-berating wake of the cold, empty clang, I turn, trancelike, to clear off the table with clumsy hands, and there they are, the divorce papers, lying on top of the newspaper like any other printout. When I turn back to look at my mother, she's half facing away, her body held slouched like a sagging tent, and I can't do a thing but stare as she hunches over the counter. Her back gives one huge shudder. A tear drips down her baggy cheek. Her knuckles fly up to her mouth, and she bites on one hard, and then she starts shaking and trembling like water under thunder, and I think she might just dissolve.

I'm silent.

Sometimes you go a long time having fooled yourself into thinking that you're as grown-up as you'll ever be, or that you're more mature than the rest of the world thinks you are, and you live in this state of constant self-assurance, and for a while nothing can upset you from this pedestal you've built for yourself, because you imagine yourself to be so capable. And then somebody does something that takes a golf club to your ego, and suddenly you're nine years old again, pieced together from humiliation and gawky youthfulness and childlike ideas like, *Somebody please tell me what to do, nobody taught me how to handle this, God, just look at all the things I still don't understand*, and you can't muster up the presence of mind to do anything but stand there, stare, silent, sorry.

Or maybe this doesn't happen to everyone. Maybe it's only me waiting to learn all this, waiting to find a place where I'll understand everyone and everything and how it all works and why I'm fumbling through life's pages with too-thick fingers, and maybe it's only me who's stuck in this emotional paralysis because I'm so busy trying to seem grown-up and feel grown-up I haven't done any growing up, and maybe it's only me standing in a small, dimly lit room, watching someone I love break down in front of me and not knowing what to do or where to turn or who I'm supposed to be.

7:15 COMES AND GOES, AND DAD DOESN'T WALK through the door. I don't ask where he is. Something's wrong with my throat.

Russ, swinging his legs at the dinner table, says, "Mommy. Where is Daddy?" and I say, "Come on, Russ, eat your dinner," and Russ turns his big, round eyes on me—Dad's eyes—and says, "Where is Daddy?" and I swallow and prod his little fork toward his hand, like, "Hush, just—here." Mom's jaw moves mechanically as she chews, her eyes trained on the saltshaker as if she's trying to count every grain inside.

I watch Russ eat, my head filling up with worries. Maybe it's stupid to worry about my brother when a million kids get brought up between two houses and turn out fine, but it's still weird to think about how different his upbringing is going to be than mine was, how maybe Mom or Dad will remarry and Russ will call somebody else his parent, or he'll be my age and look back and never remember living in the same house with the three of us. And maybe it'll fade from my memories when I'm older, too, and from Mom's and Dad's, if they can ever forget, and once we all forget what this place felt like, it'll be like this family never happened at all. We'll be a new, different set of people, only me and Russell binding us together.

After dinner, I walk Russ up to his room. We hop up the steep steps in rhythm. "*One*, two, *sound* off," I say, a little marching tune, and his hands spread out, bouncing by his cargo shorts.

A tiny bathroom, an angular closet more than anything, sticks off to the side of Russ's room. As we hunker down in it, brushing our teeth, I look down at the top of his head and get this rush of light-headedness, like vertigo, and I remember my dad standing beside me, brushing his teeth, back when I was a kid. He never missed a night, not for years.

I look back up at the mirror as my eyes start to burn, and I blink a few times, spit, rinse, swish, spit.

I usher Russ out and into his pajamas. "Read a story," he says as I tuck him in. Mom just switched him from a crib to a twin bed a couple of months ago. I settle on the fading quilt beside him, scoop up *Where the Wild Things Are* from the dark space under the bed, and crack it open to where we left off last, a page with yellow eyes and a tiny scarlet boat and a set of loving, angry, wild things gnashing their terrible teeth. As I show him the illustrations, I say in my best growl, "We'll eat you up—we love you so," and Russ's eyes are round and solemn, and he lifts his hand like the boy in the monster suit, stepping into his private boat, waving good-bye.

I WAKE UP THE NEXT MORNING AFTER THE LONGEST sleep I've had in months, dreamless, no yelling down the hall. I shower under water so hot, my skin flushes, I drive to school under the speed limit, I take actual notes in US History, I walk through the halls steady and clear-eyed, and the whole time, my head feels so empty, it's as if somebody went in through my ear with a hook and tugged my brain out in one long string.

The lunch bell rings, reminding me how little appetite I have. I don't even want to smoke. Now that I think about it, I haven't wanted to smoke since, what, last Friday? That's a long gap for me, but for some reason, I'm not missing it much.

I walk to García's classroom—empty until 1:00 for his lunch period—and dump my stuff in my seat. The back of the room, where García has a sign reading BOOK DEN, has a huge bookshelf that I always see the Poetry Society kids ogling. I draw a chair up to the front of the bookshelf and stare down the spines, all the names in alphabetical order, deep-sounding hardbacks like *The Satanic Verses* and *Crime and Punishment* mixed in with thin paperbacks in big, goofy fonts that hardly look longer than chapter books. I run my finger over the spines, remembering that half hour on Sunday when I was finishing *Inferno*, when I'd gotten so used to Dante's poetry that it slid over my eyes as gently as silk over skin, and I only had to search for word definitions a handful of times. I'd forgotten how reading felt when I was young, mental images burning brightly in my mind, my imagination smoldering above the flint and tinder of the turning pages.

I pull out a gray-jacketed book called *The Black Glass Monarch* and open it.

On Vern's eleventh birthday, the Monarch's Chief Lieutenant came for her.

The story pours over me like water, drips down onto my head until I'm immersed head-to-toe, transported between the covers. I've never read this fast, and it's no Dante, but every time the main character outsmarts a soldier or discovers something about her past, my grip tightens, and this world sharpens until I've left my own world altogether.

"Matt?" says a voice, jerking me out of the weird reading haze, and I look over my shoulder. Olivia stands in the doorway, her head tilted, her lips glossed cherry red.

I stand. "Olivia. Hey."

She heads to her desk and drops her backpack in her seat. "What are you reading?"

"It's, uh, called *The Black Glass Monarch*," I say, and she says, "Oh, I've heard of that. You like fantasy?" and I'm like, "Apparently." She approaches the Book Den shelves, glancing from title to title. I take a paper clip from the shelf and mark my page, shutting the book.

"Listen," she says, "I didn't want to say it over text, but thanks for Saturday night," and I say, "Sure. Would've taken you two forever to clean that place alone," and she says, "Oh, that, too, but I meant with Dan."

I meet her eyes, which are careful and shaded by her short brown lashes, and I say, "Sure. He was out of line," and after a second, she says, "Everything okay? You sound sort of . . ."

"Of what?"

She shrugs. "Distant, I guess," and I say, "Yeah, well."

"Something happen?"

"I don't know," I say. "I mean, yeah, but you don't want to hear it," and she says, "Sure I do."

I lean against the bookshelf. "I found out last night that my parents are getting divorced."

A dark gap parts her lips, her eyes crease with sympathy, and I stare down at my shoes. "I'm sorry," she says, and I try to sort my thoughts, which have rushed back in an eager herd, all jockeying for place. "My parents—I want them to keep trying," I mutter, embarrassed to say it, embarrassed even to want it. "They make each other miserable, so it's stupid. But I feel . . . I don't know. Betrayed? Not for *me*. I wouldn't give a shit, but it's Russ. I mean, they had a kid three years ago. I feel like that's some sort of promise to him, and they broke it."

Olivia leans against the bookshelf's other side, messing with the frayed edge of her T-shirt. She has long fingers, covered in rings. "You going to talk to them about it?" she asks.

"I don't know. It's hard to *do* anything, you know? I've just been sitting in my room for, what, five years on and off, listening to them scream at each other about jack shit, and I feel like I'm stuck there now. I feel like it doesn't make sense to break the pattern or to . . . yeah."

"No, I know," Olivia says. "Breaking patterns. Not easy. But it's never too late to try fixing them." She half smiles, and her voice turns dry. "In any case, you know somebody who's missing a parental figure, and she's turned out semi-okay, I think."

I look down at the cover of the book—the sword and shield of the heroine—then back up at Olivia, watching me with her usual calm good humor. "She's turned out sort of amazing, I think," I say, a scared, stupid thrill running down my arms into my fingertips. And then the most incredible pink tinge lights up in Olivia's cheeks, and she laughs, her fingers pulling harder at the edge of her shirt, and as she examines her dirty sneakers, I let myself look at the contours of her face, the wide, high expanse of her forehead and the uneven arches of her eyebrows that give her that careless expression and the slight cleft of her chin and the roundness of her cheeks. Every tiny thing that makes her herself. She's twisting her rings around her fingers now, and she takes a step closer, and she's hardly shorter than me, but with that step, I'm looking down into her eyes, and it's like looking down into a deep well at the very center of her, and something in there is glowing and pulsing and so alive, it swallows me like boiling water. Her thick brown hair falls over her forehead, and I see a bumpy patch where she's spread concealer over an acne breakout above her right eyebrow, and I see the clots in her eyelashes from her mascara, and I love every detail, because it means I'm close enough to know these tiny secrets. I wonder what she's seeing on my face, too, and I swallow nervously and glance down at her mouth, and God, the way her lips glimmer makes me want to lean in and kiss her until I taste what she's tasting. I want to tuck her hair behind her ear and run my thumb down her jaw and cradle the side of her face in my hand—Jesus, I want to touch her.

"I'm, um," she says, "I'm sort of," and I say, "Me too. Nervous?" and she says, "Yeah, that's the, yeah." And I laugh, and then we're both laughing stupidly and looking anywhere but at each other, and then like a light switch flicking off, we're both silent again, and our eyes are locked, and she says, "Look, I know that—"

Then the door opens, and a voice goes in my head, *Are you fucking kidding?* and we move back from each other so fast that I barge into the chair I was sitting in. García, heading for his desk, says, "Hey, Matt. Is that *Black Glass Monarch?*" And I say, "Yeah," trying not to sound too filled with rage, even though I want to take García and shove him bodily back out the door. Could the guy *be* any more inconvenient these days?

He says, "That's a fun one. You can borrow it if you want to," and I say, "I . . . thanks."

As other kids bustle in, I look back at Olivia. Her blush has turned a brilliant red. She says, "Um, I'll text you later," and hurries back to her desk, her brown hair swishing from side to side. Every muscle in my body is still tense from her proximity.

HELLO
my name is

LUCAS McCALLUM

TO-DO:

- ~~Make sure everyone knows it's not true.~~
  None of my friends were in their usual spots during break.
- ~~Eat lunch with Valentine.~~ Valentine was not by the trailers today. He is not texting me back. Figure out why.
- Place at swim meet.

I CRASH OUT OF THE WATER WITH A GASP. THE WORLD roars back into sound around me, and cool air slaps my cheeks. My heart pounding, I check the clock.

Third. I came in third—and I've beaten my old best time by two seconds.

I gulp breaths and fight back a smile. As I clamber out of the pool, my muscles tremble. The team claps, some of them, and echoes ring off the arched ceiling. My toes squelch through puddles on the tiled floor. The announcer yaps on, deafening.

I shiver my way into a towel. Usually the guys would be clapping me on the back, but they're keeping their distance today. Doesn't surprise me. I gather they're not taking the innocent-until-proven-guilty approach. If I'd been accused of being with Dr. Meyers, the very hot, very female econ teacher, would this be happening?

The meet closes well. Coach swaggers out of the building as if he swam every event himself. He whistles out of the auditorium onto the bus for the forty-minute drive home.

I'm one of the last up the bus steps. I edge down the aisle, the black-ridged rubber path, and nobody's eyes meet mine. Every so often, a backpack occupies a seat. Derek Cooper and Alison Gardner's bags. I could be sitting there, but they don't move their things.

I bring silence rippling up with me row by row, a cloak trailing from my shoulders, a sweep of averted eyes and concentrated texting. No room at these inns. As I pass Dean Prince, whose nose is weirdly swollen, he gives me an outright filthy look. I frown and move on.

Herman from Chemistry. Layna from Calc. Bailey, my relay partner. None of them says a word. My heart is deflating, a sad, old balloon.

I sit down in a seat in the back left corner, alone with my journal.

Everything I did to make these friends. Two years' worth of work, with no result. This might as well be my first day again. Fresh off the plane. A reset button, and I wasn't the one who pushed it. I wasn't the one who made the choice.

I grit my teeth and look down at the phone cupped in my hands, thinking of Valentine.

When I glance back up, I catch Sophie Crane looking away, whispering something to Bailey. Do they believe it? The accusation is so ridiculous. Under the layers of worry and hurt, I'm a bit offended that people don't think I have better taste than Dr. Norman.

I stare out the window as the bus snails through the parking lot. Why would somebody do that to me? Make that up. Who would do it? Someone who wanted to out me, maybe? But if Matt only told Olivia, and Olivia only told Claire—

She wouldn't.

Claire wouldn't.

She wears her grudges like armor. But she wouldn't . . .

Would she?

HELLO
my name is

Juniper Kipling

The key's teeth chew down on the lock.

His door swings wide, an opening lid to a treasure chest. Light spills out like liquid gold.

Hood down, head up—check around, make sure nobody saw—

Slow down, heart.

I shut the door behind me and head down the hall.

Hello? Someone there? A familiar voice, a familiar smell.

I round the corner, and it's the most familiar sight, isn't it—

a coffee mug on a glass table. Evening light in his tired eyes. His patched gray sweater on narrow shoulders, rolled up to his elbows.

Shock slathered onto his expression.

Surprise, I say.

The room expands, unfolds, unpacks.

There are miles of gray thread coiling between us.

Cavernous silence and those eyes,

those eyes.

June. What are you doing here?

(I have missed so badly the sight of you saying my name.)

It's freezing. Everything is freezing. My toes and fingers, long and pale. *I had to see you. With what they're saying about Norman—I had to make sure you're okay.*

He opens his mouth, showing nothing on his tongue but quiet. The man of words, a dry inkwell at last.

He walks step by step my way, and I watch his

purposeful strides,

worn sneakers, grayed from morning runs,

stopping inches from mine.

I don't know what to do, he says. *I don't know who said it was that McCallum kid and Neil Norman, of all people, but it's only going to get people more riled up. I . . . God, if he gets in serious trouble—the guy has a wife and kids, there's—*

It has to blow over. They have zero proof.

I guess. His voice cracks. He licks his lips. *June, I've been thinking.*

Yeah?

We can cut ties. I can delete your number, texts, emails, everything—I can make sure nobody ever finds out. I can't fix what's happening at school, but if it'll help you . . .

His ocean eyes, deep black tumults, lightning storms.

My three words, three drops of rain. *Don't you dare.*

But

If something happens, I am going to be there with you.

I can see his heart beat faster. *Are you—*

Of course I'm sure. My chest is so full, I think my ribs are cracking. *I didn't come here for a good-bye, David.*

I know.

I came here to . . . I wanted . . .

I know, he repeats.

His words light a fire under my lungs. My breaths are thick ash.

So what do we do? I ask.

I don't know.

But you love me?

Of course I love you.

The top of my heart, hinged, cracks open,

and my fears, ravens, fly out.

They spill away like black paint,

leaving me empty and pink and new.

Hopeful.

He's reaching out. I'm reaching up to take his hand,

passing through a veil of guilt,

swaying two inches before his eyes. *David.*

His hands rest on my shoulders, lightly as wings.

(your lips fall to mine, natural as gravity,

close on my lower lip, rough and sweet.

i touch, i bite, i taste.)

I consume him.

(the sounds at the back of my throat are yours. everything,

everything is yours.)

I press tight to his body. Between us is a hair-fine fault line,

hardly a fault at all.

His slender hands settle on my back and draw me in, close,

closer.

Heat tingles in every inch of this skin,

dense, thick awareness, pins and needles and blisters.

I need you, too, I murmur, flushed, aching.

His lips are a balm on mine. Gentle. *June*, he whispers, that's all.

Radiance and setting sun, bliss and blinding want.

(i feel you, cradle you, cherish you.)

When finally we break—

Missed you—

So much—

our shared words whisper and blend and merge.

A kiss, a rough kiss, the stamp of it is raw heat.

He pulls back, pulling half of me with him,

and smiles.

My own smile shrugs itself on,

wrapping me in comfort.

For weeks I have sweated,

labored,

aching to drive Sisyphus's stone up this eternal mountain,

and here: the summit.

Here they are. Here are his eyes. I have arrived

in the sunlight of his regard.

It's one in the morning when I lock us in for our thousandth
test of willpower.

His room hasn't changed an inch: bare surfaces, empty desk,
closed drawers, furniture sparse and simply made.

Blank, save his shelves of roommates:

Hemingway and Beukes, Christie and Martin, Márquez and
Morrison, Rowling and—his best friend—the Bard.

Every flavor of word treated

tenderly, every corner soft from extensive paging.

I slip into his narrow bed. We lock tight,

two-lane traffic on a one-lane street.

I trace his jaw; the stubble nips my fingers.

He brushes my hair back. *What did you tell them?*

I'm at Olivia's for the night. I don't know. We should tell them.

You've said that eight thousand times, June.

Eight thousand and one.

I curl into him. He is a brazier, blazing,

lighting me mercilessly.

He smells like apple and a touch of alcohol. My feet fold against his calves.

I know we should, he says. *But do you want to tell them?*

Of course not.

His chest collapses in a sigh under my hand. *Then there we go.*

Yeah. I guess. I touch my lips to his collarbone, his throat. He hums with contentment.

I'm excited, he whispers. A confession. *I'm excited for us. I keep thinking stupidly far into the future, you know?*

I tilt my head up, surprised. This is an edit of the usual sentence. David is the here-and-now; David is grounded and pragmatic; David is not fantasy and imagination.

Where is this coming from?

Me too, I whisper, and wonder.

I think about it all the time. After you finish college, us traveling. Brazil. India.

I smile. Let my questions fade

to haze and hope.

Greece, I say sleepily. *Mount Olympus.*

The world is here in this bed with us, continents quilted together,

the cosmos tucked against the headboard.

His finger traces my wrist, a figure skater flying in lazy figure eights. *Venice. A room this size that smells like the sea. Alaska. Lit candles, and fighting off an eighteen-hour night.*

The Great Wall, I say. *Stonehenge. The Sydney Opera House.*

He kisses me. *The moon.* Again, he kisses me. *The moon.*

Wednesday morning dawns. The air is as chill and damp as drying tears,

Autumn's last battle. (Smells like brittle sap and old fires and cold sun.)

That sun in the sky is a dream, when I leave him, when I head home.

I push the oaken door, built to loom;

my feet on the hardwood are parcels of potpourri,

featherlight and inconsequential.

I grab my backpack and stop in the foyer. My parents have materialized on the steps.

They stand like stone sentries,

unfamiliar rubies set in their eyes.

My father: *Juniper, sweetheart, we need to talk.*

But I need to go to school.

My mother: *You left your change of clothes here last night. So I called Olivia's house.*

I turn to ice limb by limb. *I . . . it's . . . I'll explain after school.*

Juniper—

After. I turn on my heel. I totter out. Shell-shocked.

Three periods' worth of thought gets me nowhere. They noticed. They're asking, finally.

Will I push them away? Cocoon myself in lies again?

In the hall between classes, I pass the door to his room. I glance in,

see his fingers wringing clouds of dust out of the chalkboard.

He catches my eye for the briefest second.

Some hand is at my throat,

choking off all sound, all breath, all air.

It should be branded on my forehead—*I'm going to tell them*—hideous, fiery letters.

I continue down the hall, gaining momentum as I go.

ON WEDNESDAY, IT RAINS AND RAINS. I CAN'T FOCUS in any of my classes, watching the droplets trickle down the windowpanes. I've hardly slept since the rumors broke on Monday about Lucas. Of course I can't turn Juniper in, but what am I supposed to do, knowing that's a lie? Lucas doesn't deserve that. Even Norman, douchebag of the century, doesn't deserve that.

García has avoided my eyes all week, and I keep busy trying not to imagine Juniper at his side. They'd be an unbearably photogenic couple, which makes it about eight times weirder. I don't think of teachers as having relationships, even friendships. In my mind, they exist in their own space: that twenty-foot stretch at the front of the room, where they're omniscient and all-powerful, where they rule our miserable lives. Everywhere else, they do not exist.

But since Sunday night, I've been thinking: what would it be like to talk to García as if he were our age? Talking about our lives and our interests and the future? It would be so weird, seeing him through that lens.

Though I guess since Juniper dropped his class, she doesn't know him through the omniscient teacher-lens. And that, more than anything, reassures me.

IT'S STILL RAINING WHEN I GET HOME. I SHUT THE
door on the sound of it, sighing.

Coming home today is the dull pain of a headache. Besides
a glimpse of Kat on Monday evening—she looked frighteningly
numb—I haven't seen her at all. All I have is the recorded messages from yesterday, and now today: *We are calling to inform you
that Katrina Scott missed one or more classes today.*

My phone buzzes. I pull it out, expecting Juni, daring to hope
it might be Claire or Matt. But the screen reads: *Daniel.*

Frowning, I pick up. "Hello?"

"Hey. Olivia."

"Dan?" I dump my backpack and my bag from the pharmacy
on the kitchen table. "How's, um, how's it going?"

"Pretty good, pretty good."

"That's . . . good?" *Why are you calling me?*

"Look, I heard about Juniper landing in the hospital. That
blows."

"It does."

"She doing okay?"

"I . . . yeah," I say in my most discouraging monotone, still
wondering what the point of this call is.

"How about you? You must be stressed."

"Sort of. I mean, she's better now." I wander into the living
room and sit on our sofa. The springs creak. "Dan—"

"What are you up to?"

"What?"

"Because if you wanted to come over later, you could. You
know, for stress relief."

I take my phone from my ear and stare at it, half floored, half repulsed. "Excuse me?" I splutter, crushing it back to my ear. "Wait, slow down. Are you seriously asking what I think you're asking?"

"I . . . don't know?"

"Okay, I'll simplify: is this or is this not a poorly disguised booty call?"

"Well, my parents aren't home. House is empty."

"Oh my God, Daniel. Let me make this perfectly, utterly clear. *No.*"

He's quiet for a second. Then he says, "What, are you with Matt now?"

"That's not—"

"Because he's not even a good guy, you know."

"*He's* not a good guy? And yet you're the one still trying to hook up with someone who has told you no, like, three times? You could ask out any other human being. What do I have to do here?"

"So the other weekend meant nothing to you. At all."

I close my eyes. "Look, this has got to be some sort of communication issue. It was fun, okay? I had fun, but it was a onetime thing. I thought we were clear on—"

"It doesn't have to be."

"But it does. *A,* I don't want to hook up again, and *B,* I like someone else, so—"

"So it *is* Matt. What's the difference between screwing him and screwing me?"

My mind stops. I have no idea what to say, but that's A-okay, because, God bless him, he keeps on going: "Besides, if you're going to let everyone and his brother get it, can't blame me for assuming you're down."

When I find words, they rush out in a waterfall. "So by sleeping with more than one guy, I've forfeited my right to hook up with who I want? Or are you saying that by having sex with multiple people, I've become, like, emotionally incapable of falling for one person? Either way, *are you insane?*"

"Hey, all I'm saying is, you can't act like a slut and expect people not to treat you like a slut. It's just false advertising."

Sweet Jesus.

I've felt my share of anger. There are some kinds you can't hold in your body. Some types burst out of your every pore at once, and you feel yourself expanding and twisting and turning into something that isn't human. You feel hot waves of rage punching their way out of your skin. Right now, I swear I could melt metal just by breathing on it.

False advertising? I am done. I'm done with the stares and the rumors and the lack of basic human decency, let alone privacy. I'm so done with being defined by this single part of me.

"I'm not advertising anything!" I yell, my words ringing off the living room walls. "My body is *not yours.* I don't owe you, I don't owe boys some fucked-up compensation for my reputation, I don't owe the public an apology for my personal life, I don't owe anyone a goddamn thing, so get out of my life and stay out!"

I punch end call so hard, a discolored spot shows up on the phone screen. For a second I tremble, my teeth buried deep in my lip. Then I make for the stairs, my hand pressed against my mouth. I feel ill.

I walk into my room, shut the door with agonizing calm, and

twist the lock. I fling my phone at the *Star Wars* pillow on my bed. The muscles in my arm ache in recoil, the phone sinks deep into Han Solo's face, and I let out a strangled, animal noise of rage. I stand there staring at myself in the mirror, my red cheeks, my sleeve askew, my torn expression. My face is hot and swollen and furious, and I feel like a melting wax candle.

Lightning flashes like a strobe in the window. The overcast day has turned thunderous.

A photograph sits on my dresser. It faces the wall 365 days of the year. I've gotten used to the sight of the black backing of the frame, a cardboard square collecting a gentle sheen of dust. But now I turn it around.

Mom, Dad, Kat, and I stand behind the glass, preserved in a summer afternoon. Every year, Dad insisted on taking our Christmas photo six months before Christmas to the day, to mark the point at which we started getting closer to the holiday. Kat's smile is radiant, Dad's grin pushes dimples into his cheeks, and I'm in the middle of a huge laugh. Mom always got a joke ready so our smiles weren't canned. That year, it was, "What do you call Santa's helpers? Subordinate Clauses."

God, I want our family back. I would kill right now for Kat's quiet understanding or Dad's gruff reassurances. I want Mom to tuck my hair behind my ear, or make up a bedtime story on the spot, or rub my back and promise it's going to be all right. She could speak quickly, quietly, for hours on end, until there was nothing but her voice wrapping me up in warmth and acceptance. I used to have the knowledge that the world could hammer at me all it wanted, but she would always be there to lift me up. Mom with her bitter-smelling perfume and her jangling bracelets and her full, wild laugh.

But the good memories of her are soured by the ones that hinted she would leave. In hindsight, it seems so obvious. She took random trips without warning, overnight drives and weekend sojourns, unable to stand Kansas for longer than a few weeks at a go. She scooped up and dropped hobby after hobby, everything from tennis to painting. She never held down friends, either, always dropping out of touch for one convincing-sounding reason or another.

I force myself not to fling the photo away. I drop the frame back into place and crumple onto my bed, trying to deaden the anger. Thunder grinds to life outside, lazy and languorous and so deep, my house shudders.

My phone tempts me. I can't call Juniper—I can't add this to her plate. Claire? God knows what she would say.

My finger hovers over Matt's contact for a second. He just found out about his parents' divorce, for God's sake. Can I load this on him, too?

Apparently I can. *God, I'm selfish*, I think as I hit call. It rings once, twice, three times before he picks up.

"Olivia?" he says. "I—hi."

"Hey," I say, my voice thick.

"What's, um, what's up?"

My throat ekes out a tiny noise, and I crush my hand to my lips. *Don't be so weak. You don't get to cry. It's bad enough that you're making this call.*

For a second, I can't talk. I can't even breathe. Weight presses on my chest, tangled up in my ribs like thick hair gnarled in a comb. My heart pounds, every beat a burst of pain.

"H-have you talked to your parents?" I manage. "About Russ?"

"No. I will after dinner, once he's asleep."

"Good. Good, great." I look up at the ceiling, breathing in and out on eight-counts.

"What's going on?" Matt says. "Hey, you can say."

"It's not—there's not—"

"Yo," he says. "Talk."

More lightning. The lights flicker. Looks like night outside already, and it's barely 5:45.

"Just . . ." I shake my head. In the absence of words, the rain splattering on my window is louder than a snare drum.

For a minute I stay quiet on the line, wondering how I can feel this outside myself.

"Sorry," I say. "I'm sorry, I just . . . Dan called me and . . ."

"Oh Jesus. What did he say?"

"That I'm a slut and deserve to be treated like one. And by 'treated like a slut,' he means 'treated like I'm open for business at all times to everyone.'" I wipe my nose on the back of my hand. This is so self-indulgent.

"He's a dick," Matt says.

"I mean, I wouldn't care if it were just him, but everyone thinks that. Richard Brown's a huge man-whore, but girls never say, 'He'll probably sleep with me if I give him the time of day, and if he doesn't, well, false advertising.' Why doesn't it work like that? Why is it just *me*?"

Matt pauses for a second before saying, "'Cause guys think

about sex all the time, so it seems normal when they see girls in terms of . . . you know. Sex?"

"But some girls think about sex all the time, too. So why do boys get to be like, oh man, bro, dude, I'm gonna get mad pussy tonight, and people are like, *ah yes, so normal*, but if a girl goes out like, yeah, I'm trying to get some dick, everyone gets all puritan?"

Matt's quiet.

"Also," I say, in full steam now, "*you* don't think about sex all the time, do you?"

"I mean, not all the time," he says. "A lot, sure. But it's not, like, a problem."

"So why do people act like all dudes are sex-obsessed maniacs? That's messed up, too."

"I guess?" he says, sounding bemused.

"Sorry. I'm ranting. I just—thinking about hooking up with Dan now is so gross. My track record is so, like, besmirched by his presence." I pull my covers over my head.

"I used to be friends with him in middle school," Matt says. "He ditched me and Burke freshman year, which is fine. I mean, not like I'm Einstein, but Dan never had more than about point-eight brain cells, so, not a huge loss."

I can't even get any vindictive satisfaction from the insult. "He's not even unique," I mumble. "He's the same."

"As what?"

I curl up around my *Star Wars* pillow. "I don't know. The other guys I've hooked up with." I sigh, sending a brush of static into the phone. "Sometimes it's, like, what's the point anymore? Why am I trying to fill this space with boys? It's—"

"What space?" he asks.

"I—what?"

"You said, trying to fill the space. What space?"

"I don't know. I guess it's kind of . . ." I bite my lip, but I can't keep it back. "Sometimes it feels like I'm not enough. For anyone to stay. You know?"

"Oh. I . . . yeah." He lowers his voice. "I don't think you're right, but I get it."

"It's stupid, anyway." I force a hard laugh. "Like guys could compensate for me feeling unwanted and whatever." The second the sentence comes out, I want to yank it back. Why am I rambling about my insecurities with the boy I have a crush on, of all people?

Matt stays quiet for what feels like several months, prolonging my humiliation.

Finally, he says, "You are wanted."

A shiver darts down my arms. His voice is low, but what's underneath comes out loud and clear: *I want you.*

I don't say anything. Can't say anything. In the commanding quiet, we lay every basic function bare for each other: the stir of our breath, the pump of blood in our veins, the air mixing in our eardrums. The softest nothing sound either of us could make. And something deep in me calms, cocooned in a wellspring of evening silence.

I open my mouth, intending to say something hopelessly witty. Instead, after a second of strangled hesitation, what comes out is, "Tell me something."

"What?" he says.

"Tell me something. Anything. I don't—it doesn't need to be a—really, anything."

"Okay," he says, clearly bewildered. "Uh, in seventh grade I broke my wrist, and this guy Adam something was like, using your right hand too much? And everyone called me 'Matt Jackoff' for, like, two years. With hand motions included. So that sucked ass."

I can't help but laugh. "God, middle school kids are even worse than high school kids."

"I don't know. High school kids are pretty bad."

"Some of them are all right." I let my usual teasing tone seep back into my voice. "Like, you're all right."

Another pause.

"You tell me something," he says, but the words sound so careful, I get the sense he doesn't mean just anything.

"Something?"

"Can I ask about your mom? Like, what happened?"

I pull back the covers, staring at my ceiling, allowing the absence of my mother to ache. Thoughts of her sit on the surface, pulsing like reopened wounds.

"Okay, so my family went to New York when I was fourteen," I say. "End of eighth grade." I still remember the sight of Mom on Fifth Avenue—it's an image cut sharp and hard, a facet deep in a gem. Her smile is stamped against the twilit gloom of the city, her blond hair whitened by the glow of a neon sign. Her hands are in the pockets of her jeans, her scarf nestling her chin in loose-woven linen. In my mind's eye, she looks so much like Kat. Sometimes I think there's nothing of Mom's face left in my mind, that Kat's snuck in and replaced my memories of her, that I've fooled myself into thinking I remember the sight of her.

"We were there for one weekend," I say, "staying at this hotel in Brooklyn. We were supposed to be flying out Monday morning, one of those stupid early flights that—we had to get up at four or something. We had two separate rooms, one for me and Kat, and one for my parents, so I woke up at four, and I heard their voices through the wall, right? They'd been fighting for years at this point, and now they were just screaming at each other in this hotel—probably woke up the whole floor. And Kat was sitting there with her arms around her knees looking terrified. So I got up, and I went out to knock on their door, but it, like, slammed open, and my mom sprinted out and ran down the hall. She was crying all the way down the stairs."

I draw my knees up to my chest. "I go into their room, and Dad's sitting there on the bed, staring at the tiny hotel TV, and there's some stupid show playing, something about tearing down old houses, and it has this obnoxious, fake-smiling host, and Dad's looking at the screen, obviously not watching it at all. God knows what he said to make her run like that. I still kind of wonder, but he's never said, so I can't help but think . . ." I swallow. "Anyway, so I ask him, like, 'Should I go see if she's okay?' and he gives me this look filled with . . . like, *wow*, little tiny fourteen-year-old Olivia, you don't understand what just happened. You don't get it at all. But I sort of got it."

My throat aches. I've spoken too long already. I rush on. "So I run down into the lobby, and I'm just in time to see the back of a taxi driving off. And me and Kat are like, okay, Dad, let's call another cab, let's go, but we can't get him to move until after the plane's supposed to take off. So we get a flight back in the evening, and by the time we get home, all her stuff's out of the house. Never saw her again. Took a few weeks for Dad to get a number she'd pick up from, but they only talked once, and apparently she, um. Apparently she didn't want to talk to Kat or me. Thought it'd be too painful."

Matt doesn't say anything.

I try to smile. I can't quite manage it. "What's your mom like?"

"I mean, not that bad. All I do is complain about her, but she's not . . . I don't know."

"What's her deal?"

He makes a noncommittal noise. "I guess all you need to know is that we visited Yale last summer for her twenty-fifth reunion, and at the end she basically said, 'I'm humiliated that U of M is your reach school.'" He sounds uninterested. "She's always thought I'm stupid. I'm smart enough to see that much. But you get used to being a disappointment when you bring home my grades every year, so at this point, not a big deal."

The resignation in his voice depresses me. Claire's got a 4.0 GPA, but she has the people-smarts of your average twelfth-century warlord. And Juniper's dad has a PhD, but God bless him, he couldn't find an ounce of common sense if it jumped screaming out of his cereal bowl. Maybe Matt's the world's best judge of character. Maybe he's one of those people you can drop into a giant city and they'll know their way around within thirty seconds. I've always thought everybody's a genius at something; you just have to dig it up and polish the hell out of it.

To me, right now, he seems a little bit of a genius at making me feel normal again.

"Matt?" I say. "Thanks for this."

"For what?" His voice lightens. "Whining about my family? I could do this shit all day."

I laugh. "Okay. I expect a five-page whine by Friday."

"No problem."

"Single-spaced," I add. "None of that making-the-periods-size-14-font shit, either. I can tell."

"Hmm," he says. "Someone's going to be a hard-ass teacher."

"Believe it."

The silence turns thick. Its back sags under what we're not saying.

"So," I say.

"So."

"Look, I don't want to mess things up, because I think this is a good . . . you know?"

"Yeah," Matt says, "it's a good."

I smile. "And I need a good right now, you know? With everything."

"Me too." After a long pause, he says, "I don't want to mess this up, either. This—thing."

"Yeah. I know. It's just, um," I say, my palms itching with sudden heat. I turn off my brain and blurt it out: "I really like you, I think, and I—yeah."

"I like you, too," Matt says cautiously, as if he's expecting me to go, *Fooled you! I take it all back!*

"Ah," I say, breathless. "Okay."

"Yeah."

I clear my throat. "Can I maybe see you tomorrow?"

"I—sure. After school? I can catch up with you in the new wing."

"Perfect. So I . . . yeah. Bye?"

"Bye, Olivia."

But neither of us hangs up, and for a while, neither of us says a word.

Finally, he says, "Raining pretty hard."

My gaze goes to the window. The thin rivulets of water shatter the outside world into an Impressionist's painting. A breeze flows through the thin opening, stirring the air. "I love the rain," I say. "Smells like waking up."

HELLO
my name is

JUNIPER KIPLING

I delayed as long as I could.

The sun has drowned in evening rain.

I unlock the door, my fingers choking the knob.

What will they say?

They'll want to make the call . . .

(*it's over uncovered my love discovered*)

Will I grovel, my voice rough as gravel

will I plead, my eyes dripping need

will I put myself to shame?

Will they forgive him? forgive me?

will he forgive me for coming clean?

(please—forgive me)

(*forgive me*)

We perch uneasily in the living room.

An hour unfolds.

Every detail I didn't detail; every problem they didn't probe—I lay it all bare.

They tick silently like time bombs.

So there it is.

And they burst together.

Juniper Bridget Kipling—

Juniper!

Five months—

You've been lying right to our faces—?

I ice over. My words detach and drift, skiffs on a calm lake.

The lying didn't take much. I've realized it would take me setting off fireworks in the house for you to even threaten me with consequences.

That is just untrue.

Do you realize how worrying—

Disbelief swims up. Yanks at my oars. *Worry? You've just been watching as I turn into a train wreck. If you've been worried at all about how I've been acting, it's been impossible to tell.*

My mother's fists are clenched.

Squeeze, squeeze, squeeze out the fear.

Squeeze us back to normal.

Dad's on his feet. *Has he hurt you? I swear, if he's hurt you—if he's forced you to . . . to do anything you didn't—*

Of course not. I'm on my feet, too. *I told you, we didn't sleep together, I told you, Dad.*

His face is stained violet and red. A watercolor terror. *I can't believe this. I am calling the school right now.*

No. You can't—

Oh, yes I can. I can and I will.

He goes for the phone. I dive for it, smack his arm away—

He yells something—

Mom's yelling, too—

(it's everything I thought it would be)

and the doorbell freezes us all with a crystal note.

We shut down. The color slides from our cheeks like cheap dye.
Mom hurries down the hallway, answers with a dazed smile.
It curdles on her lips.
Horror drips cold down my back.
David?

These couches are as stiff as court benches,
a guilty verdict clutched in our fists.
So, says the voice that sounds more like a judge's than my
father's. *So, you're him.*
*David García. Hi. I would say it's good to meet you, but under the
circumstances I'm guessing you feel differently.*
You're right. You think you can prey on my daughter and—
Dad. He didn't prey *on anybody.*
*I'm not finished. Young man, you have a responsibility. You're a
government employee, for God's sake. You have a responsibility to the
children of this country—*
I'm not a child, I point out, childishly.
My mother barrels over me. *I agree one hundred percent. You
should be ashamed to call yourself a teacher.*
I know. Something's quiet in David's eyes. *Which is why I turned
myself in.*
somebody has taken a hammer to my voice box
a broken sound collapses out of me.
teaching was his first love,
his greatest love.
(david? you—
you shouldn't have—
should you have?)

i'm wordless.

my parents sit wordless, too.

So, with that in mind, he says, *I don't know where we go from here. I understand your anger, of course. And I'll be shouldering the consequences. I'll do everything I can to keep Juniper's name out of this. I'm sure the police will be investigating, and they'll want to interview her, but that's not . . . since we never . . . it shouldn't be a legal . . .*

whispery sounds slip from my lips. *yeah, um, i told them that part.*

Right. Good.

david, why did you—you didn't have to—

I did. his hand flexes. he could slip it into mine

but he knows better. *I had to.*

the fight has fallen out of the air.

my parents look to me. they all look to me.

i stay motionless, mind churning.

he'll be fired. disgraced.

my mother's voice is low. *You will leave this house. And then, when you leave your job, and when you leave this city, you will leave our daughter alone.*

that tone of command once made millions.

he sits tall under it. stoic.

but i—

i flatten a sob beneath a fist. my voice is an explosion, spraying shrapnel carelessly. *no—Mom, don't—please, please . . .*

She's right, June, david says.

i stare at him. splintering under the surface in betrayal.

even my mother blinks her confusion.

I was wrong, he says. *I should have been more . . . I should have*

*made sure from the beginning that we—that this . . . that it wouldn't
have to be like this. That was always my responsibility, and I neglected
it for five months.*

with every word i fracture a little more, a new hair-fine line
in a ceramic surface.

with every word i am more fragile.

with every word, older.

the tears abate. *so this was a mistake?*

*No, that's not—I made a mistake, June, but you weren't a mistake.
You are, I swear, the best thing in my life. My not waiting was the
mistake.*

my mother stares at david like he is a painting she is beginning
to understand.

Juniper doesn't graduate for a year and a half, she says slowly. *And
so help me, if you get in touch before then, I will file a restraining order.*

(Before then?)

The words ring in my ears, making me dizzy with hope.

My father's balding head bobs. He takes over. *If, anytime in the
future, she has any interest in contacting you, you'll hear from us. Us
first. You understand?*

Yes, David says.

He meets my gaze. Our eyes are lifelines. In his eyes I see
myself holding him. In mine he knows I love him.

He stands.

Can I say good-bye? I ask.

No, my father says, but my mother rests her hand on his wrist.

They meet eyes, a brief and silent battle.

My mother half lifts him to his feet. They leave us.

. . . .

Juniper—

I fold myself into his arms, and he holds me so tightly
so tightly
I could merge into him, skin into skin and heart into heart.

It's okay, he murmurs. *It'll be okay. A clean break is going to hurt
less, I promise.*

It's . . . I pull back. *I mean, I can't help thinking you'll find someone
else in an infinitely larger, more interesting city.*

Yeah, no way. He brushes my hair back from my forehead.
There's only one of you.

Well. As far as you know.

The regret of making him laugh is instant—
I miss the sound already.

He kisses my cheeks, my temples.

I look up at his forgiving eyes and see everything.

I'll see you again, he says.

I know.

And with that, he walks into the hall.

It swallows him, foot by foot.

He pauses in the doorway for one moment,

a black-coated silhouette against the gold porch light,

messy hair, strong profile, disappearing eyes.

I lift my hand.

The door shuts,

the *click* of a clean break.

I sway, expecting to dissolve,

but my body holds fast.

My hands don't shake. My head is clear. My eyes are dry.
And I think—
somehow—
I will be all right.
This time, I will.

HELLO
my name is

CLAIRE LOMBARDI

THE DOORBELL RINGS AT 5:30. "I'LL GET IT," I CALL down the hall. Grace thanks me from the depths of her room.

I hop down the steps two at a time, catch sight of who's behind the glass door, and slam to a halt at the bottom of the staircase.

It's Lucas. The second I see his face, I'm sure of it: he knows.

I open the door. The sound of rain crashes in. The fact that he's not smiling terrifies me.

We sit down in the living room, his curly hair fluffing out from the dampness. The wooden mobile hanging in the alcove twirls and bobs in the air current from the heating vent, distracting me.

"Hey. Why are you here?" I ask. It feels strange to ask, given the constant presence he used to be under my family's roof. He'd pull into my driveway to pick me up every morning, and we'd drive back every afternoon talking. I kissed him on the roof, under the branches of our oak tree, in the humidity of a summer nightfall. I remember the roughness of his arms, his palms.

"I don't know," he says. "I don't know why I'm here."

What do I say to that?

I clear my throat. "How was, um. How was the meet yesterday?"

"Fine, good," he says. "I PR'ed in the 500 Free. Two seconds faster than my old best."

"I . . . congratulations."

"Thanks."

Seconds trickle by. I've never felt like I'm small-talking with him, not before now. Something is missing from us. Sometimes you can feel the detachment in the way someone looks at you, the way they arrange their body facing yours, the way they blink and sigh and put their hands on the table. Something has been subtracted. I don't know if I lost it, or if he put it away, or if someone else has it, but this isn't the pair we used to be.

Then he's saying something in a different voice, one I remember more clearly.

"I'm sorry for being so . . . you know, after we broke up. I shouldn't have acted like you weren't—hadn't been—special." The veil of friendliness slips askew from the air, and I see his face. He's saying sorry, but he means something else. What is it? This used to happen all the time. He'd make reluctant apologies, angry apologies, in the place of explanations or amends.

"Right," I say, and I know he expects me to apologize in return. Apologize for what I've done to him.

The words, though, are somewhere else, somewhere I can't reach them, because I'm looking at him and thinking, maybe it's not so much that I've lost a grip on what we were. Maybe I never quite knew what we were in the first place.

Looking at him, I don't feel satisfied, not like I did yesterday when I heard everybody talking about him and Norman. Now I remember the weight of telling him I loved him. In March, we went out on his birthday, and we spent the day hopping around Paloma's antiques shops, imagining that weird old junk was lost treasure from another world. After dinner, we drove home. He kissed me good night, and I told him in a nervous blurt, and his smile brightened and widened until it looked almost painful, and he said he loved me, too.

No, this isn't satisfaction.

"That's my last apology, I think." His voice is strangled. "I hope you got what you needed."

"Right."

Lucas shakes his head and stands. He takes a breath as if he's going to say something huge. His eyes are lit with accusation, but he shuts his mouth and leaves, and for the first time, I don't want to call after him. I don't want to say another word.

I walk back to the kitchen, my steps uncertain. For so long, Lucas was my claim to myself. For months, I've lived on some hazy gas planet of confusion and bitterness. I never understood what made me so much worse than other people, that I deserved to be alone—

But it wasn't about me, in the end, was it?

Maybe my self-blame was another kind of selfishness.

My hands go to my mouth, but I don't bite my nails. I level my eyes at my warped, dark reflection in the oven door.

Some awful, acrid taste prickles at the back of my tongue, and it finally hits me. The weight of what I did. It slams into me so hard that I sit down at the kitchen table, the breath knocked out of my chest. I stare at my trembling hands.

I am finally irredeemable.

HELLO
my name is

KAT SCOTT

ZOMBIES PILE ONTO ME.

"Shit." I hit the down key, trying to turn and run, but their teeth have already dug into my legs. "Shit, shit, dammit," I hiss, shoving my laptop forward in defeat. The zombies' decayed faces rise up the screen, loose-jawed, flaps of flesh peeling from their pallid foreheads. They overpower me. *Continue?* asks the screen, taunting me. Of course I'm going to fucking continue. It's been seven hours of me continuing.

I sink down in the kitchen chair. This level is impossible. After the miniboss, there's an ambush. None of my weaponry, let alone my armor, is strong enough to take this much undead power, but I've been trying all day. My second day of skipping school, slouching from spot to spot in our house, gaming.

Not thinking about the play.

Not thinking about Emily saying, "Please don't. Please."

Not thinking about the look on my sister's face when I said, "I don't need you."

I have not been thinking about any of that.

As I hit respawn and start again, the door swings open, ushering in the sound of rain. Dad trudges in, pulling back his poncho's hood. His facial hair has gone from stubble status to a legitimate beard, a furry salt-and-pepper shield covering half his face. He looks like a stranger.

I keep playing. He approaches the table and sets down a couple of grocery bags beside Olivia's things, which lie in an ungraceful pile opposite me. I heard her yelling at someone over the phone earlier. *I'm not curious*, I tell myself. I don't care who it was.

"Is this your sister's?" Dad says, prodding the plastic pharmacy bag.

"Yeah."

"Is she sick?"

"No clue," I say, climbing a fence. The barbed wire makes my health bar dip. I ransack a nearby dead guy for medicine as my dad opens the pharmacy bag, rustling through the contents.

"Katrina," Dad says. I hit pause and look up. His eyes, sharper and more awake than I've seen them in God knows how long, are flooded with disbelief. He's holding a small green box. PLAN B: EMERGENCY CONTRACEPTIVE.

"I . . . oh," I say. "That's . . ."

"This is your sister's?"

I'm silent.

"Go and get her, please." He sits down hard opposite me. "Now."

THE THREE OF US SIT IN DEAFENING SILENCE. MY gaze darts around the kitchen. Walls the dismal color of soggy bread. Rain still tapping halfheartedly at the glass. Sunset through the window, like firelight, simmering low under heavy clouds.

Why am I here? If they want to talk about this, fine, but why do I have to be involved?

Dad folds his hands on the table and stares at them. "How long has this been happening?"

"Maybe the start of sophomore year?" Olivia says. "Dad, please don't be mad. The point of that pill is that I'm being responsible. That's the whole idea."

"This is responsible?" he says, disbelieving. "Olivia, you're seventeen years old."

"I know, but it's—"

"This is not acceptable," Dad says.

A weird look spreads across Olivia's face. She chuckles.

Dad frowns.

"I mean," she says, "you've got to admit, that's funny. The idea of you popping in to pass judgment on, like, *this* kind of information, while the rest of the time you're totally in absentia."

Dad leans back, looking baffled. "What? What's that supposed to mean?"

She tilts her head. "Do you really not know?"

"Know what?"

"How distant you are."

His voice rises. "No, I don't know what you—"

I cut in. "She's right."

In my peripheral vision, Olivia stares at me. I don't look at her. Dad goes silent again, apparently stunned that I agree with this obvious assessment.

"Dad," Olivia says, "we have to talk. We have to. It's not just this you didn't know about. You're missing so much, you know? I made Honor Society in September, and you didn't come to the ceremony, even though I asked you. You didn't come to the plays Kat was in last spring or fall. She was amazing in both of them, and you missed them. And she's been skipping classes, and she told me you signed off to say that she was sick? That's not—did you ask her what she'd been doing? Because I can tell you. She's been getting addicted to gaming and isolating herself, and honestly? It's scary. She doesn't get out of bed on the weekends, she's not eating, and you don't see it. You don't *notice*, Dad."

I stare at Olivia. Aimed at someone else, her words don't sound like accusations anymore. They don't trigger that defensive instinct in my chest—all I feel is a tight pang at the panic in her voice. Why does it sound so different when she's telling Dad?

When it clicks, I'm humiliated at how long it took me to figure it out. Olivia wasn't trying to force me to be like her. She was *worried*.

Every time she's badgered me about something over the last year—*Are you eating? Can you get out of bed? Are you going to class?*—she was saying, *I care about you. I care. I care.* And all I heard was: *You're not good enough.*

I sit there in the silence, trying to process this. Trying to scrub off the shame that's pouring thickly over me now, like honey, smothering me. I wish I could take back everything I said to her on Sunday. Every furious word.

"I don't know what to say," Dad says, looking ashen. His arched eyebrows draw tight together. "I didn't realize . . . I didn't know you felt like this. Either of you."

"It's okay," Olivia says quickly. "I mean, I know it's hard since Mom left. It's just, sometimes I feel like we lost both of you. All I'm saying is, we need you back." My sister glances at me. "Well, I need you back, at least."

I don't need you, says that hard voice in the back of my head.

Guilt surges up. I sit in our dingy kitchen, stifled in silence, watching two people I've held back with all my might. And a million memories flutter through my mind, a storm of ticker tape. They overflow with color, like photographs edited to death. I remember trading grins with Olivia, her eyes the sort of ultra-saturated blue you see in thick paint. I remember waiting at the top of the steps on Christmas morning, back when green and red twined around the banister, and seeing Dad appear at the bottom of the steps, arms open, smile on. I remember being eight years old and tearing down the sidewalks of our cul-de-sac, the sunset a rich burgundy. Me and Olivia. Together since birth.

"I need you, too," I say. "Both of you."

My sister meets my eyes, and it's too much. Too personal, too loaded—too honest. I look down at my lap as Olivia glances toward the clock.

"Hang on," she says. "It's seven. Shouldn't you be at dress rehearsal?"

"I dropped out."

"You did *what*?"

"Yeah. On Monday. I had a sort of a freak-out." I swallow. "By which I mean I yelled at everyone. And quit the show."

Another long silence. I sneak a glance at Olivia, whose mouth is open. I guess she didn't think even I could go that far.

A long minute passes. She's clearly trying to think of something to say, but nothing comes out.

Then Dad says, "Stand up."

"What?"

He stands, fishing his keys out of his pocket. "You're going to your dress rehearsal," he says, his voice growing stronger.

"Dad, I can't go back there. I don't think you understand what I—"

"You're right," he says. "I don't understand, but I want to. I haven't been there. But that's changing now."

I stare at him. There's something familiar in his eyes. It's the fervor he used to get when talking about his weird sports finals, Wiffle Ball International or Watermelon Bowling. It's the sparkle he had when he would make a joke, wait for Mom to groan, and kiss her on the forehead triumphantly. It's from a younger year, and I didn't realize I'd missed it this whole time.

"Up," he says, heading for the door. "Let's go."

I meet Olivia's eyes. We stand and follow our father out the door.

I JOG UP TO THE GREENROOM DOOR, BUT AS I PULL it open, Emily smacks into me, about to exit. The rest of the cast stands behind her. The crew, too, all crowded into the greenroom. Did I interrupt some sort of preshow pep talk?

But nobody's in costume, and it's only a few minutes until the preshow music should start. Something in the air feels wrong. Too sober—none of the tense energy this place should have before a run-through.

I slip inside, letting the door close with a bang behind me.

"Kat?" Emily says. "What are you doing here?"

I swallow hard and look from cast to crew. Every pair of eyes stares at me with bald accusation, and I don't flinch. "I'm sorry," I blurt out. "I'm sorry for blowing up, and I'm sorry for walking out. I shouldn't ha—"

"It doesn't matter anymore," Emily says. "Mr. García isn't here."

My stomach plummets. "What? What do you mean? Is he sick?"

"No, h-he was in class and everything, but he—" Emily chews on a lock of her hair. "He hasn't shown up tonight. He said yesterday he was trying to find someone to replace you, and I guess he figured it was hopeless."

"But he wouldn't just not show," I say, but then a horrible idea sneaks into my head. He wouldn't miss dress rehearsal—unless he wasn't allowed to be here.

I remember the rumors that flooded the school on Monday about Lucas and Dr. Norman. I remember how tense, even desperate, García seemed in rehearsal that afternoon.

Did someone turn him in?

Everyone's attention presses in on me. I straighten up, filling my voice with resolve. "You know what?" I say. "It doesn't matter. So what if he's missing? We know the show."

Emily half raises her hand. "Are—are we allowed to be in here unsupervised?"

"Is anyone stopping us?"

"Well, no, but . . ." Emily says feebly, looking around at the cast. My stage husband trades a doubtful look with her.

"No," I say. "No *buts*." As I look around at these twenty uneasy faces, the empty space in my chest thickens, calcifying into a clot of determination. This is going to happen if I have to do the whole damn show myself.

I turn to the crew. "You guys sat through eight hours of tech on Sunday. Andrea, your set took so long to build. Crystal, you made all these sound effects from scratch. And, Lara, you've been in production meetings about this thing since the start of the year." I look back at the cast. "And God, you guys have put up with *me* for eight weeks, and *this* is the thing that makes you want to call it quits? That's bullshit." I fold my arms. "We all know what to do. So what if we're doing it for an empty theater tonight?"

There's a long pause. Then Emily says, "I mean . . . as long as nobody's stopping us, I guess . . . ?"

I smile at her. She looks as if she might pass out. It occurs to me that probably none of these people has ever seen me smile.

Lara says, "All right. Everyone, get into costume. Crystal, go start the preshow music. Half an hour until curtain goes up."

The cast doesn't say a word to me as we head downstairs to the changing rooms, but I catch them giving me glances. And for once, I don't wish they would stop. For once, I meet their eyes unafraid.

HELLO
my name is

CLAIRE LOMBARDI

ON THURSDAY, I WAKE UP WITH MY THOUGHTS KNOT-
ted and tangled. I hardly slept an hour.

I roll out of bed and smack my hair into place, wishing the impact would dislodge some of the clutter from my mind. I eye myself in the mirror. Have you ever felt as if your face isn't your own, but an elaborate forgery, a parody, maybe? The eyes staring out from the mirror don't look like mine. I've been disconnected from my reflection, unhooked, unmoored.

I don't line those eyes. I don't glue anything or brush anything or draw anything onto that girl. I walk downstairs barefaced for the first time in God knows how long.

"Claire bear, you okay?" Grace asks, stirring her oatmeal. She doesn't have class today, because apparently that's a thing in college, having no class for a whole day. "You look tired."

I tilt my head. My sister's sea green eyes shine. "Have you ever messed something up?" I ask, my voice gravelly with morning raspiness. "Like, so badly, it feels like you'll never fix it?"

"Of course."

"What was it?"

"That time junior year." Grace twines a lock of her sandy hair between her fingers. "I was driving home and hit Mr. Fausett's dog."

"But that was an accident."

"Still," she says, her voice shrinking by the word. "He had this look on his face . . . just, *God*, you know?"

"What did you do after?"

"Everything I could," she says. "Just everything I could, you know?"

The drive to school is a stupor. Pressure clutches my shoulders.

I consider turning back. Hiding in my bed. Hiding in the dark. Unwilling to face myself.

IN FIRST PERIOD, PRINCIPAL TURNER'S VOICE RINGS over the intercom. "May I please have your attention for the morning announcements?"

I look up at the black speaker, imagining her talking to Dr. Norman. Imagining him going home, thinking about what he might do if he lost his job. Is he married? Does he have a family? Has he had to tell them about this? And Lucas . . . I imagine myself yelling, *Lucas McCallum is now out of the closet* over that intercom, which is essentially what I did.

"Students and staff," Turner says, her voice heavy, "we have reached closure on the issue we spoke about during our assembly two weeks ago."

I freeze in my chair. They couldn't have found Dr. Norman guilty based on my twenty-second-long, cowardly impulse—that's impossible. There's no evidence.

Voices rise around me. Eager muttering. *Norman. Lucas. Norman.*

Turner goes on: "Our junior honors English teacher, Mr. David

García, has come forward and confessed to having a romantic relationship with a student."

Everything goes quiet. We all stare at the intercom, smacked into silence.

It's a testament to how much everyone liked Mr. García that people hardly joked about the idea of it being him.

"Disciplinary action has been taken," Turner says, "and Mr. García is under investigation by the police. We ask patience from all his classes while we locate a permanent substitute. A news station plans to arrive after school to ask questions of the student body. We ask that you remain respectful and truthful, and most importantly, that you disregard previous allegations, as they have no foundation in truth. Thank you for your attention."

When she goes quiet, part of me wants to cry with relief—and with remorse. Dr. Norman's job isn't on the line anymore. Maybe people will leave Lucas alone. Maybe this has undone some of the damage I did.

TEN MINUTES BEFORE SECOND PERIOD, THE HALLS are quiet. People have finally seemed to realize that this is a big deal. A teacher they liked is gone for good—is that what it takes?—but I still hear them murmuring about who the student could be. I don't hear Lucas's name once.

With every step I take toward the classroom where he sits, my insides twist tighter. My sneakers squeak on the freshly waxed floor, its chips of mica glaring at me like fireflies.

I knock into somebody and mutter a halfhearted apology without looking up. Then a hand is on my shoulder. I look up, and there's Juni, folding her arms.

"What's wrong?" she asks.

I don't bother trying to tell her it's nothing. With a pained look on her face, she steers me past the stairwell and out the side entrance.

"I have something to tell you, too," she says. "You want to go first?"

I shrug and think distractedly, *God, I need a thicker jacket. It's so cold out today.*

"Okay," she says. "Explain."

"No, I . . ." I stare down at my shoes.

"Tell me what's up, Claire. Please. Look at me."

It's hard to look up, and when I do, she has that sternness in her eyes. She cares fiercely, Juni. I feel as if she knows already. I hate her for it. I love her for it.

A plane hums overhead, leaving whiskers of white exhaust behind. The breeze sighs in my ear. "I did something bad," I say. "You know how Lucas . . . you know how people thought he was the one who . . . ?"

"Yeah."

"That was me. I turned in a form saying it was him."

Her eyes go wide.

Words keep rushing out of my mouth. "I wasn't thinking, I—I got angry, and I couldn't talk with anyone, and I—"

"You could've talked to me. I know we fought, but you still could have—"

"No, I couldn't have," I burst out. Her mouth closes, and I rush on. "I'm so tired, Juni. Don't you get it? I lost it with you two last week because I'm sick to death of you guys being so much better than me, Olivia drowning in attention, you being so fucking *perfect!*"

My words spiral out into the sky. Huge and irretrievable.

I breathe hard. White mist uncoils before me in the cold.

She's about to say we're done—I know it. Between this and my not calling her when she got out of the hospital—she's going to friend-dump me, and I'll be alone, and I'll deserve it, won't I? Won't I deserve it?

"I thought you knew me better than that," she says quietly.

I try to swallow. My tongue is harsh and dry. "That's why I didn't call on Sunday. When I heard you landed in the hospital, I . . . God, it's horrible. But part of me was like *finally*, you know? She finally does something that doesn't make the rest of us feel inadequate. Make me feel inadequate."

Her eyes crease with—is that sympathy? I can't look long.

"And it's not just that you're so smart, and that everybody's in love with you, and that you're amazing at everything you do. I mean, that'd sure as hell be enough, but it's—it's the way you *act*." I look down at my sneakers. "When you sleep over, when it's the three of us . . . even in private, you're never mean. You're never insecure or angry or . . . how do you *do* it? How are you *real*, you know? Years of us being friends, and I still feel like it's not fair, that somebody can be so—"

"Claire," Juniper says, "it was me."

"What was you?"

"Mr. García. He was with me."

Something ruptures in my chest. I stare. Her gray eyes are calm and serious.

The knots in my mind come loose, unleashing the force of a million memories.

Strangely, the first thing that comes to mind is the mess of frizzy hair I had in fourth grade; I remember wanting miles of flowing blond hair, Cinderella's or Rapunzel's or Juniper Kipling's, because even back then she was the golden girl.

I remember starting to detest my eyes in the mirror, their color, their shape, their short lashes. I remember sixth grade, the stick-thin prepubescent frames of the popular girls, Juniper the most graceful and most beautiful of all. I remember wanting to be like her so viciously, so fiercely, that when we first became friends, I dreamed that I could absorb something of her into myself, relinquish who I was and what I'd been given.

I remember last May, the end of sophomore year. One day Juniper was joking that Lucas and I would be engaged soon. The next day, he dumped me. When it ended, the choke-chain of a million clichés constricted around my throat, and I didn't—couldn't—speak about it. Heartbreak reduces you to what a million other people have suffered a million times before.

I remember feeling too much, and then feeling nothing, and when my heart turned back on, it had a blinking red light to warn off anyone who might try to get close. I remember staring at Juniper, wondering how her hair fell just so. How long had she spent on it? I started wondering where Olivia got her allure. Was it something she bought? Something she sacrificed her integrity for? That had to be it, right? Little by little, my makeup turned from self-expression to war paint, and day by day, my jokes turned into fine-tipped barbs.

And now, staring into Juni's eyes, it feels like I could summon up every tiny jealousy, every tiny hatred of the last six months. Comparing my grades to Juni's, my height and weight to Olivia's, my eyes and skin and face to theirs. As if it were a contest.

As if we were placed on two sides of a scale, and I could never measure up.

All my preoccupations, all these months, and here Juni's been, hiding the secret of a lifetime, not sparing so much as a moment to pit herself against me.

"Oh my God," I choke, tears burning at the back of my throat.

"Nobody's perfect, Claire. Everybody's got shit they want, shit they can't have, and shit they've got to deal with. You know that." Juni hoists her backpack higher on her shoulder. "I'm no different. Do you understand how often I've wished I were you or Olivia since summer? How much simpler things would've been?"

I could sink into the ground. I have been so resolutely blind.

The tears spill over. "I—I'm so sorry," I hiccup. "I'm sorry, I'm sorry—"

She hushes me gently. "I miss you," she says. "I miss *us*. I don't want you to be anybody else, and I'm not expecting you to do everything right. I sure don't do everything right." A line draws down between her eyebrows. "But what you did to Lucas, that's wrong. That's not you, Claire—who is that?"

"I don't know." I sniff. Look up at the sky. It swims. "I would do anything to take it back. G-God, it was twenty seconds and he's going to deal with that for the rest of high school. The rest of his life. It'll be one of his coming-out stories, and it'll be the most horrible one." I wipe my face. Wipe the tears from beneath my eyes. "Shit, I don't know what to do."

Juniper tilts her head. "You always know more than you give yourself credit for," she says. "I'm sure you know what to do."

Everything I can, says Grace's voice in the back of my head.

Looking at Juni, I take a too-deep breath. Tears dry on my

cheeks, and pain needles the bottom of my lungs. "I'll find you later, okay? Can I do that?"

"Yes. Yes, of course," Juni says, her voice shot through with relief.

I smile. It's weak but genuine. I feel like somebody who hasn't stood in months, finding her feet under her again. Complete with the rush of blood from my head. "Okay. I will. I'll see you."

Then I head inside. Down the hall, toward the office, gaining speed. I gather my courage, clenching it in my fists, ready to tell them that I'm the one who lied.

HELLO
my name is

VALENTINE SIMMONS

I HURRY UP TO THE ARCHWAY THAT LEADS INTO THE lunchroom. I hate eating here, hate it more than bad traffic and bullies combined, but after three days, I still don't know what to say to Lucas about Monday. My method of resolute avoidance has worked so far.

As I approach the arch, a nasal-sounding voice says behind me, "Hey, look who it is."

I turn. "Dean." I step to the side of the arch, allowing the traffic to pass us. The bridge of his nose is thick and red. I say, "I'll accept your apology anytime."

He laughs. "Apology? You think I owe you an apology?"

"Yes." I fold my arms. "I said it wasn't true, what everyone was saying about Lucas. So I was right. So you can apologize anytime."

"You are really asking for it." He moves forward, and I stand my ground, preparing to duck and run the second his curled fists move.

"Stop," says a tired voice. Lucas's voice. I turn toward him.

As people pass, they avoid his eyes. Most look embarrassed, and rightfully so, given what they've been saying since Monday. "Stop, Valentine," Lucas says. "Don't."

I point at Dean. "But he keeps saying you're—"

"He's right."

I flounder. "W-what?"

"I am?" Dean says.

"Sort of." Lucas digs his hands into his pockets. "I'm not gay, but I'm pansexual, which is like—it's a little like bisexual, but—"

"I know what it is," I break in.

"Great," Dean says. "So I was right, Simmons. So take *this* back." He points at his nose.

I round on him, narrowing my eyes. "I didn't punch you for saying he was gay, you cretin. I punched you because you were being an asshole about it."

"Whatever. I don't need this." Dean gives Lucas a scathing look as he stalks toward the archway. "Glad the season's over."

We both look after him for a second; then Lucas moves toward an empty classroom nearby. I follow him inside, and he shuts the door, locking out the sound. We stay quiet for a minute, and then I clear my throat, feeling strange. "You're . . . and you never told your swimming friends?"

He rolls his shoulders in that easy shrug. "I was scared," he says, as if it's nothing, as if admitting you're scared isn't gut-wrenchingly personal.

"Why did you tell Dean the truth, then?" I ask. "He would've believed it was a rumor."

Lucas's smile twists. It looks painful. "I wanted it back in my own hands, man. Didn't want to start lying all over again." He runs a hand through his hair. "By the way, we don't have to talk if you don't want to. I—I can go; I don't want to make things awkward for you."

"What, like I'm going to get all, *no homo?*"

"I don't know. Maybe. Yes."

"Go ahead and homo," I say dryly. "I couldn't care less."

He lets out a deep sigh. "Oh, thank goodness. After Monday, I thought you were . . ."

"Yes?"

"I don't know. Not interested."

"No," I say, not quite grasping his expression. Caution, maybe? "You're still interesting," I say. "I avoided you because I doubted you'd take kindly to my punching—"

He leans down and kisses me.

It feels like I thought it would. Skin on lips, lips on skin. Of all things, the closeness is the strangest: the knowledge that Lucas's mind is inches from mine, churning with his skipping, jumping thoughts, compiling lists and collections, cataloging everything that's happening even now. He tilts his head, his nose presses into my cheek, and his hand finds the back of my head. One of his big, sturdy arms circles my back. It is too much sensation, almost, to process.

I frown as the kiss deepens, his tongue sliding against mine. Odd feeling. I wait for something new to happen in my head, something different.

Eventually, he pulls back, and his hand falls from my hair. "You're not into it," he says as I inhale slowly. The taste of him is cold on my lips, tingling mint. Not unpleasant. Not life-changing. Just another experience.

"Because I'm into you," he says, his eyes holding mine. They are darker than I'd realized, spokes of dark chocolate on oil. "Really into you, Valentine."

I sway. My cheeks burn. "Right. I sort of gathered that from the. Um. Yes."

"And you . . ."

"I don't . . . I'm not . . ."

"Right. You're not into guys," he says, disappointment settling onto his face.

Frustration mounts in my chest. He's attractive; that's obvious. I've never connected with a human being the way I have with him. And still—*still* . . . "I'm not into anyone," I say desperately. "I don't know if it's because I've hardly had a friend, or what, but conceptualizing crushes has always been a problem, and I just—I don't." The words stick in my throat. I say them again, a broken record spitting broken words: "I don't."

"But . . . but I want you." He sounds lost and confused, like a child.

I hold my ground. "Well, I don't know what to do with that."

"Oh." Little by little, the disappointment vacates his expression, leaving him sober and unsmiling. I wait for a frustrated explosion, but Lucas just rubs his brow, seeming worlds away. "And it isn't going to change," he says.

"No. As far as I can tell."

"Right." Lucas's eyes lift to mine, hopeful. "In that case, what do you think about going back to how things were?"

I frown, taken aback. "You—you want to?"

"Why would I not?"

"Because you have feelings for me, and I don't return them."

"If you're okay with that, I can be, too," he says. "Might take me a bit, but . . . yeah." He smiles and extends a hand. "Friends?"

I look at Lucas, disbelieving. In under a week, he has lost his swim team posse, endured rumors about sleeping with a teacher, been forced out of the closet, and been turned down by *me*, of all people. And here he is with a smile on his face, one hand tucked into his North Face jacket, his journal sticking out of his backpack. Cool Lucas, handsome Lucas, overeager and optimistic Lucas. Mr. Sunny-Side-Up.

I take his hand. I want to say, *Thank you*; I want to say, *I'm sorry*; I want to say, *You are some sort of strange miracle.* "Yeah," is what I say. "Yeah. Friends."

THERE'S NEVER BEEN A SLOWER THURSDAY, I THINK, watching the clock. Usually I don't even sense my afternoon hours slipping by as my lunchtime high wears off, but I haven't smoked this whole week, and it's throwing me off timewise.

There's especially never been a slower last thirty seconds of seventh period on a Thursday. The second hand creeps sluggishly along its path, millimeter by millimeter, and when it hits *12* and the bell rings, I'm the first one out of my seat, bolting for the door.

I forge down the hall, against the tide of people surging toward the stairwell, and as I cross the arch where the old wing intersects the new wing, the halls empty little by little, leaving a few people standing at lockers, a few others heading into classrooms for after-school meetings, and one tall girl standing at the plate-glass windows looking out over the green. The light makes her eyes glint like rhinestones. The long rays of afternoon sun wash her profile in sharp relief, casting shadows from her arched eyebrows down over her eyes, and as she looks at me, she smiles, and the sight of it does something awful to the inside of my stomach.

I stop in front of her. She doesn't look anywhere near as nervous as I feel, with that easy smile playing across her lips. Unable to hold her eyes, I glance out the wide window. Paloma High is one of the tallest buildings for miles, and from here, I can see halfway across town. It seems minuscule, roads twining like veins through green little enclosures, each tiny house somebody's unknown world, and if I squint, I swear I could see my own.

"Hey," Olivia says, and I'm like, "Hi," wishing we'd picked somewhere we could be alone instead of the middle of the hall. Bit by bit, her attention erases the world around me altogether.

"Is Juniper doing okay?" I ask, once I remember that Olivia's smile isn't the only thing that exists.

"Yeah. She had to deal with the police, but she's got her head on her shoulders."

"And you're all right?"

"I . . . yeah." She twists a lock of hair around her finger. "I talked to my sister and my dad last night. Talked-talked," and I say, "Yeah?" and she says, "We're trying to work things out. I think it's going to happen this time."

"Your sister's in the play, right?" I say, remembering the lunchtime announcements. Kat's voice drawled out of the intercom, inviting us to *The Hidden Things*, by some Russian guy.

"She's the lead," Olivia says proudly. "And she found them a new faculty advisor last-minute." Her smile fades. "How about—how'd your parent talk go?"

"I don't know," I say. "I told them I was freaked out about Russ. And they were all, yeah, us, too, which . . . I never thought about that, dumb as that sounds, thought about them being worried.

They seem so angry all the time, it sort of drowns out the rest." I shrug. "I asked if they'd thought about trying again, but it's not happening. I got to the game too late."

My voice drops. "It's just . . . I thought if I tried, for once, I could fix something, you know?" I glance out the window at the horizon, at the fast-moving clouds that glide like swans across the flat countryside. "I don't know. Change is the worst. With everything happening around you, and you can't slow it down or correct it and you can't even get a hold of it, like, why it's happening, and it all feels like . . . you know, what the hell *can* you do?"

"I don't know," she says. "But just because you can't fix everything, that doesn't mean you shouldn't give a shit, and it sure doesn't mean you shouldn't try."

"I know," I say, counting the inches between us. The world is disappearing again, patch by patch, leaving only her.

"Hey, I want to show you something," she says. "Come on." She leads me down the hall. We turn a corner into a side hall, and she opens a door. I peer inside. It's a storage closet filled with old textbooks and stacks of yellowing paper, and I'm like, "What—" and then her hand grabs mine, warm and tight, and she tugs me inside and shuts the door. Darkness drops, and her other hand lands on my chest. She presses me back into the door, her head tilted up, and her lips are half an inch from mine in the dark. I feel her breath. I can hardly see her anymore. Some part of her body brushes my hip, and my body's electrified. Her hand trails over mine—fingers to palm, palm to wrist, up my forearm with torturous slowness—and fastens around my biceps.

"Hey," she whispers, and the tiny exhalation darts over my lips. "So . . . yeah? Are we . . ."

I lean forward, and the gap between us vanishes.

Her lips are ChapSticked and taste like lemon. She kisses me hungrily, her teeth pulling at my lip and her tongue flicking against mine, and I rest my hands on her waist, containing her, feeling her movement as we twist our way out of our backpacks between kisses. As they fall to the floor, I fit my hand into the small of her back and draw her close, my other hand curling around the nape of her neck, slipping up, tangling in her long hair. She's so tight against me, I feel her every curve. Her chest presses against me as she breathes. My body pulses with heat.

Olivia knows what she's doing to me; it's more obvious every second. As I lift the hem of her T-shirt, thumbing the smooth skin of her hip, her lips move down to my jaw. I tilt my chin, letting her drop kisses on my Adam's apple, letting her nip at every nerve ending I didn't know I had. Her teeth tease the juncture between my jaw and my neck, and I let out a low, frustrated sound that struggles through the silence, and when she kisses me again, I feel her smiling.

I push gently, backing her up against the shelves, and my hand's under her shirt now, sliding up from her hip to the rough lace of her bra, her breast full and heavy in my hand. My mind is a blank roar, filled with sensation. She kisses me harder, her hands wound into the back of my shirt as if she's going to tear through it, and something boils urgently in my stomach, forming clouds of steam in my head, and my heart pounds as if it's trying to kick its way through the front of my chest. The lemony taste of her is mixed with some intoxicating, bittersweet scent coming from the volumes of brown hair that fall over her shoulders. She's holding on to me so tight, painfully tight, the way someone nervous might hold on to the edge of their seat, and as my eyes adjust to the darkness, I start catching glimpses of her in shadows and grays, her strongly bridged nose and her wet-kissed lips, and when I close my eyes again and kiss her hard, she makes this high, tiny sound into my mouth that gets me so turned on, I can barely move.

"Fuck," I say, and I pull back. She says, "Thoughts?" and I say, "Thinking is sort of an issue right now," and she says, "Take your time," all casual, as if she didn't just provide me with the most life-fulfillingly hot experience I've ever had, and I feel all blushing and virginal, and words fall out of my mouth in an incompetent blob: "Hey, so can we, like, be dating?"

She grins. "Sure, we can, like, be dating," she says, "although that's the most passive possible way to phrase that question," and I say, "Okay. I want to be your boyfriend. I want you to be my girlfriend. I want you," and she says, "Hmm. Do you really?" and through her coy, teasing tone I hear something real, some tiny kernel of fear that I want something other than just to be with her, as if that were even a glimmer in the eye of possibility.

"I promise," I say. I want to say I would promise her the world, if I could make good on it. I want to tell her that nothing and no one before her could make me keep a promise, and now I never want to break one. For once, she's quiet. I kiss her forehead, and her breath on my collarbones makes me shiver. "Promise," I say. I kiss her nose, her cheeks, her lips. "Promise. Promise. Promise."

HELLO
my name is

KAT SCOTT

FOCUS.

There's silence backstage. Silence from the other actors, and silence in my head.

Everything is still except for Emily, who stands onstage, her voice brighter and more dynamic than it's ever been. She's a spot of color tracing her way through the monologue with gesture and heart, bravely carving out every second of intention.

"—and I'm tired of waiting," she finishes, triumphant. I let the silence ring for a second, her voice reverberating over the opening-night audience. Good crowd tonight. They don't laugh more than they need to. Always good, when ninety-nine percent of your show is as depressing as all hell.

I walk onstage. "*You're* tired of waiting?" I say. Emily steps back, her face filling with shame. "You're tired of waiting," I repeat. "You, Natalya, who left me in this town?"

The lines feel different tonight. I'm not using them like weapons anymore, not using them like hammers of guilt to slam into Emily's character. Tonight, something trembles in my voice and in my hands, and I feel like I'm pleading. "Look at me. Look at what I am now."

"I am looking at you," she says.

"Look harder."

"I see a loving mother, a caring sister. I see—"

"You see nothing," I insist. "I am nothing anymore except wasted potential. Nothing!"

I wait. Waiting, I realize, for her character to contradict me. But she doesn't.

I step forward, and my hands come up of their own volition, cupped as if holding water. "You were supposed to be my teacher. You said I was brilliant—a prodigy, you said. You were supposed to take me away, teach me everything, but instead you ran the first chance you had!"

My voice peaks, cracking. My heart beats hard. I haven't left myself backstage this time. Kat Scott is all here, every ugly fissure and scar laid bare by the stage lights. Every chunk of desperation and anger from the last two and a half years is here, bleeding out in front of the crowd. Every way I've ever felt abandoned is crashing out from me.

I let the silence hang for a long moment. I tuck my hair back into place, and my voice falls, quavering. "And you come back and say you're tired of waiting. You hypocrite."

"I'm sorry, Faina," she says, and as it comes out, I realize Mr. García was right. I didn't want her to say she's sorry. I wanted her embrace, her comfort. I wanted her to promise I could still have everything I ever wanted from her.

But instead she gave me a feeble apology. As if that could ever patch over what she did.

I shake my head and back offstage, still unsatisfied.

. . . .

Ani remembers every move she's supposed to make. Elizabeth hits the center of every pool of light. I don't know what we did to please the theater gods, but the show goes off like chain lightning, each line crackling one to the next, each scene tenser and more electric than the one before.

Finally, the last scene starts. I enter the old schoolhouse at sunset. The mass of gray threads that makes up our backdrop is stained with light, dappled bloody orange. As I enter, the specials up front brighten, pouring down onto me like red paint.

"Faina," Emily says. She stands at the chalkboard, writing the beginnings of an equation.

"Natalya," I greet her.

"I thought I might see you here. I thought you might be back."

"I always come back to this place."

She smiles. "Did you know I would be here?"

"I supposed." A beat passes before I add, "But I must go home soon for dinner. My daughter is awful at cooking. She'll have to marry someone who cooks, or she'll starve."

"How old is she?" Emily asks.

"Nearly fifteen."

"Is she still in school?"

"Yes," I say. "Good child, but she doesn't have my mind or my husband's determination. She does write well. That, she can do. The younger one, now—the younger one has a mind for math. I can tell, young as she is."

Bits of chalk crumble off as Emily scrawls up square roots and summation signs.

I let the words tremble at the front of my lips for a moment before they burst forward. "I thought of you as a mother, you know," I say. The momentum of it carries me toward her step by step, but she doesn't face me. "I was young. I thought the world of you. I thought you cared."

"I did, Faina," Emily says, sounding dazed. Engrossed in what she's writing. "I did care for you, and yes, there were times I thought of you as my own child. But . . ." At last, she finishes the huge equation. She stands back, admiring it, and turns to me. "What do you think?"

I swallow hard, scanning the chalkboard. My index finger brushes the last term. I pick up the chalk and trace the tiny piece of the line I erased. "It's beautiful. It's beautiful work."

"So you see why I had to go?" she says. "Why I had to resume my research?"

"No, I don't. But it is still beautiful work." I let the chalk drop to the stage. With a crisp little snap, it breaks in two. I look down at it for a moment. The space shared between Emily and me hangs heavy, and my heart beats hard. Her age makeup is dark in the spotlight, whitish bags drawn under her eyes and creases pressed in at the sides of her nose.

The apology spreads across her face. Emily approaches me, and anticipation prickles at my palms. Finally, she'll try to take me back and keep every promise she ever made.

"Do you want me to show you the rest?" she says. "I could try to find a way. I could go back and ask the other professors if you could join us at the university. I could—"

"Mama?" says a voice. I turn, and my daughter enters. "I did it," she says. "I made dinner. And—and we are all waiting for you at home."

I study Ani, struck by the hopefulness in her voice. The plea for acceptance and love. For one second, I swear to God her blue eyes look like my sister's.

All at once, I understand what García meant when he asked me to rethink the end of the show. This play doesn't close with my character's defeat. I might have hoped for something years ago, but in the meantime, I found something else beautiful. Something that I haven't valued until the closing scene.

What I saw this whole time as an obligation to my family isn't an obligation—it's a privilege. And at the end, I'm finally happy to have it. Lucky, even.

I'm lucky.

"Thank you, sweetheart," I say to Ani, choking on the words. I turn back to Emily. "No," I say. "I can't go with you."

"But—"

"I won't go," I say, and it's not resignation this time. It's self-acceptance. Here, I choose to love what I have. Here, I choose to love what I am now.

Walking away from Emily, I half smile. My cheeks are wet and cold with salt and water.

As I exit, the curtain collapses toward the stage, billowing down as if in exhaustion. The dark smack of applause thunders out in the audience like heavy, cleansing rain.

HELLO
my name is

JUNIPER KIPLING

I imagine
him next week, driving I-70 East,
steady hands, steady wheel,
steady pace,
steadily disappearing.

I imagine
myself next year, walking a stage,
steady feet, steady breath,
steady pace,
steadily myself.
And what will I remember about his eyes
besides that they had him inside,
and they made me feel some sort of way—
sick with hope?

I imagine
Hemingway and Beukes, Christie and Martin,
Márquez and Morrison, Rowling and the Bard
boxed and taped and stacked beside a spare wheel.

His emptied house would barely fill a car—
he was built to carry his home on his back.

I imagine
futures with him and futures without.
But on Thursday night, I don't dream of him.
I dream of a city made from violin strings and Saran wrap,
bubbling in the heat of a summer sun.
I dream of voices I haven't heard yet
and haven't missed yet;
of places I haven't known,
pieces I haven't played,
and people I haven't loved.
I wake up to music, an alarm-clock croon,
and I stare at my ceiling,
serene.

I think I'm beginning to understand
how hearts fit together.
Not like diseased carnations that lean against their crutches.
Not like vines that twine tight, throttling their hosts.
But like two trees:
two systems of deep, untangled roots,
two patterns of flowering branches,
whose leaves drink their own sunlight
and breathe their own air.
Two trees with something slung between them,
a hammock or a tapestry or a swing,
some third, beautiful thing

that neither would die without.
Hearts fit together like hands.
Not by necessity.
By choice.

"HO-LIVIA," SAYS A GUY'S VOICE FROM BEHIND ME.

My mouth full of green beans, I glance over my shoulder, determined to chew very angrily at whoever was responsible for the 'ho-livia' comment. But alas, the fast-moving stream of kids passing through this channel in the cafeteria has masked his identity. Resolving to chew angrily at him some other time, I turn back around.

"Yo," Matt calls after the dude.

"Not worth it," I say. Matt sighs, slouching back down, doodling faces on his History notes. On his other side, Burke Fischer has his septum-pierced nose buried in Kierkegaard.

"What'd they say?" Juni asks me over the cafeteria table. "I didn't catch whatever profoundly unnecessary insult it was."

"*Ho*-livia," I explain over the chatter echoing off the cafeteria ceiling. "It's funny, because *ho* means *whore* and also rhymes with the first syllable of my name. Ha-ha. Excellent joke."

"Don't let it get to you," Juni says. "You look tired, lady."

I make a grumbling noise. "'Tired' is the understatement of the year." I point at Kat, who sits beside Juni. "You didn't tell me your show was, like, ninety-seven percent crushing misery."

She shrugs, slurping from her juice box. "It's Russian."

Someone taps my shoulder. I turn again, wondering if ho-boy has returned, but no.

"Claire. I—hey," I say, setting down my fork on my lunch tray. Juniper told me about their conversation yesterday, but Claire never found us during lunch. I hope to God she was apologizing to Lucas.

"Mind if I sit?" she asks, every word a tentative little push.

"Sure."

She perches on the blue plastic disk to my right. A wisp of hair slips out above her ear. "I get it. I think."

"Get what?"

She lowers her voice. "Why it's not fair if guys expect . . . things from you. It's that they shouldn't respect you less whatever your choices are, and, um, neither should I." She swallows. "What I'm trying to say is, sorry. For judging you. And I'm going to stop."

Gratitude warms me. Knowing Claire, this is the hardest thing she's ever done. "You practice that in the mirror?" I tease, keeping it gentle.

The skin behind her freckles flushes deep red. "Maybe." She looks back and forth between Juniper and me. "I was also thinking, um—it's been a while since the three of us hung out. Do you guys want to come over after I get home from practice?"

Claire's cheek is puckering from where she's biting it. Jeez. I haven't seen her this nervous since tennis tryouts freshman year.

"Sure," I say. "But only if, one, we watch *Parks and Rec*, and two, you stop talking to us like we're going to break."

"What?"

"Claire." I knock her softly on the shoulder. "*Claire.* We're good, okay?"

It takes a minute for the words to struggle off her tongue: "We're good?"

"I mean, I'm good," Juni says.

"And I haven't been this good in a while," I say. "So if you're yourself again, and if you're good, then by definition our little trio is, in fact, all good."

"I . . . okay." I swear, I feel the relief rolling off her, a gentle wave. A smile spreads across her face. "Then we're good," she says, and her voice evolves back into its brisk, businesslike self. "Also, do you guys think you'll come to Young Environmentalists? Because I have all these brochures. I printed out, like, a hundred, and—"

"That's a lot of ink," I say.

Humor glimmers in Claire's eyes. "I'm aware."

"Well," I say with my cheekiest grin, "given the point of Young Environmentalists, that seems to be sort of a problematic waste of resources, wouldn't you say?"

"I would say that you're sort of a problematic waste of oxygen," Claire says dryly, and my smile widens. She's back.

Principal Turner's voice blares over the speaker. "May I have your attention for the announcement of the class presidents?"

Claire straightens up eagerly, my sister rolls her eyes, and Burke says, "Oh shit," looking from candidate to candidate.

"Twenty bucks says Juniper wins," Matt says.

Juniper grimaces. "Twenty bucks says *you* win."

"Yeah, seriously," I say. "Your posters were so terrible, they crossed the barrier into being sort of hilarious."

"Thanks," Matt says. "I think."

Turner clears her throat. The intercom whines. "The freshman president is Xavier Lee."

A table across the cafeteria breaks into cheers. A smatter of clapping drifts through the rest of the room, devoid of enthusiasm. Claire applauds politely.

"Pretty sure freshmen are incapable of self-rule," I say.

Matt nods. "Give them a dictator. Juniper can add that to the list of shit to do when she wins."

I catch the end of some kid's name. Tragically, we've missed the announcement of the sophomore president. Then Turner says, "The junior class president is Matt Jackson."

Matt's eyes widen, and I punch the air. "Called it," I say over the senior announcement. "Twenty bucks for me and Juniper. You owe us a crisp Jackson, Jackson."

"This concludes today's announcements," Turner says. "Have a happy Thanksgiving break." More people clap and cheer at the Thanksgiving break mention than they did for the presidents.

Matt swats at Burke, who seems to be asphyxiating from laughter. "What the hell?" Matt says. "How does this make sense? I didn't campaign for shit."

With a serene smile, Juniper returns to her food. "Don't let the power go to your head."

As I look around the table, a smile starts in my chest and swells up and up, lifting the world a little.

My attention wanders from our table to the next, where a girl with bleached-blond hair is frantically turning pages in a chemistry textbook, and to the table across the aisle, where two guys stir ketchup into their milk boxes. Hundreds of voices bounce off the tiled floor, off the chipping mural on the cinder-block walls, sounds lost as soon as they're made. Maybe my name is still mixed in there somewhere—I don't know—but I don't care anymore. Because I can think back three weeks to my family's silence, to Claire's resentment, to Juniper's secret, and it all seems buried impossibly deep in the past. We are always moving forward—I can see it now. We are hurtling through our lives. We are never standing still.

about the author

RILEY REDGATE graduated from Kenyon College in Gambier, Ohio, with a degree in economics. *Noteworthy* is her second novel. She currently lives and writes in Winston-Salem, North Carolina. Visit the author at rileyredgate.com.

acknowledgments

I OWE THIS BOOK TO: MY EDITOR, ANNE HELTZEL, FOR her keen vision; the team at Amulet for their talent and enthusiasm; and my agent, Caryn Wiseman, for her insight and perseverance.

I owe my sanity to: the Goat Posse, whose name is lighthearted and whose love is wholehearted; the Tumblr community, who comfort me even when I'm objectively horrible; and the amazing writers I met through AgentQuery Connect, especially Stephanie Diaz, R. C. Lewis, Mindy McGinnis, Michelle Reed, and MarcyKate Connolly.

I owe everything else to: my parents, whose love and patience are unfathomable; my sister, whose wit and vivacity I can only aspire to; and my friends, who are the world to me.

Also, to Abrams interns Lauryn McSpadden and Kristen Barrett for their enthusiasm during acquisitions. I can't thank you enough! Your support means so much.

Read on for a sneak peek
into Riley Redgate's second
novel, *Noteworthy*

ALLEGRETTO

MONDAY MORNING WAS THE WORST POSSIBLE TIME to have an existential crisis, I decided on a Monday morning, while having an existential crisis.

Ideal crisis hours were obviously Friday afternoons, because you had a full weekend afterward to turn back into a person. You could get away with Saturday if you were efficient about it. Mondays, though—on Mondays, you had to size up the tsunami of work that loomed in the near distance and cobble together a survival strategy. There was no time for the crisis cycle: 1) teary breakdown, 2) self-indulgent wallowing, 3) questioning whether life had meaning, and 4) limping toward recovery. Four nifty stages. Like the water cycle, but soul-crushing.

I scanned the list posted on the stage door for the sixth time, hoping my eyesight had mysteriously failed me the first five times. Nope. No magical appearance of a callback for Jordan Sun, junior. I was a reject, like last year, and the year before.

I moved away from the stage door with dreamy slowness. My fellow rejects and I drifted down the hall, unspeaking. Katie Woods wore a hollow, shocked expression, as if she'd just seen somebody get mauled by a bear. Ash Crawford moved with the dangerous tension of someone who itched to smash a set of plates against a wall.

All normal. At the Kensington-Blaine Academy for the Performing Arts, half the students would have slit throats for parts in shows, dance pieces, and symphonic ensembles—anything to polish that NYU or Juilliard application to the blinding gleam the admissions officers wanted. Kensington loved its hyphenated adjectives: college-preparatory, cross-curricular, objective-oriented. "Low-stress" was not one of them. Every few days, you heard some kid crying and hyperventilating in the library bathroom. I, like any reasonable person, saved the crying and hyperventilating for my dorm.

Another failed audition. I could already hear my mom releasing the frustrated sigh that spoke more clearly than words: *This place wasn't meant for you.*

Familiar anxieties seeped in: that I should be back in San Francisco, working, making myself useful to my parents. That being here was a vanity project. That, as always, I didn't belong.

There was something alienating about being on scholarship, a tense mixture of gratefulness and otherness. *You're talented*, the money said, *and we want you here.* Still, it had the tang of *You were, are, and always will be different.* I was from a different world than most Kensington kids—I'd never been the Victorian two-story in Western Massachusetts or the charming Georgian in the DC suburb. I was a cramped apartment in an anonymous brick building with a dripping air conditioner, stationed deep in the guts of the West Coast, and I'd landed here by some freak combination of providence and ambition. And I never forgot it.

I exited the cool depths of Palmer Hall onto a landscape of deep green and blissful blue. Ahead, marble steps broadened, rolling down to the theater quad's long parabola of grass. To the left and right, Douglass Hall and Burgess Hall flanked the quad, long twin buildings made of sandstone that glowed gold with noon. Nestled in the far north of New York state, a long drive from anything but fields and forest, Kensington in early autumn was the sort of beautiful that begged for attention.

Hot wind fluttered through the quad, dry heat that brought goosebumps rippling up my arms. I stood still, my too-small sneakers warming in the sunshine, as a stream of traffic maneuvered its way around me, confident hands fitting Ray-Bans over squinting eyes, shoulders shrugging off layers to soak in the heat. Neatly layered hair cascaded over even tans. Highlights snatched the sun and tossed back an angry gleam.

Over the banister, a line of backpacks wriggled up-campus toward the dining hall. I stayed put. I never skipped meals at school, but something had gone wrong with my stomach. Namely, it didn't seem to be there anymore, and wherever it had gone, my heart and lungs and the rest of my vital organs had danced merrily after it. Holding the full interior of my body was the dull roar of a single thought: *Fix this.*

I rocked forward on the balls of my feet like a racer before the starting gun. I tried to take steady breaths. All this excess energy, all this drive to get something done, and nowhere to funnel it. Zero options. I would have kidnapped the cast and deported them to Slovenia, but I didn't have sixteen thousand dollars for plane tickets. I would have sabotaged the light board and blackmailed the department into giving me a part, but I wasn't an asshole. I would have bribed the director with my eternal love, but she was Reese Garrison, dean of the School of Theater, and I couldn't think of anything that probably meant less to her than my affection.

I squinted back up at Palmer Hall, its peaks and crevices blacked out against that signature blue sky. Reese had posted the list only twenty minutes ago. If I caught her in her office, maybe I could wring some audition feedback out of the endless supply of needle-sharp comments that constituted conversations with her.

Given her entire personality, I didn't know why I was so sure that Reese, at the heart of everything, wanted us to do well. Maybe it was because she respected wanting something, and there was nothing I did better than want.

With a squeak of rubber on marble, I turned on my heel and walked back inside.

♫

Like all the offices on the top floor of Palmer Hall, Reese's was sterilized white and too bright for comfort, small lights gleaming down from on high. At best, it gave off the atmosphere of a hospital room. At worst, an interrogation chamber from a 1970s cop movie.

Behind a cluttered desk, Reese adjusted her silver-gray frames. Her lined eyes glowed up at me, amplified by thick glass. The lady had a way of making everyone feel the height of your average garden gnome, even those of us who stood five foot ten. She never got less terrifying, but you could get used to it, in the way that when you watch the same horror movie repeatedly, the jump scares start to lose their sting.

"I hope," she said, "that you're not here to ask me to reconsider."

"Heh, like that would work." It came out before I realized what I was saying, and as Reese's lips thinned, my life flashed before my eyes. It seemed shorter and more boring than I would've preferred. "Sorry!" I added. "Sorry, sorry."

I spent half my life whipping up apologies on behalf of my mouth, which I considered to be kind of separate from me as a person. I, Jordan Sun, valued levelheadedness, and also other human beings. Jordan Sun's Mouth did not care about either of these things. All it wanted was to be quick on the uptake, and the only people it behaved around were my parents. You had to be completely unhinged, borderline masochistic, to sass my mom and dad.

But the same went for Reese. Maybe I'd gotten too familiar—I'd known her from my first day at Kensington, first as a teacher, and now as a housemother. The old housemother of Burgess Hall, the frighteningly ancient Mrs. Overgard, had gotten around to retiring at last, which meant that Reese lived three doors down from me this year, tasked with overseeing the dorm. This was a bit like living three doors down from a swarm of enraged hornets. Her definition of "quiet hours" was "if I hear music even one second after 11:00 p.m., I will personally rend to pieces everyone you love."

Reese let me wallow in a long moment of sheer terror. Then her small, sharp mouth assembled a toothy smile. "You're right," she said. "I don't reconsider. But I do take bribes in the amount of eight million dollars, unmarked bills."

Before I could laugh, or even register that Reese Garrison had made an actual joke, she asked, "What's your question?"

I glanced around her office, hunting down an inspired way to phrase this. Nothing in here was inspirational.

"Spit it out, Jordan." Reese folded her hands on her desk. The collection of bracelets around her wrists rattled.

"Sorry, right," I said. "I wondered if I could ask for audition feedback. Since you—" I cut myself off. Don't accuse. Step carefully. "Since I haven't had success in casting, so far, I figured it was a me thing."

"A 'you thing'?"

"A pattern in my auditions, I mean."

Reese picked up a pen, spinning it between her nimble fingers. Tiredness passed across her face, a startling little specter of an emotion. She was so expressive, Reese, expressive and flexible— an ex-dancer who had floated on- and off-Broadway for twenty years. "As with everyone, it's a combination of things," she said. "Mostly, the parts just haven't fit. I don't need to tell you, do I? You've heard the lines. Subjective industry. Case-by-case basis."

"Sorry, but—mostly?" I repeated, picking at the single weak spot in the spiel.

"What?"

"You said, *mostly*, the parts just didn't fit me."

One thin eyebrow rose. "And you're sure you *want* to hear what I might have to say."

It wasn't a question. She was steeling herself. I waited.

Race, whispered something in the back of my head. Kensington's race-blind casting policy was meant to give everyone the same shot at a lead part, but I couldn't quite shut off the voice that said, *Of course you, Jordan Mingyan Sun, aren't getting cast as a lead, when the leads are named Annabeth Campbell, Janie Wallace, and Cassandra Snyder.* Or was it my height? The fact that I was taller than half the guys I read with during auditions?

Still, it didn't explain why she hadn't cast me in the ensemble. *Freshmen* got cast in the ensemble.

Reese set down her pen. "Then let me be frank, because this is something you'll want to consider when you're auditioning for college programs: Your singing voice is difficult to reconcile with musical theater. Firstly, there's a timbre to it—and I'm not saying this couldn't be trained out, but it's a harshness, almost an inattentiveness to the text. Like a rock singer, not an actor."

I blinked rapidly. Thoughts about race and stature evaporated with a twinge of embarrassment. "Wh—you mean my pronunciation?"

"That's part of it. It also affects your physicality." She gestured at me. "Your eyes close; you shift and sway; your hands move with the notes instead of with intention. Those tics are a challenge to eliminate."

"I can do it," I said at once. "I'll fix it. If—"

She lifted a hand. I broke off.

"Again," she said, "that's subject to change. Unfortunately, what won't change for the foreseeable future is the number of roles that fit your range. It's just so deep." She took her glasses off, massaging the bridge of her nose with her sharp fingertips. Wisps of her dark hair escaped over her forehead. "You've got a unique sound, Jordan; you don't hear many voices like yours, and I mean that genuinely. But musical theater will be a tough pursuit for a girl who's more comfortable singing the G below middle C than the one above."

For once, words wouldn't come. Instead, a horrible memory of eighth grade arrived, a middle school choir concert built of white button-ups, an array of bright lights, and a clutter of anxious feet on the bleachers. Our choir director had made every girl sing soprano. My voice had cracked down half an octave at the peak of the song, an ugly bray among the sweet whistle of the other kids' voices, and laughter had popped across the stage. My cheeks had gone as hot as sweat.

Of course this was why. Being an Alto 2 in the musical theater world is sort of like being a vulture in the wild: You have a spot in the ecosystem, but nobody's falling over themselves to express their appreciation. In this particular show, even the so-called alto ensemble parts sang up to a high F-sharp, which seemed like some sort of sadistic joke. For those unfamiliar with vocal ranges: Find a dog whistle and blow it, try to sing that note, and the resulting gurgling shriek will probably sound like my attempt to sing a high F-sharp.

"The last thing I want to be is a naysayer," Reese said, slipping her glasses back on. I bit back a skeptical noise. Naysaying was basically the woman's job description. The arts world, Kensington wanted to teach us, was brutal, so everything here was "no": no's at auditions, no's from our teachers, no, no, no, until we accumulated elephant-thick skin, until we made ourselves better.

"But," she went on, "remember. It's the greatest strength to know your weaknesses. It just means you have a question to answer: How hard will you work to get what you want? And that's the heart of it: from your career, from your time here, from everything, really—what do you want?"

I stayed quiet.

The world, I thought. *The whole world, gathered up in my arms.*

♫

Nothing kills productivity faster than feeling helpless. That night, I sat at my usual table in the corner of the Burgess common room. My hands were fixed to my laptop, which whirred frantically under my palms in the computer equivalent of death throes. The library had slim MacBook Pros to lend out short-term, but for long-term loans like mine, they apparently leased equipment dating to sometime in the Cretaceous Period.

I pressed my hands closer to the computer, absorbing its warmth. The common room was always a few degrees too cold, a perfect studying atmosphere. Even the thermostats at Kensington knew the philosophy. Don't get too comfortable. Stay on your toes.

The evening burrowed into night. Stacks of books shrank around everyone else, vanishing from the scattering of cherry tables at teardrop windows, but my work went untouched. I stared up at the brass chandeliers and out the window at the star-strewn country sky. I stared at the seat beside me, which had belonged to Michael every night last year. He'd sat with a hunch that gave him pronounced knots in his shoulders; beneath my fingers they'd felt like stone beads worked deep into bands of muscle. His hands dwarfed his pet brand of mechanical pencil: Pentel Sharp P200, sleek, black, reliable.

In the opposite corner, Sahana Malakar, ranked first in our class, was highlighting her notes. By the gas-jet fire in the hearth, Will Teagle was mouthing lines to himself, brow knitted. These were the kids I'd been comparing myself to for two years already. Kensington was divided into five disciplines—Theater, Music, Film, Visual Arts, and Dance—and the five schools hardly ever mixed, so although we had 1,500 students, Kensington could feel insular, even isolating. We lived with the kids in our discipline, went to every class with them, and spent our free hours on projects with them. "Full immersion in your craft," Admissions bragged, "and with your partners in learning!"

As my time trickled away, my brain supplied me with the usual helpful spiral of consequences: *If you don't finish this essay, you won't have time for your English reading, and you'll never catch up, and by next week you'll still be on page 200 when everyone else has finished the book, and O'Neill will look at you across the table with his bushy eyebrows doing that knowing waggling thing, and he'll realize everything you're saying is bullshit, and you'll end up with a B, and your class rank will slip, and goodbye Harvard or Columbia, goodbye to your parents being proud of anything you—*

I managed to cram in about two paragraphs around the thoughts, as they spiraled into *Why do you bother?* and *You're never going to make it* and *Give up, give up, give up.*

Finally, mercifully, my phone interrupted. Cheerful music sliced through the common-room ambiance.

The housemaster, Mr. Rollins, squat and well-postured in an armchair across the room, looked up from the play he was annotating. A few studiers shot me disgruntled glances. I mouthed an apology and stuffed notebooks and laptop into my backpack, yanking the stuck zipper so that it chewed black teeth together in an uneven zigzag. I slipped out the door.

The halls of Burgess were a maze of corkboard, colored nametags taped to doors, and embossed silver numbers. 113. 114. 115. I dashed to 119, locked myself in, and took a deep breath before hitting *accept*. "Hey, Mom."

I delayed the audition talk as long as possible, but I couldn't put it off forever. My mother took the news about as well as I thought she would: with a wandering string of Chinese and a lecture that whipped into life like a tornado.

My parents tracked my school performance like baseball nuts tracked the World Series. I never told people about it. A fun side effect of being Chinese is that people assume this about you already. It felt weirdly diminishing to admit it about myself, as if it simplified me to just another overachieving Asian kid with one of *those* moms, even if I was in fact Asian and did have one of those moms.

I weathered her tirade for a few minutes, cradling my phone between my ear and my shoulder. "Okay," I murmured halfway through one of her sentences, not thinking. She broke off.

"Don't 'okay,'" she said. "It's always 'okay' this, 'okay' that. Don't 'okay' me. How about you explain why this keeps happening?" A disbelieving laugh. "It's every single audition since you've gone to that place! It's not just singing. Why don't they put you on the, those, the regular plays?" I imagined the agitated fluttering of her hand as she tried to grab the words, put them in the right order. Mom's English tended to fracture when she didn't give herself time to breathe.

"Because," I said tiredly, "mainstage straight plays always have, like, eight-person casts, and the parts always go to seniors."

"I don't know, Jordan. I just don't know. All we get is bad news. What do you expect us to think, ah?"

"Mainstages aren't everything," I insisted. "I can find a student-led show in October. And my GPA's fine, and everything else is fine, it's just . . ." *that you've trained yourself to sniff out my weak spots.* The sentence I could never finish. Even this much talking back was pushing it. My mother and I had the sort of relationship that operated the most smoothly in silence.

She heaved her knowing sigh. I could picture the slow stream of air between her lips, her mouth framed by deep, tired creases. The sound punctured me.

Silence spread across my room. I'd been one of twenty Burgess residents to draw a single this year. It was twice the size of my room at home. Everything I owned stretched thinly across the space, making it look like an empty model room you might find, three-walled, sitting in the middle of a furniture store. I'd pinned my two posters, *Les Misérables* and *Hamilton*, as far apart as possible, thinking that it might make the white cinderblocks look busier. It hadn't worked.

The only thing I had in numbers were books. They lined up single-file on the shelves, quietly keeping me company. It was impossible to feel alone in a room full of favorite books. I had the sense that they knew me personally, that they'd read me cover to cover as I'd read them.

My mother had always been aggressive about getting me to read, scouring garage sales and libraries for free novels, plays, or biographies. She'd always wanted me to learn more.

Do more. Be more. She spent her life hoping for my way up and out.

"I'm sorry," I said, my voice tiny, and for a horrible second, I thought I was going to cry. She never knew what to do with that.

I searched the photos I'd tacked to the corkboard above my desk, trying to distill reassurance out of the patchwork of familiar faces. Near the top hung my best friends in San Francisco, the four of us, arms slung around each other's shoulders. Shanice pandered to the camera, pulling that picture-perfect sun-white grin. Jenna had her eyes crossed and her tongue stuck out, and to the left, Maria and I were in the middle of hysterical laughter, both of us shaded brown by the end of the summer.

I took a stabilizing breath. "How's . . ." I started, tentative. "How's Dad?"

"Fine. We're fine." She sounded weary. I didn't reply. If they'd been fighting, she wouldn't have told me, anyway. And what did it change, for me to know whether they were in a peace period or a war period?

"I need to make dinner," Mom said, her voice softening. "Bye. Talk soon, okay?"

"Yeah, I—"

Click.

I dropped my phone, my whole body heavy. At least it wasn't ever anger with my mom—just anxiety, a nerve-shredding worry on my behalf that made me feel inadequate like nothing else could. Every time I dropped the ball, it made visible cracks in her exterior.

It felt like my parents had been gearing up their entire lives for next fall, my college application season. Last year, I'd read a one-man show for Experimental Playwriting in which a man decides over the course of forty-five minutes whether to press a button that will instantly kill somebody across the world, a random person, in exchange for ten million dollars. If you'd handed my parents that button and told them the reward was my admission to Harvard, I swear to God they would've pressed it without a second thought.

And if you asked them why? "Because it's Harvard." Conversation over.

In a way, I was lucky that they banked on name recognition. Their faith in the arts as a legitimate career path hovered around zero, so if Kensington hadn't been nicknamed "the Harvard of the Arts" by everyone from *USA Today* to the *New Yorker*, the odds of my going here also would've hovered around zero, scholarship or not. I was fourteen when I convinced my parents to let me apply to Kensington, and—when I got the full ride—to come here. I'd cajoled them into it every step of the way. But they would never be happy until I was the *best*. Here, you were more likely to have several extra limbs than be the best at anything.

I slid off my bed and measured my breaths. *Stop thinking about college—stop thinking at all—give your brain a rest.* It was always busy in my skull, always noisy, a honking metropolis of detours and preoccupations.

I hunched over my desk, studying my corkboard. There hung a creased picture of my dad and me, his knees leaning crookedly in his wheelchair, one of my hands set on his shoulders. Beside it was a shot of my mother standing on our building's crumbling stoop, stern and stately, wearing a summer dress with a red and green print. The pictures were three years old. They seemed to be from a separate lifetime. Before Kensington, before the fighting, before Michael, a mirror reflecting a mirror reflecting a mirror, every layer of difference adding a degree of warp.

The corner of a stray picture glinted to the side, snagged behind a family photo. I swiveled it into sight and yanked my fingers back. The image of Michael's face made something clench in my chest. His dark eyes peered out at me accusingly.

Why did I even have that? I could've sworn I'd put all those pictures in the garbage, where he belonged.

The flare of hurt was swallowed almost instantly by disgust. Three months, and I was still circling the carcass of our relationship like an obsessive buzzard. The worst thing about breakups was the narcissism that trailed after them, the absolute swallowing self-centeredness. Every movie about heartbreak had turned into my biopic. Every sentence about aloneness, every song lyric about longing, had morphed into a personal attack.

I snatched the photo down, crumpled it, and chucked it across the room at the trash can. It missed, landing beneath the open window. The dark ridges of the balled-up photo shone. Outside, a yellowing harvest moon was rising over the treetops.

I approached the window, flicked the scrap of glossy paper into place, and gazed through the glass at the moon. For a second I lost myself in the sight. For a second I could breathe clearly, the first instant of clarity since that morning.

Kensington was beautiful through everything. When I didn't have anything else, I had this castle in the countryside, this oasis, this prize I'd snared. Some days it was a diamond, and I almost couldn't understand how lucky I was to have stumbled upon it. And other days it was a living thing, trying desperately to free itself from me.